WAITING FOR THE THUNDER

WAITING FOR THE THUNDER

Patricia Shaw

HEADLINE

First published in 2000
by HEADLINE BOOK PUBLISHING

10 9 8 7 6 5 4 3 2 1

British Library Cataloguing in Publication Data

Shaw, Patricia, 1928-
    Waiting for the thunder
    I.Title
    823 [F]

    ISBN 0 7472 2248 7 (Hbk)
    ISBN 0 7472 7040 6 (Tpb)

Typeset by
Letterpart Limited, Reigate, Surrey

Printed and bound in Great Britain by
Mackays of Chatham plc, Chatham, Kent

HEADLINE BOOK PUBLISHING
A division of Hodder Headline
338 Euston Road
London NW1 3BH

www.headline.co.uk
www.hodderheadline.com

To Ron and Rose Jones,
and Peter Poynton BA, LLB –
for the long haul,
with thanks.

PART ONE

October 1900

Chapter One

On a map of the Northern Territory, Black Wattle cattle station would hardly have rated a pinpoint. Nor, for that matter, would its far larger neighbour, Victoria River Downs, even though it covered somewhat in the order of eighteen thousand square miles, give or take a dusty red-ochre plain or an ancient crater, or a long-forgotten dent in the overheated landscape where once a proud river had flowed down to the now extinct inland sea; where once dinosaurs might have plodded and paddled, giant serpents stalked, and monstrous birds flapped and swooped. For the Territory, still only a part of the 'top end' of Australia, could lay claim to half a million square miles. Pinpoint or not, Victoria River Downs – or the Big Run, as it was known – and its neighbouring stations were staggering in scope, thereby causing the concept of land size, and distance, to swell in proportion for the occupants of these great estates.

To Zack Hamilton, who, as a young man, had inherited the family cattle station called Black Wattle, the size of his huge property was nothing special. He took it for granted that space was needed to support his herds in semi-arid country where ghost gums and high red termite mounds were the only objects capable of rising above the dry, spiky grasslands. It had taken Zack three days to ride over to confer with Charlie Plumb, manager of the Big Run, but that didn't bother him. Their meeting was important to set in motion co-operative plans between the stations to cope with the floods that were bound to come once the wet season set in. What did concern him, though, was Charlie's request for assistance.

'We're short-handed, Zack. Six of our stockmen took off for the goldfields last week. I've sold a thousand head of cattle and I have to get them over to the buyer before the wet sets in. His men will pick them up at Pine Creek.'

'Left your run a bit late, haven't you?'

'Don't I know it! I had to send for a droving team from Katherine. I got Paddy Milligan and his rig. Only a small team. You met them?'

'No.'

'They'll be fine, but they don't know this country too well. I just need you to take them to Campbell's Gorge and see them through it. After that they'll be right. It's only a few days out of your way, Zack.'

'On past my way,' Zack growled. 'Seventy miles east. And my wife sitting home with the hat and gloves on, ready to leave for Darwin. Not

3

to mention Lucy; I swear she's been packed for a month, with the boyfriend coming home. I've already put them off for a week.'

'Ah, the ladies! They won't mind. Plenty of time yet. How is Sibell anyway? I heard she wasn't well.'

'She's fine,' Zack said. This was no time to be discussing his wife's constitution, or, more accurately, her state of mind of late.

'That's good to hear. Now you'll help me out, won't you, Zack?'

He nodded, grudgingly. They had both known he wouldn't refuse. Could not. The unwritten rule of the outback, of this wild and isolated country, spelled survival. You gave assistance whenever and wherever it was needed; lives depended on co-operation.

'Is Milligan ready to go?'

'Yes, they're moving the mob out now.'

A few days or so? Zack groaned to himself. With a slow-moving herd of cattle? Four or five more like it.

Lucy Hamilton walked to the end of the high veranda and stared anxiously down the long track that led away from the homestead, disappearing, eventually, among the knobs of treetops, but there was no sign of movement. Nothing stirred. You could almost imagine that the dusty landscape was empty, that this house, perched on a low hill, presided over a realm devoid of constituents or their flocks. Especially now. At noon. The air practically sizzled. There was a musty smell about the station, an ancient, hot smell, as if the land itself was tired, worn out, ragged, and everything was so quiet. Deathly quiet.

Even though she knew that somewhere out there, stockmen were working, the Aborigines who lived on the property would be going about their business, native animals would be dodging about seeking shelter from the midday heat, the quiet still got on her nerves.

And where was her father? He should have been back yesterday. The dry season was almost over. Any day now, it seemed, this awful heat would have to explode, but of course it wouldn't; the wet season was due, the rains a relief.

Lucy shuddered. She hated this time of the year, waiting for the thunder, waiting for the monsoonal rains to sweep in, turning the creeks into rivers, the rivers into vast flood plains. Cutting them off if they didn't get out in time.

So where was Zack? she worried angrily. He had promised them they would be leaving for Darwin today, at the latest, and there was still no sign of him. It was hell hanging about like this. Everyone knew that the climate was trying at this time of the year, that it sent everyone a bit crazy, yearning for a break after the long dry season, yearning for the smell, the sound, the welcome wash of those first rains. Those thick walloping dollops that sent the dust dancing, the animals licking their lips, and people rushing out, arms outstretched, smiles at last. It didn't seem to help that everyone knew this was a crazy time. Knowing was not a solution. Tempers were short. Fights broke out among the men. People

4

snapped. Sulked. Mistakes were made. Gates left open. Food burned. A loss at cards, a broken plate, any little thing could cause a row. Even the livestock were edgy.

Lucy often wondered if the cattle knew danger lurked but could not define it. They had to be moved well away from the dried-up river flats and placid waterholes to the safety of higher ground before the floods came down, but it was not an easy job. Too many of them became cranky and stubborn, resenting the intrusion, confronting the whips and curses of the whirling horsemen. Thousands of cattle were being rounded up and redirected now and Lucy wished she could be out there helping; anything would be better than moping about the house, but her father had forbidden her to take part in musters at this time of the year.

'Too dangerous,' he'd said. 'No place for a girl.'

Her mother had agreed. But then Sibell Hamilton disapproved of Lucy riding and working with the men at any time, claiming it was not ladylike. Never mind that in the old days she had taken stock work in her stride when extra hands were needed. Even now Zack's sister-in-law, Maudie, owner of Corella Downs, still preferred the horse to the house and she was fifty. A tough old bird, Lucy grinned, born in the bush and proud to be a 'pioneering Territorial', as she called herself.

Lucy's mother and aunt were like chalk and cheese. English-born, Sibell disapproved of Maudie Hamilton's rough ways, and they never seemed to agree on anything, though Zack claimed they were good mates underneath the bickering. Now, at the dawn of the twentieth century, there still weren't very many white women living in the outback, and that, Sibell claimed, was all the more reason for local women to assert themselves. To show by example that their isolated situation was no excuse for graceless living. Sibell was house proud. The Black Wattle homestead was no mansion, rather a sprawling timber house with high ceilings and wide verandas and an iron roof, painted red, that could be seen for miles around, but it was comfortable and neatly furnished. With the help of her Chinese cook and black maids, Sibell liked to entertain their few visitors in style, and that suited Lucy, but she couldn't accept that her role was to waft about the house learning the duties and social graces expected of young ladies. She hated sewing, could not paint or play the piano, and loved romantic novels, instead of the 'better' reading her mother placed on the shelves. But she did love the station itself, and the outdoor life suited her.

Lucy was a tall girl, with long blonde hair, even features and a slim, athletic figure. People said she was good-looking, though Lucy had her doubts about that; she didn't feel she was actually pretty the way heroines were described in the penny novels, curls and all that. Zack always said she was beautiful, but then he would. He adored her. Proud of her really, she supposed, because she was a fine horsewoman, could ride side-saddle or astride, whatever the occasion required, and had won cups at the annual race meetings and gymkhanas. But where was her dear father now? Had he forgotten them?

Every year at this time they moved into Darwin for the summer, staying at their beach house. There was no escaping the torrential rain, or the humidity, but they could be overlooked in the congenial atmosphere leading up to Christmas, and the annual reunion with old friends from other outback stations. It was a marvellous time for everyone: a well-earned rest for hard-working country men, when they could relax with their mates and pretend it was a chore to escort the women to all the parties and dances that were already being arranged; a chance for the women to enjoy the bustle and fun of female company again; and as for the younger generation . . . Lucy smiled, feeling a little smug.

The summer months in Darwin were known as the 'meet and match' months. Romance was in the air, and love. 'And lust,' Aunt Maudie always said in her usual crusty manner. But it was exciting, and Lucy wouldn't miss this Darwin summer for the world because a certain gentleman was coming home at last, returning after nearly two years in London. A very important young gentleman who had written to her, without fail, every single month that he had been away. Lucy Hamilton had no need to join the fray of eligible spinsters in the marriage market; the love of her life was coming home. She and Myles Oatley had been friends since childhood, and before he left for London he'd asked her to wait for him.

As she'd said in her first letter to him, there was no need to ask, she would wait for him; the love they shared was only made fonder by absence.

Her parents were happy about the arrangement – they liked Myles, the only son of old friends – but Maudie, typical of Maudie, had other advice.

'You shouldn't be sitting about waiting for him. Play the field, girl. Have a good time, don't be sitting home like an old maid. Good God, you're twenty. You should have had other boyfriends by this. And don't put your eggs in one basket neither. Like as not he'll come home from London a different person, bragging about his toffy friends. He won't be a bushie like us no more, you mark my words.'

'That's ridiculous,' Sibell argued. 'His parents went on a world tour for their honeymoon, and when they came home they settled right down to work on the Oatley station as if they'd only been across the road. They never put on airs and graces.'

'Yes, but they went together. If he was so keen on Lucy, why didn't he marry her and take her with him?'

The arguments didn't bother Lucy. They amused her.

'Tell me, Maudie, why haven't you remarried?' she'd asked, to deflect the criticism of Myles. 'You were young, Wesley was only a baby when Uncle Cliff was killed.'

'Don't get smart with me, girl. I looked about, you bet I did. But every suitor that came along had a gleam in his eye for my station. They were after Corella Downs more than me, and I wasn't having anyone getting their hands on my place and thinking they could boss me around. No,

6

siree. I soon sorted them out. You should keep an eye on the ball too, my girl. You're a good catch. You'll own Black Wattle one day. You'll be worth a bit.'

'If it comes to that,' Lucy laughed, 'so will Wesley. Your son is older than me and still single. Who's he got in tow?'

That always ended the arguments. Maudie never had a good word for poor Wesley's girlfriends. Lucy pitied the girl who'd take on a mother-in-law like Maudie.

Now Lucy walked along the veranda past her parents' bedroom and her mother called to her.

'Is Zack home yet?'

Lucy pushed past the limp lace curtains in the open doorway. 'Not yet.'

She stared. Open boxes and trunks were lying about the room.

'What are you doing?'

'I'm packing.'

'But you already packed. You don't need any of this stuff in Darwin. And the trunks won't fit on the wagon!'

'I know. I'm having them sent on.'

'Having them sent on? What's all this?' She peered into another trunk. 'This one's full. We're only going for a few months, not ten years.'

Sibell emptied a drawer of underclothes on to the bed and sat down beside them. She looked up at her daughter. 'I've been trying to pluck up the courage to tell you, Lucy. I'm leaving.'

'Leaving? Where?'

'I'm leaving here and going to live in Perth.'

'What? When?'

'After Christmas.'

Lucy strode across the room and opened the large wardrobe, stunned to find it bare.

'I don't understand. What are you doing? Going for a holiday?'

'No. For good,' her mother said quietly.

'Rubbish. Zack wouldn't leave Black Wattle. What is really going on?'

'Your father isn't leaving. I am. I can't live here any more. I've decided to live in Perth.'

'Why? Have you and Daddy had a fight? I thought you were both being rather touchy lately. But you can't up and leave just because you've had a fight. It can't be that bad.'

'We haven't had a fight. Not really. He knows I'm leaving and he's upset.'

'I can't imagine why,' Lucy snapped. 'What's the matter with you? Have you gone off your head or something?'

'No,' Sibell said patiently. 'It has been very hard for me to come to this decision, but I really can't stand living out here any more. I'm tired of it all.'

'What all? I don't know what you're talking about.'

Her mother sighed. 'Oh, everything, Lucy . . . the isolation, the dust, the violence, the never-ending crises . . .'

'It was the mouse plague, wasn't it? Now I come to think of it, you've been jumpy ever since then. But that's over, it won't happen again for years.'

Sibell shuddered. 'Don't remind me. Those damn things, I feel sick every time I think of them, in the house, in the bed, layers of them. But they weren't the real cause, just the last straw. I want to live normally, in a normal climate, walk down a street, go to the shops when I feel like it, things like that. I'm nearly fifty. If I don't make the move now, I never will.'

'And what about us? Daddy and me? You're just going to walk out on us?'

'I'll be in Perth. You can visit.'

'But this is your home. You can't do this. Is Daddy just going to stand by and do nothing?'

'Not exactly, I have to admit. He's taking it very hard. I hoped you might have a word with him. Explain to him how I feel.'

'Explain to him? That his wife is leaving him? I'll do no such thing! I can't believe you're being so selfish. Put all that stuff back! I don't want to hear any more about it.'

Lucy slammed out of the room and Sibell shook her head sadly. She loved them both but they were not children. They'd have to understand that people could change, could need change. In her case, desperately. But she would not go so far as to admit that.

She'd tried to tell Zack that she'd felt her life had come to a standstill, that she needed a new outlook, but that had been met with derision.

'Fresh pastures, eh? Anyone in particular in mind?'

'You don't mean that, Zack. A remark like that is unworthy of you. I'll always love you but—'

'So you show it by leaving me?'

She felt sorry for him. He simply could not grasp her reasoning. The whole idea seemed to be beyond his comprehension.

'Is it the house then? We could renovate, make it bigger if you like. Whatever you want.'

'No. The house is very comfortable. Can't you see I need change?'

'Then take a bloody holiday if you want to get away from me. Get it out of your system.'

Why was it so hard to explain? Maybe because she couldn't put a finger on it herself. Sometimes, in a less positive mood, Sibell thought she might be searching for something that didn't exist, but she was determined to find out. Or maybe she was reverting to her earlier years, to that young girl who had been brought up in the serenity of an English village.

She sighed. That lifestyle had come to an end with a jolt when her parents made the ill-fated decision to migrate to Australia. She'd only been nineteen.

Shipwrecked. Lost both of her beloved parents. Cast ashore on a deserted beach north of Perth, only a strange man for company. Rescued, they'd thought, by a mob of Aborigines only to find their chief a vicious fellow, more interested in ransoming them than in caring for them. It was only through the intervention of a young Aborigine farm boy called Jimmy Moon that they had been able to escape from that filthy camp.

Jimmy Moon, she thought sadly. He'd been a friend. He too had come north, some years later, to escape his own troubles down there. It still hurt to think of him.

Sibell herself had ended up in Perth, living with awful people, until she met Zack's mother, a wonderful woman. Mrs Hamilton had been in the town to see a specialist who broke the news to her that her eyes were failing. Needing a bookkeeper to help her manage her large cattle station, Black Wattle, she'd offered Sibell the job.

Sibell found herself smiling. I had no idea what I was getting myself into, she recalled. What a shock that was. It took about a week to get here from Darwin. Riding! No trains in those days. I thought I'd reached the end of the earth.

But then Mrs Hamilton could have had an ulterior motive inviting a young Englishwoman to her station. About a year later I married her son.

She had no regrets though. It had been a battle at times, with the terrible loss of their little son, the elements, the distances, the fight to protect and nurture the great herds of cattle. So many things, but she'd coped, and come to like the station. But now it was time to go.

When she went in to lunch, Lucy was still angry.

'Have you come to your senses yet?'

'Can't we talk this out without rudeness?'

'Very well. Tell me this. What violence? I know my uncle was killed by blacks before I was born, but we rarely have that trouble now. And we have accidents with the men and horses, but they can happen anywhere. How can you say there's violence here, at Black Wattle?'

'I'm sorry. It was the wrong word. Forget it.'

Born here, Lucy wouldn't understand that, to Sibell, of late, distance was violence. So was the weather. The temperature, the storms. The dried-up, baking creek beds. The isolation – the nearest neighbour was three days' ride from here. Longer by wagon.

'It's more what's not here,' she tried. 'Suburbia. I'll settle for suburbia.'

'Rot. You'd be bored stiff in a week.'

'I don't think so. I feel lost here now. I don't know why, but being here depresses me.'

'It's your home. What's to be depressed about? Mother, I really think you are just bored. You'll feel better once we get to Darwin. I know you. After the summer months in town, you're always pleased to get home.'

'Maybe,' Sibell said, to close down the subject. 'We'll see.'

Tears were smarting in her eyes and she turned quickly to hide them but too late. Instantly Lucy was at her side.

'Heavens, Mother, what is it? Aren't you feeling well? Is that the trouble?'

Sibell wished she could say, 'Yes. I am ill. Pass me the medicine. I'll be better in the morning.' That would be preferable to the bouts of misery that assailed her, but she was not ill. Physically, she was in the best of health.

'I'm quite all right,' she said, 'really I am. Just a bit tired. I'm probably just run down of late.' She dabbed at her eyes, forcing a smile.

'Yes, you ought to have a lie down. I hate to see you unhappy, Mother. Maybe it's the beastly weather . . . the heat is almost unbearable today. It must be some sort of a record, well over the century I'd say. It will do you good to take a nap. Sleep away the worst of it.'

Sibell nodded. 'Yes. I'll do that. Thanks Lucy.'

Safe in her bedroom, behind closed doors, she dissolved into tears. What was the use of trying to explain the problem to anyone, when she herself had no idea what was wrong. It shamed her to think that Sibell Hamilton who had a loving family, a good home . . . so much to be thankful for . . . could be so ungrateful as to be talking about leaving. To be leaving. Her mind was made up. These miseries had been stalking her for about two years now, getting gradually worse. She was poor company these days, a cheerless person, and that made her impatient with everyone.

Zack, in his kindly way had tried to talk to her about this, asking her if perhaps she could be a little less difficult with people, especially the staff.

He wanted her to regain her sense of humour, to learn to laugh at little setbacks again, not to take everything so seriously, and of course, it was inevitable, she'd ended up in tears, her husband mystified, upset too. Several times he had tried to discover why she was so unhappy, asking what he could do, or say, to please her, gradually becoming irritated by what he called her 'moods'.

It wasn't the weather. Sibell knew that. She'd survived years of drought without falling apart, and she already knew that the holiday in Darwin was no solution. Last year she'd hoped the sea breezes would blow away this despondency but they did not, and it was then that she'd realised she dreaded returning to the station. Now she'd had a year to think about this, to try to understand why she had this awful weakness, an embarrassment, since she really was a strong person, and it had come down to one answer. There was no reason at all for her to be so depressed, none at all, therefore she felt she was losing her reason. There seemed no other explanation.

But this was not something she would dream of mentioning to anyone. Tell them she thought she was going mad? Never! She would put a stop to it, she would find the cure, and that meant the move to Perth. Sibell was certain she would feel better there, happier, more relaxed in a city atmosphere, and now she was even looking forward to the move, despite the opposition from Zack and now Lucy.

She poured water from the jug on the washstand into its basin and taking a face cloth swabbed her face and throat for a little temporary coolness, and then lay on the bed with the wet cloth over her eyes, hoping, as usual, for a miracle. That she would rise from this bed a happy sensible person again and all would be set right in her world.

After lunch, Lucy returned to the veranda and ran down the outer steps, heading for the stables, still worrying about her mother's crazy idea to leave. On the way, she met Casey, the station overseer.

'Ah, Lucy, I was coming up to see you. Your dad has been held up.'

'What's happened?'

'Nothing much. He had to help move some cattle from the Big Run over to Campbell's Gorge.'

'Oh no! How do you know this?'

'He met up with a couple of our blacks on the stock route and sent them back to let us know. In case we were worried.'

Lucy was furious. 'Worried? I'll strangle him. What the hell is he doing? Does he want us to be stranded here?'

Casey grinned. 'Plenty of time. Rains are a whiles off yet.'

'Oh really?' Lucy twisted around and pointed to a furl of grey cloud far in the distance. 'Then what's that? Smoke?'

'No, that there cloud's just for openers. Be a while before the weather hits and a good while after that for the rivers to get a go on. You'll be on your way soon.' He went to walk away and then turned back with a wink. 'I heard young Myles Oatley is due home. Is that what all this fuss is about?'

'Of course not,' she snapped, marching away. Damn. Damn. Damn! It would be days now before they could get away, depending on how close to the gorge the drovers were, and there was nothing much to do around here any more. Except to try to talk some sense into her mother.

Chapter Two

The walls of the gorge seemed to leap from the earth too fast for the eye to assimilate at one glance, massive red-streaked twin towers, reaching up and up, on and on far into the heights until the narrow band of blue above the cleavage that was this gorge became not sky, but a roof, clamped on by a hand as powerful as the great structure itself.

Down in the depths, along the two-mile sandy base of the cavern, tall palms hung loftily above a string of waterholes, lending grace and a wisp of exotica to the harsh surrounds, seemingly unaware that they were dwarfed by the sheer size of this gorge.

Yorkey stared at the trees, wondering how they could survive here. There was heat and water aplenty but little nourishment, and in the wet season they'd be battling to cling to the earth. Many of them were young trees though, skinny, grasping for the light as soon as they claimed a foothold, reinventing their little oasis, season after season. A wonder. But the gorge itself was a wonder. Awesome. This was strength, this place. Power. Bold and uncompromising. He felt like cheering, just to be here. To have found it after all.

His mother had told him about this place, famous in Dreaming legends, where the spirits had become annoyed with two tribes warring over the land, and so had cleaved the earth in two, settling the matter. But in doing so they had also separated two lovers forever, and the young man, despairing, had leapt to his death from the heights. He had been of Yorkey's mother's people, Waray, so they had claimed the gorge as their own. That was the story as far as he could recall. She'd only told him this stuff at rare times, when she was in the mood, and she'd said the gorge had several people names, being such an important landmark, all of which were lost to Yorkey by this, if he'd ever thought to hang on to them in the first place. He'd grown up in the white man's world . . .

Wistfully now, as he studied the great walls with their jutting cliffs and buttresses, he wished he had taken more notice. It would be interesting to know about that story. What spirits? Who were they? More likely, going back into the mists of time, it had probably been a battle between powerful spirits rather than a couple of tribes. He believed in the Aborigine spirits, no different from the white men's gods, who could also strike with lightning force, but he doubted many of them would take sides in wars.

His mother had told him that this place was now known as Campbell's Gorge, after the white man who discovered it, so Yorkey had remembered that name. But she had considered it an insult. Discovered! Like as if no one had ever seen it before. Like as if a thousand generations of the people hadn't known every inch of it.

Yorkey grinned. She had a point. But nothing he could do about it. All that mattered was that she'd been right about this gorge. It was spectacular. It was awesome. Dim though her memory of it had been, she hadn't exaggerated. Yorkey loved the place and he wished he could tell her. Put a smile on her poor worn face.

He sighed. Led his horse to drink at a waterhole and waded in himself, not a little shocked by the chill of the water on a warm day.

But he was here on white man's business and he'd better get on with it.

Yorkey was a drover with Paddy Milligan's team and they had a herd of cattle to bring through this gorge. A big herd, now two days' ride back there. Paddy was an experienced drover, one of the best. He had a rule when travelling through country strange to them, like this Northern Territory job, further west than they'd ever ventured before . . .

'You get the lie of the land from locals, when you can find any, then you go ahead and check it out, like you would an Irishman's directions. A yard could be a mile and a wet patch a bloody swamp.' Paddy prided himself on delivering all of his charges intact.

It was hard, though, to concentrate on the job in Campbell's Gorge. The bloody place was incredible. Though Yorkey had never seen a cathedral, he imagined they must be something like this. Only smaller. Tinier. But full of spirits. Ghosts.

Squelching about flat rocks and boulders in his wet boots he felt a tingling in his spine at that thought. It was a bloody lonely place. Eerie. A lost world. Rock wallabies clambered about the burgeoning heights, soundlessly, making no mark. An eagle soared gracefully to a safe nest on a craggy point. A large lizard slithered to a rock on the sunny side and remained still, very still, like the water in the pools.

'Hello!' Yorkey shouted suddenly, listening to the echo bouncing off the solid walls, but as his call reverberated, he thought he heard an answering sound, discordant, another voice. He looked up sharply, shading his eyes, tracking ledges, outcrops, massive shafts of rock and all the discoloration of seams that marked the ages, but saw nothing. No one.

He tried again. The bush call. 'Coo-ee!' The practised call was guaranteed to travel and was rewarded by a cacophony of echo and, to his keen ears, another distant call that seemed to clash and yet mesh with his echo.

It wasn't an animal sound. It was a voice. Someone was there. But where in this great cauldron of sound?

'Where are you?' he yelled. That echo banged and battered about but there was no intrusion this time, just his own voice. He tried again and again for a response, but in the end gave up. Some fool, somewhere, being smart. What the hell! Who cared?

The locals were right. A short cut through the gorge could save them a week. They could easily move the herd through if they took it quietly, a mob at a time. The cattle would think they were traversing heaven, tramping through a shaded gorge sheltered from the sun, and shoving on over the shallow waterholes. They'd probably drink the gorge dry, a mob this size.

But Yorkey wasn't fooled by the sharp outlines of the gorge. He'd lived in the north of this country all his life, plenty long enough to be aware of the dangers of the wet season.

'Big dry country my arse,' he commented to his horse as he swung into the saddle. 'A trap for new chums, the lot of it. But safe enough for the time being.'

Shrewdly he studied the walls of the gorge. The groaning convulsion that had rent this plateau asunder could not alter the surge of monsoonal rains, and the telltale signs were there. The walls were ribbed from the high cliffs to the base with distant pale lines tinged with green, almost as if they were hiding cracks or seams in the rock formation, but they were no such thing, Yorkey knew. They were overflow courses, bone dry now, but what a cascade they would produce in the wet.

He turned about and examined the discoloration of the walls at his own level and knew that when the overflow began, it would turn into a torrent that would flood this gorge.

The catchment area was up there somewhere and those striped rivulets would deliver falls at a thunderous pace from that height, too fast for the gorge to cope. It would hold what water it could, yards deep, and then send the runoff into the outlying plains, thereby pleasing the cattlemen in the district, but the gorge itself would be impassable for months.

'Oh well,' Yorkey said, as he spurred his horse to travel back through the gorge, 'we'd better get a move on.'

He hated leaving this wondrous place, deciding that when he had some time off he ought to come back, camp here awhile, on his own. Campbell's Gorge fascinated him. Just as it had his poor mum, he supposed, though for him it was different. She'd had her ways, her memories. Strange things. People business. For him it was something else. It would draw him back, he knew it, though he couldn't quite figure out why yet. Admiration maybe. Yorkey didn't have much in his life to admire. He was only an 'Abo' drover, just another bloke on the stock routes, and lucky to be that. There were plenty of other Abos worse off. But he sure as hell admired this gorge, whatever it was called.

'You're sure we can get through?' Paddy worried.

'Yes. No problem.'

'We wouldn't have bogs in there?'

'No. It's a sandy base. A bit narrow in parts but we can do it, Paddy. In stages.'

'You're a good lad, Yorkey. Get yourself to the cook wagon. You probably haven't had a proper feed in days.' He laughed. 'Unless you've been gorging on bush tucker.'

That was always a joke between them. Aborigine though he might be, Yorkey didn't have the faintest idea how to survive in the bush, nor did he have the taste for Aborigine fare, which he'd often tried.

He hadn't bothered to mention to Paddy the strange echoing voice he'd heard in the gorge. Mulling it over as he rode back, he'd decided that he could have imagined those sounds, that voice. No one had been there. It had been as empty as a dry pub. The gorge, a strange place, was like that. You could imagine all sorts of things.

Zack wiped sweat from his face with a rag and squinted, from under his battered hat, at the sea of cattle that swayed and stumbled ahead of him. They were moving along at a steady pace, moving well, thanks to Milligan's expertise and his willingness to take directions. On a sketch map it looked like a hundred and fifty miles or so to the gorge from the Big Run, but the terrain was deceptive. Precious time could be lost driving cattle into dead-end gullies or over rough and rocky land hidden by high speargrass, and Zack, aware of the anxieties stirring back home, was trying to make sure not an hour was lost on this drive. He had advised Milligan to break the mob up into three groups as they approached the gorge to avoid a stampede when they smelled water. The deep canyon would still have a thread of waterholes, he was sure, even after an exceptionally dry season. It was a magnificent place, and important as a short cut through a ridge of sandstone hills, but perilous. Often, for no particular reason, cattle would get spooked in there; maybe the clatter and echoes bothered them, but whatever, they had to be kept under tight control.

There was also the problem of landslides from the steep cliffs; they could cause chaos, but fortunately were rare at this time of the year. The walls of the gorge were often destabilised by the sheer weight of water that plunged from the catchment area above in the wet season, so landslides were still possible after the flooding had subsided. Always wary, Zack avoided the gorge for at least a month after the wet, to allow the area to dry out.

He was tailing the first mob, watching them spread out, crashing through the scrub bordering the old track, sheer weight ploughing the way, when a bull broke loose up ahead, leading a breakaway mob with him. As the renegades started to lumber obstinately to the left, they gathered speed, barging off into the bush. Zack wheeled his horse and went after them, but a black stockman was quicker off the mark.

Whip cracking, he hurled his little stockhorse through the scrub, straight at the escaping bull, bypassing his followers. The horse seemed to dance around the leader, harassing the hefty animal as much as the sting of the whip, and gradually he was intimidated into turning back towards the main herd, the rest of his mob swerving back with

16

him. By this time Zack had caught up with them, his own long stockwhip lashing the loiterers into line, ignoring the angry grunting and lowing.

The incident seemed to have created a ripple of unrest right through the herd, and up ahead, almost hidden in the clouds of dust, Zack could see Milligan riding fiercely on the flanks to keep them steady.

'Thanks, mate.'

Zack looked about to see the black stockman riding up to join him. He laughed.

'You were doing all right. You didn't need me, son. Fancy little mount you got there.'

'Yeah, she's a beauty.'

'You work on the Big Run?'

'No, I'm a drover. Been with Paddy's rig for two years now. We usually work out of Katherine but he got a job to bring out this mob. Pleased as punch he was to get in good with them bosses at Victoria River. Plenty of work there, I reckon.'

Zack was intrigued. This young chap was a full-blood, no doubt about that, with square, chiselled features and a tall, rangy physique, typical of the blacks around here, but he had no trace of the usual pidgin English that most Aborigines used.

'What's your name?'

'Yorkey.'

'Where're you from?'

'All abouts.'

'I mean what tribe?'

'What's it to you?'

Zack was taken aback. The owner of Black Wattle was unaccustomed to such a studied snub from white stockmen, let alone a blackfeller.

'Nothing. I was just making conversation,' he snapped.

'Yeah, well there you go.' Yorkey shrugged, then urged his horse away to shore up the stragglers.

Zack stared after him. 'Well I'll be blowed! The cheeky bugger.'

Yorkey was embarrassed. Why had he said such a stupid thing? Being smart, that was all. Trying to get the jump on the new bloke. Why hadn't he given the usual answer: 'Dunno'? That suited the whites, they didn't know one tribe from another anyway. Nor did they care. Yorkey had never known his father, he'd died before he was born, but he'd been a fine man, a great man in fact. Of the Whadjuck people. But try telling the white folks that round the campfire and all you got was chiacking . . .

'Ho! Ho! What sorta juck, Yorkey? A waddy juck? Or maybe a jumbuck? A sheep?'

All that stuff and worse. Bloody rude. Then you were a poor sport, couldn't take a joke if you got nasty about it. But listening to the white folks he'd been intrigued, when they asked one another where they'd come from, to hear that many of them had sailed here from other lands. At first he'd thought they were from different tribes, but that couldn't be,

17

because they all looked alike and spoke the same tongue. Bit of a mystery that, but Yorkey was never interested enough to enquire.

The tips of his ears burned as he sent his horse cantering through the scrub again to take up another point on the flank of the mob, at least a half-mile from that new bloke. The one who had spoken to him so politely. But the bloke himself had said he'd only been making conversation. Didn't that mean he wasn't really interested anyway? Yorkey knew he was only making excuses for himself now.

Allowing the horse to lope along, he lapsed into thoughts of his mother . . .

'Your father was a Whadjuck man, not this whitefeller we've got now. And not the one before. That first one, he threw me out bloody quick when he found I was getting a baby, not his. Too far along. He bashed me bad. I wasn't no use to him any more.'

Seemed she'd worked on a station somewhere out this way, as a housegirl, and at walkabout times she'd been able to visit the gorge with her kinfolk. Anyway, when she found she was pregnant, with no man to stand up for her, she'd been so ashamed, she'd run off with a drover.

'Your daddy had died. I was too frightened to say his name, not even his whitefeller name. And what was the use? He was gone.'

'What was his whitefeller name?'

She had smiled. Real proud she was. 'He didn't have just one name like us, he had the two, the way of the whites. He was called Jimmy Moon.'

Yorkey had often thought about that. By rights, he should have the father name too, according to the white custom; he should be Yorkey Moon. But she never told anyone else, so it would be like making it up now.

Her name was Netta. She had called the second white man her husband, but there'd been no marriage. She was just his 'black boy', what they called black gins who cropped their hair, dressed like boys, shared their beds, worked as stockmen and cooked and cleaned for them. As 'husbands' went, this drover, Alfie Dangett, hadn't been too bad, Yorkey supposed. He'd let her bring the kid along, the kid he called Yorkey after his hometown somewhere; but Yorkey and Netta had always called him 'Boss'. That was the way it was. Then, when Yorkey was twelve, Netta had been killed in a fall from a horse.

He would never forget the night those men brought her body back to camp, wrapped in a saddle blanket. He had been shocked, disbelieving for a little while, just standing gaping, until reality struck and he began to scream. But that had been cut short by the astonishing sight of Boss, of old Alfie, down on his knees beside her, crying like a baby! Who'd have believed that a bloke like him would cry over an Abo woman? He had worked her hard but he must have cared for her after all. Yorkey wondered if she'd known. Not that it mattered. The real love of her life had long gone, Jimmy Moon.

'Your father was a travelling man. A wise man. He came from way down south, from Perth. He knew languages. Some said he was a magic man. He'd crossed the big deserts where even the white men dare not go. A great man, and very beautiful. You look like him.' Funny how women said soppy things like that.

But she never said how he'd died. An accident, Yorkey supposed, him being as young as her at the time. And being that he was so well respected, his white friends had wanted to bury him, but her people, the Waray elders, wouldn't have it. They'd taken him away and buried him with proper mourning ceremonies.

Too bad all that.

After Netta died, Boss let Yorkey stay, still riding on the cook wagon, doing odd jobs round the camps, looking after the horses, mending canvas . . . plenty to do, until he was big enough to work as a stockman. In the meantime Boss took on another black boy but she was a bad-tempered girl and couldn't speak much English, always arguing and getting things mixed up. In the end he got rid of her. But then he met a white woman who would only take on Alfie if he gave up droving, so the team broke up.

By then they were way over in Queensland, so Yorkey had picked up with other drovers and eventually made his way back to the Territory because his mum had talked about it as a good place. And it wasn't a bad life, this droving.

He reached down for his waterbag and took a swig, looking forward to refilling it with cleaner water in that gorge.

Droving gave a man a lot of time to think. Here he was in Waray country, his mother's homeland, and he hadn't woken up to it until the name of that gorge came up. She used to tell him stuff about her time here, her first sixteen years, the only times she seemed to care about, as if the rest of her life didn't matter. But he couldn't remember much. Kids never listen. Lately though, to pass the time, he'd searched his brain for little corners of information that he knew were there, but they were too dim to identify. It would be good to have your own sitting-down place, your own homeland, where you belonged. Claiming to be Whadjuck had been pathetic. No one had ever heard of it. But Waray was real. He probably had kin round here.

Yorkey shook himself out of this mood. So what? Who cared that poor little Yorkey didn't have no one? Bad luck! Yorkey prided himself on being tough. He took no shit from nobody. He was a good hand, could ride rings around most of his mates. He'd even won two pounds in a tent fight against a bruiser from the south. Knocked him cold. Jesus! Did the mob cheer that night! And they all got drunk afterwards. The showman boss even asked him to join the boxing troupe, but Yorkey wasn't that dumb. So what had brought on this latest bout of maudlin stuff? That bloody gorge probably. Spooked him, he bet, like he was just some poor old Abo trying to cling to the old days. Stupid.

He put his fingers to his lips and gave a shrill whistle to Paddy to alert him. The track had widened out into a dry river course. They were only a few miles from the gorge. Time to slim down the herd, and start to hold them back. Just then another thought came to him. That other stockman, the stranger, had asked him if he came from the Big Run. Which meant that he didn't come from there either. So who was this ring-in? Where had Paddy found him?

Chapter Three

Five men were travelling cross-country. They moved fast, bare feet padding steadily over the hard dry earth, their bodies coated in dust, their faces cold and grim. On the trek since dawn, they made no detours, pressing steadily on over ochre plains scattered with pale spinifex and stunted trees. A tall willy-willy spiralled in from the horizon, engulfing them in a miniature tornado of whistling dust and debris, whipping at bare skin, almost blinding them, but it soon passed, and they emerged, undaunted, grateful for the clean air again.

They dropped down the battered banks of a dry creek bed, feet searching sand for signs of a soak, and finding it, hands dug urgently until, arm's-length down, water bubbled and they drank. Then they moved on again, covering mile after mile at the same pace, long hunting spears no hindrance to the rhythm of their gait. If they noticed that the harsh sun that had been tracking them all day was relenting, losing interest and fading into the distance, they gave no indication. Talk wasted breath. Mimimiadie was leading; they had to keep up with him, keep up, on this the fifth day of their desperate run.

These men were of the famous – or infamous, as the whites would say – Daly River mob, which in fact encompassed several proud tribes that had owned territory along that great river for aeons past. But in more recent years, war had been raging between the white settlers, drovers and miners in the Territory and the indigenous people, who would not easily give up their homelands. Though the new government, thousands of miles far south in Adelaide, urged humane treatment of the blacks, few Aborigines knew of this and very few white men agreed. This was a hidden, guerrilla war; facts rarely filtered through to southern news-papers and when they did, tales of murderous raids by black fiends were far more newsworthy, even titillating, to shuddering suburban souls. They couldn't get enough of the bloody affairs and the heroic deeds of the magnificent trail-blazers of the north, standing staunchly against the black hordes.

No matter that on the other side of the world in London, the Queen's own gentlemen had expressed horror at the news of the guerrilla war being waged in this colony, and had ordered attention to the law. Murder was still a crime, both sides should be forcibly reminded, through the courts. But how?

The administrative representative of the Government in the Territory

21

resided in Darwin, and was known as the Resident. The latest was Lawrence Mollard, a former Secretary for Public Works. He paid lip service to the hand-wringing of parliamentarians in Adelaide, while turning a blind eye to the violence still being perpetrated within his jurisdiction. Mollard found it easier to pass off such reports as exaggeration.

And so the war in the outback continued, a secretive, stealthy war.

White men carried off black 'gins', blacks slaughtered cattle. Warriors were hunted and shot. Homesteads burned. Whole families were rounded up by white posses, the adults shot, their offspring battered to death to save ammunition. Vulnerable white men were murdered in their camps. Retaliation was swift. Posses shot blacks indiscriminately, wherever they were to be found, while at the same time a hopelessly understaffed police force tracked and arrested some of the real perpetrators, both black and white, desperately trying to enforce law and order.

These men, these fast-moving travellers, were not necessarily all from the same clan, but they had gathered their families together to try to survive, making the best of skin differences which, according to their laws, were not all that distant. They had consulted an elder who had approved of the melding, under the circumstances, but had added that each should observe their traditions, where possible.

Each man, as he ran, carried grief with him. For Numinga, the oldest of the group, his grief was like a spear that had never again found earth. From the first day when he'd seen his father chained, fed – as a joke, it turned out – and then shot, that spear of pain had set out on its journey through his heart and on into the blue, searching for peace, for a place to land where the old days would bloom again. Though he was a wanted man he had tired of the war and yearned for peace with the whitefellers.

Mimimiadie was a tried and true warrior. A fighting man. Merciless. His wife had been with this small group on a hunting trip, but when they returned to camp they discovered her battered body in nearby bush. Mimimiadie had found revenge even before they'd buried the poor woman, even before the proper crying time had been accorded. Numinga knew he was a dangerous man, as were his mates, Matong and Gopiny, but what could he do? After they'd tracked two miners and killed them as they slept, though it was obvious that they'd had nothing to do with the killing of his wife, Mimimiadie had pointed out that he was simply waging war on white man's terms. His woman had been innocent too.

The young fellow, Djarama, only about fifteen, had been scared stiff, witnessing that bloody attack. He'd run off from a mission house where, astonishing though it might seem, those white Godmen had informed him that the killing of blacks by whites was wrong. Criminal. An offence against the correctness of white law. The bloody fools! Djarama would have been safer at the mission. But no. Inspired by that talk, he'd made himself a spear and run off to fight the whites. And joined up with this mob.

22

Taken in as a toddler by the missionaries at the Daly River outpost, he'd lost touch with his own kin and had been thrilled to be accepted by these men and the kind woman. But she was dead now. And the grief in his eyes began when he saw her ravaged body. He was still in shock when Mimimiadie and his two mates made short work of those miners. Heard their screams. Cringed away, revolted.

As for their leader and his men, they were not so much grieved, Numinga pondered as he matched their strides, but scarred. Irrevocably scarred. Tribal warfare in the old days adhered to sets of rules, set down by the ancients. By their understanding of the Dreaming. Land owner-ship was rarely in question because every rock, every waterhole, every hill and plain had its own history, its place in tribal lore. Intrusions, raids, insults engendered battles, never this wholesale destruction of tribes and traditions; it was now a matter that needed a new way of thinking. But no one had been prepared. Even the greatest magic men and elders had no answer, no response, where once they had been called upon to sit in judgement to avoid bloodshed.

As they forged on into the dusk, Numinga didn't need to look at the three men to enter their hearts. On average they were all about twenty years younger than him, but they were living in the past. The burden they carried was death; he could see it in the muscles straining on their backs, in the side-side, side-side fall of their hips, in the placement of their feet, step after step, in stride with each other. He sighed. They'd seen too much. Been hurt too much. They would never go in. Ask for refuge as 'tame' blacks, as so many had done. As Numinga himself had done. Work for the whites in return for food. They were warriors, but no stories would ever be told about them round the campfires over the generations; they would be forgotten in the whirlwind that had engulfed their race.

Numinga grieved on their behalf. But he had no advice for them. No solution. He himself had tried the white ways, many years ago, reaching out to the friendship offered by a white man. A cattleman. Intrigued by all this newness, by the horses that he'd come to love.

It had hurt him when Mimimiadie had speared the miners' horses too. He'd tried to intervene but had been pushed away as an old fool.

'These animals don't belong here. They have no place in our Dream-ing,' Mimimiadie shouted. This from a man who'd proudly possessed a stolen horse for some weeks, until the police spotted it and took it away.

Numinga had worked at the station, fascinated by the need of white men to build shelters of such luxury. He'd learned to ride a horse, to muster cattle, and he soon picked up their language. He taught them where to find grub and water in what they thought was an empty wilderness, amused by their ignorance of the land. To his shame, a shame that still lingered, he saw his boss bring in a new gin, as they called the Aborigine girls. The boss didn't have a woman and so he decided this one, stolen from a nearby tribe, would do. He tied her to a tree, to tame her, as if this was the most natural thing in the world. He left her there for three days, and Numinga hadn't dared dissent, though he tried to take her food.

23

She was a beautiful girl, soft of skin and fine-featured. But she was fiery. She'd spat at Numinga, refusing his help. Screaming and kicking at the smiling boss when he came near her. When she was finally released, she attacked the boss, kicking and biting, so he'd beaten her. Beaten her too hard. He told his men to let her go in the end. And so they did. After they'd taken the bandages off her head. Because she was no use any more. Her brain addled and crushed, she'd turned into a madwoman, shambling off to the bush, never to be seen again.

The shame. Oh the shame of it, Numinga grieved, though it was long ago. He'd tried to console himself with the acceptance that black men were just as cruel with their women when they broke the laws. But what had that girl done? He tried not to think about it.

Not so long after that, a party of white men had come through the station, welcomed by the boss, who was pleased to have the new company. But these men, mounted police, had brought in six black prisoners, chained by the neck, just like they'd chained his father, and Numinga had been shocked. He'd thought those days were over. Or he'd managed to forget. They were left by a horse trough through the night but not given water, so he had stolen out in the darkness, with a pitcher of water for each man, appreciating their gratitude.

But even later that night, the drunken white men, including the boss, had stumbled out into the night, set the prisoners free and then shot them, one by one, as game, as they ran for freedom, cheering and shouting in glee as each man went down.

The next morning the visitors went cheerfully on their way, while the boss, with no sign of regret, bade them farewell.

Numinga, shamed again, could have used a gun. He knew how to use one, to kill maimed cattle, to ward off dingoes. The four white stockmen had guns, and ammo, hanging on a ledge by the cookhouse door. He could easily have picked up any of the handguns or rifles or shotguns lying about. But that would not do. He found time to shape himself a spear, a killing spear with a finely honed stone point, in the old way, not the long nails filched from whites of late. It was a fine spear, the best he'd ever made, and well deserving of its mission.

Numinga rode out with his boss one day, far out into the bush, and then suddenly he speared him in his right arm, so that when he fell, his gun would be out of reach.

'You shouldn't have shot them blackfellers down like they was nothink,' he said, to let his boss know why this execution was taking place. And his new spear did the rest.

Being known to the whites, Numinga had had a price on his head for years. He kept away from his own people for fear of retribution and had drifted along with various mobs since then, changing his name at will. But to the whites, oddly enough, after all these years, he was still known as Neddy the murderer. Neddy, he sighed. That was what the boss had always called him. Strange how it had stuck. But now he was travelling east, out of the range of the posses that would come, as inevitably as

24

dawn, and take their revenge once again on any blacks they could find. Numinga grieved over that too, a burden of guilt to add to his heavy heart. Sometimes he thought it would be easier to end it all by his own hand, but his life surge was still as strong as his body, and his mind too attuned to many curiosities yet to be seen and experienced.

They had no particular destination in mind; eventually they would camp somewhere safe to sit out the wet season. High ground. The rains were due. Had they remained back there towards their own country, they could easily have been trapped between flooding rivers with no hope of escaping the horsemen and their guns. Eventually they would have to move on, and then Numinga hoped to go his own way and take the lad, Djarama, with him. They both knew the white men's talk and their ways; they could go in. Pass as stockmen. Down south somewhere, towards the desert country. He would have to concentrate on young Djarama, turn his head away from futile wars, even if he was risking his own life. He smiled grimly. White men had long memories and astonishing cleverness at learning to recognise wanted blacks. They'd caught him a couple of times but he'd escaped. If he could save Djarama from walking into the guns, his own fugitive life might have some meaning.

He watched and followed as Mimimiadie began scrambling over rocks leading to a high ridge silhouetted against the pearly-pink skies of dusk. It was a tough climb, further than any of them had anticipated over the long-drawn-out slopes, dodging crevices and dead ends blocked by rock walls, each man eventually finding his own way in the darkness, to the top.

They camped overnight and in the morning found themselves on a huge uneven plateau that seemed to reach to the far horizon, but they looked back over the low country with delight. They could see the land spreading before them for ever and ever. This was eagle country. No one could sneak up on them. It was good country too; plenty of food up here, with small animals darting about and snakes and lizards dozing in the sun. And water. They found rock pools still holding a little precious water but they knew, by examining the worn rocky heights, that this place would never be able to absorb the torrents of rain soon to come. They would be safe, though, no shortage of shelter among bulky rocks and boulders, and no chance in the world the white men would need this land. Useless for crops or for cattle. Ideal. But the seasonal rains had to escape somewhere and there had been no evidence of falls on the slopes over which they'd just travelled. They began to explore further.

They followed dry fissures, carved so sharply into the terrain that they could only have been formed by swift falls of water, until they came to the precipice, and there they stood back in awe. Dizzied by the depths below his feet, Numinga almost fell back in fright. For safety, they lay on their stomachs to stare down at this magnificent gorge, the base so far down it seemed only a hand's-width across. They studied the wall on the other side, gutted with caves that, they agreed, must have been caused by

25

ancient blowholes in the surface of the plateau, where weaker surfaces had given way. And they remained there for a long time, overwhelmed by the majesty of the gorge.

That night as they sat around their campfire, all the talk was about the gorge and the wonderment of it. Mimimiadie claimed he'd known about it all the time. Not that anyone believed him. He was a bit of a bragger.

As the days passed, the others found ways to climb over the edge of that great gap, carefully getting toe-holds to narrow ledges, and moving along to the caves, avoiding the greasy slides of future cataracts that would soon descend down the steep surfaces. Exploring the heights of the gorge had become a game to them, but Numinga would have none of it. He was a river man, born on the flats, he was afeared of heights and didn't care who knew it.

Then one day they heard a voice echoing up from the depths, and, unthinking, Djarama had responded, from his favourite lookout place.

'Hello!' he called, a white man's word, pleased with himself as his voice banged off the cliffs too.

Then he heard the bush call, 'Coo-ee!' And he was off again, shouting back, 'Coo-ee!' as he had been taught at the mission, while Mimimiadie leapt about in rage.

He hissed down at the lad to stop, to come back up. And when Djarama was up on firm ground again he bashed him with a heavy stick.

'You fool!' he shouted, laying into the cringing lad again. 'Do you want to tell the world we're up here? That's white men. Do you want to invite them up here?'

'They can't get up here,' Djarama yelled, trying to escape the battering.

'If we can, they can, you idiot!'

Mimimiadie was right, of course, but Djarama resented the assault, and as Numinga dressed his wounds, he slyly laid the seeds of dissension that could one day separate this boy from his heroes. He added a little stinging sap to prolong the pain.

The nothingness of their lives, far from their families, was bothering Djarama. Day after day they just sat up here, watching the clouds wallowing in the distance, looking forward to the great rains, content to hide out here for months. Even if they were living high in the sky it was searingly hot from the heat reflected by their rocky sanctuary and there was no way to cool off. The air was still, stifling, and they were all cranky, spitting at each other over the hunting and the sharing of meat. He was angry. They were doing women's work, gathering what little there was in the way of ground food, finding less than a piccaninny could provide. Even at the mission they'd not had to live on just meat, and yet these men said this was good country. Numinga was the only one who could bring oddments of edible berries and pods and the occasional bush apples, but it was never enough, so Djarama was sent further afield with the old man in search of more sustenance, and he resented being ordered about like that.

One morning, though, something interesting came to pass. Far in the distance they saw a cloud of dust across the plains and instantly knew the reason. White men moving a mob of cattle. Pleased with their bird's-eye view, they watched the cattle moving closer.

'Big mob,' Numinga commented. 'Biggest mob I saw in a long time.'

'Big mob,' Mimimiadie announced, as if he hadn't heard Numinga. 'And coming right through our gorge I say.'

For days they watched until the drovers began steering the leaders towards the entrance to the gorge, both the horsemen and the hundreds of cattle seeming tiny and insignificant so far below them.

'We could spit on them from here,' Mimimiadie laughed, and Numinga looked back at the grey clouds still edging in slowly from the coast.

'Soon the rains will be spouting great waterfalls down there,' he said. 'And they know it. See how fast they're pushing those animals now. It'll take more than a day to squeeze that mob through there.'

Excited, Djarama jumped up, imitating a rain dance. 'Make it rain now! Make it pour! Send down the torrents, drown them all.'

No one took any notice of him. They knew the white men were too smart to get caught like that.

But then Djarama had a better idea. 'Quick. Let's get a pile of rocks together. We could hurl rocks down at them, a hundred rocks, bash the cattle, break heads! We could cause a great stampede, wipe half of them out. Why don't we do that? Quick!'

Mimimiadie turned to growl at him. 'Why don't you shut up? I told you before, we're safe here. We cause a stampede, kill a few cattle, maybe some drovers. Then what? They'll be up here with their guns. Then where do we go? We can't go back and we can't go on. The rivers in front of us will be in flood too.'

But his mate, Gopiny, disagreed. 'Wait on. They don't have to know we're here. There's no need to be throwing rocks. We could stay hidden, we have to stay out of sight, but we could dislodge a few boulders. There are plenty out there on the ledges teetering already. I reckon they're only waiting for the next rains to set them loose.' He grinned. 'We could give them a little nudge.'

Djarama was jubilant. 'There! See! I told you so. We don't have to sit here doing nothing and let an opportunity like this go by.'

Their leader held up his hand for silence. 'I was coming to that. We could dislodge some boulders, easy, but I don't want silly Djarama out there, showing himself or yelling out like he doing now. Like he did before. He could bring the trouble on us.'

'That's true,' Gopiny said. 'He stays up here. We'll do it. Make it look like natural.'

'I won't stay here! I know where there are loose rocks. I could show you.' Djarama was furious.

At a nod from the leader, Gopiny was on his feet, his spear in his hand. He swung about, kicked Djarama behind the knees, and when he fell to the ground he stood over him, a foot on his chest and the spear at his throat.

'We don't need trouble. You stay here. Agreed?'

'Yes,' Djarama croaked. 'Yes.'

Numinga looked up as a warm gust of wind sped over the plateau. He licked his lips. 'Water in the wind already now.'

They left him there, in charge of the unpopular one, he supposed, but if Djarama decided to disobey, to climb down the rugged rim of the precipice, there was nothing he could do. He still wouldn't go near the edge. He heard a low rumbling, like distant thunder, and realised the cattle had entered the first chamber of the gorge.

Djarama was lying on his stomach by a wedge of granite.

'Come and see!' he called. 'The cattle are in there, they look like ants from here, what I can see of them.'

'I can hear them,' Numinga said dryly. Indeed it occurred to him that the constant pounding of those hooves could easily unseat loose boulders without anyone's help. And no doubt the drovers would be aware of that, looking up cautiously to save their own necks. He hoped the trio would keep well out of sight.

Djarama was fuming. 'Why don't they do something? They're just letting them pass! I'd have let them have it by this.'

'Plenty of cattle yet. They're strung out there for miles.'

'What difference does it make?'

Numinga didn't know or care. He sat well back in the shade of spindly shrubs, rethinking his plan to rescue this aggravating kid from a life on the run. Would it be worth the trouble? Would it be possible? Djarama had no respect for any of his fellow travellers, his elders. Under tribal law a few thrashings would have cured that, taught him his place. But then, by all accounts the missionaries hadn't been afraid to use the whip on him, with little success. Numinga dozed, worrying the problem, the low, persistent rumbling reminding him of welcome thunder. He was tired. He liked to rest in the middle of the day . . .

Unnoticed, Djarama lowered himself over the edge for a better view, moving carefully along the rough cliff face to a ledge hidden behind a buttress of rocks, and stepping down to another ledge. From there he could only see Gopiny, crouching quietly, waiting.

What for? Why didn't they get on with it?

Then he heard a low whistle, and he saw Gopiny pick up a stripped branch and, using it as a lever, loosen a heavy rock. When it began to move, Gopiny flattened himself on the ground as if he were afraid he'd go with it. The rock teetered, but remained in place, so Gopiny gave it a hard shove with his foot.

It was away! At the same time, other rocks near Gopiny went pounding and bouncing down, and then, disappointingly, they fell out of sight, the angle too steep to see their full progress.

Gopiny was busy trying to move another rock, not boulder-smooth like the others, but a beauty, raw and jagged, part of a cracked seam that was wedged on a ledge. He worked on it for a while but couldn't shift it, so he took his stick and moved on, out of sight. Probably to join the others. Just as he stepped away, though, Djarama saw the rock move. It definitely moved. He was about to whistle to Gopiny to go back, but changed his mind.

He would do it himself. Gopiny was a weakling!

Excited now, Djarama made his way over to that rock. He wished he knew what was happening down below. If the falling rocks had caused the chaos expected of them. But it was hard to tell. Further over he heard another rock bang loose, Mimimiadie's work, and looked up in time to see it bouncing away in a spray of rubble. But only one! He'd imagined they'd be sending dozens of rocks pelting down the chasm, not just a couple here and there. A real landslide. Well, he'd give them a hand. He'd keep out of sight, not make a sound, so they couldn't be angry with him. He'd just shove this one loose and then scramble back up to the old bloke. But it was hard to shift. Harder than he'd thought. He wished he had a sturdy stick too.

When he still couldn't move it, he inched into a crevice right behind the stubborn old thing, and managed to squeeze himself into a sitting position on the ledge, his back firmly against a good strong wall. With both feet placed midway on the rock, he shoved with all his might, stifling a yell as it gave way and hurtled into space.

But beneath him the ledge was crumbling now, and he was scrabbling with hands and feet in disintegrating rubble. Frantic, he felt himself sliding away. He clutched wildly for support but nothing would hold him. He tried to stop the slide, searching for a foothold, but the whole section seemed to be giving way, so slowly, so casually, that he expected it to come to a standstill any second. But there was no stopping it now. Djarama was caught in a landslide that was fast gathering momentum. Then there was nothing. He screamed as he was flung away from the cliff face, plunging down. His screams echoed, and echoed, becoming fainter as the life drained out of them.

Numinga was dreaming of a river in flood, of a fast-moving torrent full of debris, but he was safe in a canoe, manoeuvring splendidly, unconcerned, though they were rushing towards rapids, and Djarama was there with him, but he didn't look like Djarama; his passenger was a white man. And Djarama was screaming in fear, refusing to accept that they weren't in any danger . . .

Then he sat up. Wide awake. Had he heard screams?

Mimimiadie and his mates were back, running, collecting their spears, destroying evidence of their campfires with brush.

'What's going on?' Numinga asked fearfully.

Gopiny was trembling. 'The kid. He fell. He was screaming. It was terrible. A ledge gave way.'

'He fell! Ah no! Are you sure? Maybe he only slid down a little way. Are you sure?'

'We saw him fall.' Gopiny shuddered. 'He went all the way down.'

'And he's dead.' Mimimiadie had no pity. 'You should have kept him up here. Now he's ruined everything. We have to get out of here.'

'Where will we go?' Gopiny cried.

Matong, a sour fellow who rarely spoke, was already leaving.

'Posses coming. I'm going home.'

'You can't,' Mimimiadie hissed. 'They'll be looking for us.'

'Looking for us here too. Which way they come? You don't know.'

Mimimiadie knew that was true – the whites could come from the gorge, either end – but he had to have the last word. 'Better we split up anyway,' he yelled as Matong loped away, retreating. 'You come with me,' he told Gopiny.

'Where?' Gopiny was panicking.

'Unless you want to jump over the gorge, the only way left,' he snarled, pointing north.

'What's up there?'

'Good country.'

'For a while,' Numinga, their forager, told them. 'Then it drops down to four swamps, unhealthy. No good until the rains come and clean them out. I could smell them from miles away.'

'Then that's where we go,' Mimimiadie said stubbornly. 'We only stay for a while. The whites come up here. Find no one. Think that dead one been making trouble on his own. They go away.' He grinned at Gopiny. 'Then we come back. Sit down here. Safe.'

Gopiny wasn't so sure about that. 'How safe? Next time the whites come with their cattle, they might look about up here first, with their guns.'

'You're stupid. Once the rains come past us up here and start falling down there, no cattle, no one could get through that gorge.' He turned to Numinga. 'Isn't that right?'

'Yes. It will flood.'

Gopiny looked back across the plains that led to the open forests and on to their own rich lands along the Daly River, and Numinga guessed he would rather follow Matong, taking his chances on making it home. But Mimimiadie was the boss.

'Where are *you* going?' he asked Numinga. Not that he cared; it was only a form of dismissal.

Numinga watched them leave, their hard black backs marked, like his, with cicatrices denoting manhood, but unlike him, they were not scarred as well from the whitefeller whips.

He shrugged. They were no loss. There had been no crying for the lad who had flown to his Dreaming and perhaps, he mused, that way he could find it, the poor lost fellow. Stranger things had happened.

But what now? Obviously he couldn't stay here either. He'd be shot on sight. The whites tore into a rage if even one of their millions of cattle was killed. Those rocks must have caused that army of animals to go berserk. As a former stockman, he wouldn't relish being caught in that confined space with a mob of wild cattle, especially a mob of that size. Going on numbers, he figured, the real confusion would be at the other end, where escaping cattle would be running mad, so the drovers, when they managed to extricate themselves from a stampede in the gorge, would be out there, trying to round them up, and from there, they'd be looking up to the gorge. Matong was right. Better to go back.

He stood, limbering up for a long trek to somewhere. He would have to run the gauntlet of searchers, posses or police, who would still be trying to track the killers of those miners; they never gave up. Unless of course they'd already executed a few innocent blacks in reprisal.

That was the terrible part of this war. Reprisals. He had learned the word from the whites, discovering it meant, simply, payback. What was the use of a war based on payback? he'd wondered. Payback, according to his rules, was for individuals who insulted or broke the law, and in extreme cases via the magic men, where pointing the bone was a useful punishment. But not this endless 'you kill, I kill', with no clear result mapped out. No sit-down talks to iron out problems between tribes like in the old days; just killings. Numinga couldn't bear to look ahead to the end result. He was tired. Right now he only yearned for a safe haven.

There were still some tribes, so remote in the south, or over on Arnhem land, past the Alligator rivers, that they were not bothered by white marauders, but they were too far. He'd only joined up with Mimimiadie and his mates for company, and for his trouble had got himself mixed up in the murders. Though he really was upset about Mimimiadie's wife. That was terrible. Another crime that wouldn't have posses scouring the land. Only the distraught husband. Not the best wasps' nest to disturb.

So. The safest place right now was within the sweltering jungles still owned by the Daly River tribes, which were too dangerous for the white men to infiltrate, unless they had a death wish. The trouble was, those Daly River men, like Mimimiadie, resented being pushed back into the crocodile-infested areas. They owned the lands far beyond, where they could hunt as they'd always done had the rapacious white men not taken them. That was why stubborn men like Mimimiadie were out there. Their territory. Their hunting ground.

Numinga shrugged. Mimimiadie had been right about one thing. It was better to split up. And he had a better chance than any of them. He could speak English. And hoping that no one recognised him, he could say he was a stockman, looking for a job. A stockman wearing only a rope twist round his waist? Not likely. If he was to make it all the way to the sanctuary of the Daly River, he'd have to find some clothes.

Chapter Four

The main herd was held back as four men took the first mob, about three hundred beasts, into the cool reaches of the gorge. Paddy's son, Duke Milligan, was way up front, not so much to lead as to keep control when the herd forged out of the narrow confines on to the flat country beyond. Paddy was riding there with the cattle, keeping to the left-hand side, which provided more space between the walls and the shallow water-holes. Far from being a hazard, the watery passage was making life easier for the riders, Yorkey noticed as he followed Paddy. The heavy beasts were muscling and shoving each other to at least travel through water, aware that the shouting men and the whips were not allowing the pace to slow. Not far behind him, the stranger known as Zack was keeping his end up, feeding the cattle carefully into the narrower sections and then releasing them to move faster as the caverns widened.

It was all going well; the mob were steaming through on their best behaviour, snorting and shouldering, almost as if they were enjoying the change of air. Yorkey cracked his whip, edged his horse round a rocky patch and stood in the saddle to get a better look at the old gorge again. It would be really something to see the falls cascading down those walls, in full flood, but not possible. Not unless you were looking to drown. Then he remembered the voice that he'd heard, thought he'd heard, and craned to get a better look at the heights. Not that you'd hear an answering call over this racket. The noise of all those hooves drumming along would drown out a brass band.

He saw the movement in the flicker of an eye and shouted to Paddy to look out, waving his arms wildly, but Paddy didn't look back, nor did he look up. The boulder tumbling from above, bouncing and crashing, dislodging more rock, didn't seem to be making a sound. As Yorkey instinctively forced his mount forward, in a frantic attempt to warn Paddy, the huge rock and a shower of rubble thudded into the herd. Animals screamed, crumpled, others stumbled over them in a panic and then broke away, rampaging in all directions, causing yet more to stumble and fall.

Shouting to the stockmen behind him, Yorkey had no choice but to wheel his horse at the mob, trying to halt them, hoping that bloke Zack was doing the same, turning the last of them back until this lot could be sorted out. His whip cut viciously into the hides of the cattle still on their feet but another boulder struck and there was no holding the forward

33

mob. There was a rush for them to get out now, a stampede. He couldn't see Paddy, and his own position was too dangerous to hold, stuck right in the middle of the rush, so he pulled over to the wall, letting more pass, deciding it would be better to concentrate on the tail-enders.

Zack came up to join him, and the two of them set to work to cut off the slower, confused tail-end of the mob. They soon managed to slow them to a walk.

'Where's Paddy?' Yorkey yelled.

'Can't see him,' Zack shouted. 'He would have had to go with them, to get out of that.' He stared up. 'We can't go past that point in case there's more loose rock. You keep easing them down here and I'll go back to start turning them around. We'll take this lot outside to the other blokes.'

He backed his horse to the wall and then nosed it slowly along the side of the shivering cattle that were quieter now, apprehensive, but suddenly Yorkey ploughed forward, reaching out, grabbing for Zack's arm, almost pulling him from his horse.

Angrily Zack resisted, shouting at Yorkey, just as the landslide came crashing down on them. Not just boulders this time; a full slide.

Zack was struck by rocks but as he fell, Yorkey grabbed him, dragging him roughly from the horse before he slid to the ground himself, letting his own horse dash away in fright. He pulled the dazed man flat to the wall, in behind a mound of boulders, all hopes of maintaining control of their end of the herd forgotten. Away to their right, around the bend, a landslide was in full flight, tons of rock and rubble thundering down, and Yorkey was terrified, afraid that the whole wall was collapsing. And in among all that racket he thought he heard someone scream.

'What was that?' Zack cried.

'Someone hurt. Bad, I think.'

'Who?' Zack struggled up, groping dizzily at the wall.

'Dunno.' Yorkey was spooked. It seemed to him that the scream had not come from the ground, from a man caught under those hooves or suffering the battering of rocks. It had come from the sky and faded into the dusty mists raised by the landslides. He remembered the stories his mother had told him, of the death leap, of the spirits that still lived here, and the overwhelming feeling he'd experienced when he'd first entered the gorge. Now he felt it to be true. This was indeed a sacred place and they'd been given a warning. As they stepped out to survey the dead and injured animals that were being carefully avoided by the surviving cattle that trotted on by, their own sense of order restored, Yorkey was nervous, believing he was in the presence of a spirit. Maybe the young man who'd leapt from the heights back there in the ages was still reliving his passion and his pain. A restless spirit, Yorkey decided, still here. He would have to think on that. Later.

Zack was scrambling about, calling to other men, searching, but the slides had left huge wedge-shaped piles of rubble jutting out on to the floor of the gorge, altering the shape of the caverns, and all around him lay injured animals, moaning helplessly.

'We'd better go and find out if everyone is all right,' he said. 'I don't know who screamed. It could have been an animal.'

Yorkey nodded. 'Yeah.' He wasn't about to air his opinions to these white blokes and get laughed at. He stared at the huge extension of the wall created by the landslide. There'd be cattle buried underneath, but no humans. He and that bloke Zack had been the only ones in this section of the gorge.

'Come on!' Zack started to limp away, then turned back. 'Hey, Yorkey. Thanks. I'm beholden to you. I reckon you grabbed me just in time, I was headed in that direction.'

Paddy Milligan was badly injured, lying half submerged in a waterhole with his son, Duke, kneeling beside him wailing like a banshee.

'He's dead! Me pa's dead!'

Zack pushed him away. 'Let me see.'

Paddy was drawn up in a foetal position as if to defend himself from the pounding hooves, and his blood had turned the waterhole pink, but he was still breathing.

'Settle down, Duke. He's still with us. Help me get him out of here before he slides back in. Careful now. And someone do a count. Check if everyone's accounted for.'

They brought blankets and made a bed for Paddy by the wall, then tore shirts to make bandages while Zack worked to stem the blood and make him as comfortable as he could. He had seen men trampled by cattle before, and he knew there was a fine line between helping and destroying in these cases. Even the doctors argued about it.

'He's in shock,' he told Duke. 'Find more blankets. Saddle blankets, anything, we have to keep him warm. And get some wood to light a fire; it will get cold in here when the sun sets.'

They brought whisky when Paddy regained consciousness, and gave him some sips, while Zack gently straightened him out, resetting a broken arm and a broken leg with sticks as splints, worrying all the time about internal injuries because it was obvious that breathing caused pain.

'Go for help,' he shouted at Duke.

'Which way?'

Zack thought quickly. There were three men left with the main herd back there beyond the gorge, but they were too far from a homestead.

'Go ahead. Make for Katherine. There are homesteads on the way. We need a doctor and a wagon.'

Duke held back. 'I can't leave my pa. What if he dies?'

'Then send someone else. Move!'

It was then Zack realised that some of the men helping them were strangers.

'Where did you come from?' he asked as he eventually settled back, with Paddy cocooned by the fire.

'We're from Pop Oatley's station. On our way home. Five of us. We've been on leave. Going home to hole up for the wet.' The stockman grinned. 'We were headed for the gorge and we come across all them stray cattle wandering about and not a drover in sight, so we rounded them up and two of our blokes are keeping an eye on them. Victoria River brand, eh?'

'Yes.'

'Too good to be runnin' loose. We reckoned you must have run into strife in here. And by the way, we did what you asked. One of our blokes went on through the gorge and talked to your drovers out there. We did the count, like, and all your blokes are in one piece, except this poor bugger.'

'Thank God. I thought I heard a scream. But I'd taken a whack on the head . . .'

'I can see that. You'd better let me mop it up.'

'All right. Must have been an animal I heard back there.'

'Not surprised. It's a big bloody mess. We reckon you've lost about fifty head. Hope it's all right with you, my mates, and that Abo drover you've got, are going to shoot the beasts too beat to get up.'

'Yes,' Zack said numbly. 'Yes. It's a bloody disaster. I'm always wary of landslides here, but not at this time of the year.'

'Could have been worse. Only two or three spots. Nothing major, just bad luck for your mate here. And the Vic River station won't miss a bullock or two. Anyway, my mates reckon it was a mild quake. They reckon they felt the shiver. Can't say I did meself.'

When Zack stood up, the stockman stared at him. 'Jeez. You're Zack Hamilton from Black Wattle. I thought you looked familiar. I thought you was a drover, with this mob. What are you doing here?'

Zack couldn't remember when he'd endured a headache as bad as this, although the stockman, Johnny Wise, had announced when he'd cleaned the wound that it probably didn't need stitching. Probably not, Zack thought, but my head feels as if my skull has been stood on by an elephant. He was still waiting by the campfire when he heard the shots, heard the animals being put out of their misery. Now, as well as worrying about Paddy, he had the carcasses to think about. They couldn't be buried in rock. They would have to be burned or dragged out of here. Jesus bloody wept! Would he ever get home?

He looked at the men huddled by the campfire within reach of Paddy, who was quiet now, breathing huskily, and that reminded him. 'How is Pop? I've heard he hasn't been too good.'

'Not too good at all. Had a heart attack and then got pneumonia on top of it. William Oatley was out there for a while, until the old man was on his feet again. He tried to talk him into going to Darwin with him, but you know Pop. Stubborn old coot, he wouldn't budge. So William had to go on home. Last I saw of Pop, he was still wobbly, believe me, but he reckons he's as fit as a trout.'

Zack laughed. 'That sounds like Pop. Say hello for me when you get back. I hope he's well enough to come to town for the summer, though. It

36

won't seem like Christmas without Pop Oatley making the toasts.'

He saw Yorkey return and squat by the fire. 'The horses? Are they all right?'

'Yeah. Your feller got a gash on the rump, that's all.'

'Ah well,' Zack sighed. 'Have you had some grub, Yorkey? There's damper here.'

'I got some back there,' Yorkey lied. He wasn't hungry. Didn't even want to think about food in this place with those spirits hanging about. And that scream still echoing in his head.

That Zack, the ring-in stockman. He was a lean, rangy bloke, on the way to fifty, Yorkey guessed, and he'd taken over as if this was his show. Even Paddy's other stockmen had jumped to attention under his orders.

One of them had ridden in to investigate the delay and been shocked, naturally, at this mess, suggesting they ought to turn back, but Zack had ordered them to stay put, hold the main herd until this was all sorted out. One by one they'd come in to see Paddy, but as they did they were given jobs with the other men.

None of them were strangers to the necessity of destroying cattle in time of drought, but as they shot the injured animals and built a bonfire to burn the carcasses, they were all distressed, with Paddy lying there helpless. Paddy, who prided himself on delivering cattle, all of his cattle, in good nick. If he were fully conscious he'd hear the shots and smell the burning, and he'd know . . . and Yorkey, working with them, was upset. This was a horrible thing to have to do in the beautiful gorge. It seemed like a desecration, as if it had become unclean. And right under the noses of the spirits. Had those old spirits struck back at the white men for some reason? Not hard to think of plenty of reasons, given the way the whites had treated their people. He shuddered. He hoped they'd keep in mind that he wasn't one of the whitefellers if they decided to hand out more punishment on this gloomy night. It was cold in the gorge now. And black as pitch. For his own survival against the spirits of the night, Yorkey wondered whether he should sit with those men now huddled about the campfire, or stay apart.

Comfort won. He moved closer for warmth, hugging a blanket.

'No more landslides, eh?' Duke said to him. 'Zack reckons they've stopped. He reckons we could bring the mob through just a few at a time tomorrow. After we get my pa out. I suppose he's right.'

'Who is he?' Yorkey asked. 'Where'd you get him from?'

'Zack? He's a local. The manager of the Big Run introduced him to my pa, to give us a hand. He's a boss himself. Owns a big station out here called Black Wattle. I tell you, Yorkey, I'm bloody glad he came along. I wouldn't have knowed what to do. Jesus, he even had a bottle of whisky in his saddle pack. Good stuff, given him at the Big Run, he said, but needed now for Paddy, to ease the pain.' Duke was almost in tears. 'Bloody nice of him, wouldn't you say?'

Yorkey nodded. By the sound of things Duke had been given a few shots of the good whisky too. But what had he said just then? That cattle station? Black Wattle. Another whitefeller name for blackfeller territory. Like this gorge. Campbell's Gorge. He hitched his tobacco pouch from his hip pocket and slowly rolled a smoke as if he were rolling that name round on his tongue, then dug back again into those tattered memories, remembering with an effort his mother's stories.

'We used to go to the gorge at walkabout time, from the station, from Black Wattle station . . . I was a housemaid there, the missus . . . she . . .'

Yorkey shrugged. Might be right. Might be imagining it too. And so what? They wouldn't remember Netta now. Nor an itinerant blackfeller called Jimmy Moon. Twenty years ago. A generation of blacks had come and gone since then. He turned away from the firelight and stared into the blackness, wondering why he was even contemplating all this useless information now.

If you really want to go back, he told himself, you only have to ask for the Waray people; they'd be easy to find, some of them anyway, in the country you've just crossed. West of the gorge. The whites live their own lives. Separate. But what would be the point? What would you all do if you found relations? Sit and stare at each other? Because you're separate too. Not of them any more.

Not of anyone.

He was restless all night. Dreaming, dozing, seeing his mother weeping, but it wasn't Netta, it was a white woman, heartbreaking to hear, and he dragged himself away from her. Waking. Chilled to the bone. That was the way with dreams. They got everything mixed up. Even white with black.

There was hardly a chink of dawn when Yorkey stole quietly away from the camp, sickened by the stench of the dying fires. He sluiced his face with crystal-clear water from a rock pool and began to walk back up the gorge towards cleaner air, retracing their hazardous journey.

No doctor could be found but a wagon arrived to convey Paddy to the nearest station homestead, only forty miles away, and since word had got around that drovers were in trouble at the gorge, volunteers rode in all morning. Soon Duke had enough men for a drive twice the size.

He was nervous of taking on the gorge again but gave in to the general opinion that he had no other choice. Already clouds were encroaching on pale skies to the north. The slides had been random. Some said they were caused by a mild quake; others said it could have been blacks, but most argued against that. If blacks had been on the job they would have caused a damn sight more damage than this. It was just bad luck.

By the time they were all through, Duke was smiling.

'Jeez, Yorkey, I wish Paddy could of seen this. Those blokes nursed our mob through like they were kittens. Bloody nice of them.'

'Yes. It all went off pretty good. I heard some of them are going on with you to Pine Creek?'

'That's right. Mates of Paddy's. They're gonna see us there safe.'

38

'Good. I think I might take a break here, Duke. Go back and have a look at this country.'

'You won't get far in the wet.'

'I can always bunk in at a station. Do stock work for a while.'

'Fair enough, Yorkey. We won't have any work until the wet's over anyway. You can pick us up in Katherine, we'll always have a job for you.'

Yorkey shook hands with Duke, wished his pa well, and went in search of Zack, only to find he'd already left.

He was disappointed. He wouldn't have been asking any favours, just seeing if there were any jobs around. Maybe at Black Wattle. He could have sort of mentioned that, like in passing. Now it was too late. But he could meander out that way. Somewhere west of the route they had taken from the Big Run. He'd find it. Maybe Waray people were still there. Maybe he'd have a chance to look about anyway. Nothin' else to do.

Matong was angry. More upset than he'd shown at the death of that kid. A fearful way to die, screaming all the way down like that. And a waste. He hoped, as he ran on, that they'd killed a few whites to make up for it.

Travelling across this country was dangerous, too many horsemen on the move at this time, so he had to take shelter every so often to spy out the land, ready for his next run, watching about him all the time. Which left no time for hunting, and that made him angrier still. He had no food, and even if he fell over a wallaby or a snake, he couldn't light a fire for fear of drawing attention to himself. Rage ran with him as he faced the prospect of many days without food. He was already hungry, but he knew it was the only sensible thing to do. He would endure it, but it shouldn't be so. This was blackfeller country.

And then there was Mimimiadie's wife. They hadn't gone out on a raid, war parties never took women with them. Only to hunt for some game. The kid had begged to be allowed to go with them and Mimimiadie had brought his wife along to work; now they were both dead. Their families would have known something had gone wrong when the hunting party hadn't returned, and they'd have soon heard that two miners had been killed, but they'd have no way of knowing the rest of the story. Suddenly he realised that he would have to break the news to them that the kid and the woman were dead. The kid had no one, but she'd had a family, and three children, two girls and a little boy – Boomi, his father's pride.

Only six years old and no mother now, Matong mourned. And his father far away. But he'd be back, Matong could tell him. Mimimiadie was a brave man. He'd come home after the rainy season.

Padding along, fighting the streaks of pain that were attacking his empty stomach, he made for a creek that he knew was ahead, a sturdy little creek, deep enough to carry some water all year round. At least he could fill up on water. But then he heard horses, and dived into the shallow cover of open forest, flattening his body in the long wiry grass, listening.

39

Not horses; one horse, galloping steadily. It would soon pass. And so it did, but it slowed soon after and as Matong climbed to his feet he understood what was happening. The rider was going to that creek too. His creek! How did the whitefeller know about that? It was hidden in matted undergrowth, and in a gully too deep for horses to get to, except when it was in flood. Furious, he followed, making no sound as he edged through the scrub. He saw the man dismount, climb down and drink thirstily through cupped hands. Then he filled his wide hat with water and scrambled back up to give the horse a drink. He spilled some water on the way, so it wasn't enough for the animal. Matong watched, irritated, as he repeated the performance, but then he noticed the saddlebag. White men always had food somewhere. There could be food in that bag. Easy pickings.

When he made his move, he was almost too late. The man had his back to him as he swung up into the saddle but the horse must have smelled danger.

Just as Matong stepped out to get a clear, strong throw, the horse, snorting, jigged about, causing the rider to tighten his grip on the reins, hugging the flanks with his legs.

Matong's aim was true. His spear thudded into the whitefeller's back but it didn't dislodge him, and the horse took off, bolted away like lightning, the tall spear thwacking on low branches until it tore free from the man's back and fell to the ground.

Disconsolately, Matong went after it, picked it up and wiped it in the grass to clean off the blood. They'd got away with the food. He considered going after them, but the horse was so scared it would probably race away until it ran out of wind. Or dropped dead, Matong hoped. He should have speared that man when he was in the creek, a better chance then, but he hadn't wanted to foul the water.

Muttering to himself, he ran down, splashed across the creek, swallowed a few mouthfuls of water and leapt easily up the other side of the gully. Then he too took off, running hard now, into the glare of the afternoon sun. There were hills ahead; he could make them by nightfall if he forced himself to keep moving, and he could cross through them in the dark. He'd be halfway home by then. He glanced at his spear. He'd only been carrying it from habit, but there'd be no hunting; he could go faster without it. Regretfully he tossed it away, lowered his head and plunged on.

Yorkey had been following the cattleman all morning, hoping to catch up with him, as if by chance, and he figured by this that he'd got the directions mixed up or Zack was going at a real pace, because there was no sign of him. No sign of anyone on this lonely road. At least, Yorkey mused, he was on a track, a well-worn track, that had to lead somewhere. But he wasn't about to push his horse too much; they'd both be in trouble if the animal broke down. A man could die out here in this heat.

Right now he had grub in his pack, thanks to Paddy's cook, and plenty of water, which was just as well, since he hadn't seen a waterhole anywhere near this track, so there was no real rush. He rehearsed what he'd say when he did manage to 'stumble' on to Black Wattle station.

'Is this Zack's place? Well whaddya know? Is he about? I wouldn't mind a word with him.'

He rode on into the afternoon, getting sick of this, looking for a place to camp, preferably at a waterhole, to cool off.

'For both of us to cool off, mate,' he told the horse. 'But it's not looking too good. We better just take it quiet from now on.'

Yorkey was a whistler of note. He could whistle any tune the blokes sang to him, picked them up, no trouble. Especially the Irish songs with a lilt to them. He didn't know any of the words, but he surely got the tunes right, and was often asked to entertain in pubs or camps. He'd even whistled with a well-known fiddler once and been clapped like mad. But what Yorkey would never forget was being able to keep in tune with a real musical instrument. And to know he had it right, every goddamn note.

'Bloody hell,' he said, proud of that time.

Now, to entertain himself, and the horse, who liked him to whistle, Yorkey began to work through his repertoire, pealing out notes that would make a magpie green, as a publican had once told him.

But down the track the whistling came to a breathless halt. A lone horse, still rigged, its bridle dribbling to the ground, was standing nervously by the wayside.

Yorkey slid from his mount and approached it carefully.

'Whoa, boy, whoa, boy.' He held out his hand and inched forward as the horse shied away.

'Whoa, boy. It's all right. I'm not gonna hurt you.'

There was blood on the saddle and its rump. Dried blood.

'Good boy, you're all right, aren't you? Good boy, now don't you be worrying about me.' His voice was soothing as he moved closer, whispering. This was Zack Hamilton's horse! But where the hell was he?

'Don't turn away, I'm not gonna hurt you. Come on now. You look at my mate back there. He's a good horse too, a real good feller. What say we go back and talk to him?'

Horses were curious, Yorkey knew. It didn't know what this chat was, though it was listening carefully to the soothing voice, ready to bolt. Rather than have to chase the animal down the track, Yorkey kept talking, a few feet back, and when the horse finally turned its head to see what this was about, curiosity having got the better of it, Yorkey lunged and grabbed the bridle.

Quickly he hitched both horses to a tree and ran along the burning track, calling to Zack; then he turned and ran in the other direction, noticing as he passed that Zack's water bottle was still strapped to the saddle. When there was no answer he began again, up and down the track, still calling, searching the soft thick dust for footprints, even for traces of blood.

When he finally spotted a disturbance in the dust, not footprints but thick drag marks that led into the scrub, he soon found Zack resting against a tree that at least offered some shade.

'What the hell . . .'

'I fell off,' Zack muttered, as if that was a stupid thing to do.

'You more than fell off.' Yorkey ran back to fetch him some water.

While he gave him the water, Yorkey could see that Zack was badly hurt. There was blood seeping from his back right down the side of his dungarees, and his face was grey. He hadn't even the strength to hold the water bottle for himself.

'Hang on,' Yorkey said quietly, putting the water bottle aside. 'Let's just see what's wrong here.'

Zack groaned and fell to his side as Yorkey drew him away from the tree to inspect his back.

'God almighty!' Zack's shirt was drenched in blood, so much so that it was difficult at first to discern skin from cloth, but as Yorkey gingerly pulled away the torn material he saw the gaping wound, already under attack by flies. He brushed them away, shocked to see that this man's back looked as if it had been torn, just like the shirt.

'What happened to you?' he asked as he ripped half the shirt away, dousing it with water to try to clean the wound.

'Spear,' Zack whispered. 'Bloody spear.'

'Christ!' Inadvertently Yorkey peered about him. His own back felt very vulnerable as he worked. He managed to get the rest of the shirt off, trying to cause as little pain as possible, though he knew that was a faint hope. Then he squeezed out the material and placed it over the wound, using the rest of the shirt as a makeshift bandage that would at least cover the wound if not hold the cloth in place for too long.

His mind was racing. Blacks on the warpath around here? The horses half a mile down the road with rifles and ammo in full view? I'd better get them first.

'I won't be long.' And he wasn't; he sprinted down the road, relieved to see the firearms still in place, and galloped the horses back to lead them into the scrub. Yorkey doubted he'd be able to kill kinsmen anyway, but at least he had the guns, not them. And maybe he could parlay with them to get the bossman and himself out of this mess.

'Go for help,' Zack muttered through clenched teeth.

'I can't leave you here.' He supposed he could build a shelter of branches to protect Zack from the heat, but he'd be a sitting duck if his attackers were still around.

'How far on to your place?'

Zack was lying flat on his stomach, and he seemed not to hear.

'Are you still awake?'

'Thirty miles,' Zack replied irritably. 'Go.'

'It'll be dark soon. I'd never find it.'

He heard Zack sigh in frustration and lift his head to stare at him.

'We better camp here the night,' Yorkey said, but then realised he'd be faced with the same problem tomorrow. He couldn't leave Zack stuck here alone. Maybe he could make one of those stretcher things from saplings that horses pulled along. He'd seen a man brought into Katherine on one a couple of years ago. But he knew that was fanciful. He didn't even have an axe to start with, let alone the rest of the wherewithal.

It was Zack who made the decision. 'Get me up. I'll ride.'

'You can't ride.'

'Get me up.' That was an order.

The struggle to get Zack on to his horse was a slow and excruciatingly painful operation for him but they finally managed and Zack flopped, exhausted, on to the horse's neck.

Yorkey gave him some water. 'I'm gonna have to tie you on, you can't go through that again. I'll try not to hurt.'

Once Zack was roped down, Yorkey mounted his horse and, leading the other, set off slowly. He was sure that Zack had passed out several times as they covered mile after long mile, but once they plodded into the darkness he must have forced himself to stay awake, issuing the occasional instruction.

'Branch off here. Right.' And later on, other turns as the track followed the terrain. Yorkey thought it would be hard enough to find the place in daylight. Every so often he stopped to check on his patient and share water with him and the horses until it was all gone. He munched his rations and chewed tobacco to keep himself awake.

Had he dozed off? He felt Zack tugging at the lead.

'You all right there?' Yorkey asked.

'Stop here.'

'Ah, too soon, mate. We got a good way to go yet.'

'Call!' Zack grated.

'All right, I'll call.' He shouted. 'Hey! Black Wattle! Hey, anyone there?'

Dogs began barking, and soon dark figures began to drift through the trees.

'Ah, Jesus,' he said miserably, when he saw they were blackfellers, 'I shouldn't have listened to him. He's ravin'.'

'What's up?' a voice asked. 'Who you be?'

'Looking for Black Wattle station,' Yorkey said nervously.

Then there were shouts as the other men milled about. 'That the boss he got there! What you doin', mister?'

Yorkey almost cried in relief. 'He's hurt bad. Can you help us?'

Gravely he watched as the camp came to life. Fires were lit, and firesticks to lead the way. Yorkey fussed about as two men carried Zack down a track to a bark humpy where someone had proudly placed an old mattress 'for the boss'.

'He been shot?' a big woman asked as Yorkey made sure Zack was laid on his stomach.

'No. A spear.'

'Ah.' She took over, ushering him out of the way.

43

'Where are we?' he asked.

'This Black Wattle here.'

'Shouldn't we have taken him up to the homestead?'

'Big house ten mile from here, mister. My boy, he gone up tell 'em. Doan worry. He got a horse, he go fast. He a stockman,' she added proudly.

They were all very efficient, moving about quietly. Someone had taken care of the horses so Yorkey was left with nothing to do but squat by a fire and light a smoke. Weird country we live in, he mused. Boss gets speared by blackfellers and us blackfellers get to pick him up.

A woman brought him a mug of scalding black tea and he drank it gratefully, and then the tiredness got the better of him, and he dozed.

The white men woke him, plunging noisily into the quiet of the camp, looking for the boss, hurling questions about. Giving orders. A girl was with them, a fair-haired girl, all weepy, demanding to see her daddy.

Yorkey walked through the camp to where a half-dozen horses were hitched, all of them still heaving and puffing from their ten-mile ride down here. His horse and Zack's were standing quietly by, relieved at last of their saddles, heads drooping, ignoring their excited companions.

A bloke called Casey came looking for Yorkey. 'What happened?'

'I dunno. He got speared is all I can tell you. I found him by the road.'

'You shouldn't have put him on that bloody horse. It must have given him hell. Why didn't you just come for help?'

'And leave him out there for the bushmen to finish him off?'

'Eh? You on your own?'

'Yeah.'

Casey backed off. 'Ah . . . right.'

They brought down a wagon for Zack, a big heavy wagon for a smoother ride, not like the rackety cart that Paddy got taken away in. How long ago was that? Yorkey couldn't recall.

Then they were gone and the camp settled down again. Even at this early hour of the morning there was a hot wind blowing, so Yorkey took off his boots, collected his saddle blanket and sought shelter behind a thicket of tea trees. It had been a long day.

He stayed on at the camp. No one minded. Built himself a lean-to on the outskirts, down along the billabong, with a few saplings and tree branches and the enthusiastic assistance of giggling children. They pointed out that their elders were preparing for the wet by thatching humpies and scavenging for scraps of canvas and corrugated iron, even old bits of carpet, but Yorkey told them he wouldn't be staying long. Their faces fell. The stranger, he learned, was a hero for bringing the boss home safely.

They were content, these people. Accepting. Living the way they wanted in a tiny corner of land that their tribe had once owned, with the permission of the boss. Strangely too, some of the men bragged that Black Wattle station was big, bigger than the Big Run next door, which Yorkey knew wasn't true, but he didn't argue. They were proud of the fact, claiming they had more cattle, more stockmen, more horses, more everything, and Yorkey smiled.

'Just you lot?'

'No. More blackfeller camps on this station. Long ways off. All sit down near water.'

Then he understood that the size of the camps was restricted to the availability of water, and wondered idly who had made that rule, saddened that their lives were so restricted, but not bothered about it. Everyone had to do the best they could. Like himself. He'd always worked hard, sometimes being paid only half what the bosses gave white drovers, but he knew better than to complain. Give Paddy his due, he paid him the right money. Not that he ever needed much, but it was good to always have a pound in the hip pocket.

He told the men here that he was no good at grubbing for food, which they thought was funny, coming from a blackfeller, but he offered some shillings in a tobacco tin to pay his way.

'For my laziness,' he grinned, because lazy days like this were like a holiday for him, though the food was grim. Yorkey knew he wouldn't last too long here.

An old crone came down to talk to him, a woman he'd seen bossing people about, so he guessed she was a matriarch of the clan. Power in various clans descended from the female line.

She spoke to him in her own tongue and was surprised he didn't understand. She reverted to English.

'People say you Waray man. You don't know your own language?'

'I never learned. I always lived with whites.'

She hissed disapprovingly, then reached out and felt his face, as if the rheumy eyes could not provide enough information. She touched his hair, long and lank, tied back with a string, then the coarse hands went back to his face, to his forehead, his sharp nose, his firm jaw, and rubbed across his lips.

'That not Waray face, mister. No fear. We Waray people. Us.'

Yorkey, cross, pushed her away. 'So am I. My mother was Waray.'

She grinned, baring broken teeth. 'Waray mother but wrong face. No white man there neither. What tribe your daddy?'

Yorkey steeled himself. 'Whadjuck. From down south. Long ways.'

'Ah.' No recognition. No interest. 'You fine feller. Good face anyway. You married?'

'No.'

Her face lit up and Yorkey guessed the reason for this visit.

'Yes, fine feller. Good big man. I got a girl for you, make the best wife, pretty . . .' She threw up her hands in delight.

'You and her make best babies, you see.'

Yorkey saw his days were numbered. He changed the subject, trying to form the question without breaking the rule of mentioning the dead by name, which was an offence in some tribes. But maybe the whitefeller name would suffice.

45

'I think my mother used to work up at the homestead. They called her Netta. Did you know her?'

She shook her head impatiently. 'This girl my own kin. She seen you. Shy girl. She think you pretty though.'

'Mother,' he said gently, 'I can't stay. I have to go soon. Can I talk about my daddy?'

She shrugged.

'My mother said he was a great hero. I never knew him. He was killed, out here somewhere.'

The woman clucked sympathetically. At least he had her attention.

'He was a black man, but he wore a whitefeller name. They called him Jimmy Moon. You ever heard of him?'

He saw those old eyes lift in recognition, then they shifted away, lids shutting down to a half-stare at the ground. A few seconds later they snapped back at him, clouded, anxious.

'Doan know them peoples! You talk old stuff!'

Yorkey tried to make light of it. 'That's true. But you're a good old woman. I bet you know plenty of old stuff.'

'Forget now.'

'But you knew Jimmy Moon.'

'Nebber!' she said angrily. 'You go. We doan want no trouble.'

She scrambled to her feet with surprising agility and hobbled away without a backward glance, and Yorkey was dumbfounded. Somehow he had offended her, maybe by mentioning those names or maybe by not displaying interest in the prospective bride, but what was this about trouble? He wasn't about to cause any trouble. Surely a man could ask about his parents. And had she known Jimmy Moon? Hard to say. Why would she lie? He wandered over to the track that led up to the Black Wattle homestead.

'Might as well go up there tomorrow,' he muttered to himself. 'Take a look around. See how Zack's getting on.'

But he wasn't finished at the camp. The old woman's reaction had made him curious. One of these days he'd have a talk to the older men when she wasn't about. They might remember the hero Jimmy Moon, or better still Netta. He was only asking for his own interest, nothing to make a fuss about. The old crone was probably a bit mad.

Chapter Five

The mailman came through, carrying newspapers as well, and the last of the small orders and parcels for station folk before he stored his wagon in a shed behind the Pine Creek railway station. After this he'd be doing his rounds, wherever possible with a packhorse until the wet season was over.

When Lucy heard he'd arrived she rushed inside to write to William Oatley, in Darwin, to advise him that the Hamilton contingent had been held up by unforeseen circumstances, but would be in town shortly, hopefully in time to welcome Myles home. She made the letter sound light-hearted, joking about the 'never-never' train they planned to catch in Pine Creek – 'If we ever get there, at this rate,' she muttered to herself – so-called because not only was it notoriously slow, it only made the journey of a couple of hundred miles once or twice a week, and then it could be not hours, but days late.

'I suppose I shouldn't complain,' she wrote, 'since we have a train, of sorts, and don't have to suffer wagons or horseback all the way. Though come to think of it, horseback would probably be faster.'

She addressed the envelope carefully and handed it to the mailman, watching to make sure it went in the bag, since he was apt to be a little careless.

But where was her father? Surely he should be back from Campbell's Gorge by this. It wasn't fair.

Even before Casey came to the house to tell them there'd been an accident, Lucy was out of bed throwing on a shirt and trousers, pulling on boots. She'd heard the dogs barking, sharp, snappy sounds in the stillness of the night, but hadn't taken much notice; anything could have disturbed them, a stray animal or a dingo prowling the chook pens. But then the barking had changed to that excited yapping. Something different was happening out there.

She ran out on to the veranda, peering into the darkness, the dogs sounding louder than ever, and then she saw lights beginning to flicker from the men's quarters down the hill. Mystified, she stood listening, hearing clearly the jingle of the bridles. Someone was saddling a horse, no, horses. More lights, shouting. Lanterns swaying outside. Then horses galloping away into the night.

Sibell, clutching her nightdress, was at the door.

'Something has happened to Zack.'

'No, Mother. There's some sort of fuss down there. I'm going to see.'

But then Casey was at the door. He saw the worry in Sibell's face, and with a warning glance at Lucy, announced that Zack was home.

'Thank God,' she said.

'Where is he?' Sibell demanded anxiously. 'What's all the fuss about?'

'It's all right. The blacks have got him down at the Ten Mile camp. They're looking after him.'

'What for? Is he sick?'

'Sounds like it. Some of the men have gone on ahead.'

'Why? Why would they go down? Have you sent for a doctor?'

'Yes, I have. There's no need to panic.'

'I am panicking, Casey. How long has he been there? A sick man in the blacks' camp! Are you out of your mind? And why are we hearing about this in the middle of the night? What the hell is going on?'

Casey was apologetic. 'Now take it easy, Sibell. The blacks found him on the road—'

'Oh my God! When?'

'Tonight. Just a while ago. Darky Mick came up to tell us he's there. Now don't take fright, but Mick says he's been speared. Too crook to move. They're hitching up a wagon to get him now.'

'Let's go,' Lucy said, running down the steps.

'Maybe you'd better wait here, Lucy. Not much you can do. We'll bring him up.'

'Let her go,' Sibell said. 'I'll get the room ready.'

The station was unusually quiet until Maudie Hamilton burst in, leaving her horse to trample the remains of the front garden.

'How is he? Why wasn't I told? Sitting there like a knot on a log, waiting for you people to get around to collecting me, bags packed, thinking I'm going to Port Darwin and we're going nowhere.'

Aunt Maudie, Zack's sister-in-law, was a widow, sole owner of an adjoining station, Corella Downs. She was a trim, hardy woman with sun-browned skin, sharp eyes and an abrupt manner that befitted her role in life. Maudie managed her cattle station with an iron hand. Her son Wesley, two years older than Lucy, was her overseer, but, as everyone knew, in name only.

She usually wore checked shirts, dungarees and bush hats but today, allowing for travel, she had donned a black riding habit and looked quite smart, if you excluded her treasured old black felt hat with the cockatoo feather.

Lucy took her into the parlour. 'He's very weak, Maudie. The doctor says the spear struck his lung, and he has lost a lot of blood.'

'So it *was* a spear! Jesus wept! Is there no end to this? Did you get the police? Have they found the mongrels? It's been three days, hasn't it?'

Lucy sighed. She wished she'd remembered that Maudie had been waiting for them. She was sorry about that, but right now she could do without this bombastic woman crashing into the house, unless . . . Lucy remembered her mother's threatened departure.

'We have to keep him very quiet, Maudie,' she warned. 'Mother has been marvellous.'

'Why wouldn't she be? He is her husband.'

Lucy closed the door. 'Listen to me, please. I'm so sorry about keeping you waiting, and I really thought someone would have let you know Daddy was hurt. I suppose it was my responsibility and I should have seen to it. And I apologise for that too. But I'm glad you're here. I want you to have a talk to Mother.'

'What's the matter with her?'

'You're never going to believe this. She's leaving Daddy.'

'Why? What's he done to her?'

'Nothing, Maudie. For God's sake, he loves her, you know that! She has just decided she doesn't want to live here any more. She's moving to Perth.'

Maudie took off her hat and dropped it on a sofa. 'People don't just up stumps and leave for no reason. Something must be wrong.'

'That's just it! She says there's nothing wrong. She just wants to go. She says she's fed up with living on a station.'

'So she's walking out? Leaving her husband? Leaving you? For no reason? I mean, I've known women who've bolted, and I wouldn't blame them – got beat up by their husbands or starved out on failed properties – but there's no excuse for Sibell. Zack's good to her and she wants for nothing. What's got into her?'

'I don't know. That's why I'd appreciate it if you'd talk to her quietly. Find out what we can do to make her stay. She has packed all her things. Everything.'

'Surely she won't leave with Zack laid low?'

'No. She plans to stay with us until after Christmas.'

'Big of her. Where is she?'

'In the kitchen, I think. But take her quietly, Maudie, I've been arguing with her for days now . . .'

Lucy might as well have been talking to the wall. Maudie marched out the door and stamped into the hallway, calling for Sibell.

Her sister-in-law came running. 'Shush, Maudie. Please. Zack's sleeping. I'm so glad you came over. He'll be pleased to see you.'

'I had to come over. I thought you lot had gone to town without me.'

'We'd never do that. It's just that we've been waiting for Zack to come home, and then this terrible thing happened.'

'But he'll be all right, won't he? Lucy is very worried.'

'Yes. So the doctor says. He's coming back tomorrow.'

'Good. Now what's all this about you leaving?'

'Maudie, if you don't mind, I don't want to discuss this right now.'

'I do mind. I'm family. I'm entitled to know what's going on. You sit right down here and tell me what's going on.'

With Sibell trapped in a chair in the hall, Maudie dragged over another one and sat opposite her, lifting her skirts to undo her riding boots while she waited.

'Well?'

'There's nothing much to tell, but since you insist, I am leaving. Station life is too much for me.'

'What's wrong with station life? You're a bloody lucky woman to be living here. Hundreds of women would give their eye teeth to be living in a place like this. And with a lovely man like Zack.'

'I know that. And if you want me to answer you, please don't interrupt. You were born in the bush, Maudie, you'll always be happy here, but I can't cope any more. I've tried to explain this to Zack and Lucy. I know I've nothing to complain about, but that's not the point. I don't want to live out here any more. I want to live in a town . . .'

She went on with her explanations, which didn't make any sense to Maudie until Sibell mentioned that she'd been thinking about this for a long time and had finally decided that, at her age, if she didn't make the break now, she never would.

'Ha!' Maudie said, as if she'd found the root of the problem. 'Change of life. That's all it is. You're going through the change of life. I'm older than you. I know about these things. Fortunately, it never bothered me, but then I'm a more active person. A lot of women go quite mental at this time. I don't think you are but you've got the symptoms, the fancies. Suddenly you think you want to run off—'

'It's not sudden, Maudie.'

'Neither is the change of life. It creeps up on you. Now what you have to do is talk to that doctor tomorrow. Get him to give you a tonic. Mrs Walsh swears by it. And ride more. A brisk ride every morning. You never ride much any more, do you?'

'No, it's too hot.'

'Then go early. Get up and get about and stop thinking about yourself. That's the real trouble. A lot of women do that, they spend too much time thinking about themselves, getting the fancies. Now I don't want to hear any more about this bolting business. You're upsetting everyone. Lord knows, your poor husband doesn't need this worry now, of all times.'

'I suppose so,' Sibell said meekly. It was easier this way. This was not the change of life; it was to be a change of lifestyle, but it was no use arguing with Maudie. Zack would recover, he was a strong man. They'd all go into Darwin eventually, and once there she would book passage on the first ship leaving for Perth in the New Year. No matter the upsets or consequences, this was what she had to do. She had money of her own, thanks to the investment left to her by Zack's mother, but apart from that, Zack was a generous man. While he was upset and angry about her leaving, still hoping she would reconsider, he'd been appalled when she'd told him she wouldn't ask anything of him financially.

'This is not about money!' he'd fumed. 'My wife will never want for

50

money. This is about whether you care for me or not.'

'But I do care for you . . . I do. I just can't stay here.'

He didn't understand, any more than Lucy did, or Maudie. Or, when they heard, any of their friends would. She had no one to turn to, but that was all part of it. They loved the outback life, they revelled in it. The distances, the space, the high adventure of cattle drives and musterings, and watching the herds multiply, and their horses, the stock horses and the Thoroughbreds, and the interminable wrestle with the weather . . . Ah, but what was the use? There were no words to explain the course she was determined to take. Before it was too late.

At least Maudie had the grace to be quietly cheerful in the sickroom. She took Zack's hand, edging a chair closer so that she could sit by him.

'Well you are a one, old chum. I heard there'd been a landslide in the gorge and you were over that way. Thought you must have got a bump on the head, but the head looks all right to me. Are you comfortable there?'

He managed a smile. 'I did get a bump on the head. Then a spear.' His voice was weak, weary.

'So they say.' Maudie looked at him fondly. 'Got you in the back. Lucky shot, I reckon, they'd never have got you front on. Miserable bloody thing to happen, love, but you're going to be all right. Up and around soon . . .'

Lucy took her mother outside. 'Maudie can sit with him now. Go and have a rest.'

'I can't leave her in there. She might upset him.'

'No she won't. She's not that silly. You have to rest, I'll bring you a cup of tea.'

Sibell shook her head. 'I'm not tired, really. I might just go for a walk. Stretch my legs. I haven't been out of the house for days.'

'Good. Do you think he'll be all right, Mother?'

'Of course he will. The wound's clean now, and the doctor said we have to let the healing process do its own work. The same goes for his lung.'

'I hope so.'

Lucy went to her own room, glancing forlornly at the suitcase, still packed and ready for them to leave, but those plans were now postponed. No one was making any plans at all. And Myles Oatley was due home any day. Lucy wouldn't desert her father at this time but she'd been so looking forward to being in town to welcome Myles home – fantasising about their romantic meeting after all this time – that she was thoroughly depressed. Why did everything have to go wrong now?

When Maudie came out, Lucy had tea ready for her on a side veranda shaded by an ivy-covered trellis.

'You want to get rid of that trellis,' Maudie observed as she sat down. 'It stops the breeze.'

51

'Maudie, there isn't any breeze, the air's like lead. How do you think Daddy is?'

'How would I know? The room stinks of laudanum. They've got him so dosed up he's too woozy to know where he is.'

'That's for the pain.'

'Pain my eye! There's a reason for pain. The man needs to be able to think for himself. To tell us how he got speared. You don't know, do you?'

'No. One of the blacks found him on the road and brought him in.' Lucy poured the tea and handed Maudie a slice of cake. 'But what was that about a landslide?'

'There was a landslide in the gorge when they were taking a mob through. A drover was injured and they lost about fifty head of cattle. Zack was there too.'

'Yes, but we didn't hear anything about a landslide. Who told you?'

'Syd Walsh came by my place. He's always sniffing about other people's property. He said he'd heard that Zack was hurt – so I took it for granted it was the landslide. It wasn't until I was halfway here that I met some stockmen, who told me he'd been speared.' She finished the cake and took another piece, grumbling about Syd Walsh.

'I hated leaving that bloke hanging about my place. I'd swear on a stack of Bibles that he's behind that last mob of cattle that disappeared from Pop Oatley's station. And a few more over the years.'

'Oh, Maudie. You shouldn't say that. Syd's a bit rough, but he's not a cattle thief.'

'I'll say what I like. He's no good and he never was. I warned that silly Joanna not to marry him when her husband died. He was only after her station. And I was right. He treats her like dirt. And,' she said angrily, 'he had the cheek to send his regards to Zack and Sibell.'

'That was nice.'

'You reckon? Well, don't mention him to your mother or she'll have another attack of the vapours. But what about you, my girl? When are you going to town?'

'I can't leave with Daddy so ill.'

'Zack will be all right, if they stop addling his brain with that stuff and let him get a grip on himself. I heard your boyfriend's on his way home. About bloody time. You'll want to be there to meet him, won't you?'

'Yes, but I'd rather wait until Daddy can travel.' She shrugged. 'And by then the rivers might be up.'

'Rot. We'll wait until Zack is a bit better then I'll take you to town. You're not going to leave Myles loose with all those young heifers rolling their eyes at him. You have to be there.'

Lucy shook her head. 'I can't just go and leave Mother and Daddy here.'

'Why not? It won't be the first Christmas they've spent at home.'

Lucy was in no mood to argue with Maudie; it would only add to her own distress about Zack and Myles. Nor did she want to mention Sibell right now. She believed it was important for Sibell to go to town for a few months, see her friends, enjoy herself, forget that other business. A holiday would cheer them both up. But how long would it be before Zack could travel? The doctor had stitched the wound in his back and insisted that he remain still, propped up on pillows, until it was time to take the stitches out.

Lucy was resigned to staying home for Christmas. Maudie could go if she wished.

Yorkey took his time covering the miles between the camp and the station headquarters. Though much of this vast outback seemed monotonous, grindingly boring in its sameness, to Yorkey, drover and stockman, there was always something to learn as he rode through new areas, as if a map of the terrain was forming in his head, more from habit than a conscious effort to retain the information. He followed the dusty red walking track for a while and then veered off across the plain, riding through the dry grass, through the spindly trees and high anthills which always looked to him like strategically placed sentinels, mysterious beings dreaming of ancient times.

He detoured round a rocky outcrop and went on across the open country, watched by listless cattle that couldn't even be bothered to turn away. Yorkey grinned, whistled at them for the fun of it. He liked cattle. Mobs were never the same. There were always personalities among them, from the very shy to the bold and batty, just like people.

In the distance he could see the homestead resting on a low hill, surrounded by a commune of outbuildings. Plenty of them too, like a small town. Must be a lot of blokes working there. He began to follow a wider track leading in that direction, coming first to a small fenced cemetery.

Yorkey sat awhile, staring over the fence at the tombstones and crosses, reading the name Hamilton on some of them, idly contemplating the tranquil scene, then he set off again.

He avoided the homestead area, making for the maze of stockyards. They were empty, not much doing at this time of year, but the fenced paddocks nearby were of interest. Yorkey nodded approvingly; there had to be about eighty horses corralled here, stock horses, in good nick too, and up ahead long, well-kept stables for the élite among horseflesh.

A couple of dogs ran out, growling at the stranger, alerting a burly blacksmith, who glared from his open forge.

'Who are you?'

'The name's Yorkey. I'm looking for Darky Mick.'

'He'd be out workin'. Won't be in for an hour or so. What's your business here?'

Yorkey wasn't about to admit he'd only met Darky Mick the day before and was using his name to gain entry to this fortress. He had his pride.

'I'm a drover. Just moved a mob for the Big Run.'

The blacksmith looked at him curiously. 'You speak good English for a blackfeller.'

'Yeah.' Yorkey shrugged. 'Any chance of a cuppa tea while I wait?'

'Down there.' The blacksmith jerked his head towards some buildings past the stable and went back to work.

There were other men wandering about but nobody took much notice of him after that, so he hitched his horse to a railing and went in search of the cookhouse.

Yorkey knew the ropes. Station cooks always had tea stewing in big pots on the stove, and white men could sit in the adjacent mess hall, but not blackfellers.

The cook was obliging. He handed Yorkey a mug of tea and a bun. 'You're new here?'

'Only passing through, mate. Thanks.' He took the tea and, munching on the bun, retreated to the shade of an awning outside. There he squatted in the dust, waiting for Darky.

That night Yorkey was the centre of attention. A hero. His new friend Darky Mick made sure of that, dashing about in all directions, calling to stockmen and station hands to come and meet this 'pfella'.

'He the pfella done pickmeup sick boss,' he boasted. 'Done findem in the bush, else boss he be bloody dead pfella. This here Yorkey!'

Men gathered, patted him on the back, brought him a bottle of beer, listened eagerly to the full story. And as a bonus they heard first hand of the drama at the gorge. It was a heady hour for Yorkey, and for Darky Mick, who was as proud as he could be at all this excitement. But the best part for Yorkey soon followed; the cook brought him out a great feed, telling him there was plenty more where that came from.

Yorkey enquired after the boss and was told he was still pretty sick, which didn't surprise him, but they said the doctor would pull him through, and that was a relief. He liked Zack, admired him really, but was a bit shy of saying that in front of all these blokes.

Instead he commented: 'He's a tough bloke, your boss. The pain must have been killing him but he stuck it out all the way on that horse without a peep, and even knew where he was going.'

Zack's men nodded, agreeing, and Yorkey knew the story would go proudly into the folklore of the district, to be told and retold over campfires, to grow and be embellished, as was the way with good yarns. Yorkey grinned to himself. He'd be forgotten but Zack Hamilton would have to live with a tale of fantastic bravery. And knowing Zack as he already did, the laconic, laid-back boss would hate that.

Then the number two bossman, Casey, came down from his house to hear the stories all over again.

'You did good, Yorkey,' he said. 'And when he's well enough, I'm sure the boss will want to thank you himself. In the meantime if you want to bunk in with Darky Mick and his mates, you're welcome to stay as long as you like.'

'Thanks, Mr Casey, but I'm no freeloader. If you've got a job for a stockman I could earn my keep in the next droving season.'

Casey grinned. 'I can't very well say no, can I? You show him around, Darky.'

And that was how Yorkey got himself on the payroll at Black Wattle station, as easy as that, sharing a good dry bunkhouse with Darky Mick and two other Aborigine stockmen. He was even able to spell his tired horse and pick a fresh mount from the paddock. He was on top of the world. Set for the wet season.

Sibell was frantic. 'Maudie has poured Zack's medicine out the window! Lucy, send someone to get some more. I'm not expecting the doctor back for a week. You have to find him.'

'How could you do such a thing!' Lucy cried, but Maudie was unconcerned.

'I told you they shouldn't keep him doped up like that.'

'It's not your place to make such decisions, you're not his doctor!'

'Pity I'm not! Sibell can go on wringing her hands. I'll look after him.'

And she did. She bathed Zack to keep him cool, she kept him comfortable by rearranging his pillows so that he wasn't lying on the wound, at the same time insisting that he remain upright to help his lung breathe and ward off pneumonia, ignoring Sibell's complaints that he couldn't be expected to sleep like that; and before the new bottle of laudanum arrived, two days later, Zack was wide awake, grumbling about the constant pain and the necessity to remain in bed, swaddled up like an old woman, but recovering. When Sibell brought him the laudanum, to Maudie's delight he refused to take it, although his objection was the taste.

But the boss was in control again. He insisted that he'd been attacked by a lone man, probably out to rob him, not by a war party as the police were inclined to believe.

'They're too quick at blaming everything that happens on war parties. They like their bit of excitement. I got a glimpse of that bloke, I won't forget him in a hurry. He was on his own and he wasn't wearing any paint at all, not a dab.'

'Well, it was a war party that killed those miners,' Maudie said.

'How do you know?' Zack asked. 'More than one that time, agreed, but the station blacks say there were no war parties out anywhere. Blacks don't just come out on the warpath for no reason, there has to be something to upset them first, and then look out. I reckon the mob that killed the miners were only hunting and something went wrong.'

'Like what?' Maudie demanded.

'I don't think we'll ever know. And you can bet the bugger who attacked me, and saw me escape, will be a hundred miles away by now, so I don't want the police picking up innocent tribal men just to make themselves look good.'

'They're only doing their job,' Maudie muttered.

'Yeah,' Zack growled. 'Anyway, Maudie, when are you going to town? I'd like you to take Lucy with you.'

Sibell, who'd been sitting quietly by the open French doors, was out of her chair in an instant. 'They can't go. It's too dangerous.'

'No it's not,' Maudie declared. 'Dear God, if we jumped at every shadow we'd never leave home.'

'I don't call worrying about the attack on Zack jumping at shadows.'

'Sibell, he just told you that bloke would be long gone by this. And the police got the men who killed the miners.'

'What?' Zack jerked around to her, and grimaced in pain at the sudden movement.

'Don't upset yourself,' Maudie said. 'I didn't mean to tell you that just yet. The police found them in one of the Daly River camps.'

Zack sat back and sighed. 'I see. They just rode into the camp, asked who did the killings, and the murderers stepped forward. Brilliant!'

'They had to arrest someone. They couldn't just let them get away with it. And they say they've got the right ones, Zack, so I wish you'd stop carrying on about these things. It's not our business.'

Zack made no comment because Sibell was listening. He wondered what the truth of it was. Here was a reason for payback of some sort, if the Daly River blacks took umbrage. He decided to double the guards accompanying Maudie and Lucy to Pine Creek.

'I want to be on my way,' Maudie was saying, 'but Lucy wants to wait for you and Sibell.'

'No need for that. We'll come along later.' He smiled at Sibell. 'We might get our feet wet, love, but it won't be the first time, will it?'

'We're not going at all until you are quite well,' she said.

Later, Zack talked privately with Maudie.

'To be on the safe side, take two of our men with you.'

'What for? Wesley and two of my stockmen are waiting, ready to go.'

'Good. That'll make four. They won't object to time off. Our wagon is packed ready to go, with all the stuff you'll need. You go on ahead. Sibell and I will ride.'

'If the doctor says you can.'

'Let me worry about that. Lucy has been so looking forward to the holidays . . .'

'And Myles,' his sister-in-law grinned.

'Yes. It'd be a pity to keep her for no good reason. But take care through the gorge. Let the men take the wagon through, you ladies ride, and don't mess about. Get in and out of there as quickly as you can. As a matter of fact, I'd prefer you took the roundabout route. Give it a miss altogether.'

'We'll be all right. We'd be unlucky to strike another landslide.'

'Be careful, that's all I ask.'

Maudie didn't waste any time. The wagon was hauled out again and repacked, Lucy fussing over her clothes, Sibell making sure they had everything they needed to reopen their house by the beach in Darwin, and the cook loading hampers for their journey.

At first light the next morning, Maudie was down at the stables, checking the horses, the wagon, and giving orders to the stockmen, who had heard them all the night before. Then she hurried back up to the house, where Sibell was waiting for her.

'You were so busy last night, I didn't have a chance to talk to you. I got the shock of my life yesterday. I thought I saw Jimmy Moon riding by the house paddock.'

'So now you're seeing ghosts. You do need a holiday.'

'Don't be so rude. I only meant—'

'I know what you meant. You're living in the past. Jimmy Moon has been dead for years. I think that's half your trouble, going on about the violence here – that's all in the past.'

'Lucy told you that, I suppose. She misunderstood what I meant by violence. I hadn't dreamed that Zack might be attacked.'

Maudie was unimpressed. 'We're having a hard time understanding what you do mean. That attack on Zack – are you going to use that as another excuse to leave him?'

'Of course not.'

'Then why don't you go in there and tell him that you were only fooling. That you're not buzzing off to Perth after all. That would be better medicine than the stuff you were giving him.'

Angrily Sibell walked away from her. 'I hope you haven't mentioned this to him.'

'Oh no. I didn't bring up the subject. Neither did he. Zack would never criticise his wife. He's very loyal.'

Sibell caught the caustic remark as she left the room, but she wouldn't turn back. There was to be no turning back.

Jimmy Moon's son settled in easily. He rode with Casey the first day, searching low-lying scrub areas for roaming cattle that had been missed in the first roundup and driving them up to the stockyards to await removal to higher ground.

Casey didn't say much to him – they were kept too busy – except to remark that he'd take him up to see the boss when he was feeling a bit better. Later, though, he heard Casey tell two men that the new boy was 'a good hand', and he saw them nod their approval. He could have told them that himself. And so could Zack, when he was on his feet again, but it was good to hear. He wasn't just a visitor, he wanted to stay. They were a friendly lot on this station, unlike many other places he'd come across where the station hands, for all sorts of reasons, were at each other's throats.

But he was still interested in Jimmy Moon, especially since the old woman had gone so cold on the subject, as if he was taboo or something. He knew about Netta, and what had become of her, but Jimmy Moon was a mystery. A hero, his mother had said. So how come? What had he done to deserve such an honour and to have a real white-man name? She had said he was a full blood, like her, so he hadn't taken his name from a whitefeller father.

After a couple of days Yorkey sought out an old bloke called Dodds, because he'd heard that Dodds had been on the station a long time. Dodds, they said, was a retired stockman, now an odd-job man, who lived with his missus in a fancy little hut up by Casey's house, but was mostly found around the stables.

It wasn't hard to pick him, Yorkey grinned to himself when he saw the bandy-legged old greybeard locking up a shed. Nor was it hard, he found, to strike up a conversation with Dodds when he asked how long he'd been on this station.

'Just about all my life,' Dodds said. 'Came here as a raw kid, got dumped here you could say. You got a smoke?'

'Sure.' Yorkey rolled a smoke for him, and handed it over.

Dodds lit the cigarette and inhaled. 'This is good baccy. Where'd you get it?'

He meant where did a blackfeller get such good tobacco, but Yorkey wasn't concerned. 'Casey gave it to me.'

'He did? Ah . . . you're the bloke brought Zack in. Good on you. What did you say your name was?'

'I didn't. It's Yorkey.'

'Well, Yorkey, the good Lord will smile on you. He's a fine feller, Zack. Known him since he was knee-high to a grasshopper.'

'Is that right?'

They settled on some packing cases outside the shed for a yarn, and Dodds, obviously glad of an ear, held forth about his old man, who had tried to set up a cattle station out here but went broke in a matter of months.

'Had no bloody idea,' Dodds said. 'Overlanded his cattle, lost most of them on the way, then the dry took all the rest. Now me, with what I know now, I'd have made a go of it, but that stupid bugger . . . he didn't even get to build a hut. Me and me brother, we was just camped with 'im in the bush. Bloody starving we were, living on snakes and bush grub like bloody Abos. If you'll excuse me to say.'

'That's all right,' Yorkey allowed.

'Yes, well . . . Then he brings me and Stan here – Black Wattle wasn't such a grand place then – and leaves us with Charlotte, Zack's mum. Said he was going back east to get his wife, our mum. The bastard never came back. Never saw either of them again.'

'What happened to your brother?'

'Stan? Hard to remember him now. He got drowned. Mad as his dad. Trying to ford a bloody river in a flood. But I didn't have none of that harum-scarum in me. I went on working for the Hamiltons. I was head stockman for fifteen years, and I could tell you a tale or two about this place.'

Yorkey had met men like Dodds before, earbashers, king-sized ear-bashers, but he gave him another smoke and listened to all the dreary

58

tales, hoping there'd come a mention of Jimmy Moon.

Finally he had to ask. Interrupt. 'Do you remember a bloke called Jimmy Moon? I think he worked here.'

'If he was here I'd remember him. Now let me think. Jimmy Moon. Can't say I do. When would that have been?'

'About twenty years ago, I think.'

'Twenty years. Jeez, big trouble those days. Charlotte died, lovely woman. Did I tell you she took Stan and me in hand and gave us some schoolin' because we never had any? And bought us our first pair of boots. Jeez, how we treasured them boots.'

'About Jimmy Moon. He worked here. Probably a stockman. He was a blackfeller.'

'Ah well, I wouldn't remember them. They come and go. If you don't mind me to say, mate.'

'Ah well, it was just a name I heard. Strange name for a blackfeller anyway. The blacks say there's some story about him. Made me curious, like.'

'Yeah, I suppose so. They like their stories. But wait on. Jimmy Moon. The blackfeller! He didn't work here. I remember him. No fear, Jimmy Moon didn't work here. He just came a-visiting, like you, I suppose.'

'Living down with the station blacks?'

'No bloody fear. He was a bit of a toff as blacks go. In with the white bosses he was. Gawd knows where he came from. Good stamp of a bloke, though. Even mates with Colonel Puckering.'

'Who's he?'

'The Colonel was the boss of police in the Territory. Retired now, probably dead.' Dodds' eyes twinkled. 'The Colonel, he married a lady of the night, best whore in Darwin. Brother, was that a scandal and a half!'

'So Jimmy Moon just came to visit?'

'Yeah. Rum story. The missus liked him. Mrs Hamilton. He was a friend of hers.'

'How did that come about?'

'If you'd stop asking questions I could get it together. They think old Dodds is doddery but they've got another think coming. I'm as sharp as any of the blokes here, you mark my words.'

Yorkey sat patiently while Dodds, maybe to assist his memory, drew lines in the dust with his boot.

'Yeah now. Jimmy Moon. That was a peculiar day. We were all called out to watch the big presentation. Mrs Hamilton, Sibell that is, she had this horse brought in all gussied up with ribbons, and presented it to this blackfeller. That was the first time we really took notice of him.'

Yorkey sat very still, remembering his mother's words: 'He had his own horse.' Important for a blackfeller in those days.

'Dunno what Zack would have made of it. We all wondered at the time,' Dodds continued. 'But he was away droving. That's why I remember. Peculiar that was. But she said she owed Moon a horse, for a

59

promise she made to him some time back. So there's your story. Told you I don't forget people. Maudie was here at the time too, living here with her husband. But he was killed, so she took her pa's station, Corella Downs. Been there ever since. Listen, mate, I gotta go. My missus will have the dinner ready.'

He stood up to leave, but Yorkey had another question.

'Do you know what became of Jimmy Moon? They say he was a hero.'

Dodds stopped and looked back at him. He scratched a thatch of grey hair that engulfed a lined face as it met his beard.

'Hero? Dunno about that. They hung him.'

Yorkey stood, open-mouthed. Shocked. His mind shut down with a clang. He was speechless. He couldn't utter a word to call Dodds back, to ask more, to cry that he was mistaken, to say anything. He stood watching Dodds amble away into the warm seduction of that night, as if Dodds himself was a sly, mournful spirit, intent on upsetting the dead. Intent on reducing a chance for glory into nothingness. For it was a nothingness that Yorkey felt now.

And later, foolishness. Netta had led him on, making up stories to suit herself. Kidding him about a father who was never a hero but had run foul of the law like so many other blackfellers before him. What was the use of that? Why had she bothered him with this mischief? Why couldn't she just have said he'd died, and left it at that? Why did women have to invent romantic tales? No wonder the old crone at the camp had recoiled. Hanging was a horrible death, greatly feared by tribal people. It was a horrible death in anyone's book. Yorkey shivered, wishing he could erase what he'd heard. Put it out of his mind. One thing was sure, he wouldn't be asking any more questions about his father. He'd been better off not knowing.

'You're doing all right on your own,' he consoled himself as he tramped down to the bunkhouse.

On the Sunday morning Casey came looking for him.

'The boss wants to see you, Yorkey. Get yourself shined up.'

Yorkey rushed to shower and shave, borrowed a clean shirt, did his best to clean his battered boots, and combed his wet hair into a small plait at the back, threaded with string, all the time wondering what he should call Zack, wondering why he was so excited. After all, Zack was just another bloke; he wouldn't bite.

Mrs Hamilton met them at the back door. She was a nice sort of a woman but seemed very nervous. She stared at him as if he might suddenly turn into a bogeyman and go rampaging through her house.

'This is Yorkey,' Casey told her, and she seemed bewildered.

'Is that your name? Yorkey?' she whispered.

'Yes, missus.'

'Where do you come from?'

'Over Katherine way. Thereabouts.'

60

'I see.' She smiled suddenly, reminding him of the white woman he'd seen in the dream, the one he'd confused with Netta.

Casey stepped in. 'He's come to see Zack.'

She nodded. 'Yes. Of course. Come on through.'

Yorkey loved the smell of these houses, of polished timbers and plastered walls and floor rugs and a faintly scented air that had room to move about under high ceilings. As they travelled along the passage and then went up a fine staircase, Yorkey didn't turn his head, so as not to appear nosy, but his eyes swivelled into open doorways, glimpsing a fine dining room and a couple of posh sitting rooms, even some bedrooms with linens as white as paint, then they were in a big bedroom looking straight out through open doors to a veranda and on over the valley. A good room to be stuck in bed if you had to be, he mused as they wheeled him about to face the boss, who was propped up in a cosy heap of lace-edged pillows, looking so out of place in the pretty bed that Yorkey grinned at him.

'Taking it easy, eh?'

He saw Casey frown, but Zack laughed. 'Not by choice. How're you going, Yorkey?'

'Pretty good.'

'You want to stay on here?'

'Yes, until the droving starts again.'

'You could stay longer if you want. Good steady job, no more travelling about.'

Yorkey was surprised. He hadn't given a thought to a permanent job; he'd always been a drover.

'I dunno.'

'Plenty of time to think about it. By the way, I heard that Paddy is on the mend.'

'That's good. You too, eh?'

'Yes. And about time.' Zack turned to Casey. 'I just thought . . . we should have sent Yorkey with the escort for Maudie and Lucy. He's seen what can happen in the gorge. Too late now.'

'They'll be all right,' Casey told him. 'Maudie will see to it.'

For a while they talked about this and that, and Yorkey began to feel out of place, the audience over. He wished he could leave, but Zack had other plans.

'Have a look out on the veranda, Yorkey.'

'What at?'

'See what's on the veranda.'

Mrs Hamilton was standing by the door, beaming now; she seemed more relaxed. 'Out here, Yorkey.'

Mystified, he trooped out and found a brand-new saddle hung over a chair, but couldn't see anything else of interest.

'It's yours,' Zack called from the bed.

'What is?'

'The saddle, you goat. I noticed you needed a new saddle, so there it is.'

'It's his way of saying thank you,' Mrs Hamilton whispered. 'He wants you to have it.'

'Mine?' Yorkey had never owned a saddle as flash as this and he was dumbfounded.

Somehow he managed to thank Zack, who shook his hand, and Casey picked up the saddle and dumped it on his shoulder. It was light, the leather soft and smooth to the touch, but well cut and hardy, and the steel stirrups gleamed. Yorkey couldn't believe his luck.

'Let's go,' Casey said. 'You'll be wanting to try it out.'

At the door, Yorkey bobbed his head feeling he ought to say something else.

'Hope you're walkin' about soon, boss,' he called and followed Casey downstairs and out along the path that led away from the house. Later he realised he'd got it right without thinking about it. Zack was now the boss. His boss.

Chapter Six

Matong had made it through the dangerous country and into the homelands of the river people. The outlying swamps had dried up, slabs of mud pancaked into uneven patterns under forlorn marooned mangroves, their evergreen foliage hitched high, like skirts above spindly legs. Though there was food here in plenty, he ran for another half-day, on to the lush green woodlands that bordered the river, and, with a cry of relief, dived from a high bank into the warm depths.

For a while he just wallowed, drinking, resting, keeping an eye out for crocodiles, drifting, watching the shores for signs of any of the people. But then the hunger cramps returned so he set about finding a feed with eager anticipation. He lit a fire, poking at the steaming wood until it was well underway, and left it to begin his search. Soon he was back with yabbies and mussels to throw on the coals, leaving them while he raided a fish trap he'd discovered a little way upstream.

His meal was a feast worth waiting for. He devoured two fat fish, gorged on the other delicacies and lay back, content at last. Sleep was upon him in no time.

In the morning he found some of his kin, but before he could tell them of the death of Mimimiadie's woman, they wailed their bad news. Troopers had come through their country searching for the killers of two white men, and had dragged off three young men, ignoring the pleas of the elders, who had insisted they were innocent.

On hearing this, Matong decided not to mention that he and the others had killed those white men in retaliation; instead, he only related the circumstances of the woman's murder, causing more distressed wailing as more gathered to hear his awful news.

'We are greatly saddened to hear this,' one of the elders told him. 'But I would speak with Mimimiadie. Is he not with you?'

'No. He and Gopiny were afraid to make the journey back. I was not,' he boasted. 'The white men will never catch me, though Mimimiadie says we have become too well known to the whites.'

'I don't know about you and Gopiny,' the elder said. 'But it is true, the troopers claim Mimimiadie is a ringleader, and they were looking for him. When will he be back?'

'After the wet season. He is at the gorge. I must find his family and tell them about the woman.'

The old man shook his head. 'More tragedy for them. When the troopers couldn't find Mimimiadie, they took his son, little Boomi.'

'What?' Matong was shocked. 'Why would they do such a thing?'

'They said they'll give him back when Mimimiadie gives himself up. If you can believe them.'

'It's just a trap. When they take the children they never give them back.'

'I'm afraid this is a true fact,' the old man said wearily. 'I'm afraid this is so. But Mimimiadie must be told.'

In all the angry discussions that went on after that, it came to Matong that he'd forgotten to mention the death of the lad who'd been killed at the gorge, but since he had no kin here, he decided it wasn't relevant at present. No point in frightening them further by crowing about their exploits at the gorge. It was better that they didn't know.

There was talk that night about payback, about attacking a station homestead, or making a major attack on a mob of cattle, in retaliation for the arrest of the three young men, who would surely be imprisoned or hanged. As more men gathered round the campfires, arguments raged about payback. Some said it would cause even more trouble; others insisted a swift attack was the only honourable course; while still more suggested that they appeal to the white missionaries to help them. Ask them to go to the white bosses and swear to them that the wrong men had been arrested. Demand that they be returned or the tribal people here would have to think payback.

In all of this, they agreed on one point. That someone should go immediately to inform Mimimiadie that his little son had been taken. He would know what to do. The vote was unanimous. Matong was chosen as the messenger.

He was sorry now that he had boasted about how easy it was to traverse that dangerous territory. Plain stupidity. But he couldn't refuse. He had been directed to go. A refusal was out of the question.

Unaware that Matong's actions had placed him in jeopardy, Numinga trotted on resentfully. He was disappointed at having to leave that great plateau, where he could have sat like an eagle watching the world change beneath him, high and dry in a cave, out of the reach of enemies. Now, thanks to those hotheads, he was back where he'd started from. A hunted man again. So, the only thing to do now was to stick to his plan. To cross over to the white man's world again.

He allowed himself a few more days of leisurely travel, the hot and humid air pleasurable on his bare skin now that the great monsoonal clouds were banking up far to the north. Though barely discernible yet, just a few loose clouds wafting on the horizon, Numinga could feel the difference that canopy was making and smell the dampness all about him.

Even then he was in no hurry when he sighted a station homestead because he'd found water in a wide, deserted riverbed. He examined his surrounds, pleased to note that there were no recent tracks of cattle or

He heard a mutter of irritation from stockmen watching from the high fences. The joke had misfired.

'That settles that,' the bossman said. 'He's a stockman all right.'

'A bloody renegade, though,' the old policeman with cropped grey hair replied. 'I still say he's the one. Zack said his attacker was out to rob him and this bloke fits the picture even better now. If he'd killed Zack he'd have had the horse and all.'

'You bloody liar,' Numinga shouted, but they shoved him aside while they discussed this.

In the end it was the bossman who made the decision. 'It's easily solved. Take him over to Black Wattle station. Let Zack get a look at him. He'll say you yea or nay.'

'No can do,' the boss policeman said. 'Black Wattle is days away from here; we've got to get back on track. Our orders are to report in to Darwin before the monsoons set in. You know that, Pop. They need every copper within shouting distance to handle that place when it fills up with every rowdy in the Territory. I'm surprised you haven't left already.'

'Not going in this year,' Pop said. 'A bit tired. Not up to the ride nor the shenanigans.'

'Sorry to hear that. They'll miss you.'

'They'll survive.' He shrugged. 'But what about this bloke? If you won't take him out to Black Wattle, you'll have to arrest him and take him to Darwin. Sling him in jail there until Zack can get a look at him.'

'I dunno about that. He'll slow us up.'

'Put it this way,' the old man sighed. 'There'll be no hanging on my land. He won't slow you up; you can rope him and stick him on a horse. But you listen to me: he could be innocent. Certainly half his story is true. So I will hold you two responsible for getting him to Darwin in one piece. I don't want to hear that an accident happened to him. Do you understand what I'm saying?'

'Yes,' they replied, unwillingly, glancing at each other for support.

'Then see you do. You can rest up today. My guests until the morning, so make yourselves comfortable. But you mark my words, gentlemen. You do your job and get him to Fannie Bay jail or I'll want to know why.'

The other stockmen thought it was fair enough that Zack should give Yorkey a new saddle but they ribbed him about the way he treasured it, forever cleaning and polishing it, and they threatened to dip it in the horse trough, or worse, drop it in manure. 'To give it character, Yorkey,' they laughed.

He took the teasing in good part and soon they turned their attention to the wagonload of supplies that had just arrived. A special load that contained 'the necessities', as he was told.

Yorkey was intrigued to learn that these vital necessities were extra bottles of beer and rum, groceries, new clothing, books, a parcel of decorations – paper streamers and the like – and a large mysterious box.

Then he realised they were preparing for Christmas. Though months away, they were making certain the 'necessities' got through before early rains isolated them.

'That sounds like a real good show,' he said to Dodds. 'Just as well I stayed.'

'You can say that again, son. But listen. You was asking about Jimmy Moon, and I was telling my missus. Now, she remembers him, got a memory like an elephant she has. You come on over with me and she'll tell you all about it.'

Yorkey had managed to put Jimmy Moon out of his mind by concentrating on the job and his new surrounds. He had no wish to hear any more, but Dodds insisted.

'We've got her going now. You started it, you can't duck it now. She loves a good yarn. Come on . . .'

Unable to think of an excuse, Yorkey followed him down the track to the little one-roomed cottage on the other side of a dusty paddock from Casey's neat bungalow.

Mrs Dodds was out the back chopping wood when they approached her, splitting blocks into firewood with the expertise of long practice. A small, scraggy woman, she pushed back a battered straw hat and leaned on her axe.

'What are youse two up to?'

'This is Yorkey,' Dodds said. 'Come to talk to you about Jimmy Moon.'

Yorkey was wondering what he'd say if she asked why, but she had other matters on her mind.

'Didn't the supply wagon come in this afternoon?' she asked Dodds.

'Yes. It's in.'

'Well, where's my order?'

'I'll get it later.'

'You'll get it now. I don't want that cook grabbing my stuff. Last time I only got half the tea I ordered and missed out altogether on golden syrup. The list is still on the wall in the cookhouse; you check every ounce. It'll be too late tomorrow. Now get going.'

Thinking to escape with Dodds, Yorkey turned away, but she called him back.

'It doesn't take two. You stay, Yorkey. Sit yourself on the back step till I finish here. If I waited for Dodds to cut the wood we'd never get the stove lit.'

'I'll cut it for you,' he offered, but the contrary woman declined.

'That's real nice of you, son, but I'm nearly finished.'

He sat moodily on the single step for a few minutes, feeling a right fool for getting himself into this – the last thing he needed was a gory tale about the villain they'd hanged – then, unable to stand the wait, he jumped up to stack the wood she had cut on to the neat woodpile.

Eventually she finished, but then said he had to wait longer while she carted some wood inside to fuel up her stove. But she returned with a mug of black tea for him. Yorkey appreciated that; his mouth was dry and his forehead felt numb, as if it were turning into stone.

'So you wanta hear about Jimmy Moon?' she asked, hitching her skirts to settle herself on the chopping block.

'Not if it's any trouble, missus. Just a name I heard drovers talking about one time. Nothin' much. Your old man shouldn't have been bothering you.'

'No bother. I knew him all right. I was working up at the house at the time. One of the house gins was sweet on him. Netta, if I recall. Never forget a name, I don't. Good girl she was, but silly. Left a damn good job to run off with a no-good drover. A whitefeller, of course . . .'

Yorkey shifted uncomfortably; he didn't want to hear this.

'. . . you know how the gins are. Think they're smart taking up with a white man. You married, Yorkey?'

'No, missus.'

'Yeah, well, don't let those black mummas down there push you into it. You stay fancy-free. All the gins had eyes for Jimmy Moon, 'cos he was a smart feller. Not from round here, though. Not him. I remember he rolls up here looking for Sibell. At the front door too, if you don't mind, a blackfeller an' all. Gave Maudie quite a turn. She tried to chase him away but Sibell goes flying out and claims him like a long-lost son.'

She laughed. 'You wouldn't forget that row in a hurry. Those two was always arguing, but this was just about a box-on, because Sibell invites him in.'

Despite himself, Yorkey had to ask. 'Why would she do that?'

'Turned out she'd known him down south before she was married to Zack. He was working on a property where she was staying. I never quite got the story straight, you know how tales get about . . . You want some more tea?'

'No thanks, missus.'

She sat back, discarded her hat and rummaged through her grey hair as if searching for the details. 'Best I can make of it is that she fell into the hands of bush blacks, a real bad lot who would have done her harm, but Jimmy Moon found her and brought her back to her own people. So he was the hero of the day. Like you, Yorkey, with Zack. But don't let it go to your head. People forget easy.'

Yorkey was intrigued. 'Did he follow her up here? The white lady, Mrs Hamilton?'

'No, no. He came north for some reason and was working for the police in Katherine as a tracker. Did a good job there; the coppers had a lot of time for him.'

'I thought they hung him?'

'No fear they didn't. Who told you that? See how stories get mixed up over the years? No fear. Everyone liked Jimmy Moon, he was a nice feller. Even,' she grinned, 'old Maudie, eventually. And that takes some doing.'

Yorkey's head cleared. He felt better, relieved. Now he could afford to listen. Even to tell the woman that Netta was his mother and . . .

But Mrs Dodds was enjoying her yarn. Her sharp green eyes held his attention. 'What happened was this. While he was working for the coppers he heard that Sibell was living out here, so he just decided to look her up. See how she's doing.'

'Sounds like a bit of a cheek for a blackfeller,' Yorkey suggested, fishing for compliments for his father.

He wasn't disappointed. 'Not if you knew him. He was polite, but he had the air of a chief, if you know what I mean. The blacks used to say he was the chief of a tribe that must have got scattered by the whites down south, but that was only talk. He never said much about himself at all. I could tell you this, though: he treated the blacks and whites as equals, among themselves if you get what I mean. He never talked down to our blacks nor up to us whites.'

'And he worked here?'

'No. He was just visiting. And Sibell was happy as a lark. She was lonely. Zack had been away for months, and this feller could tell her all the news of folk down south, I suppose. Anyway, he became like her pal. Lived down in the bunkhouse where you are, but took her riding, took her on walks with young Wesley, Maudie's son, and Netta and other girls trailing along. But he was always interested in tribal folk. That was his undoing.'

'So *they* killed him?'

'Gawd, no. Just as well you came to me. It annoys me to hear these stories getting all mixed up. I can write, you know. I was always going to write about life in the outback – the papers pay for stories about that – but I was kept too busy, and I'm sorry now I didn't. It's history going past us fast as a train.'

'Is that right?' Yorkey said, to be dutiful, though he couldn't see anything out here that could make it into a history book.

'Yes. And Jimmy Moon understood that.'

'Why did he have a whitefeller name? Like two names?'

She shrugged. 'No idea. I talked to him sometimes. He wasn't interested in our station history, though; he wanted to know about all the tribes out here, who they were, what language they spoke. He used to talk to an old blackfeller there for hours on end, asking questions about all the tribes and clans.'

'Why?'

The question irritated her. 'Because he wanted to know,' she snapped. 'Because he wanted to know about all of his people, not just his own mob like you blokes.'

Yorkey accepted the chastisement rather than admit he didn't even know anything about his own mob.

'Then he went walkabout,' she said. 'He wanted to meet the Daly River mobs. To learn about them. He was warned they were dangerous, they didn't take to strangers, but he had no fear of them. So off he went. Said he'd be back.'

'And he didn't make it back?'

'You want me to tell the story or not?' she complained. 'Hang on, I've got corned beef on the stove, it'll be boiled away to nothing.'

Yorkey took the opportunity to stand up and stretch his legs. He felt an overwhelming sadness for Netta, for the pride that had caused her to run away from a safe place like this. Pride engendered by exposure to white men's rules. In her own society, pregnancy was not a sin but a joy. Even if Jimmy Moon had disappeared out there on the Daly River, or gone further west in his travels, she should have been able to bear the child with dignity. But not in the white world. Yorkey knew about the shame visited upon unmarried pregnant white women; he'd seen them whipped, he'd heard the jokes about them, but he'd never taken much notice. Not his business. Nor had it been his business to hear from his mother that she'd run off with a drover to escape the humiliation of a black housemaid living in a white household having to admit she was carrying a 'fatherless' child. For that was the peculiarity of the white folk. Fatherless? That was their word all right. And they would have sent Netta down to the blacks' camp to see out her time.

Loss of face, the Chinese called it, he recalled, but there was more to it, as he had recently discovered. Like Netta, he had become accustomed to the white men's style of living and their food. He had not enjoyed winding the clock back for those few days in the blacks' camp; even though those gentle people, his own people, had made him so welcome.

He wished he hadn't taken Netta's story for granted, without a second thought, without hearing her pain, only the boast about his proud father who had been highly regarded but had died too soon.

Mrs Dodds had said Jimmy Moon expected to come back. Maybe Netta had taken fright and bolted with the drover by then.

Yorkey was sad and weary, ready to leave, when she came back complaining about the weather.

'It's so bloody hot,' she said, wiping her face with a rag. 'I could kick a bloody cat if it would stand still. There's rain in the air but where the hell is it? I tell you, Yorkey, when it comes, I'm going to run outside and stand right here in the nuddy as long as it lasts. I suppose you blackfellers are used to it, but me, I come up here when I was only a bit of a girl, from Perth, and I never knew what it was like to yearn after rain, though I soon found out. Look at that bloody country out there. It'll crack wide open soon if we don't get rain. Now where was I up to?'

'It doesn't matter. I ought to be getting along.'

'Typical of you young bucks. Didn't I just say that? Only interested in your own mob.'

Yorkey mumbled an apology. 'Sorry, missus. I thought you were finished. I don't suppose the rest matters anyway.'

'Not to you it don't. But it did to me, and the rest of us round here. There was a great injustice done!'

'To Netta?'

'Who?'

'Netta.'

'Her? Gawd, no. Didn't I tell you she ran off? No. To Jimmy Moon. Now here's something you ought to know. I can write, I told you that. So when Colonel Puckering came out here, after the event – he was the Commissioner of Police for the Territory – I wrote down in my own hand a letter of reference for Jimmy Moon, and got all the station workers to sign it. We figured it was the least we could do.'

'Why did he need a reference if he was so in with the white folk?'

'Ah, I dunno. It was just something we wanted to do. You see he went off to have a pow-wow with them strange tribes and then he came back. He was crossing Black Wattle land when it happened.'

She sighed. 'Sit down, Yorkey, you're giving me a stiff neck standing over there.'

She waited until he resumed his seat on the steps and glared at him as if he was the cause of her sudden anger. 'Here he was, coming home, riding on a horse Sibell had given him, and what happens? He runs into a posse of louts. They was out there searching for outlaws who'd robbed and killed a white man. From that ambush there was a survivor, and he said there was a blackfeller among the outlaws. They didn't find the outlaws – who, years later we found out, had wandered into Daly River country and got chucked to the crocodiles – but they found Jimmy Moon.'

Yorkey steeled himself. He knew about posses, legal and illegal. He knew what was coming.

'Those bastards, one of them brother to the man who was killed in the raid, were not on a legal search; they were out there making big fellers of themselves. Full of booze and by-Jesus, they came across this blackfeller on a horse, and by all accounts were more interested in the missing gold from the robbery than anything else.'

She looked at him sadly. 'They beat him up, Jimmy that is, trying to find out where the gold was hid, and in the end they hung him.'

Mrs Dodds shook her head. 'Bloody bad all round that time. Sibell was hysterical. On our own land, you see, bad enough. Maudie, I have to say, was ropable. She called in the police. She laid charges against the men who killed Jimmy Moon. Oh God, it was a terrible time. Poor Jimmy. He probably had no idea why they hung him.'

They sat there in silence. The moon was up, a full moon with a ring around it – a sign of rain – the rest of the sky was dark, stars outshone by a stronger power. Yorkey's face was stiff and strangely cold but his hands, clutched together in fists, kept him under control. He couldn't form the questions he still needed to ask nor even acknowledge that he'd heard her.

Then Dodds came rattling round the corner pushing a wheelbarrow piled with stores.

'You got enough here to feed an army,' he whined.

'I got the same as always, if it's all there.' She began removing the smaller items, handing them to him. 'Here, take these in, put them on the table. I don't want nothing put away until I do my count.'

Yorkey jumped up out of the way and she heaved a bag of flour at him. 'You take this, and the tea . . . Where are the sultanas? I can't find the sultanas.'

'They're there!' Dodds shouted. 'Use your bloody eyes!'

She buzzed about, picking over the supplies on the table, examining bags and boxes to make sure they hadn't been tampered with, short-changing her; ordering her husband to tip the flour into a bin so she could check for weevils, and Yorkey glanced about the room. It was a tight fit, with a huge fireplace, a table and two old chairs, a bed, cupboards and bamboo shelves, but they nipped about without any trouble.

They were still arguing so he decided to leave.

'I better go now, missus. Been nice talking to you.'

'Righto,' she said over her shoulder, and he edged outside, but then stopped and poked his head in the door. 'That was a good story. What happened to those blokes? In the posse, I mean.'

She looked up, blinking at him. 'Who? Oh, them. They was charged. Colonel Puckering didn't muck about. They was charged with murder. But they got off.'

Dodds nodded. 'See. Didn't I tell you? She remembers things.'

'That I do,' she said, pleased. 'Everyone knew who did what, but you get to court and suddenly no one knows nothin'. They disappeared after that, all four of them.'

Suddenly Dodds came to life. 'Ha! That's where you're wrong. One of the four came back years later, when it was all forgot.'

'Who?' she demanded, annoyed at being upstaged.

'Syd Walsh. He married the widow woman what owned Glenelg station.'

'He wasn't one of them.'

'Bloody oath he was!'

She scratched her head, frowning. 'You could be right. Yes. He married her, didn't he? Gave her and the two kids such a bad time, her lads took off as soon as they were big enough to run. He never comes here, though. Wouldn't want to. I reckon Sibell would put a bullet in him.'

They went back to their sorting, which seemed to be a major operation for them since there'd be no more supplies for months, and Yorkey wandered away.

His mother had said he looked like his dad. Maybe that was why Mrs Hamilton had been staring at him. He felt closer to her now, a fondness for the woman who had been a friend, and who had mourned his dad. Maybe one day he ought to introduce himself to her, proper, as Jimmy Moon's son. He thought she might like that. Feel better about the whole thing.

But anger was building in him.

All the next day he brooded. He worked with three other men clearing creeks, building rock walls to keep the rushing waters on course, when they came. Hard work, just what he needed to keep his head clear, levering rocks from the dry soil and setting them firmly and carefully in place, while he deliberated his next move.

Late that night, Yorkey saddled up his horse and rode quietly away from Black Wattle station.

The monsoonal clouds had finally come together, forming a green-black canvas across the northern sky, a fitting backdrop to the flicker and glow of sheet lightning. Keeping pace, thunder rolled ominously, giving fair warning as the great storm advanced on the pink-streaked skies of dusk.

Suddenly a shaft of lightning struck with a deafening bang and Mimimiadie quaked.

'That was close,' he muttered and ran from their cave to check.

'Look over here,' Gopiny shouted from their lookout, and Mimimiadie hurried to join him. Awed, they peered out over the plain at a burning tree that was now igniting the tinder-dry grasses around it.

'I thought it was close,' Mimimiadie commented.

'But it's still a bad omen,' his friend said. 'We must be careful.'

'Of what? It's clear no white men came up here after the landslides, there wasn't a stick or a speck of dust disturbed. And they won't be coming now.'

Gopiny was confused. 'I still can't understand why not. They have a dead blackfeller at their feet and they don't even bother to see where he came from.'

'Why should they? They probably thought he was already in the gorge and got run down by their cattle. And they wouldn't care about a blackfeller. They would have spat on him and kicked his horse aside.'

He watched a flock of squawking cockatoos flying low, fleeing inland, and grinned. 'This is the best place in the world to be now. It doesn't matter how much it rains, we'll be dry; the waters will run off, pass us, down those crevices and over the top, and with the rain the earth will come alive again. We'll have plenty of food. The good spirits are with us, Gopiny.'

'There'll be plenty of food back at the swamps. Maybe we ought to go back there. It's a bit exposed here.'

Mimimiadie shoved him, teasing. 'You're scared of lightning, you big baby.'

'I am not.'

'You are so.'

All around them now the thunder rolled incessantly, lightning flashed and heavy drops of rain began to fall. Mimimiadie was glorying in it, throwing his arms wide, shouting greetings to the rain spirits of the storm.

'You can run and hide if you like. If you're too scared to stay out here and watch the fun.'

Gopiny shivered. 'I'm not scared.' He turned to watch the tree crumble as the fire died away, disappointed that the grass fire, too, was petering out. Then carefully he settled his gaze on one spot, pointing.

'There's someone coming.'

'Where?'

'Down there. This side of the tree. I saw movement.'

'It could have been an animal. A cow. Or a kangaroo.'

'No. It was a man. Running.'

They waited, eyes skimming over scattered trees on the plain until Mimimiadie saw the man too.

'It's a blackfeller. He's making for the gorge.'

They followed his progress, picking him out from the dark shadows of the trees as he crossed open areas, moving fast, but then they lost him as the black cloud cover defeated the short twilight and plunged their world into darkness.

Lone birds shrieked as they flew by, caught by the sudden change, and a dingo howled, calling his family in, rewarded by an answering howl. Then all was quiet except for the thud of rain that sounded heavier on their rock eyrie than it really was. Too soon yet for the torrents; they could be weeks or months away. But they would come.

In the morning they were astonished to find Matong sitting angrily by the sodden embers of their campfire. They didn't have to be told that his keen sense of smell had led him to this spot. Either of them could have done that; day-old embers still held the smell of cooked meat and fat. But what was he doing there?

Matong informed them that since he'd run cross-country for days and nights to bring them messages, he would not utter a word until they fed him.

Their plateau was steaming in a mist of light rain which did nothing to alleviate the increasing heat of this season, so Mimimiadie proudly escorted him back to their cave, which, so far, was kindly cool.

Impatiently he built a fire at the entrance, haranguing Matong with demands that the message be delivered, and a forest of questions, but the stubborn clansman would not budge.

By the time Gopiny returned with a rock wallaby, which he threw into the hot coals, fur and all, along with a fat lizard, Mimimiadie was shouting at Matong, threatening to bash his brains out.

The smell of the meat cooking seemed to satisfy Matong, and he began with the tale of his death-defying dash back to Daly River country, which didn't interest them at all.

'You didn't have to go,' Mimimiadie said caustically.

'Do you want to hear the story or not?' Matong retorted.

'Go on,' Gopiny said, turning the meat with a stick.

'When I got home there was great sadness among the clans. They knew that someone had killed the two miners because troopers had been in, on the warpath. They took away three young men, blamed them, one of them your second brother, Gopiny.'

'Ah no! He was never a fighting man. He was being trained by the elders for higher things. What happened to him? To them?'

'No one knows. They just roped them and dragged them off, like always.'

Gopiny was shattered. 'Did you tell the people why we had to kill the miners? That Mimimiadie's woman had been cruelly murdered?'

Matong was eyeing the meat, so Gopiny took his knife, politely grated fur from the cooked wallaby leg that he'd torn loose and handed it to Matong. Then he served Mimimiadie too, observing status.

'I told them about your woman later,' Matong told Mimimiadie nervously, 'and they all went about their crying for her. She was much loved.'

Mimimiadie's face was stone. 'She was that. A better woman I never knew. But her ordeal is over and her spirit can rest easy, for the payback was twofold.'

'This is true,' Matong said. 'We know that and so does she. I did not deem it necessary therefore to tell them who had killed the miners.'

'Why not?' Gopiny cried. 'You could have saved them. You could have saved my brother.'

Mimimiadie shook his head. 'No. It was too late. We all knew there'd be payback. You knew they'd arrest someone. Anyone. And more. So don't be such a weakling. The troopers had taken the men. What was he to do? Try to run after the horsemen, blurting out the truth?'

'But my dear brother . . .' Gopiny mourned.

Mimimiadie lashed out at him, a savage blow across the jaw with the back of his hand, sending Gopiny flying.

'Stop your whimpering! We have to live with these risks or give up the fight. If you want to do that, you go and live on a station like a tame dog.'

He stood up, pacing about, obviously distressed, but still defiant. He turned back on Gopiny.

'We are of the dingo clan. He is our totem. The dingo never gives in. They can't tame him and they won't tame us. You heard the dingoes last night; they are here with us. They mourn our brothers, and your brother, who could be dead by this.'

Gopiny dropped his head in his hands and muttered: 'It's all very well for you to talk. The people are dying. There has to be an end to this somehow. The more we fight, the more innocents we're putting at risk. I don't like your risks.'

'Then get out! Drop your tail between your legs and run to the nearest station for handouts and permission to dwell on a bit of land the size of my foot.'

'I haven't finished,' Matong said calmly, casting away bare bones, and licking his fingers. 'Since I had made the dangerous journey to the river people, they chose me to come back with the message for you. I get no thanks for my bravery in making this journey, though I'd rather be safe there with the people. I just have to listen to you going on like a couple of old women. I don't care about anything right now, not who wins or loses—'

'Shut your mouth unless you've got something to say,' Mimimiadie shouted at him.

'If you'd shut yours I'd tell you. The troopers don't know the names of Gopiny and me. But they know you, Mimimiadie, and they're on the lookout for you.'

'That's not news. They know me,' he said proudly. 'They know Mimimiadie is a warrior. I'll never be a tame dog.'

Matong nodded. 'That's true. They left a message for you. They want you to turn yourself in.'

'Me? I'm not that stupid. They're spitting into the wind this time. Why would I do that?'

'Because they've got your son.'

Mimimiadie didn't seem to hear him for a minute. 'Can you see me walking up to a police house asking them to come out and . . . Whose son?'

'Yours.'

'That's Boomi! He's only a little boy.' He was perplexed, then it hit him. 'They took Boomi?' he shouted. '*My* boy?'

'Yes. They said they'll give him back if you surrender to them.'

'They let him take my boy? Why didn't they stop them?'

Gopiny shook his head sadly. 'They can't fight guns. What could they do?'

'But an innocent little boy. What could he ever do to them?'

'My brother is innocent too,' Gopiny said, moving quickly aside as Mimimiadie raged at him.

'Shut your weak mouth about your brother. He's a grown man; Boomi is only six. I'll kill them, I'll find those troopers and kill every one of those dirty cowards, those dung-eaters. If they hurt my son I'll find theirs, I'll strangle them with my bare hands . . .'

He slammed away from the two men and strode out into the rain, still shouting curses and threats.

'Do you think he'll go in?' Gopiny asked.

'I've been thinking about it all the way back here. Can't see him doing that. They'd hang him from the nearest tree.'

'It is said they're not allowed to hang blacks any more.'

'So they shoot him instead. What use is a dead father? They won't give Boomi back anyway. He'll be sent off to live with whites somewhere.'

'You don't think they'll kill Boomi?'

'No. And they probably won't kill your brother. He'll get worse, he'll be locked up in a jail until he goes mad. They all go mad in those jails.'

Gopiny shuddered. 'I don't want to hear such a terrible thing. But I don't understand. What if they do mean to give Boomi back? If they arrest his father, who could they give him back to?'

Matong grinned meanly. 'You. You go in with Mimimiadie, leave him with the troopers and you take the boy in exchange. You can take him back to the people.'

'But they might arrest me too.'

'That is true. And that is why Mimimiadie can't go in, no matter how dearly he loves his son. It's just a trap and he knows it.'

They worried the subject for a long time, for it took a great deal of discussion, and in the end Matong stated the only two possibilities.

'Mimimiadie could give himself up and trust them to send the boy back to his own people.'

'Not much hope of that,' Gopiny sighed.

'Or he bides his time and finds out where the boy is and tries to rescue him.'

'We already talked about that. The white men are too smart. They will have the boy well hidden, probably far away. We'd never find him. We wouldn't know where to look.'

'Then he will have to accept that nothing can be done.'

Mimimiadie didn't return until late that afternoon and he was in such a dangerous mood, his two friends treated him with care. They had a good meal ready and offered him the biggest share. Gopiny promised him that on the morrow he would go foraging, women's work, but he could do it, the way Numinga had taught him.

'Numinga. Where did he go? Did he go back to the river people also?' Mimimiadie asked suddenly.

'No. He went off on his own.'

Mimimiadie scowled. 'The son of a crow. Gone walkabout just when I need him.'

'What for?' Gopiny asked.

'Because he speaks the English, you fool.'

Gopiny nodded, though he had no idea why that was important. Unless . . . He steeled himself to ask the question.

'Why? You're not thinking of giving yourself up, with Numinga to do the English speaking for you?'

'Even if Numinga was here, not a wise thing to do,' Matong said.

'You think I'm stupid? Mimimiadie growled. 'I'm not going in. I'm not giving myself up to those pigs. I wouldn't live to see my son again and they would never let him go home.'

Gopiny sorrowed: 'It's a terrible thing, Mimimiadie. We are with you in your grief, but there seems no solution to the challenge they have thrown at you.'

Mimimiadie climbed to his feet and stood tall at the entrance to their cave, flexing his muscles.

'Who says there isn't? I will bring them to their knees. I will have my son back. You wait and see.'

The word went out. This was secret men's business. Only a few highly respected elders were told the reason for the search, but that was enough. They passed on their instructions to people, whether they be station- or bush-dwellers, or even clans on walkabout, making their diligent way along the traditional routes to pay their respects to the land. Communication among the Aborigine tribes, clans and kin across the Territory far outclassed the efforts of white settlers, for this system had been in place for centuries. Elders were obeyed without question, rather with enthusiasm, for it was not often these days that a message of such urgency went forth.

The name was whispered, passed on; runners took it in their heads and delivered it to camps where it was relayed and sent on, the net widening by the hour.

Not one word of this was spoken to white men, not to friends or bosses, nor even their women and children. They had no idea that right across their great stations and beyond a search was in progress.

Find Numinga.

Information came back. Numinga was a Waray man. He had gone in. Worked as a stockman. Known to the white men as Neddy. He had killed his boss. Disappeared. Became a lone traveller. Sighted every so often by friends. All this was sourced back to Mimimiadie, who was waiting in a secret place with his father-in-law, father of his murdered wife, grandfather of Boomi.

The two men, united in their grief and their desperate plan, accepted the information without a flicker on their war-painted faces. They waited for the real news, that Numinga had been found. For then he would be approached by the magic man of the Waray people and told he was needed in a certain place. Even an old loner like Numinga would not dare to risk the wrath of a magic man, Mimimiadie said smugly. It was only a matter of time. He was surprised to hear that Numinga, whom he had considered to be more of a dreamer, had actually killed a station boss, but that was all the better for his purposes. All the better.

Yorkey travelled across the stations, following stock routes, accepting the easy hospitality of stockmen round their campfires. His shiny saddle caught their attention, and though he knew it would make him a marked man, he had no qualms about telling them it had been given to him by Zack Hamilton. He was on a mission and didn't want to be turned aside by suspicion of theft. There had to be a reason why a black drover would have such a prize.

That admission, though, made him even more welcome, since the story of Zack's encounter with a bush black had got about, and these men were pleased to meet the man who'd rescued him. It wasn't difficult for him to learn the way to Glenelg station.

He'd given the impression he was just drifting, and that was acceptable, especially for a blackfeller, but in between camps Yorkey rode hard.

It took him four days to reach the property owned by the man called Syd Walsh, and as he rode boldly down the track towards the stables, he gazed angrily at the imposing homestead with its screened verandas and red-painted roof. Obviously the bastard lived in style. The bastard who had hanged his father. Yorkey hadn't made up his mind what to do about Syd Walsh yet. At first he'd decided to shoot him, kill the bastard. The rifle, holstered by his saddle, was tempting. He could pick him off with one shot. But as the days passed he realised he probably wouldn't be able to do that, kill a man in cold blood. Not even Syd Walsh. He didn't have the stomach for it.

Yorkey slowed the horse to a walk. Better decide what to do before you go barging in there, he thought.

Then he grinned. He'd beat him up. Let him know why. Revenge would be sweeter that way.

But what if Walsh, though an older man, was more powerful than a skinny young black? This was a fact to be taken into account. What if Yorkey lost?

Was that a fair fight? he asked himself. When four men grabbed Jimmy Moon and hung him?

No. So there was no reason why he should engage in a fair fight with Walsh.

Yorkey had seen many an unfair fight that had quick results. Weapons and the element of surprise would do the trick. An iron bar, an axe handle, a chain. Now that could be nasty. And he'd choose the time and place. Ambush the bastard the way they'd ambushed Jimmy Moon. Bash him senseless, and ride off. At least that would be payback of a sort.

He nudged his horse and rode in, soon making the acquaintance of station hands and answering the usual questions. There were no black stockmen on this property but the cook sent him out some grub, a greasy stew, and he was allowed to sleep in the stables since a light rain was falling. That had everyone in a good mood, so after the initial introductions, no one took much notice of Yorkey.

On the second day he commented to a stablehand that he hadn't seen the boss around.

'No. He and the missus have gone into Darwin to sit out the wet.'

Yorkey was stunned. Why hadn't he thought of that? White men's habits! What a bloody fool he was, to come all this way for nothing. Depressed, he hung about the stockyards all day, idly watching Walsh's men branding a mob of cattle. They were laughing as they worked, and that drew his attention; roping and branding angry cattle was hardly a laughing matter. Then he realised they were altering brands, adding a bar to brands already in place. Cattle duffers! He ambled away, as if he hadn't noticed. It was none of his business, but interesting, from a drover's point of view, to know about it.

So there was nothing he could do but leave. Go on his way. Back to Black Wattle. He'd make some excuse for going missing. Walkabout. They expected blackfellers to just go walkabout when it suited them. Not that Yorkey had ever exercised this right, having no homeland to speak of, but they wouldn't know that. Anyway, who cared?

But it just didn't seem right to creep off back to his corner after that long ride to Walsh's station. No. That wouldn't do at all. Left to his own devices, he stole a tin of kerosene and hid it in the scrub.

The unoccupied homestead was in darkness when he opened the squeaky wire door and slid along the veranda from one end to the other trailing kerosene. Then for good measure he sprinkled the rest along the side of the house before throwing the tin into the garden. His horse was waiting, a hundred yards down the slope.

Yorkey took a deep breath, then, holding the wire door open with his foot, struck a match and tossed it on to the veranda. At the first whoosh of fire he was running to his horse. He jumped on, urging it away, and was soon galloping down the track that had brought him into Glenelg station. He heard the crackle and roar as the timber house went up, and unable to resist, turned back with a smile of satisfaction.

'See how you like that, Mr Walsh.'

Men were running, shouting, but Yorkey knew that there wasn't enough water within reach to put out a great blaze like that, not at this time of the year. Even the drizzle of rain would not help. That house was finished.

'Time to go,' he told the horse, and put it to the gallop again, but as the track rounded a clump of trees he almost ran into two riders racing towards the fire.

'Whoa!' they shouted, as surprised as he was, but Yorkey kept going; he had to, they'd be wondering why he was riding away from the fire.

The men were already suspicious. They wheeled their horses and went after him.

Yorkey's stockhorse was no match in speed for their mounts, much bigger, flashier horses. He considered breaking away from the track and making for open country where the stockhorse would have the advantage, diving around the sparse trees, but by then it was too late. He was suddenly jerked from his horse with a crash. One of them had roped him, and was hauling him in like a calf.

It turned out that the two men were the manager and his brother, returning from a visit to another station. They dragged him in and tied him to a fence while they went to investigate the damage, and it was a good hour before they returned. They didn't have to ask how the fire had started; the air was thick with smoke and fumes. Nor who had lit it. But they did ask his name.

'Yorkey Moon,' he said proudly, though it didn't mean a thing to them.

'Righto, Moon,' the manager said viciously. 'You've had your fun. Now it's my turn.'

An audience gathered, braying about his ingratitude, as he was dragged away again and tied, facing a hitching post. Someone ripped his shirt off and the manager stepped up.

'This is what we do to black bastards like you,' he said, waving a whip in Yorkey's face.

The first stroke seemed to cut his back in half, the next was even worse, and Yorkey screamed. He heard a satisfied mutter from the watchers, so clamped his mouth tight, trying to count to take his mind off the excruciating pain. But as the whip kept slashing and tearing at him, he lost track. Then it was all over. They cut him down.

He must have passed out for a short time, because he awoke lying in the dust, tied to a fence by his neck and ankles.

'Leave him there until the morning,' he heard the manager say. 'We don't want the coppers out here, so you two lads take him to the police outpost at Bald Hill, and hand him over for arson. Tell them he burned down the house and leave it to them to break the news to Syd. That'll make his Christmas, he'll be ravin' mad.'

Chapter Seven

The police outpost consisted of two sandstone buildings in desolate country with a horse paddock at the rear. The first, long and low, with slits for windows, looked like a miniature fort, as indeed it was. Years back this had been a staging camp and remount station for troopers, but it had been attacked by blacks, and the two policemen who happened to be in residence were killed, their hut burned to the ground. To provide more protection, this sandstone house with an indoor fireplace for cooking had been erected, and beside it a small, solid lockup with a single barred window.

Few of the police who patrolled this western area recalled that attack. It had gone into the folklore of the district, and since there had been nothing similar in recent times, security was lax. These days manning the lonely outpost was considered a miserable assignment, dodged by all mounted police except for new chums who knew no better, or constables sent there to cool their heels as a disciplinary measure.

Police Constable Second Class Wally Smith was enduring his last weeks in this hellhole. Crossing off each day on the calendar was the most important of his chores, after caring for the six horses in his charge and filling in the log. He rarely had anything to report beyond an ongoing account of the health and attitude of these horses, all of whom he knew by name.

Even when other police came by, they never wasted time here, only staying overnight, lodging their reports and pushing on, preferring to head for the comfort of station homesteads. To them, his predicament as a new chum was a joke, and he had to put up with their constant teasing about black gins under his bed, and such obscene remarks that he would have to turn away for fear of having them notice his blushes. He was always pleased to see visitors, and just as pleased to see them go, knowing that he'd wished this on himself by volunteering. Fresh up from Adelaide and his cadetship, Wally had seen this job as a great adventure, working in this wild, exciting country, and had been proud to hear that he would be in charge of an important outpost.

He now knew that the tough police patrolling the Territory likened this post to that of the old-time shepherds, a throwback to the European and English style of minding livestock, which didn't work here because of the huge distances involved. The shepherds on their lonely vigils were either killed by blacks or went mad. Armed with that unsettling information, Wally had gone back through the old logs, kept in dusty cabinets, and found that several of his predecessors had been either boozed or loony, judging by the crazy scrawled reports.

One fellow wrote that he was visited every evening by an old man kangaroo who sat by the fire with him and told him stories of great anthropological importance, which he had described in the accompanying notebook. Wally never found the notebook, but he did stop writing about the horses and their idiosyncrasies for fear he might be thought to be obsessive. And he also prepared a sane and sensible report for his superiors suggesting that this outpost was obsolete, that it should be shut down. That there were now enough cattle stations and their substations, known as outstations, operating over this great territory, right through to the border with Western Australia, that it was no longer needed. That accommodation for policemen and their remounts was readily available at these stations therefore saving urgently needed funds for the Department of Police. He knew that whining about the conditions wouldn't work, but cutting back on expenses would appeal to the bureaucrats, safe at their desks.

Armed with this carefully written report, Wally waited for the last days of his six-month stint, when other police were due to come by and join him in closing this place down for the wet season. Signing it off. Collecting all the horses and heading back for civilisation.

'And God rot the place,' he said, over and over again, while he waited.

But instead of the police, he was confronted with a prisoner. The first he'd had since a sergeant had come by months ago with a miner who had gone berserk with a pickaxe. Prior to that there'd only been stockmen accused of theft, and one of rape. But they'd all moved on the next day. Wally never heard the outcome of the charges, nor did he care. But this prisoner was a blackfeller. A young chap. Brought in by station hands from Glenelg station, on a charge of arson. He'd burned down Glenelg station homestead.

Wally thanked the stockmen profusely for doing the right thing, though the prisoner looked in pretty bad shape. He gave them tea and invited them to stay over, but they declined, having been instructed to return to work at the earliest.

He locked up the prisoner, took careful note of the stockmen's statements, had them sign the log and waved them off, then hurried to check on this fellow Yorkey Moon.

He threw back the bolt and peered at the prisoner, who was lying, hands still bound, on the dirt floor.

'Are you all right?'

The response startled him.

'No, I'm not bloody all right. The bastards flogged me. My back has to be cleaned or it will fester.'

Wally was no stranger to flogging, but he was not accustomed to being addressed in this manner by a blackfeller. He had to concede, though, that the man was right about the aftermath of the whip. He would enter in his log that the prisoner had arrived in this state, so that he could not be blamed, and that he himself had treated the injuries in the usual manner.

'Hang on,' he said.

For all he knew, this bloke could be playing possum. Best to get him properly secured first. He grabbed manacles and leg irons from the hook inside the house, the last he had left, since police passing through had marched off with the rest. Wally reminded himself to add their loss to the stocktaking forms that had to be completed before he left.

'Hold still,' he said, as he clamped on the irons.

The prisoner protested. 'What's this? Rope *and* irons? Do you think I'm some sort of magic man?'

Wally untied the ropes and discarded them. 'Procedure,' he said firmly. He helped him up. 'Now come outside and I'll have a look at your back.'

'How?' the prisoner snapped, sarcastically. 'Through this stinking old shirt? I can't take it off with handcuffs on.'

'One thing at a time.'

The 'shirt' was sleeveless, more of a waistcoat made of rawhide that had successfully kept most of the wounds covered. Wally sat him on an empty crate and gingerly lifted the stiff hide a little, and the prisoner winced.

'The bloody thing is stuck to my back.'

'Yes. I'll have to cut it off.'

He whistled when he saw the mess this man's back was in, and apologised that it was taking so long to separate the hide from the torn skin as his knife worked its way up, but eventually that was done, so he cut across to the armholes as well to remove the garment altogether.

'All right now.' He went inside, poured some warm water from the kettle into his enamel washbasin and threw in handfuls of salt.

'This is going to hurt,' he told the prisoner, who nodded.

Gently he swabbed the wounds, gritting his teeth at the sight of the spongy, bloodied flesh. The lacerations were deep.

'You might as well sit here for a while and let it dry out,' he said. 'I think that's the best I can do.'

'Thank you,' the prisoner gritted, slumping forward over his knees. 'Could I have some water?'

When Wally returned with the waterbag, the prisoner seemed to feel better.

'I want to make a statement,' he said.

'Why? They said they caught you red-handed. You burned down Syd Walsh's house. Are you denying that?'

'No. But I still have the right to make a statement. Get a pencil and paper.'

Wally shrugged. He had nothing else to do. 'Righto.'

The prisoner dictated: 'My name is Yorkey Moon. I burned down Syd Walsh's place because he killed my father, Jimmy Moon.'

The policeman was intrigued. 'When was this?'

'Twenty years ago, thereabouts. Before I was born. And that is a true fact.'

Wally shook his head, disappointed. Syd Walsh was a nasty piece of work. 'That won't do you much good now.'

'Write it down just the same. Folk at Black Wattle station can testify to it. He hung my father, an innocent man.'

His warder didn't like to say that hanging blackfellers wasn't unusual twenty years ago.

'And that's why you burned down his house?'

'Exactly. I'm a law-abiding citizen or I'd have shot the bastard.'

'I don't think a judge will see it that way.'

'It doesn't matter. I want people to know.'

'Very well. Is that all?'

'No. I own an expensive saddle and they kept it at Glenelg station. I want it back, and my horse too. You saw my horse, it's a good stockhorse. They took it with them.'

'Don't like your chances there either.'

'And one more thing. While I was out at Glenelg I saw them branding cattle. Changing brands. Those blokes are cattle duffers.'

Now that interested Wally. Rumours were rife that Walsh and his men were behind cattle losses throughout the district but there was no proof.

'Did you see what brands?'

'I sure did. Some of the cattle had a Bar C and they were changing that to a G. Bar G. Glenelg. And some had a W. I don't know what they were going to do about that.'

'W would be for Walsh.'

'Then why is he using a Bar G for Glenelg too?'

'I don't know. I'll look it up.'

The prisoner insisted on signing the statement, which Wally thought was a waste of time, except for the last bit, and the interview was over. Moon was returned to his cell, and Wally set about his own duties, entering all this in his log with pen and ink and attaching the statement to the back of the page.

Constable Smith inspected his uniform, brushing off the dusty mould that gathered on the dark serge every day or so, and hung it up again, ready for his departure. He never wore it out here; shirts and dungarees sufficed for this place. He worried that he shouldn't have been wearing his boots either; they were shabby, the soles paper-thin. Though he'd filled in the correct forms, requesting new boots and socks, none had been sent, and that annoyed him. When he did return to civilisation he wanted to look smart in his uniform. No chance of that now.

He shaved, and trimmed his fair hair with the razor, sticking to his routine and his self-made regulation of keeping himself spruce, despite the fact that other policemen came through here looking like shaggy bushmen.

Or because of it, he thought, frowning. Smith was ambitious. He felt that the police should look the part, whether in or out of uniform, and he was always ready for scrutiny. When the Superintendent had come by, he had commended Smith for keeping the post in good order. The constable hoped he had remembered to put that in his report.

He stepped outside into air like hot treacle and gasped at the shock of it, sweat already stinging his skin.

'God almighty,' he said. 'A man wouldn't want to stay out here too long, if this is only the beginning of their summer.'

The constable hadn't minded the dry heat of the previous months. Adelaide could produce ferocious heat too. But this was awful, and getting worse by the day. Low clouds sweltered overhead and there was an ominous stillness about the trees beyond the clearing. Nothing to see out there at all. Even the birds, the huge flocks of brilliant birds that used to brighten his day, had long since disappeared.

He took the rake and combed the red sand between the white-painted rocks that he'd set in place from the front door of the house to the hitching posts, but soon lost interest, deciding he might as well get breakfast. Not an appetising thought. Tea, hard duty biscuits and cold corned beef.

When he served the same meal to his prisoner, Moon was full of complaints.

'This rathole stinks. Don't you ever clean it out?'

'I sweep it every day.'

'You should hose it out. It stinks of piss and animal droppings.'

'I can't hose. I don't have enough water.'

'You don't expect me to eat in here.'

'No one else has complained.'

'They must be used to jails. I'm not. Never saw the inside of one before. It wouldn't kill you to let me out awhile.'

This conversation was being carried on through the open barred window. Wally supposed he could think about it, but he had to see to the horses first.

'Food's not much anyway,' he said. 'You might as well have it and I'll come back.'

He dawdled about his chores, then made a stew of chopped beef and potatoes from the remains of the weekly stores sent over from an outstation. While that was cooking on the stove, he turned his hand to a damper of flour and water. Wally was getting quite good at dampers, with all the time in the world to pound some air into them. He was thinking that Moon wasn't a bad sort of chap. It wouldn't hurt to have someone to talk to for a change. Over lunch. Even if the prisoner was an Abo.

Yorkey thought that if any of his mates could see him now, they'd roll around laughing. Here he was sitting up for a meal in a police station, with a nervous chump of a copper not much older than himself, his ankles in heavy leg irons and handcuffs on, making it hard to scoop up the food. And all the while the copper was making polite conversation, as if he were a real guest, not a guest of the Government.

He heard that Constable Smith had joined the force in Adelaide, and that it was a beautiful city but there were more chances of advancement up this way for police volunteers, and so on. He heard that Smith had lost his dad – how wasn't explained – when he was a kid and he'd been brought up by his mother, who'd married an older man, but then she'd run off with a young lover . . . By this time, Yorkey had lost interest, but he let the constable rattle on, realising the poor bloke was lonely as all get out.

'How long have you been in this dump?' he asked.

'Six months. My time is nearly up, though.'

'Jesus, is it worth it?'

'Oh yes. I feel sure it is. Actually I haven't minded it that much. I've learned to cook. Would you like some more stew?'

'Yes, I'm starving. But let me tell you, mister. If you were a drover's cook, we'd have drowned you by this.'

When Sergeant Riley rode in with Constable Grimm, and a prisoner tied on to his packhorse, he was astonished to find another blackfeller, fully constrained, sitting at the table in the house, drinking tea.

'What's he doing here?' he demanded.

'I was just going to sweep out the cell,' Smith said quickly. 'I couldn't have him loose.'

'Forget that now. Put this bastard on a charge of attempted murder.' He jerked his head at the native Grimm was minding outside. 'Have you got some spare duds? He's been whinging all the way that he wants clothes, and we can't take him in bollocky like he is now.'

Wally rushed to his trunk to pull out some old clothes for the native, trying to decide which were the worst, since it was obvious he'd never see them again. Or want to. He was in a fit of embarrassment at being caught out like this, with a prisoner actually inside his residence, wearing one of his shirts.

But Riley took command. Both prisoners were soon in the lockup and the kettle was on.

'Moon is still in irons,' the constable said nervously. 'Should I go and take them off?'

'Later. Damn smart of you to keep him restrained. That's a mistake a lot of coppers make when they've got no backup. Open the cell door to feed 'em, and get bashed. Same thing when the bucket has to be emptied. You pay attention, Grimm! Wally here has got a head on his shoulders. Now who is the bastard anyway?'

'His name's Yorkey Moon. Two men from Glenelg station brought him in. He burned down Syd Walsh's house.'

'He what?' Riley began to laugh. 'Burned the bugger's homestead, did he? We ought to give him a medal.'

'It's all here in the log,' Wally said, much cheered by Riley's appreciation of his security measures. He handed it over, together with pen and ink for the sergeant to add his report and, he hope, favourable comments.

'More tea, sir?' he asked. 'Or some stew?'

'Rather have a drink, Wally. Got any booze?'

'Sorry, sir. They never send me much.'

'All right, tea.' He was reading the log and the statement. 'What's this about Walsh murdering his father? I like that. Can he prove it?'

'I think so, but it was twenty years ago.'

'Oh, for Christ's sake! What's it doing in here?'

Wally shrugged nervously. 'I'm sorry, sir. He insisted on making a statement.'

Riley sat back. 'I don't know what the world's coming to with upstart blacks talking back like they own the place. He sounds as uppity as the one I've got out there. Friggin' bloody native wearing a belly band for trousers, giving me bloody cheek all the way. Smart Alec talking English, if you don't mind.'

Wally poured the tea. 'I suppose it had to happen with us here, so many white people I mean. That Yorkey Moon, who made the statement, he's black but was brought up by white people, I think. He says he's a drover.'

Riley laughed. 'One up on my bloke; he reckons he's a stockman! Ran out of duds. But there's more to him.' He peered down at the log. 'Wait a minute. What's this about cattle duffing?'

'It's all in there. I took careful note. Moon saw them changing brands.'

'And he's a drover?'

'I'd say yes, he is. He knows what he's talking about, though I'm not familiar with brands.'

'Well I bloody am. Bar W is Pop Oatley's brand, from Warrawee station, and Bar C is Bill Connor's brand. They've both lost cattle to duffers. Maudie always reckoned it was Walsh . . . How long ago was this? How long has Moon been here?'

'Only two days.'

Riley was on his feet. 'We've got them.'

'Syd Walsh isn't there, though. He's gone to town for the wet.'

'Lucky for your customer,' Riley snorted. 'Syd would have had him shot and buried by this. He'd have disappeared off the face of the earth. And he wouldn't have been the first.

He pushed the log aside. 'I want a word with your prisoner.'

The constable shuffled about his tiny residence, tidying up, stirring the stew. He thought it might be nice to make a fresh damper for the sergeant and Constable Grimm, remembering that Yorkey Moon had said his recipe needed more salt.

Then Grimm came in, furious. 'What the bloody hell do you think you're doing? Why did you tell Riley about them cattle duffers?'

'I didn't tell him. He read it in the log.'

'You shouldn't have put it in your bloody stupid log. Do you know what happens now? We're not heading home after all. Riley's draggin' me back over to Glenelg station to catch the cattle duffers so he can get another feather in his cap. And you, you stupid bastard, you're stuck here until we return. We were all set to leave this stinking country tomorrow.'

The constable was stunned. 'I don't understand. How can you do that? Two men can't go bowling into Glenelg and arrest those blokes, even if you do find proof.'

'Of course we can't. We'll need fresh horses, so we're crossing back to Pop Oatley's place first, then we sign up a posse, then we all converge on Glenelg. Riley's raring to go. There's no stopping him now, thanks to you! Can I have some stew?'

Wally realised then what he'd done. If he hadn't inked in that story he could have rubbed it out. But it was there forever. Walsh accused as a cattle duffer. If Riley hadn't read that, they would have been leaving this desolate post, headed for Pine Creek and Darwin in the morning. He was so disappointed he could have wept. More days here sounded like months, a sentence, with supplies and water running short. But Riley was a man who enjoyed the bush. His hunting ground. He was famous for tracking a murderer, a white man who had raped and killed two housemaids on a lonely station, right down past Alice Springs, and bringing him in.

Nothing Wally could do now, though. Riley was after the cattle duffers, and he would be stuck here with two prisoners. He went in search of the sergeant to ask him to enter the name of the second prisoner and the charges against him in the all-important log.

But Riley was busy interrogating Yorkey Moon.

'Tell Grimm to fill it in,' he said. 'And see he gets it right. That prisoner speared a station boss.'

His name was Numinga, he told Yorkey, but he'd given them a name that sounded like Mooboola and let them figure out how to write it.

'I was only trying to pinch some clothes from a line when they grabbed me. Well, I got the clothes,' he said, sniffing at the shirt and trousers the constable had dug out for him. 'What's this smell?'

'Camphor,' Yorkey said. 'They dragged you in for stealing their clothes?'

'No. They reckoned I speared a boss.'

'And did you?' Yorkey was very interested.

His cellmate was squatting across from him, gingerly touching and inspecting his bruises.

'You a station black?' Numinga asked suddenly.

'No, I'm a drover.'

'What are you in for?'

'I burned down a house.'

Numinga grinned. He liked that. He had burned down a few places in his wilder days too.

'I didn't spear the bossman,' he admitted. 'I give up that stuff long back.'

'Who did?'

'Not my business, mister. Not yours neither,' he growled.

Yorkey apologised. But then he explained that he'd found the station boss lying by a track with a spear wound and taken him in.

'Did he die?'

'No, he's getting better.'

Numinga nodded. 'Good. No use this spearin' and shootin' no more. You tell the police boss I never did that, eh?'

'I don't think he'll listen to me.'

Numinga scowled. 'You bin talk to him plenty.'

'No. I was just making trouble for a white boss who has been stealing cattle,' he explained. 'They steal cattle from one boss and sell to another one.'

Now he'd offended Numinga again. 'I'm no blackfeller fool,' the older man snorted. 'I know that. I was a stockman younger time.'

More apologies. Yorkey found this granite-faced bloke heavy going, and touchy as hell. He couldn't make out where he fitted in and thought it prudent not to ask. Though he was in his forties, Numinga had a powerful frame, no fat on him, his muscles lean and stringy. Yorkey had noticed all the tribal markings on his bare body when they brought him in, before the clothes had been tossed to him, and yet Numinga had not asked the immediate question of tribe or clan. Important to bush blacks. They wouldn't sleep within miles of wrong totems.

It was Yorkey's back that saved the day. Numinga's mistrust of him disappeared when he realised why Yorkey was lying flat on his stomach. He was upset to see Yorkey's wounds. His turn to apologise. There were cures, he said, for the savaging of skin, and mourned that he was not able to help.

So they talked, locked in the small, gloomy cell. Yorkey told him a little about how he'd found the injured bossman, part of it anyway; that he'd happened to be following the same route from the gorge, where there had been landslides, causing huge problems for the drovers, and one man almost killed.

Numinga stopped him. 'This was a blackfeller?'

'No. My boss. A drover.'

'Ah. He didn't fall to the ground then?'

'Who?'

'The boy who went over the cliff into the gorge. I bin there. His heart was weeping to be a true tribal man because they took him to a mission as a little one and he lost his Dreaming. Ah, yes.' Numinga nodded, dropping his head to chant a monotonous song that rose and fell like a dirge, and the hairs stood up on Yorkey's neck. The sounds were familiar, but too far back in his memory for him to fully understand, and they unsettled him. This was spooking him now. He could have sworn they were not alone. He cringed back into his corner until it stopped.

'I didn't understand that,' he said, shaken.

Numinga sighed. 'He went over the gorge; his body him still there, but the spirits, they catch him, save him and take him on to his Dreaming. This is a good thing. This is what the spirits have been hanging on to tell me. We never did the proper crying or we would have knowed that.'

'You, not me,' Yorkey said.

'Not true. You were there. You walked past the empty body. Doan you think the spirits know? You a lost boy too, you are.'

'I am not,' Yorkey said angrily.

'Your spirits know you,' Numinga said gently. 'They was here. You are Waray but of the ancient lizard people who dwelled in that gorge, lizards who were more powerful than puny men . . .'

Yorkey was tired. Exhausted. He didn't want to hear this. He pulled back into reality.

'Someone fell down the gorge? Is that right?'

'I just tell you that.'

'And he got killed?'

'Yes.'

'This was the time of the landslide?'

Numinga smiled. 'No landslide. To bugger up your cattle.'

'Oh shit! And you were there?'

'I watch. I doan like that gorge.'

It took time for Yorkey to piece it all together. Numinga and other blackfellers had been up top when they'd been trying to take the cattle through. One man, a young man, had fallen to his death but others had been there besides Numinga, all busy creating a nuisance. No mention was made of those names. And Yorkey didn't want to know.

None of his business. But at least he now knew that scream had been real, and some poor fellow had been killed, and was still lying there buried under tons of rocks. And maybe the spirits *had* come for him. Best to let him rest there. And it was better not to mention any of this to the drovers or cattlemen. It would only cause more trouble. Let the gorge keep its secret.

They found Numinga. But he had been arrested for spearing a white man. Now in the custody of two armed mounted police.

The news caused dismay, and decisions had to be made on the spot. Was the matter so important he had to be freed?

It seemed so.

The mounted police had taken him from Warrawee station and were heading east. To free him, an attack would have to be made on those policemen.

There were mutterings against this. Station blacks were terrified. They knew the consequences of violence against lawmen, and wanted no part in it.

Finally an elder sent two men to track them, keep after them, and when they caught up, watch for an opportunity to free Numinga and give him a message. It was days before the trackers sighted the riders far ahead of them, but they guessed they were headed for the police outpost and followed cautiously.

92

When the constable stepped out the next morning he had no idea that his every move was being observed. His mind was on the weather, on the wind squalls that were raising clouds of hot dust to make his life even more miserable. That fine dust got in everywhere, even into houses with windows, and in this place, with no glass in those slits of openings, it was hopeless.

He went about his chores as usual, but with two prisoners to contend with, took the precaution of strapping on his revolver. Moon didn't worry him too much, but that other one was obviously dangerous. Once he'd fed and watered the horses he turned his attention to feeding and watering his prisoners. He studied his larder. They could have the rest of the stew with some biscuits. He would make a fresh damper and fry up some bacon for himself, then he'd really have to do some cooking to cater for them and for Riley and Grimm when they came back. Damned nuisance all this.

He delivered their food on metal dishes, handing it to them through the horizontal bars of the window, ignoring Yorkey Moon's complaints and demands.

'All in good time,' he said frostily.

When they returned the dishes to him, he outlined his orders.

'I am throwing in the handcuffs and the leg irons. You will put them on, Moon, after which I will unlock the door. Make them fast or I will shoot you. That other man will stay back because I have a gun on you both, and will not hesitate to shoot. You will bring the night bucket with you as you step out the door.'

'You mean the shit bucket?' Moon laughed. 'I can't carry it with my hands in cuffs, and tripping over these bloody leg irons.'

'Please yourself,' Wally retorted. They had to be given water and that bucket had to be emptied every twenty-four hours, and this was the method outlined in the manual. It also said the cell had to be cleaned out daily, but they could forget that.

'All right, I'm ready,' Moon said eventually.

Wally undid the lock, put the key and lock in his pocket, slid the heavy bolt and ordered Moon to step outside.

'What about the bucket?'

'Step outside first.'

When Moon opened the door and stepped out, the constable had his loaded revolver trained on him. He moved forward quickly to check Moon's restraints. Finding them in order, he was pleased with himself. This was the way he'd done it before, step by step, and it worked. No one would have the opportunity to rush him.

'Now you can get the bucket. Tell your mate to keep back.'

This was the easy part. With Moon outside, he slammed the door to the cell and slid the bolt again.

'The bucket gets emptied in the scrub round the back,' he said. 'So start walking.'

'Trying to walk,' Moon snapped as he shuffled along at a snail's pace, hanging on to the handle of the bucket, while Wally followed with his revolver at the ready.

Numinga's rescuers had seen the two policemen ride away, but another was at the post, and no doubt well armed, so they stayed clear until nightfall.

When all was quiet they slipped down to the lockup, only to find it had a key-lock as well as a sliding bolt; disgusted, they departed without a word. Numinga was in there, but he was not alone; better not to alert him as yet.

The same problem arose. Did they attack the lone policeman, take his keys and free Numinga? No. It was a dangerous move and would have the same result. Big payback for wounding or killing a policeman. They decided to wait until the policemen were on the road again with their prisoners. This was only a temporary jail. And this time the police didn't have a head start on them. They would keep up and free Numinga at a night camp. They discussed all sorts of plans during the night, including the possibility that they might somehow steal the policeman's weapons, thereby rendering him harmless. They could then tie him up and release the prisoners. Both of them. That would be funny.

The watchers were up and prowling about long before they saw the smoke coming from the chimney that morning. Too late they realised they'd missed an opportunity to steal the weapons. The policeman had walked out briskly to fork hay over the fence to the horses and take water to the trough. Any minute they expected him to turn back to his house, but he did not. He took his time, talking to the horses as they came over, patting them . . .

The two men looked at each other and grinned. Agreeing. They knew the horses would be fed again in the evening, or at worst the next morning, and they'd be ready. They hoped the other policemen didn't come back before then.

In case of some other development, they took up their watch as close as possible to the lockup, keeping to the edge of the scrub, witnessing the food delivery and then the other interesting bits of police activity, paying particular attention to that heavy lock. The thing that had kept them out last night. They also saw the revolver, which depressed them, and the fetters being thrown in . . . all of that. And they watched, interested, as the policeman shuffled the chained man away with the shit tin.

They both saw their chance and in an instant one man was running swiftly, silently across the clearing, the other man cutting back through the scrub towards the horses.

It only took a second. The lock had not been replaced. He slid the bolt, opened the door and hissed: 'Numinga. Out. Quick!'

Numinga took an extra second to shut the door behind him, and slide the bolt into position, and then he was gone.

The chore completed, Moon used the opportunity to take a piss before he was marched back to the cell.

'My back needs swabbing,' he said. 'It's on fire.'

'I'll get some salt water and you can take it in with you. Your mate can do it this time.'

'We need some fresh water.'

'I know. I'll get that too.'

'And what about a clean shirt for me? The flies are bad, I'll have maggots.'

'I thought you blokes reckon they're a cure for open wounds?'

'Not me. I want a shirt.'

'All right. Stay there.'

Wally left him standing in the shelter of the lockup wall while he went to the tank for water, and then he panicked! The gate was open and the horses were galloping away. No accident this, Wally knew; the gate was wide and they'd been chased out. Someone was stealing the horses. He ran, shouting, yelling, firing his revolver as the precious mounts scattered into the bush.

'Oh Jesus!' he cried. 'Oh no!' There wasn't a horse left in the paddock.

He fled back to Moon, jabbering his distress. 'What am I going to do? The horses are gone!'

'All of them?' Moon was as stunned as he was.

'Yes. All of them. Someone opened the gate.'

'Then there's nothing much you can do.' Moon shrugged. 'You'll just have to wait for the sergeant to come back. Jesus! You won't be too popular.'

'What the hell could I do?'

'I dunno, mate. It's just the way it goes.'

'You'd better get back in the cell,' Wally said, remembering his duties, waving his gun about.

'Unchain me first and put that bloody gun away before you shoot one of us. I'm not going anywhere in this bloody country without a horse. I'd be dead in a day.'

Still trembling with shock, Wally took the small key from his pocket, undid the manacles and released Moon's leg irons. He unbolted the door and shoved Moon in, glancing about as if he half expected the horse thieves to jump out at him. He was slamming it shut when it dawned on him that the cell was empty. Disbelieving, he staggered back, turning on Yorkey, screaming at him. 'You did this! You let him out!'

Yorkey hardly heard him. He gaped, suddenly cold, his mind reeling. Numinga was gone. Had got out, past a bolted door. It had been bolted all right. He'd seen the constable do that. Then Numinga had dashed round the back and let all the horses out. Or maybe he didn't even have to do that. Yorkey's imagination was running wild. He recalled Numinga's chanting, his accord with the spirits. Was he a magic man? Could he have used the same magic to free the horses that he'd used to free himself?

He realised that Smith was shouting at him, blaming him.

'Don't talk rot,' he said, following the constable outside, unhindered. Smith was in such a state he seemed not to care that his prisoner was walking free.

'I suppose I walked over, in chains, while you were watching and let the horses out too?' he asked sarcastically.

'Someone did.'

'Unless it was magic. Spirit stuff. He's a weird one, that Numinga.'

'That's not his name. Not the name he gave. Is that his real name?'

'No,' Yorkey lied. 'That's just a blackfeller word for magic man.'

'How did he get out then?' Smith examined the bolt again, sliding it back and forth, but Yorkey, standing in the wind, feeling the sting of the dust, glanced down and realised with a pang of disappointment that there had been no magic involved. Deliberately, he walked over the footprints in the dust, footprints that led to and from the scrub, peering about him, as if searching for intruders.

'You ought to see if any of the horses have come back,' he called. 'I'll go round this way.'

It was clear to him now. The prints weren't from boots but bare feet. Some blacks had released Numinga, and scared off the horses to draw attention away from the escape and, he guessed, stop any efforts to chase after them.

That knowledge irritated him. They could have waited and released him as well. He was a blackfeller too. Bugger them! Where was their loyalty?

Nevertheless, he did his duty and tramped over the tracks, obliterating them. He'd be willing to bet there'd be no horses missing; they'd be wandering about the scrub and would probably come back in their own time. Not his problem. Right now he needed some water and a shirt.

Yorkey was right. Within a few hours the first few horses came trailing back and Smith woke up to what had happened. He locked Yorkey up again, locking and bolting the cell door this time, and saddled a horse to round up the rest.

The wind dropped and rain began to fall first in slow, heavy drops, then it teemed and the thunder rolled. Safe in his dry cell, Yorkey felt sorry for poor old Smith out there in the scrub. Thunder spooked horses, they'd be hard to catch in this weather.

Two days later, a posse of three station men rode in with Riley and Grimm, and with them were two more prisoners, the manager and his brother from Glenelg station.

They were all pleased with themselves for catching out cattle duffers, but Riley was furious that Smith had let the other prisoner escape. From his cell Yorkey could hear him berating the constable.

But now it was Yorkey's turn to suffer. At first the new prisoners refused to share a cell with a blackfeller, but on recognising him they changed their minds, placing Yorkey in danger. To solve the problem,

Yorkey was chained to a tree for the night, within sight of the cattlemen camping nearby.

In the morning he and the other two prisoners were tied on to their horses. The spare mounts were haltered and brought forward and the police station was shut down. The station men, anxious to make sure the two cattle rustlers had no chance to escape, volunteered to join the escort to Pine Creek and Sergeant Riley accepted.

He was still angry with Constable Smith for allowing the other blackfeller to escape, so Yorkey put in a good word for him.

'That feller didn't spear Zack Hamilton. You had the wrong bloke anyway.'

'How do you know?'

'Because I talked to him in the lockup. He was only trying to pinch some clothes so he could go in.'

Riley was even more suspicious. 'How do you know it was Zack Hamilton?'

'Because I'm the one who found him. He'd collapsed by the side of the road. I got him home.'

Hearing this, the cattlemen told Riley he ought to let Yorkey go.

'Who cares about Walsh's house? It might give him the hint to quit the district.'

But Riley would not hear of it. 'Arson's still a crime in my book. He's for jail and that's that.'

Eventually they moved out, a small procession heading briskly across the open plains.

Yorkey was angry with himself, not for setting fire to the house, but for getting caught. That had been downright stupid. He began to concentrate on how he might escape before he was taken into Darwin. There was a long way to go yet; he'd just have to watch for an opportunity.

Then, he realised, he'd become a wanted man, an escaped criminal, but that wasn't so bad. He could make his way back to Queensland. Once he was out of the Territory he'd be safe. And there was plenty of work for drovers in that big busy state.

PART TWO

June 1899

Chapter Eight

The Oatley Mercantile Company was located in a single-fronted shop premises in Smith Street, across a wide expanse of dirt road from the stone archways of the Commercial Bank. It was a hot, windswept corner with barely a tree to offer shade, and not enough buildings in the adjoining street for protection from the relentless sun. Surveyors had done an admirable job in planning the town of Port Darwin, streets laid out neatly in blocks on the sandy flats left bare by sweating labourers who had cleared the rugged bush for their town.

Almost thirty years had passed since the first allotments were meticulously pegged, and many commercial and residential buildings were in place, but half of the allotments were still vacant, overgrown with weeds, giving the town centre an odd, gap-toothed appearance.

William Oatley, the owner of the Mercantile Company, leaned back in his chair with a mug of tea and studied the cloistered façade of the bank. One of these days, he decided, he would pull down this flimsy building and replace it with a cool stone building like that, extending it over the two neighbouring blocks that he also owned. He would have a footpath too, even if he had to set one in himself, since the district council was short of cash, and an awning to cover the footpath for the benefit of pedestrians. One day. But not just yet; he wanted to finish the house first, the one he'd always promised to build for Emily May. Though it was too late for her. She'd never get to see the 'town' house she'd designed with such loving care.

He sighed. Never mind, my love. It has been a long time coming, but I'm building it exactly as you wanted. It'll be a fine house. It was hard to believe that five years had passed since she'd died. He still remembered that terrible day as if it had only been a week or so ago.

He and Emily May had been childhood sweethearts – just like Myles and Lucy, come to think of it – both station kids; they'd lived all their lives in the bush. The Oatley station, Warrawee, was more than a hundred miles from Emily May Mills' family holdings, known as Millford station, but their parents were friends, so they all kept in touch by letter, occasional visits, and shared holidays in Darwin at Christmas.

While he and Emily May were away on their honeymoon, tragedy struck. Mrs Mills was washed into a flooded river as they were trying to ford a causeway in their buggy, and her husband drowned too, trying in vain to save her. It was a sad homecoming and meant their plans had to change. William had expected to return to Warrawee station where they would live with his parents, but it was decided that he should take over the Millford station instead. He'd been twenty-one at the time, and as Pop Oatley said, old enough to know what he was doing.

Running a cattle station of that size had been a challenge for a young man, but William had always been a resolute person, so with his beloved wife at his side and Pop Oatley ready with advice and assistance, he set to work. Within a few years he'd gained a reputation as an astute cattleman, welcomed into the heady ranks of these northern pastoralists who administered properties larger than counties.

Myles was born at Millford, and then a daughter, Constance. William shook his head sadly, watching a little girl in a large hat trail across the street with her mother. Constance had been about that age when she'd died of whooping cough. He remembered that Zack Hamilton's boy, Simon, had died of the same ailment only a month later. Emily May had held up well at that loss, relying, as she said, on God's will, but Sibell Hamilton had taken Simon's death hard, even though she still had her daughter Lucy, who'd been spared.

Some said Sibell never got over the boy's death, but then 'some', he thought, didn't take into account that Sibell had encountered her share of troubles already. Her parents had been lost at sea, and Sibell, only a young girl, had struggled ashore from the shipwreck.

William's clerk came in from the back office. 'Is that all for today?'

'Yes, Leo. You pack up and call it a day. But if you see Myles, tell him I'm waiting for him. I need to know if Mr Chen arrived today from Singapore.

'Should have gone myself,' he muttered when Leo left. Mr Chen was a wealthy Chinese financier who would expect to be met and escorted to the Hotel Victoria, the only decent hotel in town. Myles should have come back to tell him that the Chinaman was settled and available for a dinner meeting this evening. They had much to discuss.

William decided to wait a little longer before trotting around to the hotel to make his own enquiries. He took a whisky bottle from the cabinet behind his desk, located a glass and poured himself a few inches of the Scots' best, allowing himself to reminisce to pass the time.

Myles had never known either of his grandmothers. Or wouldn't remember. Mother Oatley had died of cancer when he was three. Pop Oatley, too, had borne the loss as God's will, and his son, broken-hearted, had suffered in silence rather than further upset his bereaved father.

But when his own wife, his dear Emily May, had died, that was a different story. Myles had been fifteen, he recalled, working with him mustering cattle more than twenty miles from the homestead, when a stockman had come galloping across the plains to tell him the missus had been bitten by a snake.

'What sort of snake?' he yelled even as he wheeled his horse around, shouting to Myles to come with him.

'Tiger snake I reckon, boss. Black girls say it was a tiger, but she's real bad . . .'

'They don't know what they're talking about,' he shouted to Myles. 'Bloody tiger snake. They call everything a tiger snake now. It's a word they've picked up. I've never seen a tiger snake in my life. It might not be venomous but we'd better get back.'

Father and son rode recklessly over the longest twenty miles of their lives, hurdling the low fence of the kitchen garden to leap down from their horses, tossing the reins aside.

As William took the steps to the back veranda in his stride he saw the dead snake, probably brought in by the black girls, hanging over the rail. He stopped, shocked, to stare at it.

'A king brown,' he whispered. 'God help her. God help her!'

But God did not help his darling wife. God allowed the sweet woman to puff up in agony before slipping into a coma and then eventually to drift into death without a word, without hearing his voice, his comfort, his love, without ever a chance to say farewell.

Even now, his sigh of nostalgia was a sob. He had been devastated. Distraught. Oddly enough, of all the faces that surrounded him in those days, trying to comfort him, the only one that he now remembered clearly was Sibell Hamilton. Sibell. She had been there, with Zack he supposed, but he could still recall his agony somehow reflected in her face, though if she'd spoken to him, said something, he couldn't recall it now.

After the death of Emily May he'd lost control for a while. A good while, he corrected himself . . . drinking too much, neglecting his work, hanging about the house nursing a grief that had become precious to him, so much so that he resented the intrusion of family and friends.

Eventually Myles had rebelled. He'd accused his father of being a self-pitying, selfish drunk.

'You're not the only one who misses her!' he shouted. 'She was my mother. Doesn't that mean anything to you? Or do I have to get on the booze too, just to show how sorry I am?'

'Shut your bloody mouth!' William roared at him. 'Get out and leave me alone.'

'I'll bloody get out! I'm going over to Pop Oatley, he can do with an extra hand on Warrawee station.'

'Do what you like!'

Even though those months had been mostly a blur, it was scenes that he'd rather forget that remained in his memory. Myles had gone. He'd watched him ride away, knowing that the journey of a hundred miles was hazardous for any lone man, and especially for a fifteen-year-old, but he'd let him go without a qualm.

Grief, he pondered. A contrary business. Like an illness, except that with some people the wish to be cured could be suppressed by the need to remain in the mourning state, to howl into the night, taking solace from pain. Looking back, it still surprised him that a man who had always considered himself to be a strong, reliable person should come crashing down like that.

Myles hadn't returned and the drinking had increased. His men complained. He ignored them. Some left. He didn't care. Afraid of his rages, the black housegirls kept away, leaving him to ramble about in a mess of his own making. Then one day, old Dubbo, the black retainer who had been with him for years, had the temerity to shake him from a drunken sleep.

'Time to get up, boss. You done enough of this drinkin' stuff. Better you put down your cryin', this no good. Long enough cryin' now.'

William had pulled himself up, sitting shakily on the edge of the sofa, gradually grasping what Dubbo was saying, and then he hit him. A savage punch that sent the old man flying across the room, colliding with a heavy cabinet. He slumped on the floor for a few minutes, then struggled to his feet and shambled out.

It wasn't until the next day, when he saw Dubbo working in the vegetable garden as usual, that the incident came back to him. William hoped he'd dreamt or imagined it. He went down to the old man and turned him around, mortified to see the lined face swollen and bruised.

'Oh Dubbo. I'm so sorry. I'm so sorry. What did I do to you? Come inside and I'll put something on that face.'

'It's all right, boss. Girls they fixem.'

William felt his face. 'Let me see. No bones broken here?'

Dubbo grinned awkwardly. 'Don't tink so. Just as well you drunk, eh? Not hit too straight, else face get broke.'

'Oh God, I'm sorry. You leave this work, go and lie down.'

Dubbo shook his head. 'Tink you done 'nuff lying down for all us, boss. I gotta get these cabbages in 'fore them wallaby get 'em.'

That was the turning point. William cleaned himself up and took charge again. His apologies to his men caused them some embarrassment, since they obviously agreed that it was about time he smartened up, but he soon had the station working smoothly again, and the housegirls singing as they worked.

A month later he too rode up north to Warrawee station.

'If you've come for Myles,' Pop growled, 'he's staying here. He won't go back to you.'

'That's all right, he can stay. But I can't stay on at Millford.'

Pop looked at him in surprise. 'Why not?'

'Too hard. Too many memories. I'm installing a manager and moving to town.'

'Town? Darwin?'

'Yes.'

'What the hell will you do there? You're a cattleman. You can't sit on your bum in town. It's not right.'

'Yes it is. I feel like a change, that's all. I'm thinking about opening a business. That port's getting busy. I'll probably start a mercantile agency, something like that.'

'Sit in an office? You're mad!'

William shrugged. 'We'll see. I can always come back to the bush.'

He'd meant that, because in truth he had only been seeking a temporary change. He hadn't envisaged himself being much shakes in the business world, but even before he opened the office he had clients lined up. Unsure of himself, he'd begun by seeking advice from friends as to the viability of a mercantile agency, turning to bank managers, mine owners, wily Chinese merchants, even Lawrence Mollard, Government Administrator, and they were all anxious to assist. Few knew the Territory as William Oatley, they insisted, and overseas investors would do well to seek him out.

It helped of course that he and Pop Oatley were already wealthy men. William smiled. You couldn't argue with the old adage that money makes money. He underwrote successful mining ventures, co-operated with exporters and importers from Singapore and Hong Kong, and vetted their investments in the Territory. He invested in the Canton Shipping Line and became a trusted adviser to British mining and pastoral interests, and within a couple of years he had become known as the man with the Midas touch.

All very well, he thought, but money wasn't the bottom line for a former cattleman. He had become thoroughly immersed in the world of business and found the people he was dealing with fascinating, people he'd never have met had he stayed out on the station. Most were honourable, decent men; others hard-liners, pushing deals to the last penny, ready to double-cross, given the blink of an eye; yet others, flaunting their overstated credentials, were confidence men, barely a cut above card sharks. That was the challenge. Sorting the wheat from the chaff, not easy in an isolated outpost like Darwin. It was accepted that the town was a haven for southern criminals, north of the law, but from William's experience, he'd take the bad lads, the outlaws any day in preference to the natty characters who came to his door with their sleeked hair and 'honest' eyes and their grand plans to make a mint.

Whoever said you could tell an honest man by his eyes ought to try this place, he mused. Some of these buggers, with their smooth talk and amazing confidence, could and did sell nonexistent cattle stations or pearling leases. You had to keep on your toes ... Fortunately the Territory was his back yard so he could usually trip them, or sense mischief.

Myles interrupted his meanderings just as William was about to give up on him. For the last year Myles had been living in town too, working in his father's office, but it wasn't panning out very well. Office hours didn't seem to mean a thing to him. His father sighed.

'Where have you been?'

Myles tipped his Panama hat back on his head. 'I collected Chen. Took him to the hotel. He's looking forward to dining with you tonight but not at the hotel. He doesn't like our food. So I went round to Charlie Wong's café and he's arranging a banquet. His food's good.'

105

'It might be. But I can't talk business to Chen there. Not in all that racket.'

'I know. But the problem's solved. He'll close the café for the night and put on a real bang-up feast.'

'What'll that cost?'

'Who cares? Chen's big-time and he's got his major-domo with him. We'll have a good feed, you can bet on that. I told Charlie if we didn't get the best I'd drop a word to the Resident about his opium den out the back.'

'That's a stupid thing to do. You don't threaten Charlie Wong. You never threaten Charlie Wong. He won't forget that.'

'Who gives a damn about the Chinks? You worry too much. But now that I'm here, I wanted to have a talk with you. I have a favour to ask of you.'

He dropped into a chair. 'I see you've been having a nip, what about offering me one?'

'Help yourself.' A favour. What now? William wondered. Short of cash again, are we? Though he was paid a wage, more than Leo Lavelle, William's excellent clerk, Myles was always broke. Too many parties and pals. When Myles first asked if he could come to town and learn about the other side of the family business, the Mercantile Agency, his father and his grandfather had agreed it was a sensible move. In time Myles would inherit the cattle stations and the agency so he ought to be introduced to the world of finance, having already proved his worth as a station hand. Lately, though, William had been giving serious thought to sending him back to Pop Oatley.

Myles poured himself a whisky. 'Pop's getting on, you know. Are you planning on staying in town?'

'Yes.'

'So I take it I'll be needed to run Warrawee when he starts to slow down.'

'I was hoping you would. It'll be a load off my mind.'

'Good, that's settled.' He turned his chair about and sat astride it, facing his father. 'So . . . I was wondering if I could take a bit of a detour before settling down at Warrawee.'

'A detour? Where to?'

'Ah . . . London.'

'London, you say? You want to go to England?'

'Well, you and Pop keep saying that the stations are a big responsibility. I accept that, and when I come home I'll toe the line. Believe me. But I'm twenty, I would like to see the world first, just as you and Mother did.'

William was delighted. 'Dear boy! What's this I'm hearing? Wedding bells, is it? Well I'll be blowed!' He leapt up and rounded the desk almost in a bound to shake Myles's hand, risking the whisky. 'Of course you shall go. You and Lucy can go anywhere you wish. Just as we did. I'm so happy—'

'Whoa! Hang on!' Myles pulled away from him, scraping the chair on the floorboards. 'You're going way too fast for me. I haven't proposed to Lucy. Not yet.'

'A foregone conclusion, though,' his father chortled.

'No. Please. Listen to me. Sit down.'

Chastened, William worried that Myles and Lucy had had a tiff, and was preparing to offer some fatherly advice.

'This has nothing to do with Lucy,' Myles said. 'I do intend to marry her, we're both set on that, but I want time on my own. I've always been surrounded by family and friends. I've never been anywhere by myself and I want to do this. Lucy will understand.'

'I hope so. How long do you want to go for?'

'It would have to be a year, it takes so long to get there. Does that sound unreasonable?'

'No. I'm disappointed, thinking of a wedding, but it sounds as if you've made up your mind . . .'

'Then can I go?'

'Of course you can. With my blessing. But don't go sowing too many wild oats. I only wish I could spare the time to go with you. But a year . . .' He looked over to see Myles shaking his head.

'Oh yes,' he laughed. 'You want to be the lone adventurer. Very well, we'll have to start making plans. The better ships sail from Perth, we'll have to check coastal ships to make the connection. I've got some business to do in Perth, so I'll come down with you, to see you off.'

'Thank you, Dad, I'm very grateful to you.' Myles gave a sigh of relief. He'd expected his father to insist he wait until he and Lucy were married but that hadn't happened. He'd taken the request rather well.

And now he really was going! He could hardly contain his excitement. A better ship? Why not? First class, of course. Then London and all those fabulous continental cities; it would be marvellous to be on his own, free to go anywhere he wished. And one thing about the old man, he was never stingy. He would want his son to have the best, stay at the best places, meet the right people. Fantastic! There was Lucy to be considered, though, he hadn't mentioned any of this to her yet, but she would understand. She would have to. Then when he came home they would marry; William could have his wedding.

Merle Cunningham, wife of the manager of the Bank of Western Australia, in Perth, was known to despair of her daughter Harriet. Despair! For years she'd been endeavouring to arrange a suitable marriage for the girl, without success. Her friends, both conspiring and consoling during the ebb and flow of her plans, concluded that Mr Cunningham should be called in to insist that Harriet co-operate. After all, the girl was now twenty, they reminded her, on the very doorstep of spinsterhood, with younger, prettier girls coming on . . .

'It's not that she's plain,' Merle's best friend Anna lamented. 'She has nice long hair and a kind face.'

'But she is too tall and busty.'

'I wouldn't say that,' Anna mused. 'Svelte, maybe.'

Merle was cheered. 'Svelte? Really?'

'Oh yes indeed. Quite svelte. Graceful too, the way she walks and holds her head. Haven't you noticed that?'

'Don't remind me. It's that attitude that puts the boys off. I keep telling her not to be so standoffish. She might be graceful as you say, but she's not gracious. Did you know Clive Benning called on her? Now he is quite a catch but our Miss Harriet wouldn't have a bar of him. Said he was boring.'

Anna giggled. 'He is a bit.'

'That's not the point. He was a genuine suitor. I told her straight she's not so damn interesting herself, with her nose in her books all the time.'

'Oh dear. That's a bit harsh.'

'Harsh nothing! The stupid girl agreed with me. Said it was quite true that she was boring, she'd never been anywhere interesting. She even thinks Perth is boring, so suburban and insular.'

'But Perth is not boring! My dear, it's a fine city!'

'You try telling her that.'

'Then you should explain to her that marriage will change all that. She'll have her own home. And children . . .'

'Children!' Merle squealed. 'Children! She says she doesn't want children. You won't believe this but she claims there are enough children in the world without us producing more. I never heard the like, going on about India and the Far East . . .'

'Oh goodness!' Anna whispered, feigning shock though her eyes were brimming with excitement. What a tale to tell the ladies this afternoon! A delicious piece of gossip.

'Do you think there's something wrong with Harriet?' she murmured.

'Yes, I do. Her father's spoilt her, that's the trouble. Always let her have her own way. Now see what it has come to. I get so angry when I hear those ugly Slater girls crowing about their engagements to the Bignall brothers, when it was Harriet that Albert Bignall liked. Only she wouldn't have him.'

Anna was gathering up her gloves and parasol.

'Now Albert has his own farm and a piggery and my husband says he'll do well. Didn't you say he's built a charming farmhouse for his bride?'

'Yes. We went out to see it. Very pleasant, with a river view. But I must go, dear. Cheer up. It's not the end of the world to have a daughter home for care and comfort in your old age. You might be glad one day.'

'Humph!' Merle rang for the maid to see her friend out.

Mr Cunningham did listen to his wife's concern about their daughter. He smiled patiently at her outrage.

'Don't upset yourself, my dear. You should know Harriet by now. This week she never intends to bear children. It's only a phase. Not so long ago she wanted to go to India as a missionary. Prior to that she was clamouring for womanhood suffrage and nagging me to move to Adelaide so that she would be granted a vote when she's twenty-one.'

'She's not far off that now.'

'True. But there's light on the horizon. You remember my old friend and associate William Oatley?'

'Yes. He lives up north, doesn't he?'

'Not only lives there, my possum, he owns vast grazing properties in the Northern Territory, as well as his very successful mercantile business. In short, he is a very wealthy man. Very few gentlemen in Perth could hold a candle to him in the money stakes.'

'Yes, but . . .'

'Bear with me. I had a telegram from William. He is coming down to Perth and bringing his son. His only son.'

'How old is the son?'

'As good fortune would have it, as far as I can recall, about the same age as our daughter.'

'Heavens! When are they coming?'

The dinner party in the bank residence was a success, it could be said. William and Myles, who were staying at the Palace Hotel, were delighted to be invited by the Cunninghams for a home-cooked meal, and Merle made sure her menu – which, naturally, included roast beef, since these gentleman were cattlemen – would appeal to manly appetites.

Her large round table, without the extensions, was ideal for the chummy family occasion. Just the five of them. She sat Harriet next to Myles, with – hold your breath, she prayed – the prospective father-in-law on the other side of her daughter, keeping in mind that his opinion would carry great weight.

Oscar Cunningham was in good form, bless him, joking happily over sherries before dinner. Harriet too was less reserved on this warm family occasion, knowing that Mr Oatley was a business associate of her father's, and entitled to respect. And Myles was charming . . . so handsome, with strands of straight fair hair falling lightly across his forehead in a dashing sort of way. He had the most delightful smile too, it lit the room. So nice. So very nice. And again, so handsome, Merle herself felt a bit giddy just looking at him. He reminded her of an actor she'd seen in *Twelfth Night* at the Lyceum Theatre. She'd been quite overcome at the time.

It was a jolly little group that trooped into the dining room. Merle was wishing by this that she had invited her widowed friend Anna, just so that she could meet this Adonis. This calmly cheerful young man, fresh from the wilds of the north. Another lady at table would have evened the numbers. But that didn't matter now.

When her husband said grace, she was a little disconcerted to see Mr Oatley fiddling with his napkin and glancing up at her newly installed chandelier – just a small one, in keeping with the small dining room permitted by the architects of the bank manager's residence – but she supposed millionaires were entitled to their eccentricities.

And then it happened. Even before the soup was served, Merle's special oyster soup, a carefully guarded recipe from her mother's collection, Mr Oatley announced the reason for their visit to Perth. Myles was leaving for a protracted stay in London.

'And probably,' he beamed, 'those other great cities over there.'

'You can be sure of that,' Myles added with a grin. 'I'm not going all that way to miss out on a thing.'

'How marvellous,' Harriet was saying, the stupid girl, when she should have done something. Been coquettish, beguiling. Something. To prevent him. To make him want to stay. It was all wrong. Merle was in such a state of despair again that she hardly heard the Oatleys, father and son, praising the soup. Her soup. The oyster soup. Delicious! Well, she knew that. But now Myles was telling Mr Cunningham, on his other side, all about his proposed tour of those faraway places, and there was Harriet – Harriet! – talking to the wrong man. Listening to Mr Oatley expand on his own world tour and the places he hoped his son would not overlook. The son who, with his father's riches at the back of him, could easily ensnare a duchess or a countess or whatever. The son, she'd been pleased to note the minute he walked in the door, who stood a head taller than her tall daughter.

'I mean to say,' she'd rehearsed telling Anna at the time, 'no way Miss Snooty Harriet could be looking down her nose at Myles. Or his father, for that matter. Both men are at least six foot two. That puts her back in her box.'

Dully, dulled, Merle went through the motions of the hostess throughout the meal as the maid served, accepting the compliments then listening to the main topic of the evening, sea voyages, hoping for a miracle. But worse was to come.

After dinner, with abject apologies, Myles took his leave.

'Do forgive me, Mrs Cunningham, but my time is so short now. There are people I have to see. I have to fly. I'm sure my father will more than compensate for my absence. But do believe me, I can't recall when I've so enjoyed a meal and such excellent company.'

Then he was gone. With only a light, a fleeting farewell to Harriet, a warm handshake for Mr Cunningham and a request, jokingly, that they keep an eye on the old man in his absence.

Merle was glad she hadn't invited Anna after all.

'I wish I could go to England on my own like that,' Harriet said. 'It would be simply marvellous.'

Her mother shook her head. 'I don't know where you get your ideas from. Ladies don't travel alone. Anyway, they say it's an icy-cold place, and they have pea-soup fogs that last all day. Quite dreadful.'

'At least it would be interesting. Better than here. This place is so boring.'

'It wouldn't be boring if you got about a bit more.'

'I play tennis.'

'But you never go to their dances.'

'One needs a partner, Mother.'

'You'd have partners if you weren't so fussy. Now, your father and I are going out to Fremantle to see the ship off. It will be nice to farewell Myles. Are you coming or not?'

'I might as well.'

'Don't put yourself out!' her mother snapped, but Harriet ignored her, still smarting from the indignity of that dinner party. Myles must have known his hostess was making an attempt at matchmaking, thanks to Merle's ingratiating utterances, so Harriet wasn't at all keen to line up with his cheer squad. He had sent the appropriate letter of thanks, but apart from that the Cunninghams had not heard from him again. And worse. He and his father were staying at the luxurious Palace Hotel, and his send-off party, to be held there, had been the talk of the town for days. Several young people that she knew had been invited but obviously Harriet's name was not on the guest list. The function was last night. Although she'd never admit it, right up to the last minute Harriet had hoped an invitation would arrive at her door, but it was not to be. So why should she put herself out? Indeed! Except that she did love to see those great ships, to walk the decks and swan through the public saloons as if she were a passenger.

Which was exactly what she did. Once aboard the ship, Harriet avoided the throng at his cabin and wandered about, dreaming of sailing the great Indian Ocean and of the excitement of the first port of Cape Town. She was unashamedly jealous of Myles, and wondered, seriously this time, if she could persuade her father to allow her to go to London. Or even Cape Town. That would be a start.

Don't raise your hopes, she told herself disconsolately; not much chance of success.

While she was standing on deck, gazing towards the open ocean, she was joined by Mr Oatley.

'A fine harbour now, isn't it?'

Harriet smiled. 'I was looking rather further afield.'

'Oh? Where to?'

'Colombo, maybe.'

His eyes twinkled. 'You can see it from here?'

'Of course. It's very green, and there are palm trees along the shore . . .'

'And longboats are pulling away from the ship to take you to shore where natives are waiting to sell you pretty saris and "pure gold bracelets, memsahib", for twenty pence.'

'Really?'

'Yes, but you'll find they're duds.'

'You've been there?'

'A long time ago. I don't travel much these days, except to Singapore.'

'Why Singapore?'

'Business. I have business interests there.'

'You don't sound very impressed with it.'

'With Singapore? Oh no. It's a fascinating place, believe me, but I do find it lonely between meetings and social duties, hanging about the hotel, filling in time.'

'I should have thought that would be the best part. You could explore.'

'Not very amusing, pottering about on one's own.' He shrugged.

A Goanese steward came by, ringing a bell. 'That's the bell for all ashore who's going ashore,' Mr Oatley said. 'We'd better get down to Myles, if we can get through the mob.'

'I shouldn't like to intrude now, Mr Oatley. You wish him well for me.'

'I'll do that, dearie. Please excuse me, I must hurry.'

Harriet thought 'dearie' a funny, old-fashioned expression, but she forgave him. He was a very nice man.

She joined the crowd leaving the ship and stood with her parents for an interminable time as streamers were thrown from ship to shore, sad streamers that broke as friends and family were parted, and fell to the wash, the gap between the pier and the lumbering ship widening slowly, relentlessly. The gaiety was over; it had run its course, leaving tears and stricken faces in its wake. People were walking grimly away from the lonely pier; others stood stolidly, silently, holding out for that last glimpse of the departing ship.

Even Merle Cunningham was moved. 'These things can be such a letdown, can't they? All fun and champagne aboard, but an absolute nothingness when we're left to get back to Perth while all those people on board are enjoying themselves.'

'I hardly think all,' Harriet said. 'I imagine many people on board that ship are quite shattered at having to leave their loved ones, probably for years, or even for good.'

'Oh my, Harriet! How you do dramatise things. I'm sure Myles Oatley will be breasting the bar already.'

Her husband admonished her. 'Kindly don't say that in front of William. He's standing over there on his own and he seems quite distressed.'

'What's he got to be distressed about?'

'Myles is his only child. He's a widower. Of course he'll miss the lad.'

Oscar Cunningham was right. William Oatley was a forlorn figure, obviously deserted by Myles's pals, who had so eagerly toasted him on board but had made for the Fremantle pub as soon as the gangway was up, to continue their revelries. Harriet appreciated her father's kindness in inviting the gentleman to join them on the ferry that would shortly take them upriver to Perth.

Mr Oatley accepted gravely.

The town hall clock was chiming six as they walked up Hay Street, and gaslights were flickering. The gentlemen had talked quietly of their own affairs on the ferry, leaving the women to their private thoughts and observations, but now Mr Oatley turned to Mrs Cunningham.

112

'If you have no other engagements this evening, I wonder if you would all like to dine with me at the Palace? The dining room will open any minute, and they have excellent fare.'

Mr Cunningham intervened. 'That's kind of you, William, but I'm sure you'd prefer to be left alone this evening. It has been a long day for you.'

'Not at all, my dear fellow. I'm feeling rather low, I'm sorry to say. I didn't realise what a wrench it would be to see Myles go off like that. I should very much appreciate your company.'

Harriet was impressed by his honesty. She was often lonely, very often, in fact, but never would she come out and say so. She wouldn't dream of admitting such a thing. Here was food for thought.

'I promise I will not inflict my sadness on you,' Mr Oatley was saying. 'I will cheer up. And besides, they do have a pleasant string quartet playing in the dining room to entertain you if I don't make the grade.'

Harriet laughed. 'I'm sure you would, Mr Oatley.'

Her mother frowned at her boldness. 'I don't think my daughter appreciates your loss—'

'Myles hasn't died, Mother!' Harriet cut in, but Merle ignored her.

'And I don't think we're dressed for the Palace Hotel.'

'Why ever not?' Mr Oatley said gallantly. 'I think both of you ladies look charming. Now, Oscar, what do you say to dinner?'

'We'd be honoured to accept.'

Harriet was relieved. They rarely dined at the Palace; a bank manager's salary did not run to such extravagance. For a while there she thought her mother would resist, and only because they weren't formally dressed, such nonsense. Merle fussed far too much about clothes and so-called fashions, always nagging her to dress up more, despite her daughter's preference for plain, sensible clothes. After all, Harriet mused as they proceeded to the elegant hotel lobby, she was a tall person, and tailored clothes suited her. Right now she was perfectly at ease in her well-cut grey suit, quite pleased, in fact, at the way the skirt had turned out, with a slight flair at the ankle.

As they took their places at a table in the dining room, she could see her mother looking nervously at other ladies in their swish dinner gowns, but Harriet was unconcerned.

They had a jolly evening. A delightful evening. Mr Oatley was a fine host with a wonderful sense of humour; he even had her mother laughing at his tales of the bush and of that northern outpost where he lived.

'They say Darwin is awash with the most dreadful characters,' Merle Cunningham had to say, to her daughter's disquiet, but he didn't seem to mind.

'It's true,' he nodded, without a qualm. 'You can bet your life that any outrageous stories you hear about Darwin are not only true, but probably watered down.'

'And you have no plans to leave there?'

113

Mr Cunningham lent support to his friend. 'Mr Oatley's properties are inland and his business is located in Darwin. It might be the Northern Territory, but it's also his territory.'

'But such a place! For a gentleman!' she insisted.

Harriet looked to Oatley, to the older edition of Myles Oatley, with his fading fair hair and square-jawed features, the skin lined and tanned from the sun. She noticed his keen blue eyes, jovial blue eyes, barely touched by age though he had to be fifty at least.

'You're quite right, my dear,' he smiled. 'Absolutely no place for a gentleman unless he knows what he's about.'

'And what would that entail?' Harriet asked.

He put down his glass. 'Miss Cunningham. That is a very good question. I'm not sure how to answer it. To outsiders it is a very strange town, a frontier town one could say, but an Asian port too. We're closer to Singapore than any other Australian town and we have a large number of Asian residents and Aborigines, as well as our country people. Then we also have odd sorts like buffalo hunters and crocodile hunters – one just has to learn to deal with them all.'

He called for the waitress. 'Now I'm beginning to bore you. One cannot describe that town. You'd have to see it for yourselves.'

'Crocodile hunters?' Merle exclaimed, hands to her throat.

'But you like it?' Harriet persisted.

'You wouldn't consider transferring your business to Perth?' her father asked.

'Oh no. Darwin gets in your blood. It's a great town. I can tell you now, no matter where his travels take him, Myles will be back. There's no place like the Territory to one born there. He'll be back.'

As they were leaving the dining room, he turned to Harriet. 'I hope you enjoyed yourself.'

'Oh yes, thank you.'

'I feel a little guilty dragging a young lady in to dine with me, with no notice. I'd like to make it up to you. Do you think your parents would mind if you dined with me tomorrow night?'

Once outside the hotel the two men lit their pipes, having a few last words together while Merle stamped impatiently.

'Why is it that men dawdle so? It's quite breezy now.' She nudged Harriet. 'Tell your father to come along.'

'He's coming now.' Harriet hoped Mr Oatley hadn't mentioned his invitation to her. She had accepted but didn't want her parents to know because she was already regretting it. He'd taken her by surprise, hadn't given her time to think. Her response had been a nodding politeness. 'Oh! Yes. All right. Very well.' Hardly enthusiastic. Only a reaction to the pleasant evening. Quickly said. To the host. More of a mumble, she agonised.

Oh God! What have I done now? she worried, as she fell into step with her parents. Oh God. I'll write him a note tomorrow and slip into the hotel with it. Apologise. Previous engagement overlooked. Dreadfully sorry. Please forgive. Leave it at the desk. And run! Hoping he wouldn't catch her. Lord! How stupid.

Her father was in a chirpy mood. 'Good fellow, William! Good fellow. Step out, ladies, it's past your bedtime. All together now! One, two . . . one, two . . .!'

Merle shook her arm free. 'Stop that. You've had too much to drink, Oscar Cunningham. You're making a spectacle of yourself!'

'And not easily done in an empty street,' he grinned. 'But what about you, miss?' He leaned heavily on Harriet. 'You're the quiet one. Dining with William again, eh?'

'What's this?' Merle was instantly beside him. 'Who is?'

'Harriet. She made quite an impression. William is coming to call for her tomorrow evening.'

'Oh no,' Harriet moaned. 'It was a mistake. I'll apologise tomorrow.'

'What was a mistake? What are you talking about, Oscar?'

He drew a deep breath and turned to his wife. 'As I was saying before you interrupted . . . interrupted me . . . my friend Oatley has invited Harriet here, our Harriet, to dine with him tonight, no, tomorrow night. On her own. So naturally, as one would expect, Mrs Cunningham, he will call for her. Am I making myself clear?'

As he staggered a little to the left, Harriet hung on to him and Merle took his other arm. 'Let's get him home,' she grated. Then she peered over to Harriet.

'Is this true?'

'Yes. But he was probably in his cups, like Father.'

'But he did ask you?'

'Yes.'

'And you accepted?'

'Sort of. I wasn't expecting it, I didn't get a chance to refuse.'

'Refuse? Are you mad? We'll talk about this at home.'

With Oscar tucked away in bed, Merle put the kettle on.

'We'll have a cup of tea.'

'Not me, Mother, I'm tired. I'm going to bed.'

'You sit down there, girl. What's this about refusing William Oatley?'

'I don't want to go. I should have refused there and then. I'll send him a note in the morning.'

'You'll do no such thing. William Oatley is one of the richest men in the west. You have accepted, and you will go. Now, what can you wear? We ought to get out in the morning and buy you a new dress . . .'

'I don't want a new dress. Just because he's a business associate of Father's, I shouldn't be trotted out as a handy companion for the evening. The man might be lonely, missing his son, but we've done our duty. Let him find someone else to keep him company now. Or go home, for that matter.'

Merle slopped hot water into the teapot, not caring that it was hardly boiling yet.

'The Oatleys have plenty of friends,' she hissed. 'Even you might have noticed that, since you were not invited to Myles's send-off. But it could be that the father has taken a fancy to you. You seem to have got along quite well at dinner.'

'Mother! He's twice my age. And some.'

'So what? He's in the prime of his life. And I'll tell you what, he's a fine stamp of a man.' She turned the teapot, twirling, thinking. Harriet knew the signs.

'Oh no! Don't you dare, Mother!'

'Why not? He's a widower. He won't stay single for much longer, a fine country man like him. Every spinster in town will be after him. I'll speak to your father in the morning. Here's your tea.' She poured two cups and sat down at the kitchen table with her daughter, her eyes alight with excitement.

'Just imagine, Harriet! What a catch! William Oatley. Oh my heavens! Everyone will be green with envy.'

'A catch? The man asked me to dine, not to meet him at the church. And he was probably in his cups at worst, or at best needing someone to share a meal with. Either way, I don't want to go. I wouldn't know what to talk about. He's old. I'd feel a fool. And I told you, I don't want any tea.'

Harriet rushed up to her room and slammed the door, dreading the next encounter with Mr Oatley for there was no way her mother would allow her to renege. She could only hope he would forget.

He did not forget. Harriet did not buy a new dress. In a fit of pique she wore the blue silk that had long been relegated to the back of her wardrobe, left her hair long and plonked on one of her mother's hats.

Merle was furious. 'What are you doing in that old dress? Do you want him to think we're paupers? Go back and put on your taffeta.'

'It's too dressy.'

'Then the voile, the Swiss voile. It's a beautiful dress.'

'This will do.'

Merle appealed to her husband. 'Oscar! Do something! Make her change.'

'Why? I think she looks nice.'

So did Mr Oatley. He said she looked charming.

The evening was not a success. Far from it. They struggled to make conversation from the minute they left the house to stroll up to the hotel. He seemed shy this time, uncertain of himself, so obviously trying to please her. Harriet was embarrassed for him, but unable to extricate herself from the awkward silences that gaped between the courses. Mercifully, the service was swift, and though the time had seemed to drag, they were on their way back through the foyer well before eight.

As he escorted her home, William apologised. 'I'm sorry, Harriet. I shouldn't have put you through such a boring evening.'

'Oh no, Mr Oatley,' she said, remembering again that he had asked her to call him William, another stumbling block for her during the meal. 'I had a lovely time.'

'No. I appreciate your kindness but it's not necessary. It's my fault for rushing you like that, placing you in a difficult position, stuck with a man you hardly know.'

'It's all right, really.' Harriet felt better now that she knew the ordeal was over.

He grimaced. 'I hope this hasn't struck a mortal blow to our friendship.'

William left it at that. For the time being. But he was not to be put off so easily. He liked Harriet Cunningham. Though the dinner had been a mistake – he had seen from the beginning that she was uncomfortable with him on her own, and rightly so for a young girl – all was not lost. In the right circumstances, as he had already seen, she was a bright girl, and forthright, somewhat different from the pack. She was also fine looking, without fussiness, tall and slender. He thought they made an attractive pair together. Until meeting this girl, he hadn't given a thought to remarrying, but she intrigued him. He admitted to a gulf of loneliness at parting from Myles, as he'd told the Cunninghams, but that wasn't the whole truth. After all, he still had Pop back home, and his various business dealings kept him busy, but on the ship that day, looking at Harriet, he had felt cheated. Cheated that he'd lost his own dear wife, who had always been young to him, and reminded that a man shouldn't go on denying himself the pleasures of a wifely companion.

He delivered Harriet, dutifully, to her parents, relieved that her bout of shyness had been overcome, took a glass of whisky with Oscar, and left. Of one thing he was sure: her parents would raise no objections to the courting of their daughter.

Heading for the hotel, William cheered up. His next drink would be a pleasure, a comfort after the stress of the last few hours. A time to think how to redress the situation. For he had made a whopping mistake, charging at the girl with the enthusiasm of a bull at a gate.

By the time he was settled in the wide canvas chair on the veranda outside his hotel room, with a good strong whisky, taking in the cool night air, he was able to apply himself more sensibly to the problem. With first a prayer for understanding from Emily May.

Harriet reminded him a little of Emily May. It was the curve of her lips, the wide smile, the promise of good nature. But also she had an adventurous soul. Emily May had been like that. She adored to travel, and even when they'd settled back on the station, she was always looking about for something different, something new. Women like that were rare, women of his acquaintance anyway. Maybe that was the way to Harriet's heart, to offer her a more interesting life than some young swain could, than years spent in suburban Perth with kids underfoot.

Apparently there was no boyfriend on the horizon, unusual for eligible girls of her age, or they wouldn't have trotted her out for Myles. Poor Harriet. How were any of them to know that Myles was already spoken for, that Lucy Hamilton had pride of place.

On the debit side, he reflected, fifty must seem old to her, very old. Depressing to think that the first lady he had admired since he lost Emily May could reject him without a qualm because of his age, although he didn't feel old. Not for a minute.

But then, he decided, finishing his drink, I have to try, I am quite fond of her already; if she would give me a chance I'm sure we could make a go of it.

The next day William began his plans for the seduction of the Cunninghams, *en famille*, resolving to remain in Perth until he had this matter sorted out, one way or the other. This time he would not invite the daughter alone, but she would be included in his plans. He hoped she would accept. Prayed, because he deplored time-wasting.

But it had to be done. He chartered a boat to carry business friends upriver to a specially arranged luncheon at the leading winery, sparing no expense, choosing a Sunday so that Oscar and his ladies could attend. They sat at his table but he made no extra effort for Harriet. She was simply a friend. He saw to it that they were invited to a luncheon at Government House, and were placed by him, at the Governor's table. Graciously he accepted Merle's invitation to dine with them again, and enjoyed their company. They went to the races together, and with Oscar's party to the bankers' picnic. He met their friends, who were pleased to include the well-known William Oatley in their social circles, and he found himself in a whirl of activity such as he hadn't seen since his travelling days with Emily May. And all the time he was placing Harriet at her ease, listening to her, befriending her because he knew she was a lonely girl, occasionally mentioning that he would have to leave soon, for Darwin. For Singapore. For anywhere. But that ploy had no effect.

Too late William realised that by casting himself in her company so often, he had become completely besotted with her. He adored her. She was so right for him. She was strong in mind and body; the rigours of the tropics would not daunt a woman like this. He no longer thought of her as a young girl, or just a girl; she was a very desirable woman and he looked like failing at the task he had set himself. That hurt. He was astonished at how much it hurt, as if he were already suffering an unbearable loss. In the meantime Harriet was cheerful in his company, treating him as a family friend, giving no indication that a closer relationship might be considered.

Time was running out. He really did have to leave. Business affairs were pressing, he couldn't handle a mercantile agency by mail.

The day he spotted her walking down to the fish market on the riverfront, he dived across the street and went after her. Something had to be said, and this was a chance to catch her on her own.

Home had become intolerable for Harriet. She was even thinking of running away, of taking the train to York to stay with her aunt to escape her mother's nagging and Oscar's silent disapproval.

'You can see he's keen on you,' Merle argued, over and over. 'Why do you ignore him?'

'I don't ignore him. You're the one I have to ignore with your humiliating innuendoes; you embarrass him. Don't you think he knows you're trying to throw me at him because of his money? The man's not stupid.'

Obviously Merle had discussed the matter with her friend Anna, who whispered advice to Harriet:

'My dear. It's better to be an old man's darling than a young man's fancy.'

That enraged Harriet even further and brought Merle's wrath down on her friend.

'Shut up, Anna! How can you say such a thing? William Oatley is not old! He's just the right age for a girl like Harriet.'

'I was only trying to help.'

'Then don't help!' Harriet snapped. 'And I'd be obliged if you would cease gossiping about me. Mr Oatley is a friend of the family, nothing else, and I find the tales you are spreading quite disgusting.'

'How dare you speak to me like that!'

When her father finally intervened, Harriet was shocked. 'If this situation is making you unhappy, dear, then I will ask William about his intentions. It's a perfectly natural thing for a father to ask. That will sort things out.'

'No,' she cried. 'No! How awful how you people are. Why can't you leave him alone? Leave me alone. I heard you talking to Mother the other night, about what a catch he would be. You're as bad as she is! Worse, if possible!' She slammed out of the room.

The situation was awful. To my dying day, Harriet thought melodramatically, I will regret my coldness to that man the night he asked me to dine with him. Because, day after day, William had gone up in her estimation. He was such a pleasant man, such good company, and quite attractive.

Truly Harriet had become fond of William – more than fond – but there was nothing she could do about it if she were to preserve her dignity now. William had tried to find common ground between them, by the sudden invitation to dine with him, Harriet was sure of that, but her cool behaviour had put a stop to it with a finality that he had accepted right away. No more invitations had been forthcoming. And why would they? Meanwhile, she'd been forced to keep her distance from him because she was under scrutiny all the time from family and friends. It was horrible. It was easily seen that Oatley, who was due to leave Perth shortly, had no interest in her now. How humiliating it would be to have William respond to her father's advances with a resounding no. Thanks to Anna, that would be all over town in an hour. Harriet cringed.

On the Friday morning, Harriet was appalled to hear her mother, Anna and another woman in their sitting room discussing her prospects – with William Oatley. She grabbed a basket and rushed out of the house, heading for the fish market, determined that on her way back she'd detour to the railway station and find out when the next train was leaving for York. Because she'd be on it, without a word to any of them.

He caught up with her at the first stall.

'Shopping?'

'Yes. I have to buy some fish.' What else? she wondered, cross with the world.

'We have some marvellous fish up north. Barramundi is the prize, a river fish too. So succulent, it melts in the mouth.'

'That's nice.' Almost in tears, she stared at the fish laid out on the slab, unable to choose, unable to think.

'Are you all right, Harriet?' he asked gently, and she turned on him, tears brimming.

'No, I'm not all right if you'd like to know. I'm not all right at all. Damn the fish! I'm going down to the station.' She turned to storm away but he grabbed her arm.

'Whoa there! Hang on. What's wrong?'

'Every damn thing is wrong.'

'Come with me, perhaps I can help.' He led her away from the crowds to a bench on the jetty. 'Now sit down here and tell me about it.'

Harriet dabbed her eyes with a handkerchief. 'Not much to tell. I hate Perth. I really can't stand it any longer. I'm leaving. Today. I'm going out to York to stay with my aunt.'

'York.' He nodded. 'Hmm. Pretty little town. Over the hills and far away. But I should think it would be rather dull.'

'I don't care. I just want to get away.'

He considered that for a minute, and then took a deep breath.

'If you want to get away, Darwin would be more interesting.'

'Darwin?' she echoed.

'Why not? A sea voyage first and then the port. Something different for you. You'd enjoy it.'

Harriet nodded defiantly. 'Darwin? Yes. Why not? That's where I should go.' Then her shoulders slumped. 'That would take some arranging; they'd never let me.'

'But if you had a chaperone? Surely you could find a lady to accompany you. And I could arrange accommodation for you. At a hotel. Or even at the Residency.'

'What's that? Sounds like a manse.'

William laughed. 'No, dearie. Not at all. It's our equivalent to Government House. The Resident and his wife are friends of mine, they'd be only too pleased to invite you.'

Harriet looked up, delighted. 'Would they really?'

'Most certainly. They enjoy company.'

But then the dream faded. Her mother would jump at the chance to chaperone her. And she'd make things worse, it would only increase the problem. Harriet could hear her crowing now.

She shook her head. 'I'm not getting along with my parents, William.

I need to get away. If I went to Darwin my mother would insist on accompanying me and it just wouldn't work.'

'What a shame. Why aren't you getting along?'

She shrugged. 'It's nothing really. But they run my life, I get stifled.'

'So York is the answer?'

'I suppose so,' she said dully.

'You could still come to Darwin.'

'How?'

'If you married me.' There! It was out, William told himself. Do or die. The race was run, win or lose, he'd had no other option since she was threatening to leave town. Turning the tables on him. He clutched his hat. After this harrowing experience it would be a relief to return to the Territory, where he knew exactly what he was about, instead of dithering about here. He looked at her, wishing she would say something, anything, and saw tears running unchecked down her cheeks.

'Oh Lord, Harriet. I'm sorry if I've upset you.'

She grabbed for her handkerchief again. 'So you should be! You're as bad as they are. Do you think I would marry you just to make use of you? As an excuse to leave home? Is everybody so insincere that the true meaning of marriage is lost in these self-serving attitudes? Let me tell you, William, I am not like that and it's hurtful that you think so little of me.'

The tears had disappeared, dried up in the heat of her anger, and he was shaking his head, trying to calm her. 'No. No. You're wrong. I didn't mean to hurt your feelings. God almighty, Harriet, I'd never do that. I love you. I was only trying to help, but I can't seem to do anything right. I want you to marry me. I do. Oh Lord, what am I saying now? I mean, if you'll have me.' He stopped then, giving up. 'If you'll have me,' he repeated, staring dully at a yacht becalmed on the river, its sails limp, waiting for a breeze.

Harriet watched it too, and eventually she spoke.

'You're a very nice man, William Oatley. If you can forgive my accusations, I should be proud to marry you.'

That night William called on Oscar Cunningham to formally ask for his daughter's hand in marriage, taking him by surprise because Harriet hadn't mentioned the morning meeting, and when she came downstairs looking neat and polished in a new white blouse and navy skirt, Merle gaped.

'Did you know about this?'

'Of course I did, Mother. William and I had a long talk this morning. We hope to be wed as soon as possible because he has to return to Darwin.'

William was happy to leave all the arrangements for the wedding to Merle, who was so excited she could hardly contain herself. He only had one stipulation.

'I am not a religious man. I hope this doesn't disappoint you, Harriet, but I would prefer to be married in a civil ceremony.'

Merle was shocked. 'Oh no. You can't do that. There's the cathedral. It's just wonderful for weddings. You can't deny a bride her day. Oh, definitely not.'

'I'll still be a bride,' Harriet said firmly. 'The registrar's office will do perfectly well.'

William smiled. 'Thank you, my dear. I have no objections to you following your own religion, nor to your attendance at services, but I will not join you. I hope you don't mind.'

'That's fair,' she said. 'I'll abide by it.'

The initial congratulations and discussions over, William was the happiest man in Perth, he was sure, as he rushed back to the hotel to write to Myles with the wonderful news that he was to marry Miss Harriet Cunningham, who, fortunately, Myles had already met.

He could hardly sleep that night, his head spinning with excitement and a lurking fear that Harriet might change her mind. By sunrise he was back at the desk rushing off another letter, this time to Pop Oatley, out on the station, whom he had almost forgotten. Then he remembered that Harriet ought to have an engagement ring, so well before the shops opened, a jeweller saw the tall, sun-tanned fellow pacing up and down outside his shop. He took no notice, guessing him to be another of those back-country men who had no regard for business hours, until he realised it was William Oatley himself, and rushed to open up.

'I wanted to buy a ring for a lady,' William informed him. 'A special ring. What have you got?'

'For your wife, sir?'

'No. For my fiancée,' William grinned. Then he stopped. 'Just a minute. I'm a little out of touch with these niceties. I suppose I should bring the lady in to choose for herself. Get the size and all that.'

'If you wish, Mr Oatley. But I have some beautiful diamonds here. I could deliver some of these superb rings to the lady at her home, so that she might choose . . .'

William was tapping the counter impatiently. 'No. I don't think so. I'll bring her in myself, then you can show her the best you have. She mightn't like diamonds.' He peered about him. 'But I might as well buy something, didn't want to waste your time.' He spotted a rope of pearls on a black velvet stand. 'What have we here?'

'The pearls, sir? They are superb. Flawless and perfectly matched.'

'Let's have a look at them.'

No stranger to pearls, since he'd had business dealings with pearlers working out of Darwin and Broome, William studied them carefully. They were of high quality, he acknowledged, but he could probably buy pearls much more cheaply up north. Then again, it would take time to match up so many into a long rope like this.

'Any lady would be proud to own them,' the jeweller was saying. 'The quality is guaranteed.'

'I can see that, they're excellent. How much?'

'Well, of course, there are so many on the rope, and all chosen with such care . . . Four hundred pounds.' The figure came in a whisper.

'Three fifty.'

'I couldn't part with them for under four hundred, sir . . .'

'Three sixty, then.'

'Well, I suppose I could stretch a point, Mr Oatley. After all, as you say, you'll be back for an engagement ring . . . Yes, I think we could say three sixty.'

William grinned, knowing the extra forty pounds would somehow find its way on to the cost of the ring, but he liked a bit of bargaining. With so many Chinese and Japanese in Darwin, haggling over prices was much more intense than this, and almost a way of life.

When he presented the pearls to Harriet, she was stunned.

'Oh no, William! They're so beautiful. I couldn't accept them. Where would I wear them? They're too much for me, really!'

'You can wear them on our wedding day,' he smiled. 'You have to keep them, I can't take them back.'

'Of course you can't,' Merle cried. She was ecstatic. All thoughts of further argument about the registrar's office were lost in the glow of the lustrous pearls.

The lady didn't choose a large diamond after all. She preferred a facet-cut sapphire set between two small but worthy diamonds. The jeweller was delighted, since he had several tiny sapphires of the same indigo blue, not the best in the range that colour, but a sale was a sale. Quickly he produced the matching gems, pointing out that he could set three of them deep in a lovely gold band, the very best of course. Then they would have the set. Matching wedding and engagement rings.

'Perfect!' he announced, and the shy couple agreed with him.

Chapter Nine

Their honeymoon in Singapore was a great joy for both of them. William had arranged for them to stay in a beautiful rambling house with an ocean view and magnificent tropical gardens, the most romantic setting Harriet could ever have imagined. She was dazzled by the luxury of the house, the colour of the exotic blooms that gleamed in the deep green of the grounds and the delicacy of the same flowers when set in shallow dishes by unobtrusive servants. Everything was perfect, not least her husband's tenderness.

The marriage was not consummated on the ship because, as William explained to her, their sex life was far too important to have a beginning bundling together in hard narrow bunks; they needed more pleasant surrounds. And how right he was, Harriet rejoiced, as she strolled along a garden path to her favourite spot by a softly flowing waterfall. The bedroom was large and airy and the carved mahogany bed a dream, with its misty white curtains. Mosquito nets they might be, but to her they accorded sweet privacy for a girl suddenly very shy when faced with what some older women had referred to as 'the inevitable'. But William had been so patient, so loving, there had been no 'inevitable' at all. Practised in the art, he had had her wanting him. Aroused, she reflected, a word she'd once found repulsive, but now delighted in. She spun about, twirling her parasol, extremely pleased with herself, knowing she had made the right choice of husband. She loved William, and she adored having him make love to her, deliciously aware now of her own sexuality and the effect it had on him. For William, her lover, was madly in love with his beautiful bride, as he called her, and overjoyed that he could make her happy. She had teased him that they spent so much time in bed, even during the day, as to be not quite proper, and he'd laughed.

'As it should be, my darling, as it should be.'

She truly was his darling, Harriet smiled, idly fluttering her fingers to allow the sun to catch the glint of her wedding band and superb engagement ring.

She'd had no inkling of the extent of this man's generosity. Here in Singapore he was spoiling her outrageously, her every wish his command as he was wont to say, and Harriet was overwhelmed.

They explored the town together, investigating the bazaars, where they bought trinkets and souvenirs and bolts of cloth, beautiful silks and cottons and crêpe de Chine for Harriet; and visiting William's tailor for his suits and shirts, in a strange little shop deep in an alleyway. They went further afield in a light carriage, servants following behind in rickshaws with the necessities for elegant picnics, servants who laughed and giggled as they set up the table and presented the food and wine, making the occasions jolly events, and Harriet was charmed.

There were times when he had to leave her at home, to attend business meetings, but Harriet didn't mind. The house was so lovely she was content to roam about or find a comfortable corner in which to read. To make up for his absence, William always returned with a gift: ivory carvings, magnificent china figurines, even a complete dinner service of the most marvellous china Harriet had ever seen. She kept telling him that this wasn't necessary, but his pleasure was in the giving.

'I think about you every minute, my darling,' he told her. 'I have to tell you that I was very much in love with Emily May, and when she died my life seemed bleak. I managed to adjust eventually but it was a grievous time for me. It never occurred to me that I might marry again, until I met you. Until I fell in love with you. Even on our wedding day I was a bundle of nerves, wondering why I was so presumptuous in thinking a man of my age could please a lovely young girl like you. I was terrified waiting at the registrar's office, convincing myself that any minute I'd receive a message that you'd changed your mind.'

'William, I love you. Why would I change my mind?'

'Because you never actually said so. In those weeks when I was pouring my heart out to you, you never said the words . . .'

'Oh my dear. I was too shy. I took it for granted you knew.'

'But you do love me, Harriet? You do?'

'I adore you, my love. I truly do.'

'Then you've made me the happiest man in the world. Whatever foolish things I find for you in these little shops, Harriet, they don't count. They could never express the joy you have brought into my life. You're the most wonderful companion I could ever have hoped to find.'

'Not just a companion,' she twinkled, and he grinned.

'Oh no. I've found I'm not so old after all.'

His Chinese business friends invited them to banquets at the most luxurious homes Harriet had ever seen in her life. They made their honeymoon house seem like a bungalow. The food, more than ten courses, was strange but Harriet gallantly took a little of every offering because she was being careful not to offend.

She didn't dare tell her husband that she found the banquets difficult. He was so much at home with the Chinamen and their dainty wives, who simpered behind tiny fans at remarks that the men found were hilarious, but that were lost on Mrs Oatley. Right from the start Harriet had felt gauche, standing head and shoulders over these tiny women, trying to make conversation. Some of them, she discovered to her horror, didn't even speak English, their responses only play-acting, which they seemed to consider sufficient. But they were beautiful women, like dolls, like

126

expensive dolls, exquisite in their gorgeous *cheong sams*, with flawless skin, almond eyes and cherub mouths.

English style, they met for sherries first in the drawing room, or whatever they called them in this country, Harriet told herself caustically when she saw herself reflected in mirrors, standing there in her new evening dress, a dark blue taffeta, off the shoulder, which she had thought attractive and alluring until that night. She felt like a big ox among gentle does.

The next time she tried to be less obtrusive, in the palest pink crêpe de chine, a charming dress that William had ordered to be made for her, right here in Singapore, but it didn't help. The problem was size.

In desperation, when they were dressing for the next function, Harriet poured out her woes to William.

'Don't worry about it,' he said. 'Those girls aren't wives. They're concubines. Wives at this level don't associate with foreigners. We're beneath them, my love.'

Harriet was shocked. 'Concubines? What are they?'

William shrugged. 'I don't know. What does it matter? Extra wives, I think. Something like that. They're there to pretty up the show.'

'Oh my God!'

'Don't let it bother you. They're there because you are. Female company to support your presence. Balance, my love.'

'Their wives won't receive us?'

'Definitely not.'

'Then you should be insulted. How dare they?'

'Don't worry about it. They have their rules, same as we do. Now hurry along. I'm looking forward to the banquet. Feeling rather peckish.'

'I'd settle for a chop and a sausage.'

'What?'

'And mashed potatoes. I'm becoming rather tired of oriental food.'

'Oh Lord, don't say that. Our cook at home is Chinese.'

Disconcerted, Harriet turned to stare at him. 'You're joking!'

'No. Billy Chinn's an excellent cook.'

'Billy? A man?'

'Yes.' William ran a comb through his thick white hair and ducked to view the result in the mirror over the dresser, too low for a man of his height.

'William. I won't be able to cope with a male cook.' Let alone a Chinese, she thought. 'We've always had women.'

He gave her a peck on the cheek. 'Don't worry about it. Billy's the best cook in Darwin.'

She was to learn that 'don't worry about it' was William's easy-going response to matters that bothered her and he regarded as unimportant. It was difficult to make him pay attention without making a fuss.

On the way to the banquet William pointed out a large warehouse. 'That's where I bought our furniture. Good for you to know where it is if you need anything else. Quite the best stuff in Singapore.'

'I thought you said the house was empty.'

'I did. Fortunately we finished building it before we left for Perth. You can't imagine how thrilled I am to be able to take you to a brand-new house. But I chose the furnishings last time I was out here and notified the manager from Perth that my order could be forwarded. It should be in the house by this.'

Harriet laughed. 'Oh William, you are so funny. Having furniture delivered when you're not even home. It will probably all be stacked in one room.'

'No. It'll be just fine. Tom will arrange it for us.'

'Who's Tom? Your clerk?'

'No, that's Leo. Leo Lavelle. Tom's our houseboy. Tom Ling.'

Harriet hardly dared ask. 'A houseboy? What does he do?'

William blinked. 'Tom? I don't know. Let me see. He runs the house. Cleans up. Serves the meals. All that sort of stuff. He and Billy have been looking after me ever since I moved to Darwin. I was living in a bungalow near my office prior to this.'

'You mean he's the housekeeper?'

'Sort of. Yes. Good little fellow, Tom.'

Harriet was silent. Realising she now had a male cook and a male housekeeper, both Chinese, made her feel very uncomfortable. How could she live in a house with strange men wandering about? It wouldn't do at all. What would people say?

Even William found this last banquet tedious. As usual, the English-speaking Chinese gentlemen carried the conversation, translating for the benefit of other guests, and William assisted, since, to Harriet's surprise, he was able to make himself understood in their language, so they all got by. But this time there were speeches. Long-drawn-out speeches where Harriet guessed that two of the Chinese gentlemen were showing off their prowess in the English language, rambling on and repeating themselves.

When at last they arrived back at their residence, William ordered the driver to stop at the gate and climbed down.

'I need to stretch my legs. Do you feel like a walk up to the house, my darling?'

'Yes, I'd love to.'

They dismissed the driver and strolled up the drive hand in hand. It was a beautiful starry night, the air rich with the perfume of jasmine, palm trees silhouetted against the sky and a gentle breeze rattling through tall clumps of bamboo as if to remind them of the lovely surrounds. When the house came into view, Harriet sighed. It would be a shame to leave this elegant white stone building with its wide pillared veranda. All the lights were on, welcoming them home, and fine curtains drifted languidly in the open French doors all along the front.

'Doesn't it look romantic?' she said. 'I wish I could take it with us. But then we've got our own home to go to. I'm so happy, William. Thank you for a wonderful honeymoon.'

★ ★ ★

Darwin was not Singapore. Far from it.

The ship sailed down the vivid green coastline of Sumatra and Java, then struck east across the Timor Sea towards the mainland of Australia.

Darwin harbour was a huge bay, a sea in itself, and Harriet was surprised by the lack of colour that she'd become accustomed to in the more northern tropic lands. The great empty harbour was bordered by a low line of grey-green foliage that seemed to crouch dismally by the shores. Gums, she realised, plain old gum trees, and probably casuarinas. No waving palms here.

She was even more surprised when informed that they would be going ashore in very choppy seas in a longboat. Had she been wearing less formal attire she wouldn't have minded, but because she'd wanted to make an impression on William's family and friends, she was wearing a tailored suit specially made for this important occasion. She was tightly corseted into a jacket with a nipped-in waist. Her long skirt was tight and slim at the front, with an overskirt of neat pleats at the back. Not very manoeuvrable, she thought anxiously. And she would have been better off wearing a bonnet in this wind, instead of the hat she had chosen, burnt straw with grey rosettes to match her outfit. Her hair was pinned up and the hat was fitted in place by more hairpins. She sighed as she waited her turn on the windy deck. How was she to have known that she wouldn't be able to step elegantly to the wharf as in other ports? Now it was too late to change.

'Come along, darling, your turn,' William said happily, as she watched a young girl in a light muslin dress and bare feet leap nimbly from the short steel ladder into the rocking boat. 'Dorothy has made it.' Dorothy, though, was returning home, and she'd known what to expect.

Harriet had difficulty even climbing on to the ladder until finally sailors grabbed her and handed her on stiffly, like a corpse, she thought. But at last she was in the boat, her hat knocked sideways, her legs stuck out in front of her to ease the strain on the stitching. Then, as the boat left the shelter of the ship, a blast of hot wind caught her unawares and her hat flew off.

'Whoops!' William yelled, laughing as he strove to catch it, but it shot past his hand, whirled merrily about and came to rest prettily on the waves, well out of reach.

Unperturbed, William grinned. 'Poor old hat. We'll have to get you another one.'

Everyone else seemed to find the incident amusing so Harriet forced a smile as she tried unsuccessfully to contain long strands of hair that had escaped their pins.

They seemed to be making for a pier and Harriet stared at it in horror. It was high above the water, and she dreaded having to scale a ladder right up to the top.

'Do we have to get up there?' she asked William.

'Goodness, no. It has to be that height because we have huge tides.

129

But it's low tide now so we'll just pull up on to the beach.'

Bypassing the pier, the sailors made for the beach, jumping out to drag the boat as far as they could into the shallows. Everyone began clambering out, happy to be on firm ground again.

But to Harriet it wasn't firm ground; waves still rippled around them. William took her arm and helped her up the beach, and by the time she reached dry sand her shoes and stockings were squelching and the hem of her skirt was limp and soggy. Her husband's boots were soaked too, but that didn't bother him; he was already calling gaily to a group of people hurrying down stone steps set in the cliff.

The first man to approach was elderly, but tall and straight as a ramrod, and Harriet guessed this was her father-in-law.

William hugged him. 'Pop! How marvellous to see you. I didn't think you'd be here. Is everything all right at the station?'

'Sure it is. You didn't think I'd miss out on welcoming your bride.' He turned. 'So this is Harriet. How are you, my dear?'

She blushed. 'I'm a bit of a tangle right now, Mr Oatley. I must look a sight.'

'You look pretty good to me. I don't know how he managed to catch a fine lassie like you. Now you call me Pop, and if he doesn't look after you, just you give me a yell, do you hear?'

Other people bustled about them, and although they were introduced, Harriet lost their names immediately in all the excitement and the gradual movement towards the stone steps, which seemed to be the only exit from the beach. It was a steep climb but William took them slowly for the benefit of his father, who found it quite an effort. Harriet was touched to see the fondness that was obvious between father and son, the same fondness she'd noticed between William and Myles. It gave her a good feeling to be part of such a warm and loving family.

No one, it seemed, was the slightest bit bothered by her untidy appearance, nor had anyone noticed, as far as she could see, her elegant tailored suit. The women were all in skirts and blouses, and boots rather than shoes, and the men, including Pop, weren't wearing jackets. It was hot, for June, blazing hot, especially as she climbed those stone steps, and it was a dry heat like Perth in December, hardly tropical weather at all.

As they walked around a long shed, it was William's turn to groan. 'Oh no!'

There was a crowd waiting for them – half the town, he told Harriet later – and with whistles and a great cheer it parted, revealing a fine black gig garlanded in white ribbons and rosettes for the newly-weds. This meant more introductions, laughter, teasing, short speeches, a huge bouquet of flowers for the bride and a shiny white satin top hat for the groom. Gravely William removed his Panama and donned the hat, and he looked so funny in it that Harriet gave up trying to play the part of the shy bride in all this confusion and doubled up laughing.

Pop ended the proceedings by climbing into the driver's seat and calling for them to hop in.

Once aboard, waving to their well-wishers, William called to him: 'Home, James.'

'Not yet,' Pop said. 'We have to show Harriet the town.'

It was only a bush town, with wide, unshaded streets, dressed up here and there with the odd brick government building and narrow church, flat-looking shops, several hotels – one two-storied, quite large, embracing a deserted corner – and some plain houses, contrasting sharply with a lot of shanty housing that Harriet thought was an eyesore, more derelict than habitable.

Pop insisted on driving up one of the cross-over streets which William had told her was the Chinese sector, and here Harriet expected to see more of those exciting crowded bazaars, but it was only more shanties, even worse than the others, set around a long shop that had shutters instead of the usual windows. This was the dreariest town Harriet had ever seen, but as William told her, they were keeping the best to last.

They drove back towards the port, only a few streets, and showed her the Residency, on the Esplanade, where the Government Administrator lived. Immediately Harriet began to feel more cheerful. This was a very unusual house, in white stone, with several high gables, surrounded by a lush tropical garden. Here at last were the waving palms she'd come to expect.

They followed the Esplanade along the front. On the left, gardens with massive old trees lined the sandy road but the few buildings she saw were uninteresting places of white timber.

Then she realised they'd stopped. In the middle of a large cleared block was another white-painted timber house, standing beside a vacant plot overgrown with weeds.

'Here we are at last,' William told her. 'We've had enough sightseeing. Not a step further, Pop. Come on in and have a drink.'

'No,' he said firmly. 'This is where you try to carry your wife over the threshold.' He turned and grinned at Harriet as she stepped down. 'I wouldn't risk it if I were you, love. See you tomorrow.'

With that he was off, ribbons flying in the wind. Only then did they see the large sign: 'JUST MARRIED'.

'They're a bit late,' William grinned. He unhitched a wire gate and ushered her forward. 'I didn't have time to plant a garden, but it's just as well. You can have a say in it now, my darling. There's plenty of room at the back too.'

Harriet nodded. 'Oh yes. I see.'

But there was no chance for him to attempt to carry her over the threshold, for two Chinamen came rushing out, pigtails flying, grinning, talking wildly, bowing, grasping their hands, thrilled, absolutely thrilled to have their master and his lady home, and together they bundled Mr and Mrs Oatley into the house.

★ ★ ★

131

Looking back, Harriet could only blame her ignorance for the disappointment that had almost overwhelmed her at the time, but she still found Darwin deadly dull.

The house was large and roomy, with high ceilings for coolness. A wide veranda enveloped the front and both sides, and some of the rooms could be accessed from it as well as from the passageways inside. But the verandas were shielded from the sun by fixed bamboo shutters, so they had a closed-in feeling about them. Where Harriet came from, verandas and porches were for sitting out, to watch the world go by, but here they needed protection from the fierce sun and torrential rains, and one had to open the bamboo louvres for light.

The cedar floors were polished like mirrors and William's furniture was arranged carefully, just as he had said it would be, but it was all oriental in style, and on being confronted with it, Harriet was embarrassed, wondering what people would say. Her mother would have been appalled at this assortment of carved beds and dressers, delicate lacquered cabinets, carved armchairs and sofas plumped with plush cushions. The long dining room featured an astonishing mahogany table with twelve high-backed chairs that were inlaid with ivory.

Harriet shook her head now, remembering that day. The lacquered screens and side tables she'd stared at, the beaded doorways, the madness of a half-baked attempt to emulate those lovely Singapore houses ... She remembered looking about the house, her home, and saying to him, sarcastically:

'All we need now are the punkahs.'

William hadn't taken the comment amiss. He was remarkably naïve about things like that. Or maybe so open, so good-natured, it wouldn't occur to him that anyone was being offensive.

In time Harriet had become secure enough to talk to him about the house.

'I'm not complaining – we're very comfortable here – but it intrigues me. You're a wealthy man, so why would you choose one of the best blocks in town, away from the shops and shanties, and build a plain timber house? You could have built a mansion here, William.'

'That's true. I could have built a mansion that would have made the Residence look pale. But would it have fitted in here?'

'I don't know. It might be fun.'

'Bloody lonely fun. Who are our friends? Cattlemen, bushies and their wives, government clerks, miners, police, shopkeepers, Chinese. It's hard for you to adjust to the social scale that operates here, hard enough for you to find appropriate friends among the women. I'm aware of that, and I appreciate your patience, but my darling, believe me, it would be a lot harder for you if you were sitting up here, queen of the castle. All wrong for Darwin, and at my best guess, it always will be. People here are more interested in survival and in the bonus of friends than in posh.'

She understood then, but wondered about the homesteads out on the Oatley cattle stations.

132

'Are they luxurious?'

'God, no. In the bush you look for comfort. There's no one to impress.'

'I see,' she said, feeling like the blind man who said the same thing but didn't see at all.

'Besides,' he laughed, 'what about Mollard, the Resident? If I built a house better than his fancy Residency, he'd never forgive me. He can be quite pompous at times.'

And that had Harriet laughing too. She agreed. Mrs Mollard was worse. On one occasion, with William well out of earshot, the Resident's wife had said to her haughtily, 'I believe your papa is in trade.'

Harriet knew that in high-ranking social circles being in trade was unacceptable, so to her later mortification she'd tried to rise above the slur.

'No, Mrs Mollard, my father is a bank manager.'

The woman had fluttered a lacy handkerchief at her, murmured, 'Oh, dear God!' and wafted away.

Harriet never got round to telling William about that episode because too many other things were happening. She simply could not cope with two Chinamen running her house. Billy objected to her entering his kitchen and rarely produced the menus she had requested. He was a good cook, an excellent cook, and William had quite an appetite. He'd grown up with English and Chinese cooks on the cattle stations and had no preference, as long as the meals were tasty, and aplenty. But for Harriet, when she asked for roast beef and Yorkshire pudding, that was what she expected to see on her table. Not fish and rice with a promise that roast beef would be next week. The daily battles made Billy sullen and silent and drove Harriet to standing over him, slamming down beef or pork cuts, demanding they be cooked intact, not shredded into his version of meat dishes.

Then there was Tom Ling, the non-stop, shrill, talking, chattering machine. He never shut up. He drove her crazy. She demanded he stay out of her bedroom but he managed to dart in when her back was turned, grabbing clothes 'for the wash', even fresh clothes she'd laid out to wear. In her eyes he was a fanatical housemaid. Floors were polished to danger level; he even waxed the washbasin and bath on one occasion. If she moved furniture, lamps or even decorative articles on display, the next day they would all be returned to their original places. He was always underfoot, wiping, dusting, fussing, padding about after her like a keeper. And worst of all he would insist on lighting special candles to combat mosquitoes, candles that gave off a suffocating aroma of incense and some sickly perfume, even though Harriet argued she'd prefer the insects.

None of William's friends, who were all very kind to her, saw anything odd about the furnishings in the Oatley household, and at first Harriet thought they must all furnish their homes in this style – for the climate, perhaps – but this was not so. Houses they visited had very ordinary furniture. It took a while for her to realise that these matters were not a priority, not even of much interest.

But the ladies were impressed that Harriet had such an efficient houseboy – though they expressed no surprise at his gender – since it was so difficult to keep house in this climate, what with mould and armies of insect invaders. She gritted her teeth and smiled, accepting their compliments, but she knew the time was coming when she would have to speak to William about their servants, because the daily arguments, the lack of privacy, and the desire to be fully in charge of her own household were always on her mind, at a time when she should be looking outward, taking more interest in the town itself and getting to know people.

The weather was deteriorating, becoming hotter, temperatures reaching the century day after day. The air was oppressive, almost ominous, Harriet felt, and she was on edge though she could see no reason for it. This was November and she was looking forward to her first Christmas in Darwin, when, as she'd been told, the town came alive with the annual pilgrimage of outback and station people coming to spend a few months by the sea. A great time for socialising and parties galore. And yet she was depressed and unhappy. Not with William, who was just as kind and cheerful as ever, but with things in general.

Harriet was to come to know well that feeling of being in the doldrums, a very real malaise, associated somehow with the wait for the rains to come and break the hold of a dry heat that was becoming unbearable; but of course she hadn't known then, and that was when she began to make mistakes.

She'd had a particularly bad day with Billy and Tom Ling. She'd tripped over a hoe in the garden and banged her knee; in a garden that was an obvious failure, plants burned by the sun or ripped out by destructive cockatoos. And she'd forgotten, again, to collect a parcel at the post office for William, a parcel of his favourite cigars.

When he asked for them she burst into tears.

He was upset. 'My dear. Don't worry about them. It's not the end of the world.'

But the tears had taken hold. She wept over the garden, over her inadequacy, and William smiled. 'We'll get a gardener in.'

'I wanted to do it myself,' she sobbed.

'So you shall. But it's hard to get it started here with the sandy soil and all. You design it, he can do the digging, prepare the soil – that's men's work anyway – and when he's got the plants established, you can take over. It's a big job, this is a large block. With a gardener by your side, you'll enjoy making a really good fist of it.'

Harriet sighed gratefully. 'You're right. I should do that. And William, I'm so sorry about the cigars.'

'Don't be silly. You should have sent Tom for them.'

But that was entirely the wrong thing for William to have said.

'Tom? Send Tom?' she cried. 'And put up with his jabbering arguments about the why and where? It's easier to do it myself. He drives me mad.' She was crying, raising her voice, but she didn't care.

'Have you seen the library, William? Your books, my books, all placed on the shelves the way he wants them. Set up in groups of colour, not authors, not subjects. Colour . . .'

She saw William grin and that enraged her. 'This is not my house, this is their house. They do what you ask, but not what I ask. I have no control over my own kitchen. I can't sit down to read, if I can find my books, because that damned Tom is always banging about, opening and closing shutters, doing everything he can to annoy me. I never get any peace, I have to battle with them all day.' She was shouting. 'When I order fish I get meat. When I order vegetables I get rice. I have no say in this house. It's just not good enough, William. It's just not!'

He took her in his arms and kissed her. 'Now, now. Don't worry about it. Leave it to me. You sit down here on the veranda and we'll have a nice glass of wine before dinner. And I'll serve,' he added.

At dinner, he looked mildly at Tom. 'I thought the missus ordered pork tonight?'

Tom bowed. 'So sorry, boss. Billy say no pork. Get good fresh fish. And extra-special tasty rice for you, plenty good green veggie and sweet sauce you like.'

'I see,' William nodded, while Harriet sat silently, worrying she might have gone too far and offended her husband.

He had nothing more to say on the matter over dinner, instead turning to other subjects. A consortium of British investors were interested in a copper-mining venture in the Territory; there was some talk of a meatworks being built in Darwin, which would be a boon for cattlemen; and best of all, he'd had a letter from Myles, who was enjoying London and of course sent his best regards to Harriet.

'I'll read it to you later,' he said happily, as if nothing untoward had happened in his household. As if he hadn't heard a word his wife had said about the servants.

The next morning he sacked them both.

Within a week Harriet had hired a cook and a housemaid. Both women had responded immediately to the advertisement she'd placed in the post office window, so for fear no one else would reply, she engaged them. Before she remembered she should have asked for references. Too late she discovered the older woman had been a shearer's cook, not a good sign, and the stews and slops that came out of the kitchen proved the point. The maid was useless, a sixteen-year-old, neat in appearance but with no idea of what she was supposed to do, which Harriet found strange until she heard the girl lived with her family in a tiny shanty house.

From then on maids and cooks came and went, some after just a week's pay, and Harriet had to roll up her sleeves and work, not only in the house but as her own cook, to try to maintain a standard. She complained to William about the unsuitability of these women and he commiserated, explaining that it took time, up here, to find women with the background to understand what was required of them.

'It has been suggested,' she told him, 'that I should hire black girls and train them.'

'I wouldn't recommend it, Harriet. Not town blacks. Station blacks are another matter; they've grown up on the job and station women understand them.'

He was patient about the meals set before him, which were sometimes excellent, but most times odd and unappetising.

'A lucky dip,' he used to call dinner. 'I never know what to expect, so I'm beginning to regard our meals as little adventures.'

She was mortified. 'Oh William, I'm so sorry. I'll try to do better.'

'Not to worry. You'll get the hang of the servant scene in time. But I do wish you'd remember that I worked on our station. We'd be out mustering for months at a time, living on salt meat and damper and billy tea. A meal's a meal, my dear.'

'But you're accustomed to better now, and I'm letting you down.'

'I was always accustomed to better, but when you're hungry you eat. The food you provide is fresh, even though it isn't cooked to your satisfaction, and it won't poison me. So don't fuss.'

She realised then that it would have been easier to just sit back and let Billy Chinn serve whatever he liked, because with Billy in charge, the kitchen was clean and the meals were excellent. What did it matter if the roast dinners or cottage pies turned up on nights when she'd requested fish? But it was too late to be thinking about that now.

Then the rain set in. It had rained in Singapore, every day in fact, about noon if she remembered correctly, but they'd been cosseted from the weather in their cosy little honeymoon world. This was rain as she'd never seen it before. It poured, teemed incessantly, blanketing the town, day in and day out. The house seemed perpetually damp. She never could get clothes dried, and that mould that Tom Ling had always been whining about permeated closets and clothes, accompanied by huge cockroaches that scampered across the floors and bred in dark corners. Tarantulas took up residence in the house, huge dark spiders that seemed to follow her from room to room, glaring balefully from high walls, and geckoes marched across the ceilings, their huge eyes dewily innocent but their presence unnerving. They were still lizards, miniature versions of the big thick reptiles that plodded about the garden. Such as it was. Work had ceased out there, weed and high grass prospering in swampy undergrowth.

By this, William's station friends were in town – the Hamiltons, the Westons, the Grogans, and dozens more – and Pop Oatley came in to stay with them. Harriet was relieved that William had closed down his office for some weeks, because she needed him by her side to cope with the endless run of visitors. People were always dropping in unannounced, at all hours, sometimes whole families at a time, with children and grandchildren; such was the informality of Darwin life.

136

William was delighted to receive them and inevitably asked them to stay for meals, throwing Harriet into a state of utter confusion.

Despite incompetent cooks and maids, who fortunately accepted the sudden influx of guests as normal, she struggled on, until some of the station women, recognising her predicament, came to her rescue, Sibell Hamilton and Aggie Weston 'leading the chase', as they called their efforts on Harriet's behalf.

Suddenly her larder was reorganised, the latest cook given a jolt by Aggie, who set to cleaning up the kitchen while Sibell's daughter, Lucy, bullied the maid into straightening up the house.

Harriet found Sibell Hamilton a vague sort of woman, but very kind. She always had a batch of scones, or pies, or cakes in her basket, waving aside Harriet's reluctance to accept them.

'My dear. We have to feed the hordes when they turn up. You can't be expected to work out the catering yet.'

Harriet loved them. They were the nicest women, easy to talk to, and often very amusing. They teased Pop Oatley, pretending to flirt with him and suggesting ladies who had their eyes on the wealthy old widower, and they adored William. They congratulated him on being smart enough to find such a lovely bride, and not once did Harriet hear them refer to her as a 'young wife', as Mrs Mollard did. At every opportunity.

Of course the hospitality was reciprocal. They visited people in the same easy-going manner, they dined with parties of twenty or more at the hotel and the Chinese restaurant, and had a jolly time. So much so that Harriet stopped noticing the rain. She knew she would miss all of these cheery people when it came time for them to leave Darwin.

Sibell Hamilton sympathised with Harriet. She could feel her panic.

'Not surprising,' she reflected, 'since I seem to be in a constant state of pandemonium myself. I feel so panicky inside.'

Because of that she found socialising an extra burden . . . having to smile, to give the impression all was well, when she'd much rather stay home. Keep out of sight. Sibell tried not to think too much about the reasons for her depression. She was certain that too much introspection would only add to her confusion. Then again, there was always the hope that her miseries were only a phase. That one day they would disappear of their own volition. Maybe . . .

She sighed. She sighed far too much and had tried to check the habit, but that one had slipped out. One thing was sure. She couldn't cope with the outback life any more. There was a possibility that all the heartbreak associated with living out there, taken for granted by the hardy inhabitants, could have triggered her depressions in the first place, and not just a single event, so she had to get away.

Her spirits lifted at the thought of living in Perth, far enough south to enjoy a temperate climate at the very least. What a pleasure it would be to live in a city again after all these years in the bush!

Spurred on by a rare lightness of mood and sympathy for Harriet,

Sibell took a deep breath and went in search of William.

She chastised him for throwing his wife headlong into such a busy time without proper support.

'Good lord, William, the poor girl must feel as if she's running a hotel. She's not accustomed to the concept of daily open house. I mean, who would be, if they didn't know this town? She doesn't know what liquor to buy, let alone food, and those women she has working for her, they couldn't run a blacks' camp.'

'I know,' he said. 'It has been difficult for Harriet for quite a while. But I never complain or criticise, Sibell. I wouldn't upset her for the world. What else can I do?'

'Did she have problems even before we arrived?'

'Oh yes. Servants have come and gone like flies. You know how hard it is to find good staff here.'

'Why aren't you using the Chinese? Where are Billy Chinn and Tom Ling? They've been with you for years.'

'They didn't work out either. They overwhelmed Harriet. They got too pushy and she was nervous about having men working for her.'

'I see.' Sibell gave this some thought. She tapped her fingers on the table. 'I think you ought to get them back.'

'I can't do that. It's Harriet's home. I can't override her wishes.'

'Let me talk to her.'

'Very well. But you know the Chinese. If she asks for them back, she'll lose face, and she'll get no sense out of them at all.'

'Then it's up to you.'

His wife appeared in the doorway carrying a tray of cups and saucers. 'I'm serving tea on the veranda. Would you rather have yours in here?'

'No, we'll come out and join the others,' William said, noticing the creases of a frown that had almost become permanent on Harriet's face through her determination to please. He felt guilty. Guilty that this girl had lost the spontaneous smile that had so attracted him, in only six months as mistress of his household.

He grinned at Sibell. 'Maybe I could let them know that their term of punishment is up. They're both working at Murphy's Hotel these days, and making pests of themselves there because they hate it. Beneath them, you know,' he laughed. 'I could inform them that if they were prepared to apologise to Mrs Oatley she may consider taking them back.'

'Excellent. I'll tell Harriet she has to look surprised when they appear, and very businesslike. Now that's done, tell me, William, what about Myles? When is he coming home? He's been away so long and Lucy misses him so much.'

'Not that long, my dear, Not even the full year yet.'

When the guests had left, William noticed a break in the cloudy weather and walked across to the bayside parks as the skies cleared, to view the sunset.

He wasn't disappointed. The sun, lowering through skies awash with pink and gold, was creating a spectacular show across the harbour as ripples of colour tipped the waves, and bronze-winged birds glided gracefully to rest. Gazing fondly at the sunset, William thought of his son. He'd always loved him dearly, and since his self-pitying lapse, he had gone out of his way to make it up to Myles. Until recently they had been the best of friends, but now a problem had arisen.

Myles had been shocked to hear that his father was engaged to Harriet Cunningham. To put it mildly. His response had been to urge William to reconsider. To remember that the Cunninghams had practically thrown their daughter at *him*, and with no luck in that direction had obviously turned their ambitions towards the father. Hadn't he realised that money was at the back of their plans? The Oatley wealth. What a coup for a mere bank manager to ensnare one of the Oatley men for his plain daughter, who was almost as tall as William was. By the end of the letter, Myles had bypassed 'reconsider' to demand outright that his father extricate himself from this situation, even with a quiet payment if necessary.

William shook his head sadly. By the time Myles's letter reached him at his Darwin office, he and Harriet had returned from their honeymoon and were settling into the new house. He wrote a long letter to Myles, expressing his disappointment at his son's reaction. However, he continued, he was married to Harriet now, they'd enjoyed a wonderful honeymoon in Singapore and words could not express his good fortune and great happiness in finding such a loving wife. He rebuked Myles gently for the unfair assessment of his in-laws, reminding him that Oscar Cunningham was an old friend and a gentleman.

On receipt of that letter, he had lied to Harriet, conveying best wishes and congratulations from Myles, and waited nervously to hear an apology from his son, but the next letter was worse.

'Am I to come home to a stepmother my own age?' Myles had written bitterly. 'Making us a laughing stock? It didn't take you long to forget my dear mother. So much for the great love you felt for her, the love that caused you to collapse and totally disregard the shock and suffering I was experiencing at that young age.'

So there it is, he mused. There it is. The past can never be undone.

Their correspondence continued. William never failed to mention Harriet, to reassure Myles that he was completely content in the marriage, and Myles retaliated by refusing to acknowledge her presence, simply remarking that since his father was so immersed in his business and charming domestic arrangements, he had decided to extend his stay overseas.

And William went on lying. He read the letters aloud to Harriet – about Myles's travels through France and Italy – and she enjoyed them immensely. She was particularly touched by Myles's greetings to 'your good wife'. She was so much looking forward to meeting William's son again, to welcoming him home.

But Myles couldn't stay away forever, living on the generous funds supplied by his father. Pop Oatley was complaining that the boy had to be brought into line. That no father in his right mind should allow his son to wallow about in such profligacy for so long. Eventually William explained the problem to him, expecting his father to understand the situation and the reason for his own lenience.

'Bloody cheek!' Pop roared. 'Bugger him! You married Harriet and she's a good woman. What you do is your own business. You tell that brat to get home. By Jesus, I'll tell him meself. What's his address again?'

'Don't upset him, Pop. I'm just waiting for him to adjust to the situation.'

'Adjust? It's Christmas. He's been gallivanting about long enough. What are you talking about, adjust? Where did you get that bloody word from? He comes home. He works on my station until we think he's got the brawn and brains to run Millford and then he gets on out there. No more to be said.'

All very well, William thought, but he had no intention of insisting that Myles come home, no matter what it cost, until his attitude changed. Until he could extend the hand of friendship towards Harriet.

The sun had exercised its right, in this tropical locale, to sink swiftly into oblivion, the show over, a few lonely clouds retaining a soft orange glow, the sea dark and restless, wondering what the night would bring in this switchover to stormy weather after the day's respite, and William turned away, as if turning from his own problems.

'Oh well,' he said. 'I'd better get home.'

Billy Chinn and Tom Ling were back, bearing deep apologies to the missus for previous 'badnesses', and exquisite bouquets of frangipani and orchids and delicate ferns for her home.

Gravely Harriet reinstated them and within a few days serenity was restored to the Oatley household. On William's advice, Harriet no longer concerned herself with menus, leaving the decisions to Billy; after all, she now realised, he shopped for the provisions so he knew what was available and fresh, and what was not. She was afraid he might complain about the influx of visitors, and the difficulty of preparing meals for extra guests at short notice, but he was unperturbed, taking pride in the compliments that the ladies heaped on him. Harriet wondered how she could have been so foolish as to resent these treasures, because now she had to restrain herself from falling about them in heartfelt gratitude.

At last everything had fallen into place. Freed from all the nagging household worries she was able to enjoy being with Pop and William, both good-natured, amusing men, and to appreciate the company of all these new people. Even finding the time to take an interest in the town.

Aggie Weston invited her to the annual meeting of the Quilters' Group where she was encouraged to take up the craft. Their work was of such excellence that Harriet was immediately enthusiastic and happy to join, but she noticed the ladies were only station ladies, none of them town-dwellers.

'That's why we call it our annual meeting,' Aggie laughed. 'Distance prevents us from having any other meetings.'

'It's an honour to be invited to join them,' William told her later.

'But why don't they have local women?'

'Not a lot in common I suppose,' he said vaguely, and Harriet began to take notice of the social divisions in the small community.

Lucy Hamilton took her for a stroll through Chinatown, crowded streets of shops and shanties that Harriet wouldn't have dared investigate on her own; and stranger still, Sibell Hamilton collected her one day, in her buggy, to help with charity work.

Next thing she found herself inside the big Fannie Bay jail, handing out food and blankets to Aborigine prisoners, the most miserable wretches she'd ever come across in her life. They were chained to the walls of a stinking hall in the filthiest condition, but Sibell seemed not to notice. Nor was she afraid of these unkempt savages. She knew quite a few of them by name, speaking gently to them, taking their hands, listening to their moans and woes, promising to speak for them, as Harriet stayed close to her, almost retching from the stink, having the food she proffered snatched from her hands.

Warders stood by – for their protection, she supposed, hoped – but otherwise seemed bored, even amused at this intrusion. It seemed to Harriet, by the look of these half-mad men, that their efforts would do little to mitigate their misery, but then they were criminals, after all.

She was relieved when the gates clanged behind them and they could breathe clean air again.

'What a horrible place!'

Sibell nodded. 'It's disgusting and inhuman. White prisoners are not chained like that and they get better food. I have been complaining to the Resident about the treatment of Aborigine prisoners but he has no sympathy for them.'

'What crimes have they committed?'

'The same crimes as white men, if they're guilty. But most of them are just rounded up and thrown in here on any old charge, to get them off the streets.'

'That's so cruel. Are you sure?'

Sibell laughed bitterly. 'I'll admit I'm not sure about a lot of things these days but I'm damned sure about this. It's common knowledge, Harriet, no secret. I hope you will continue to visit them after we go home. William can arrange a permit for you.'

'Yes,' Harriet mumbled, meaning yes, no doubt William would be able to arrange a permit for her. But this was not the sort of charity work she had envisaged. She stole a glance at the hem of her skirt, now darkly soiled from contact with the dirty, damp floor of that prison hall. The foul smell of the place lingered too, so much so that as soon as she got home, Harriet put all of the clothes she had been wearing into the wash.

And then she had a much more interesting invitation. Mollard, the Government Resident, was calling for donations to build a tennis court, to be completed in time for the dry season, and so his wife was forming a tennis club. She now extended an invitation to Harriet to join 'our exclusive Ladies' Club.'

William was happy to donate but passed on registering as a player.

'I was never one for tennis, but you join the ladies, my dear,' he grinned. 'If you feel exclusive enough!'

Harriet nodded. 'She really is a silly woman to write that, but I can't be worried. I'll join. Actually I'm quite good with the racquet.'

And so the days went on. The rains eased to an occasional shower, making way for the hot, dry winter. The station people began to pack up for the long treks to their homes, and William arranged a farewell party at the Victoria Hotel for Pop Oatley.

The day Pop left, travelling with the Hamiltons and the Westons, there were crowds at the station to wave goodbye and cheer as the lumbering steam engine puffed down the track.

Harriet was still a little confused about their journeying.

'A lot of station people came to town in wagons. Why don't they all use the train?'

'Some are going in different directions,' William told her, 'and some say the train isn't much faster, which is true enough at times, but at least it's more comfortable. Then again, old habits die hard. If we had a train going fifty miles an hour, old stagers would still stick to their wagons.'

'But the train only goes to Pine Creek. Pop's station is still a long way from there, isn't it?'

'Yes. A couple of hundred miles. He'll ride on from there.'

'Ride? At his age!'

'You wouldn't catch him sitting in a wagon,' William smiled. 'Beneath his dignity. But he'll meet up with a couple of dozen or so of his own men, station hands who pull out in the wet season too. They'll be waiting for him at Pine Creek. Then away they go. He's looking forward to it, do him good.'

The town seemed quiet after they had all departed, but there was renewed energy in the air, as if the lethargy of the monsoons was at last shaken off. Mischievously, William had renewed energy too, and more time for their lovemaking, rewarding his darling wife with a gold bangle set with a fiery opal.

Harriet was thrilled. In fact she was so content, so happy, she decided to write a long letter to her mother, about the town itself for a change. No more sobs and sighs about the difficulties of running a household in this tropical outpost. An amusing letter even. It only took one evening to compose.

My dear Mother,

Believe it or not, one can become accustomed to a monsoonal climate, despite the croaking of frogs and the house becoming a haven for all sorts of creepy-crawlies. At least the rain is warm and everything dries quickly, except, of course, the washing, but I no longer have to worry about that since the return of my clever houseboy.

You asked about the town. Well, I have to say that it is not an attractive place by any means, not in the drab grey of the wet season,

142

and not when exposed to the cracking hot winter sun. Like the populace, the architecture has a pecking order, with the Residency overlooking the harbour being first up, followed by white-stone buildings dedicated to government and banking, then a few decent houses, of which I may state, thanks to its newness and the sure hand of my husband, the Oatley house is modestly fine. There is one good hotel, two-storied, some long, low buildings which house respectively the police and the staff of the Cable Company, and we have a town hall.

Shops are old-fashioned, unshapely premises that appear to be temporary. They feature awnings in some cases but are enclosed, with no window displays to give hint of merchandise beyond. Thence, deterioration. Mephitic shanties and hovels rudely occupy main streets, crowding beside sweeps of vacant blocks. Therein lies a tale to which I shall refer later in this epistle.

Botanic gardens of some note lend a civilising tone to the town site which was cleared ruthlessly of trees for a metropolis not yet evident, though I can say some have survived and others are creeping back.

Beyond the gardens we have a jail, placed delightfully on a splendid spot overlooking Fannie Bay, though I cannot for the life of me see merit in the view for the wretched inmates imprisoned behind high walls. Nor why such a fine location should be spoiled by such an unfortunate choice of establishment.

A long sandy road is the only ingress to the Great Outback. To travel only a short way out there is to enter the bush, a steely grey-green surround that makes it very plain by its density and known immenseness that we are indeed remotely perched on the edge of this great continent facing Asia beyond the sea. A little frontier town with Chinese and Aborigines living in such squalor as you could not imagine, right at the feet of the white populace, and a Resident Governor who sees nothing amiss in this situation from his lofty sea view.

With my dear father a respected banker, you'll understand my astonishment at discovering that the social set here considers commerce to rank low, on a par with tradespeople. It appears that supreme status remains with the Resident and his wife, a few government officers and bureaucratic members of the Cable Company and their ladies. The Cable Company gentlemen operate and maintain the telegraph line from London, via Java, to Darwin, on to Alice Springs and so forth to Adelaide. These people, with their Indian servants and fancy buggies, really do 'bung on' outrageously, in a manner that I should regard as ill-bred. However, their ladies, in concert with the Resident's lady, call the social tune. All the rest are 'hoi polloi' in their self-aggrandising eyes.

Except, that is, for the station owners and their families, called variously squatters, graziers, pastoralists, cattlemen . . . or just plain

143

bushies. They come to town in force in the wet, the high summer, and upset the status quo. These people are the real backbone of the Territory, not those itinerant government officials and civil servants jollied up by their own self-importance in such a tiny community. The station people work hard, they control vast estates and 'run' herds of cattle in such thousands that one becomes distracted trying to envisage the numbers that they refer to so casually.

They have a languid social status of their own, leaning more towards friendships and having a good time than a concern with who's who. But our town's social lights suddenly become syco-phantic, scrambling for their company, and a handshake closer to real wealth, prospecting for invitations to their almost closed shop of entertainments.

As town residents, locals, if you please, William and I lead a charmed life. He may be 'in' the dreaded commerce, but he and his father are notable station owners as well, so he cannot be over-looked in the social scene. William, with his democratic bent, is not keen on social favouring, believing it has no place in a struggling town like Darwin, but as you would agree, Mother, these situations, pecking orders, as previously mentioned, do exist, and one has to observe them.

There are often functions in the great hall at the Residency, soirées, luncheons, dinner parties, even balls, though the stone slab floor is hardly conducive to enjoyable frolics. And I have to say here that all the colourful silks and satins I bought in Singapore are now languishing in my camphor trunk, since the order of the day here is white. Because of the heat, ladies claim, white is the only sensible colour, so white it is. White silk, muslin, cotton, calico, dimity, organdie, the lot – and it is such a bore. We swan about on a sea of black and white, black for the gentlemen, white for the ladies. There we all sit at luncheons at the Residency, in white dresses and huge white-adorned hats, but a couple of the older station ladies either don't own, or won't indulge in, the acceptable hats, so they sit sourly in their white, of course, with black felt hats like tea cosies crammed down on their heads. I must admit they do look funny and out of place.

But referring now to those vacant blocks.

We do have a district council, with six elected members who meet regularly. They are mostly businessmen. One is a Chinaman! And one member has been unable to attend meetings for the last six months because he has been in jail for some financial misdemean-our. Say no more!

The main problem the council has to face is lack of money, due to the fact that few residents or absentee owners of land in the town pay their rates. They simply don't pay. At last count fewer than fifty people had their rate bills paid up to date. Some have never paid any, including (and don't you love this?) the Earl of

Rosebury and the Duke of Manchester, who both own large sections of the town centre, all vacant blocks.

William is greatly concerned about this situation and was considering standing for the council himself, to see if he could find a way to enforce payment since letters and threats of legal action have failed. He gets so angry with people who complain about the lack of facilities in Darwin, insisting that the council is hog-tied without finance.

I told him, however, that he would be wasting his talents on the council. That he should speak to the gentlemen he knows so well in the South Australian Government, which annexed the Territory, and present himself to be appointed the next Resident. No one in the Territory is better equipped than my William to take up this post, and if I may say so, no one could do a worse job than the present fellow, who rarely visits Pine Creek or Alice Springs or any of the outback stations in the lands he is supposed to administer, and seems devoid of the integrity necessary to make important decisions about the fate of this outpost and its surrounds. Too busy socialising with his simpering wife to care about the town, the frightful clashes between whites and Aborigines that are daily occurrences in the outback, and the miserable state of our port. William would make his mark, I can proudly declare, but then I'm only his wife.

Who, you'll be relieved to know, still attends service on Sundays at the Protestant church, which is a prefabricated building, since the previous one, along with many other buildings, was destroyed a few years back by a cyclone. In the wet, my husband kindly takes me to church in the buggy but still will not participate. I am sorry to say he is soundly on the side of the anti-religionists, so I pray for him. The Reverend Walters gives a good service, when one can hear over the noise of the rain and the interjections of grizzled bushmen who feel it is their place to correct him, when they do not concur with his opinions. Some of them, who also have their dogs sitting stoutly beside them, can be quick-witted and amusing, but then one should not condone such behaviour by even the hint of a smile. William laughs outrageously when I tell him of the goings-on in our little church. I was amazed last Sunday to see him raise his hat to a couple of those bushmen, informing me that they were crocodile and buffalo hunters!

Such is my tale of the Far North. This is a peculiar place but by no means dull, so you must visit us. When weather permits, we are going inland to visit the Oatley cattle stations and that will be an adventure in itself.

I leave you, dear Mother, with my fondest regards to all.

Your affectionate daughter,

Harriet.

145

Chapter Ten

Feeling in the best of spirits this Sunday morning, William decided to stroll up to the church and escort Harriet home, taking a detour to view the American brigantine lying at anchor in the harbour. Two businessmen, prospective investors, were on board and William had arranged a meeting with them on the morrow. The gentlemen, from Seattle, USA, had been corresponding with William for almost a year now, and their plans to invest in Territory copper mines were nearing completion.

Cautious men, they had requested the presence of the 'Governor' at the meeting; and the senior official in the Department of Mines, and William hadn't raised objections.

'Fair enough,' he explained to Lawrence Mollard. 'They only know me through correspondence, though I think they've probably made a few quiet enquiries of their own, to come this far. Your presence will calm any fears they might have.'

'As well as my cognisance of the legalities of mining leases. New chums like this would find my advice invaluable. I could probably act as a consultant to their enterprise. What did you say was the name of their firm?'

'Garfield Perdoe Incorporated.' William coughed quietly. 'I'm acting in the capacity of consultant.'

'I know that. And I believe you get a fair slice of the action. But you're talking copper. My expertise is in the field of gold mines. Serious investors would do well to take my advice.'

'I'm sure they would, Lawrence, but we've already covered the possibility of gold mines, and they're not interested.'

'Are you sure? There's still gold at Pine Creek. Keep in mind, William, that I have to encourage investment in the Territory; we're desperately short of funds . . .'

'I quite agree, so perhaps we could close the copper deal first. Leases of the size they're mentioning will put thousands of pounds into the government coffers. Will you bring Barlow from the Department of Mines? He already knows all about this and has maps and assayers' reports on hand, so that he can provide any extra information they require.'

'Very well. What's the form?'

'A meeting at the Victoria Hotel, a private room, the day after their ship berths, followed by a luncheon.'

'You're paying?'

'Of course.'

'Good. Count my aide in too. Christy's a smart chap. He can talk to them and arrange a night for a reception at the Residency for our American visitors. That should impress them.'

William doubted that. The Mollards were known for their mean table. However, protocol would be observed. These Americans, who had chartered their own ship for this voyage, were big time, easily matching, according to William's enquiries, the wealth of Britons he'd welcomed to Darwin. Their investments were important to the Territory, which was suffering badly from the negligence of its seat of government far away in Adelaide, and its refusal to provide funds for the barest facilities. The town was run down, the hospital a disgrace, the port primitive . . .

'A forgotten town,' William sighed as he walked along the Esplanade. No wonder people wouldn't pay their rates on town blocks. Nothing to show for them. No pavements or gutters, no street lighting, and no organised arrangements for disposal of sewage. 'And we're the capital,' he added, pleased that the Esplanade did at least give the impression of genteel living, with its tidy sea-front park.

He checked his fob watch and quickened his step. One thing he could do to please his guests: give them a hearty meal. No matter the luxury of ship's quarters, good fresh food would be appreciated at the end of a long voyage. William had asked Mrs Ryan at the Victoria to give of her best. And her best was outstanding.

'Come to think of it,' he smiled, 'I'm looking forward to it myself.'

He rounded the corner and walked up towards the church. It wasn't just Emily May's death that had turned him off religion. That had simply been the trigger, causing him to question his beliefs. As he had done with his reckless overreaction to the death of his wife, William had set out to examine his behaviour. It had all begun with a fury at a God who would allow one of his flock, a woman who dearly loved the Lord, to die so young. From there he'd drifted into a sort of no-man's-land as he'd listened, dissatisfied, to pastors and friends giving him the same patter about God's will, and how it was not for men to question the ways of the Lord.

Then one morning, after he'd moved to Darwin, it occurred to him that nobody really knew what they were talking about on this subject. Least of all himself. For two years William studied religion. It was something to do in quiet times, in his lonely dwelling beside his office. He read books on all major religions and a few on less-known groups, appreciating goodness as the basic concept, but finding all the man-made rules and rigmaroles insufferable.

He met some Daly River missionaries who were risking their lives to convert some of the most militant Aborigines in the north.

A bushman at heart, William had grown up with Aborigines. He knew so many of them and was so steeped in their culture that he was amazed when one pale-faced, pious missionary called Walters assured him that

148

they were succeeding beyond their wildest dreams. That within a few years they would bring all the tribal blacks to Christianity. It was only a matter of time.

'Bullshit!' William had exploded. 'How do you expect to do that?'

'By teaching them love, sir. Love of their fellow man. The Christian way as opposed to their pagan habits.'

'Yeah. Christians are a great bloody example. Murdering whole bloody families, raping and stealing their women, killing the kids . . . They're not stupid, Pastor. You won't convert them. The Christianity you're selling hasn't got a lot going for it. Love? What love? They haven't even glimpsed it. Give it away, Pastor.'

'And are you without blame, Mr Oatley?' the pastor asked, his whiskered face trembling with rage.

'We are all intruders, but some of us are doing our best, as my family does. They're protected on our lands.'

'In which case the Bible says it behoves you to bring these wretches to Christianity or you're failing your duty to the Lord. God help you, Mr Oatley, if you don't grasp this opportunity.'

'God's got nothing to do with it,' William said wearily.

And that was the end of his foray into the dreamworld of religion, into the silliness that came down to ladies wearing hats in church so as not to displease a being who, by the last calculations, must be millions of years old.

To spare Harriet's feelings, William kept his opinions to himself, nor had he told her that the missionary, that Daly River missionary, had been promoted to the vicar of her church, and was now the Reverend Walters, ministering to the Protestant community as opposed to the Catholic, the only other denomination in town.

When he arrived at the church, a little late, thanks to his saunterings and meditations, Harriet was waiting for him outside with none other than Walters himself, his bushy whiskers trimmed, and the tropical whites replaced by a portly black cassock. He'd put on weight.

'William!' His wife greeted him with a smile. 'Reverend Walters has been waiting to talk to you. He has news for you. We are to be neighbours.'

'Neighbours? What do you mean?'

'We have bought the vacant block next door to you,' the Reverend said excitedly. 'We are to get our new church at last. An Anglican church. Our Bishop in Adelaide finally approved the funds last week.'

William was nonplussed. 'What vacant block? I own the blocks either side of my office building.'

His wife laughed. 'No, silly. The Reverend means the big block beside our house. I'm delighted, that block is so overgrown with weeds it must be harbouring whole families of snakes.'

'Next door to my house?' William was almost apoplectic. 'You're building a church there? The hell you are!'

'Really, William, don't take on so,' Harriet cried, but he turned on Walters.

'Think again, Reverend. I'll not be looking out my windows at a bloody church and a mob of God-botherers. The Esplanade is no place for a church. Stick it back in Smith Street or some other place; no shortage of vacant blocks in this town.'

Walters stood his ground. 'I'm sorry you feel like that, Oatley, but we have made our decision. The land belongs to the Church now and an architect in Adelaide is already drawing up the plans. As for the Esplanade,' he said caustically, 'if it can suffer a hotel as it has done for years, then there can be no objection to a church. If indeed zoning requirements existed here, which they do not. The matter is not open to discussion. I bid you good day, sir, and you, Mrs Oatley.'

'We'll see about that!' William called after him as he strode away. 'They'll not build a church next door to my place,' he told Harriet.

But she was embarrassed. 'How could you? I've never known you to be so rude. And to Reverend Walters, of all people. I don't know what you're making such a fuss about.'

'Weren't you listening?' he grated. 'I won't have a church next door. I won't have my Sundays ruined by psalm singers.'

'It could be worse. What if they put a hotel there?'

'I wouldn't have that either. And kindly refrain from arguing with me. I don't need your feather-brained opinions!'

They walked home in silence, William forgoing his original plan to take her to see the brigantine, so that he could hurry home and compose letters of complaint to the authorities, and Harriet almost in tears. Her husband could be a little crotchety at times, but he'd never been so angry and cruel to her before.

The first inkling of real trouble began on the following Monday morning.

William found his visitors, Theodore Perdoe and his son Jay, a jovial pair, thoroughly enjoying their trans-Pacific cruise and the island-hopping that had brought them across to Darwin, calling it an unbeatable adventure.

He had met them at the port and walked the short distance with them to the hotel, pleased to see how interested they were in everything about them.

Perdoe Senior was far from disappointed in Darwin. 'By God, this is a real frontier town, isn't it? Looks like we're in on the ground floor all right, Jay. Nothing like the other ports we've seen. Reminds me of our wild west in the old days. Cowboys and all riding through the town.'

William laughed. 'We call them stockmen.'

'Stockmen? Is that right? Yeah, that makes sense. You'll have to learn the lingo, Jay. He's a geologist, William, and a damn good one too. If we get this show on the road, he'll be back, working out there on our leases. Keeping an eye on things.'

'I'm glad to hear it,' William said. 'If there's anything you need at any time, you let me know.'

Jay grinned. 'I reckon the first thing would be a couple of good horses.'

'That's no problem. I'll see to it personally.'

'Thank you, sir. I'd appreciate that.'

There was no shortage of talking points while they waited in the hotel for Mollard and his offsiders, since these two men were still full of their travels and exploits, with William an interested listener, but the Resident was late, very late, and William began to feel uncomfortable.

Eventually he made his apologies. 'If you would excuse me, gentlemen, I'll see what's keeping the Resident.'

'Who's he?' Perdoe Senior asked.

'Mr Mollard is the Resident, which is what we call a governor up here, since we aren't officially a state, rather a territory, annexed to South Australia. He's the chief administrator really.'

'I guess time doesn't really mean much in these parts,' Perdoe allowed kindly, lighting a cigar, and William nodded, escaping to ask Mrs Ryan to take them in coffee, or drinks, whatever they wanted while they waited.

He was about to send one of the hotel staff across to the Residency to remind Mollard of this meeting, and race across to the Mines Department himself to find Barlow, when Captain Christy Cornford, the Resident's secretary, marched in the door.

'Thank God!' William said. 'You people are nearly an hour late. Where is he? Is Barlow with you?'

Christy, a tall, elegant fellow, ex-British army, was apologetic. 'I'm sorry, sir. His Excellency will not be attending your meeting. Nor will Barlow.'

'What? Is he mad? These gentlemen are serious investors with the highest credentials. He can't snub them.'

'Mr Mollard seems to believe he is being used to put money in your pocket, Mr Oatley. I can't convince him otherwise.'

'Bloody rot! Doesn't he understand that opening up copper mines on the scale proposed by Garfield Perdoe is far beyond Australian resources? More important to the Territory than they are to me. Tell the man we're waiting for him.'

'I have my instructions, sir. Mr Mollard is now otherwise engaged. Where are these gentlemen?'

'Inside . . . I'll have words with Mollard over this.'

William took a few moments to compose himself, then remembered to tell Mrs Ryan that there would only be three for lunch.

'What happened to Mollard and company?' she asked.

'He let me down, the idiot.'

She shrugged. 'Never mind, he's no loss.'

'In this case he is. These people need official reassurance before putting pen to paper on investments costing them hundreds of thousands of pounds.'

But when he returned to the private room his two visitors were cheerful.

'Looks like the boss couldn't make it,' Perdoe said. 'But he's giving a reception for us tonight.' He waved a handwritten invitation, obviously delivered by Cornford. 'Good of him at such short notice. His aide said we'd be dining and dancing at the Residency, the house you showed us on the way up, William. Formal too, Jay. Looks like we'd better get the stewards to air our dinner suits.' He rumbled a laugh. 'We haven't seen them since Honolulu. And we'd better not get started on Honolulu either. I had to drag Jay away from there. What a place, William! Dancing girls laid on. A mighty time we had there!'

William took them to lunch, where their enthusiasm overflowed as he'd expected as they tucked into the excellent meal and fine wines, so much so that they invited Mrs Ryan to join them, congratulating her on her table. Before she arrived he did manage to discuss the mining problem with them for a while, and they were still on course, but as Perdoe Senior said, there was plenty of time to discuss business.

'It's just great to be on solid ground again,' he said, 'and to sit about a table that's not rocking, with good food and good company. Drink up, William, my son and I are having a whale of a time. You've got a son too, haven't you? Where is he?'

'He's in England.'

'Shame about that. We'd have liked to have met him. Now Mrs Ryan, how did a lady like you come to own a hotel way up here in the wild west, or should I say wild north . . .'

William gave up. Perdoe was a powerfully built man with a personality to match. He was in charge, and in a good mood, his son matching him with hilarious tales of their adventures. Despite his anger over Mollard's behaviour, William was enjoying himself. In fact they all were. William couldn't remember when he'd laughed so much and Mrs Ryan had such a good time, she invited all three to dine with her again on a night of their choice, 'on the house'.

Jay accepted with a sweeping bow, on condition that she join them again and tell them more about her gold-mining days, when she and her husband had earned enough to buy the hotel.

They went back to their ship and William climbed the steps from the port to the Residency, his head aching from an unaccustomed indulgence in wines at midday, from a sun that seemed unreasonably hot, and from his anger at Mollard's non-appearance.

Cornford came out to meet him as he strode towards the front door. 'What can I do for you, Mr Oatley?'

'I should like to see Mr Mollard.'

'I'm sorry, he is not at home.'

'Then what time is the reception this evening? I have already been informed, by the guest of honour himself, that there is to be dining and dancing. What may I tell my wife?'

Christy tugged at his starched collar, settling a bow tie as thin as a bootlace, glancing nervously over his shoulder as if hoping for rescue.

'I really don't recall your name being on the list of invitees,' he said anxiously.

'What?'

'Do you wish me to check?'

'Check it immediately.'

'Very well.'

William paced the path angrily. He'd have a few things to say to Mollard tonight. The fool was jeopardising the best offer the Territory had had in years by snubbing a director of Garfield Perdoe. Had the man no common sense?

'I'm afraid I was right,' Christy informed him.

'I am not invited!'

'That is correct.'

'I see. Then you tell him this! If he bungles the Garfield Perdoe deal, I'll see to it that the Premier of South Australia is made aware of his incompetence. And you may have my word on that!'

William tramped home, furious. It was obvious what that bastard Mollard was up to. He wanted to be consultant on this deal, he wanted the commission, in flagrant disregard of the law, of the requirements of his high office. And worse. What if he wrecked the delicate negotiations? Organising mining ventures took a lot of preparation, rock-solid information, and a great deal of goodwill. Plus the incentive of government subsidies, in this case from Adelaide, which were hard to come by, though William had that offer in writing. All he needed was the signature of Theo Perdoe, as representative of Garfield Perdoe, on the other side of the complicated contracts.

By the time he slammed his front door and threw his hat on to the peg, his headache had reached the pitch of a kettle drum.

Tom Ling was there to minister to him.

'I have to lie down,' William told him. 'Bring me something for a bad headache and be quick about it.'

'So sorry, boss, dear dear, you lie down, yes, lie down. I fixee. You see. Lie down. Tom fixee poor boss.'

He shuffled away, at speed, and William went through to the bedroom, casting aside his jacket, his tie, his shirt and his shoes, throwing himself on his bed, hearing only the pounding in his head until Tom ran in with a white mixture for him, and though it had a foul taste, William swallowed it. He'd had Tom's potions before, and knew they worked.

Soon he was sound asleep.

The dose must have been stronger than usual. William awoke to the sound of roosters crowing and padded over to the window for his morning regime of deep-breathing exercises. Thoughts of Mollard still rankled but he had slept so long and so well he was in good spirits this fine morning. Time enough to sort out that gentleman.

He decided to go out to the kitchen in search of a cup of tea, but Harriet's voice startled him.

'So now you're sneaking out on me.'

William turned. 'I beg your pardon. I thought you were asleep. Would you care for morning tea? It's a bit early, but since you're awake . . .'

'I don't want anything,' she snapped. 'Nothing at all. Except for an apology from you.'

He smiled. 'Yes. I'm sorry, I slept right through. You should have woken me.'

'Really? First you abuse me in the street. Then you come home drunk—'

'Excuse me, I did not abuse you, and I was not drunk.'

'You were so. You came in and collapsed on the bed. I didn't even know you were home until I walked in here. Then I had to dine alone. Tom Ling had to undress you. It's disgraceful.'

William blinked. He remembered that now. Tom had lit the lamps and handed him his nightshirt. 'Boss can't sleep in clo's, too much tight.' And he'd sleepily obliged. No doubt with a snort of opium in his system. But whatever Tom's cure, he was in no mood for tantrums at this hour. He left the bedroom without a word, closing the door quietly behind him.

William sent his clerk to make contact with Theo and Jay and arrange another meeting at their convenience, then went back to the Residency to talk to Mollard, but once again he was met by Christy, who informed him that His Excellency would not see him.

'What does that mean? Won't see me today, or tomorrow? And what about the Perdoes?'

'That was the message I was instructed to convey, sir.'

'Then make an appointment for me.'

'Very well. I shall advise your clerk later.'

Leo returned to report that the Americans were unable to see their way clear for a meeting just yet, and by the end of the day there was still no word from Mollard.

Then William heard that the Resident was arranging a safari for the Perdoes, taking them to visit a cattle station and some of the spectacular springs and gorges en route, and he realised that he was being effectively shut out of negotiations with Garfield Perdoe.

Unfortunately he met Mollard in the street, and, controlling his anger, asked him courteously when they might begin business discussions with the Americans.

Mollard stared at him. 'I wonder that you keep pestering me when you obviously believe you could do a much better job as Resident yourself.'

'What are you talking about? I told Cornford I am not asking for your assistance for my benefit, but for the Territory. I would willingly forgo my consultancy fees to see this venture come to fruition. The contracts and all the details are ready—'

The Resident interrupted him. 'If you have any complaints about the way I conduct business, then you speak to Adelaide; in the meantime, you could stop pestering Mr Perdoe. I am quite capable of managing this matter without having to suffer your criticisms.'

He strode away and William, thunderstruck, was left standing, convinced that Mollard was using some imaginary insult to sever his connections with Perdoe and usurp them for himself. But how could he do that? The contracts he was holding had been drawn up and approved by the Mines Department in Adelaide. The head office.

And what was this about William believing he'd do a better job as Resident? Admittedly, like most businessmen in the town, he wasn't impressed by Mollard's poor showing, but he had no ambition to take on the job himself. Obviously all his double talk was a red herring, designed to undermine William's standing with the Americans.

He charged back to his office and wrote a long telegram to the Minister for Mines in Adelaide, asking for his position to be clarified. He had Leo send it off immediately.

The response came two days later. A curt reply, stating that the Resident had the matter in hand and all contracts and relevant material should be handed to him forthwith.

William shrugged. 'All right. If that's what they want. So be it. Pack up all that stuff, Leo, and take it to his office. Let's see if that fool can sort it out. I don't want to hear any more about it.'

But Mrs Ryan was troubled. 'Mr Perdoe called on me before they left for Mangalow station. He apologised that he and his son would not be able to accept my invitation to dine if you were included, because there appeared to be a protocol problem, and he didn't wish to offend the "Governor". He also sent you his regrets and best wishes.'

William decided to let it all pass. His good name stood. He would not enter into correspondence with Garfield Perdoe again unless they contacted him, and he certainly would not stoop to defending himself against whatever mischief Lawrence Mollard had introduced into the scene.

'Protocol my eye,' he muttered as he left his office, heading home to a wife who was still in a mood from the other night. He had refused to apologise for his 'inebriated state', as she put it, nor would he explain. It was enough that he had told her he had enjoyed a merry luncheon with guests, but had not come home drunk. William was startled that Harriet chose not to believe him, realising it was her way of retaliating for his calling her feather-brained in a fit of ire, and would have apologised for that had she not gone off at a tangent. Annoying him further. He really couldn't be bothered with this domestic trivia.

'And anyway,' he muttered to himself as he cut through to the Esplanade, 'so what if I was drunk? I was no nuisance to her.'

Though she was still cross with him, Harriet had decided to forget the unpleasantness and welcome her husband home cheerfully. Only then did she learn that he'd had a falling-out with Mollard and that an important deal with the American visitors had collapsed, or rather been taken over by Mollard himself. That would account for William's ill temper, but she couldn't understand why he was still upset. What did it matter? It wasn't the first time he'd come up against Mollard, and besides, he was involved in other business deals. It wasn't as if he needed the consultancy fees.

But all week, while Mollard and the Americans were out of town on their safari, her husband was despondent, self-absorbed, obviously still worried about the copper mines, or, she thought, cross that he hadn't been included in the safari; after all, he knew that area better than Mollard or any of the other gentlemen he'd invited to join them. They were probably all having a marvellous time. Not that Harriet would dare remark on that, any more than she would mention the subject of that vacant block next door. Every time she looked in that direction it made her nervous. William hadn't said any more about it, so she hoped he had calmed down and accepted the inevitable.

William had not. He had lodged objections with the district council. Engaged a solicitor to look into the matter and sent a letter to the relevant bishop in Adelaide warning him that the construction of a church on that site would spark off vehement objections in the town. He was also in the process of advising owners of other blocks in the vicinity, one of whom was Zack Hamilton, that they needed to submit their objections right away.

Eventually the travellers returned to Darwin and there was a gushing article in the local paper about the success of the safari but not a word about the proposed copper mines.

Two more days went past. William, on principle, would not enquire as to what was happening, only scouring the paper for news, so he was stunned when he looked out over the harbour to find the brigantine had sailed. He couldn't stand not knowing what terms had been agreed to, so he rushed off to find Barlow.

'None,' Barlow said coldly. 'We lost them. Nothing settled. They've gone.'

'I know that, but why? We had it in the bag.'

'You tell me. You were supposed to be setting this thing up but you pushed it over to Mollard.'

'I did no such thing! He elbowed in. Cut me out completely.'

'That's not what he says.'

'I don't give a damn what he says. What happened?'

'Well, we had a meeting but couldn't do much until you handed over the contracts, so I went on the safari with them, trotting after them with all my stuff, trying to get a word in, ending up with the only real meeting the night we got back, at the Residence. Mollard didn't know what he was talking about. When I put my nose in, trying to shut him up, he pulled me into line in front of the Yanks. To give Christy his due, he tried to maintain some order but it was confused, what with Mollard talking consultancy fees, me talking assayers' reports and the copper grade, them peering over the fine print, cost of equipment and transport to the port . . . and finally Mollard getting the figures all mixed up or wanting more financial input from them. Hard to say.'

'So! Then what?'

'Well, I had a meeting with Jay the next morning. He's all right. Everything was back under control. We handed out joint figures to the bosses, Perdoe Senior and Mollard. I wasn't invited to that meeting. Apparently they couldn't agree on subsidies and God knows what—'

'But I had all that worked out.'

'Then you should have stuck with it,' Barlow snapped. 'We needed them.'

William was furious. 'How many times do I have to tell you Mollard cut me out? I was ordered by Adelaide to butt out.'

Barlow shrugged. 'Well, it's all over now. Jay dropped in on me before they left, to say they were disappointed that we'd moved the goalposts out of their reach. That's what he said, the goalposts, and I reckon he's right. The whole thing got buggered up and the Territory is the loser.'

'The copper is there, isn't it?'

'Yes, tons of it.'

'Thank you. I was beginning to think I might be over-enthusiastic. Send me over your figures again and I'll put them to some Melbourne investors. They might come to the party if I can turn them away from their obsession with New Guinea gold.'

Barlow nodded. 'Yes. That's the trouble. It's hard to compete with gold, and we've had our day. I'll give you the figures but don't mention it to Mollard. I don't want to lose my job.'

Harriet was confused. The tennis court in Knuckey Street was completed and it looked splendid, the grass trimmed as neatly as a carpet. There was even a white-painted shelter-shed at one end with two rows of long benches awaiting players and watchers. Harriet was waiting too. Her mother had sent her two good racquets from Perth and she'd had some white skirts and blouses made to accord with the rules. In her eagerness for the games to begin she'd gone out of her way to watch the progress of the court.

But then one day she saw some ladies playing. That was a shock at first, but she told herself they were probably trying out the court prior to the official opening. Then, on a Monday morning, she read in the local paper that Mrs Mollard had officially opened the Darwin Tennis Club the previous Saturday, 'with afternoon tea in the grounds of the Residency before retiring to the court to watch exhibition games between some of our finest exponents of the sport'.

Harriet was upset, and bewildered that she'd somehow missed the great event, but then the paper listed the inaugural members and her name wasn't there. No sign of it. She was dreadfully disappointed, finding no reason why she shouldn't have been included, and then it dawned on her. William! He'd been so involved in all that copper business, not to mention his barrage of objections to the building of a church next door, that he'd forgotten! No wonder his wife had missed out. Members were expected to support their club; making a tennis court from a rough old town block took money. And it would have been such an honour to be listed as an inaugural member; tennis clubs were part of the history of small towns.

By the time he came home she was almost in tears as she charged him with this oversight.

'How could you be so forgetful? It's the only thing I ever really wanted to do in this town. I love tennis, I play very well. You must give the donation immediately! And find out if there are membership fees as well. Maybe they have to be paid. Probably they do! I'm really humiliated, William,' she cried, giving way to a flood of tears. 'It's just not good enough of you to be so selfish.'

'Now, now,' he soothed, 'there's no need to be so upset. I did give them a donation. I don't know, ten pounds, twenty pounds, something like that, I'm sure I did. Yes, I gave the cash to Leo to deliver to them. So don't be bothering yourself. If Mrs Mollard's in charge of the club ledgers they're probably a mess. I'll look into it tomorrow. Leo can go over there and ask Christy what happened. You'll be reinstated in seconds.'

But Harriet, already miserable, conjured up another scenario.

'You haven't been getting along with Mollard lately. You don't suppose he's taking it out on me?'

'Nonsense! No. I haven't actually fallen out with him. Not more than usual. He took over one of my projects and he knows that perfectly well. The powers in Adelaide will be aware that he messed up, and it serves him right. I'm just looking elsewhere now. No point in vendettas, he is the Resident and we have to live with him.'

'So you don't think this oversight is anything to do with your business?' she asked shakily, unconvinced.

'Of course not. By the way, there's a concert on at the town hall on Saturday night, a nigger minstrel show. Would you like to go?'

'I thought you didn't like them.'

'No, but some of them have good voices. I have to warn you they get a hard time from the audiences here, because the black greasepaint runs in the heat and they look all streaky. Funny to watch greasepaint dripping off them. I don't know why they bother with the blacking at all.'

Harriet smiled thinly. 'I'll try not to watch.'

'That's better, my dear. We'll just listen. I do love to hear those players harmonising all the old tunes. What say we go for a walk before dinner?'

Harriet agreed, but she knew there was no way of retrieving her position on that inaugural list. Too late now, and such a pity.

On the following day, though, more trouble, more confusion. Tom Ling brought her a letter from Mrs Maudie Hamilton, sister-in-law of Sibell.

Harriet smiled, wondering what the formidable woman had to say. Probably a reminder that she had promised to visit the Hamilton stations as soon as the weather cleared, or rather, when William could find the time to escort her. But the Oatley stations had priority. Maybe they could make a round trip of these stations. It would be wonderful to see several of them in their travels, and the Hamiltons were known to be so hospitable to guests.

'Dear Madam,' the letter began harshly, and Harriet checked the envelope to make sure it was addressed to her. It was.

As one of the women able to please herself in what she chooses to wear on her head, whether it be black, white, brindle or a tea cosy, I suggest that as an upstart newcomer to our town you keep your opinions to yourself, or at least seek the advice of the gentleman who is your husband before insulting his friends.
Yours faithfully,
Mrs M. Hamilton.

'What?' Harriet's eyes popped as she reread the letter. 'What on earth is she carrying on about? When did I insult her? The stupid woman.'

She reread the letter yet again, focusing on the nastiness about hats. Maudie Hamilton did wear old black felt hats all the time but Harriet had never remarked on them here. Never. Someone else must have made the same comment and blamed it on her. There was still no excuse for such a rude letter. How dare she?

Harriet tore the letter up, tore it into tiny little pieces and threw them into the waste bin outside the kitchen, as far from her as possible, as if the pieces were contaminated. It would be dreadful if William came across it. What would she say? She worried about a response. Should she write a note, patient, yet reproving the woman for her unfair and uncalled-for remarks? But the more she rehearsed possible wording, the angrier she became. Damn her! Why bother to reply at all. How dare Maudie call her an upstart. It was all very distressing. Harriet had counted the Hamiltons as friends. Perhaps it would be better to write to Lucy and ask her what it was all about. Lucy wouldn't want upsets with the Oatleys because of her boyfriend. She liked to keep in touch with William, exchanging news of Myles's travels.

The worry lodged, though, firmly set, bothering her all day. Harriet wished now that she hadn't torn up Maudie's letter. Maybe it wasn't so bad after all. She might be overreacting. Then again, she might not.

It was Leo who began to unravel the mystery. At William's request he sought out Christy Cornford, finding him at the bar in the Cable Company recreation hall.

'I have the receipt for Mr Oatley's donation to the building fund for the tennis court, but it seems Mrs Oatley's application to join the Ladies' Tennis Club has been overlooked. Do you think you could look into it?'

Christy grimaced. 'No need to, Leo. She's been blackballed.'

'What? They can't blackball Mrs Oatley!'

'They can and they have.'

'Why?'

'I don't know the whole story yet, but it appears she has insulted the Resident, and Mrs Mollard. First heard was a telegram from Perth. Now I didn't see it, haven't read it, because it has been whisked out of sight, but it was enough to send His Excellency into a right royal rage.'

Leo was always irritated by references to 'His Excellency' since he was certain that Mollard's rank did not warrant it, but for now the title was unimportant. 'You must have some idea what was in that telegram. It has to be a mistake. Mrs Oatley is a very nice woman, she wouldn't insult the Mollards. I can't believe that.'

'Well something's up, and it doesn't augur well for your man Oatley. If I recall, that telegram came the morning of Oatley's meeting with the Perdoe father and son team. Though I did not know it at the time. I was only told the Resident was withdrawing from the talks.'

'That's why he pulled out!' Leo shook his head. 'I don't understand this. It doesn't make sense.'

Christy looked at him quizzically. 'There's a story abroad that Oatley wants to be appointed Resident.'

'Rot! Where did you get that from?'

'My office actually,' he said, being deliberately vague. 'But Mollard is waiting for a full report from Perth.'

'About what?'

'About whom, I gather. Seems the telegram was but a tip-off from a friend in Perth. Letter following, so to speak. But it must contain some interesting information to have put both Oatley and his wife in the bad books.'

'And yet whatever it is,' Leo said acidly, 'neither Mr Oatley nor his wife know anything about it.'

Christy shrugged. 'We'll see. Personally, I can't wait. Care for another drink?'

'Yes.' Leo nodded thoughtfully. Christy, he knew, received only a small salary, less than most civil servants working in Darwin, another victim of Mollard's frugality. Though he seemed content with the perks of the job, free tickets to functions and some prestige, Leo wondered . . .

He paid for the two whiskies and took the plunge. 'Oatley's entitled to a fair go,' he said. 'If someone's sending information of some sort about him he ought to have a chance to look at it.'

'It might be classified,' Christy said, with a wry smile.

'In which case I wouldn't dream of asking you to let me see a copy, but if not, I could make it worth your while.'

'In what manner?' Christy asked carefully.

Leo was cautious, feeling his way. Cash? How much? Then he remembered some months ago Christy had been enquiring after the price of a block of land in Bennet Street, owned by Oatley, but had found it out of his range.

'What about those blocks on Bennet Street? You could have one of them,' he said easily, as if tossing it away.

Christy was surprised. 'For how much?'

'For a copy of that report. Nothing said. No money involved. Time's more important. We'd need a copy first up.'

Christy noted the change. 'We?'

'Well, it's Oatley's land. He'll approve. He owns half the town anyway. I'll have the title deeds signed over and hand them to you personally.'

'Bit dicey,' Christy worried.

'Why? No one need know how much you paid. For that matter, I could give you a receipt for the going rate if you feel anyone would be impertinent enough to ask. You'd be covered.'

'Oatley will agree to this?'

'He just might. Especially since his wife's upset.'

'Good. You fix it with him and I'll see what I can do.'

'You're giving him one of my blocks?' William yelped.

'What's the block worth? Ten pounds at most. Christy's touchy, full of himself. If I'd offered him ten pounds he might have balked, soiling the fingers rather with a cash bribe. You wouldn't miss ten pounds,' Leo laughed. 'Let him have the end block. By the sound of things, you're seriously maligned by someone, and you just said you need to know about it.'

William was mystified. 'And he can't tell you what was in that telegram?'

'No. But it was enough for Mollard to cancel that meeting, and to cut you out of the Garfield Perdoe deal.'

'To wreck it,' William growled. 'Cornford must have been in a talkative mood.'

'He'd had a few drinks, but he likes to show off what he knows and he's as interested in that report as we are. And it also seems that Mollard's nose is out of joint because he thinks you want him out of the job. That you want to be Resident.'

'Me?' William stared.

'Well, that's what Christy heard, from whom he wouldn't say, but I'm betting it came from the boss himself.'

'And where did he get such tripe from?'

'That's what you're paying to find out, as soon as possible.'

William shoved some papers out of the way and took the application for transfer with the title deed that Leo handed to him, glaring at it.

'Giving this to Cornford!' he scowled.

'You don't have to, William, I can say you wouldn't approve. It's no skin off my nose. I just saw an opportunity to find out what's going on there, since you're being kept in the dark. Mollard's keeping his cards real close, even from Cornford, so I don't think this is the end of it.'

'All right. Give him the bloody land. But not until you get that report. If it exists.'

'A copy of it,' Leo corrected.

Fuming, William lit his pipe. 'And all this came out of your enquiries about that damned tennis party. So this is why my wife missed the opening?'

'Ah,' Leo said, remembering. 'I think she has missed more than the opening. They've blackballed her.'

161

William sat bolt upright, stunned. 'They've what?' he shouted. 'They've blackballed my wife from a prissy little tennis club?'

'I'm afraid so,' Leo said, wilting.

'My wife!' William could hardly believe his ears. 'By Jesus! Get that title deed to Cornford. Give him anything he wants. And if he's got any more information about those bloody Mollards, the wife included, he can have a house on it for all I care. Keep at him. And not a word about this to Harriet. I'll tell her it was just an error. A mistake. Which the whole thing seems to be, a typical Mollard mess. I ought to go round and see the bugger right now.'

'Better to wait until you see this so-called report. It's not a government matter, we know that, so it must be some personal mix-up.'

'I'll wait then,' William growled. 'Mollard will keep.'

Christy justified his forthcoming misdeed, if it eventuated, by mulling over just how much he had suffered at the hands of Their Excellencies. As the aide, he was expected to be in uniform on official occasions but no allowance was provided for its upkeep; nor for the donations to charities that were too often begged from him by Mrs Mollard's friends. And as for his hours, he'd been unable to pin Mollard down to any set time, or day. It was a beck-and-call job, at their service any time the selfish pair required, like the lowliest of servants. When he did have time off, they thought nothing of sending a lackey to call him back for the most trivial things, even to play draughts with Mrs Mollard when she could find nothing else to do.

'And I have to let her win every second game,' he muttered to himself.

They seemed to think he should be grateful for the social life they provided, including being loaned as escort to frightful female friends of theirs who lacked partners. As if the aide were not entitled to a private life of his own.

So no. Christy had no bad conscience about this little arrangement with Oatley's clerk. Why should he? It was time he started to look out for himself. When Mollard's term was up, in a year or so, he might not renew, or he might not be reappointed, in which case he would have no further use for Christy. He'd have to hope the next Resident would keep him on.

Christy was envious of Leo Lavelle. Fancy a clerk being in a position to make decisions like that. He wasn't even permitted to change the position of his desk without Mollard's permission. And Lavelle was well dressed too. It was said that Oatley was not only hugely wealthy, but a generous man too. No doubt he paid his clerk well.

Come to think of it, Christy mused, what a change it would be to have a wealthy man in the Residency after years of the penny-pinching present gentleman. Maybe Oatley was thinking of seeking out this appointment, the very thought of which had sent Mollard into a funk.

He had refused to think of the arrangement with Oatley as a bribe; more as a service, a business arrangement that could do no harm, but now he saw it in a much better light. More sensibly. It would simply be a political move, essential for his own survival in the shifting sands of an aide's career. Essential to keep on the right side of the incumbent *and* the possible replacement.

A coastal steamer had hove to in the harbour during the night and it would be sure to be carrying mail, so when Mollard appeared for breakfast, his aide suggested that he might pop down and collect the Resident's mailbag, as he often did when he had time, only to be told a servant had already been sent.

Christy whistled to himself as he waited at the gate. Seems that Himself is just as keen to look at this lot as I am, he reflected.

As soon as the servant had laboured up the hill with the bag, Christy rushed it into his office, an alcove off the Resident's office. He unlocked it quickly and began sorting. Nothing unusual. Some departmental mail, catalogues, private letters, nothing bulky enough to be seen as a report. Disappointing. Very disappointing. Since Mollard always opened his own mail, and his wife's, Christy arranged them neatly on the blotter with the fine ivory letter opener and went in to advise the Resident.

'What? It's in? Why wasn't I advised? I've been waiting.'

'All on your desk, sir.'

'Dammit, bring it all here. No, wait a minute. I'll see to it myself!'

He slurped the rest of his coffee, dabbed at his lips with a napkin before throwing it down, and rushed out.

Christy stood waiting as his master slit open envelopes, tossing letters aside until he came to one which was only a note enclosed with a newspaper clipping.

'Ha!' Mollard said. 'Ha!' As if he'd collared a poacher. 'Let's have a look at this.'

He settled his glasses in place, and as he began to read the long printed article, his bulbous face took on shades of green and purple.

'By God!' he shouted, almost choking. 'By God!'

'Is there anything wrong, sir?'

'Wrong! What do you call wrong? This is libel! I had no idea it would be as bad as this! It's disgusting. It's libellous! Get me a drink of water!'

Christy rushed water to him and watched him gulp and splutter, until he pushed the glass away. 'That woman's a menace. I'll have the law on her, that's what I'll do.'

'What woman?' Christy asked, bursting with curiosity.

'Get Judah Forrest here, my solicitor. Get him here now! I want to see him right away.'

'Excuse me, sir. You have an appointment at the bank, sir, at ten, and it's nearly ten now.'

'Bugger the bank.'

'It's very important. If the bridging loan isn't signed and sealed today, public works will have to cease until the South Australian Government budget goes through.'

'Why do they have to leave everything to the last minute?' Mollard asked furiously.

Christy sighed in sympathy. 'You know how they are, sir.' Though Mollard had postponed the last two appointments.

'Well, I'd better go,' Mollard said reluctantly. 'But you get Forrest here just the same. Immediately. Have him sit here and wait until I get back.' He shoved the newspaper clipping into a drawer. 'And leave that there. I'll attend to it when I get back, by God I will. Oatley needn't think he can get at me through the back door.'

'The back door, sir?'

'Never mind. Find my wife. Isn't she supposed to attend a morning tea somewhere this morning?'

'Yes. With the ladies' committee for the new church on the Esplanade.' The building that Oatley is dead against, he almost said, but with his newfound attitude, decided it would be more politic to hold his tongue.

'Then get her! She can come with me.'

Christy thought they'd never leave. Mollard was in a vicious mood, yelling at his valet, tearing off a stiff collar that wouldn't sit right, shouting at his wife to get a move on . . .

'What's the matter with you?' she cried as he bundled her out the door to the waiting carriage.

'What's the matter with me?' he shouted. 'I'll tell you what's the matter with me. Oatley has libelled us, he's libelled the town, and why? So he can take over, that's why. Using his wife as a front.'

'I don't understand,' she said. 'Was Mother's telegram right? Has Harriet Oatley published awful things about us?'

Her husband shoved her bulk into the carriage. 'Get in! Get in! I'll tell you about it on the way. And shut up about it in front of Pastor Walters.'

Dutifully Christy waved them off, then sauntered back to the office, where he rushed over and tore open that drawer.

He grabbed the note and read:

'Dear Maggie and Larry . . .'

That made him grin. Marguerita and Lawrence, if you don't mind.

This is the piece in the paper I thought you ort to see. It's just terrable I think and everyone is reading it all the time and saying things that is why I thort you ort to know and sent you that telegram which cost me three shillings. Makes us wonder what is going on up there. Hope you are orlright.

    Your loving mother and in-law,
    Jenny Shilders.

Quickly Christy dropped the note. He'd seen Jenny's letters before – before 'Maggie' burned them. The clipping would be more interesting.

The headline, from page seven of the *West Australian* newspaper read:
LETTER FROM THE FAR NORTH.

He scanned it, eyes popping. 'Oh Lord. The woman is a menace,' he muttered. Good God! Sending this to a leading newspaper! There had to be more to it. Oatley was at the back of it for sure. In amongst all her prattle, there it was, clear as a bell. Oatley for Resident. No wonder Mollard was pooping his pants. Money talked. And influence. Oatley would have the station people as well as the local businessmen behind him, *and* he was sweet with the Chinks.

He grabbed a pen and began to write, copying the note and the article as fast as he could. But halfway through he stopped. Oatley would already know all this, even though it purported to have been written by Harriet Oatley.

But no. This was the 'report' Lavelle and Oatley had wanted and he was delivering. He wasn't expected to divine the political machinations behind it. He would simply deliver a copy, as requested, of a letter Mrs Oatley had written to the Perth newspaper. Her letter from the far north. Explaining that the Resident's mother-in-law had telegraphed a warning to him about it before posting it on. And this was why Mollard was highly insulted, and Mrs Oatley had been blackballed from the tennis club. Nothing to do with him. Not his problem. He had delivered his end of the bargain and would expect it to be honoured.

Christy began writing again, filling a couple of pages. When he'd finished, he returned the originals to the drawer, placed his copies in an envelope, and prepared to leave the office on his errand to summon the solicitor. He would make a short detour en route, to Oatley's office. Timing was all-important now. He had to have a guarantee of those deeds before he left Oatley's office or it would be too late. That same ship would be carrying back-copies of the *West Australian* newspaper, and the edition in question was bound to be among them. When they were distributed it would be too late. And, he sighed, poor Harriet wouldn't be the most popular lady in town.

'Goodness me, what a to-do!' he chortled as he flicked his blond hair back and set his top hat in place before departing the house.

Leo took the thin sealed envelope. 'Is this all?'

'It's enough,' Christy said gravely. 'It's a very serious matter. Now if you'd be so kind, I'd like to see the papers you promised.'

'They're here. I need your signature on this contract of sale.'

'And a receipt goes with it?'

'Yes.'

Christy signed with a flourish and watched as Leo slipped the papers into an envelope. 'Is that the title deed?'

'Yes. And the relevant forms. You can take them to the registrar and he'll issue a new title in your name.'

'Thank you.' Christy reached for them but Leo held back. 'Not so fast. The boss has to view your offering first.'

Christy was nervous. 'I'm in rather a hurry. I'm very busy today.'

'That's all right. Come back later.'

'Can't do that! Really, I thought this would be just a simple exchange . . .'

Leo looked past him. 'Here's the boss now.'

The next ten minutes went by so slowly, Christy could hardly control his nervousness. What if Oatley already knew of the letter? What if he decided the information didn't match up to the value of the payment? What if he just changed his mind? His head was swimming as he endured Oatley's cheerful morning greeting to the two men, watched him hang up his hat, take off his jacket and hand it to Leo, and finally take his place at his desk.

'Sit down, sit down,' he said to Christy, who would have preferred to stand but dared not disobey. He sat stiffly, all attention.

'I have to tell you,' Oatley said, 'that no matter what business disagreements or misunderstandings I might have with Mollard, these are matters for men. I will not tolerate insults aimed at my wife. I will not tolerate them. You are free to repeat that to the gentleman.'

Christy's hand fluttered to his sealed envelope now sitting on the blotter before Oatley. It seemed the only answer to that statement.

Leo stood by the window, his intense curiosity almost crackling in concert with Christy's taut nerves.

Oatley picked up the envelope addressed to him. 'This is your report, Mr Cornford?'

'Not exactly a report, sir. But you have your answers in there. And,' he blurted, anxious to please, 'Mr Mollard is referring the matter to his solicitor.'

'Is he now?' Oatley said comfortably. 'Let's see what he has to say for himself.'

He took out the note and the newspaper clipping. Read them quickly with no change of expression, then put them firmly on his desk and turned to Leo.

'Have you drawn up the necessary forms and contract for Mr Cornford?'

'Yes. They're all there.'

Christy held his breath.

'Good. Give them to him, Leo.'

The clerk stared, hesitated, still curious as to the mysterious contents of that slim envelope, but then, with an effort, he hurried to fetch the papers and hand them to Christy, who thanked him effusively and turned back to Oatley.

'Thank you, sir. You're very generous. I can't tell you what this means to me. I regret being the bearer of bad news.'

'It is not bad news, Mr Cornford. A storm in a teapot I daresay. But you did your part as requested. Good day, Mr Cornford.'

Christy almost bowed to him as he backed away, glad to be dismissed so quickly, marvelling that for such a minimum of effort he'd gained the right to place Esquire after his name, a man of property according to colonial lore, though back home in England it denoted gentry. Whatever, the solicitor could wait. He rushed over to the registrar's office in a corner of the crumbling government buildings, and staked his claim impatiently, wondering where else he might be able to feather his nest while jumping to attention for tight-fisted Mollard and his dreadful wife. Their Excellencies!

Leo had been working for William Oatley since the day he'd opened the office. And what a happy day that was. What great good fortune had come along just as he was despairing, ready to leave on the next ship, broke and disillusioned.

A fool he'd been, Leo readily admitted now, but he'd been seduced by the temptress of all, gold fever, leaving a good job in Perth, selling all his possessions to mount his own expedition from Darwin to the Pine Creek goldfields. Arriving too late. The rush was over. Never finding enough colour to fill more than a matchbox or two. Hanging on, he sold all his belongings and eventually his horse, as he descended into the purgatory of starvation and blazing heat well known to failed diggers, until he was forced to pull out, to walk the two hundred miles back to Darwin, where, thin and frail, he collapsed in the street and was taken in by a kindly Chinese family.

They fed him, cared for him, until they discovered that he had been trained for office work, and before long he was writing letters for them, filling in forms, attending to paperwork that was a great mystery to the Wong family. And they introduced him to their friend, William Oatley.

Right from the beginning they worked on a first-name basis. William was quite clear on the nature of the business he was establishing, but he was a cattleman, and Leo had been a Grade Three clerk in Perth's seat of finance, the West Australian Treasury Department.

'Champion!' William had said. 'You're for me, Leo. You watch the nuts and bolts and I'll see to the customers. We'll do all right, you and me.'

At first Leo had thought that this business was just a hobby for William, something to do while he overcame his grief for the wife who'd died. Everyone knew he'd taken it hard. So he made the best of it, working hard and loyally for his new friend and employer, expecting the good times to end with William deciding to go back to his cattle station. But it didn't happen. In time Leo realised that his boss was a real whiz when it came to setting up deals, whether they be worth a few hundred or a hundred thousand pounds. Money didn't impress William; he'd been born to it. A lovely man, he was honest and respectful, and, Leo eventually realised, a rolled-gold, dyed-in-the-wool patriot. He loved the Territory, his home territory, this wild, awful country, and often backed losing ventures with his own money to try to save them, to create employment, to keep folks from walking away in despair. As Leo often said, he could write a book about his mate William Oatley.

Clerk though he might be in name, Leo was paid more in a week than he'd received in a month in Perth, and William was generous with bonuses. And to Leo's great joy, William had stood up for him when he'd married Sue Tin Wong in the Chinese temple.

They went to Singapore for their honeymoon, and when they returned they were escorted by family and friends to a large bungalow in Bennet Street decorated with coloured streamers and bunting, bought for them as a wedding present by the conspirators, Sue's father and William Oatley.

Leo had found happiness in this odd frontier town, and though he missed the cool, sweet air of Perth, and the gracious living that he couldn't afford when he'd resided there, he was settled now. Darwin, with its cosmopolitan community, would do him.

While he waited and waited for William to make some comment about the contents of the pages that Christy had delivered, to say *something*, Leo pretended to be interested in what was going on in the almost deserted street out there, but for some reason he was thinking about Mrs Oatley. Harriet Oatley.

Leo couldn't take to her. She was a big girl, much taller than him, polite, respectful, even a little gushy to him. As one would be to a good servant. A valued servant. And she loved her husband, that was plain to see, she looked up to him as a wife should. But there was something hard about her. Brittle. She talked gaily, always enthusiastic about anything William proposed or mentioned. But sometimes Leo felt her enthusiasm was a trifle forced. Overdone.

Sue Tinny Wong, as he called his pretty wife, thought Leo was unkind to have such thoughts about Harriet Oatley. She even teased him that he was being old-man jealous of a wife intruding on his friendship with William.

'You give her little time,' she giggled. 'That Billy Chinn and Tom Ling frighten the poor English lady.'

'We're not English, we're Australian,' he said.

'Then why you talk English? You English all right,' she'd said, and would not be dissuaded.

In the end he couldn't stand this waiting any longer.

'Well?' he said, turning to William, who hadn't bothered to reread or even pick up again the contents of Cornford's envelope. 'Well? Did he deliver the goods? He must have, since you approved the payout. What's our Resident up to?'

William slid the note and newspaper cutting across the desk.

'You might as well read it. We'll all be reading it soon,' he said dully. 'I think I owe Mollard an apology, Leo. That's gonna hurt.'

'The heck you do,' Leo said, reaching over to scan the pages.

The article was headed: LETTER FROM THE FAR NORTH, by Mrs William Oatley in Darwin.

His expression was troubled as he read her comments about the town, but when he came to the uncomplimentary remarks about local society, the flimsy piece of newspaper shivered in his hands. Reading on, he gulped. She was downright scathing about the Resident, and Mrs Mollard, claiming her husband would be better suited to the job.

'Oh my!' was all he dared comment, though his mind was racing. The stupid woman! What could she hope to gain by flaunting such outrageous opinions? Gingerly he handed the note and the offending piece back to William, who took it and slid it quietly into a folder. His face was grey and cold as stone.

'What do we have on Caleb Moore's outstation?' he asked Leo, deliberately shutting off discussion of the letter, for which his clerk was grateful. He'd expected an explosion with Christy out of the way.

'He still wants to sell,' Leo replied. 'He wants to keep his head station and dispose of that section, which comprises half his land holdings, to raise the cash to keep going.'

'Will he be selling it stocked?'

'No. He writes that he is cutting back on herd numbers and moving as many as he can run on to the head station. I think water is the problem.'

'I suppose so. It's very dry that far south. But write to him again and see how he's fared over this wet season. He might have had better luck this year. I don't want to sell trouble to a buyer. He might be better served to borrow enough to divert some water courses and dig more substantial waterholes on the outstation.'

Leo wasn't convinced. 'He's deep into the bank already.'

'I know. But he could add the cost to the sale price. We would have a better chance of selling it for him. Caleb has never had much luck with outstation managers, that's half his trouble. He'll be better off pulling back, letting the outstation go.'

And so their morning went on. As usual, it seemed. Mail to be answered, contracts discussed, maps to be studied with assayers' reports, a meeting with Japanese pearlers and their translator.

William always went home for lunch. At midday he donned his jacket, picked up his hat and turned to Leo.

'I won't be in this afternoon,' he announced, and left the office.

Leo watched him go down the street, the long stride of the tall country man slower today, almost jerky, and he worried about him. But William waved cheerfully to a group of stockmen riding by, doffed his hat to two ladies and disappeared around the corner.

I wouldn't want to be in his house today, Leo thought, and went back to his desk to wait for Sue Tinny to bring his lunch.

'Oh my!' he said again.

Tom Ling was so fascinated with her quilt-making that at times Harriet felt she ought to tell him to go make his own, since, in truth, he was so much better at it than she. But she'd come to rely on him. Heaven alone knew where he managed to find them, but he'd turn up every so often with bags of material for her to use, some of them containing such gorgeous satins that they decided to separate them into Number One quilt, for the cotton cottage style, and Number Two quilt, which was to be far more elegant.

Harriet designed the cottage quilt, but Tom Ling brought her his own design for Number Two quilt, which had a peacock drawn in the centre.

'I can't do that!' she cried. 'It's too difficult.'

'Yes, missy, we make it, you see. Velly nice, you see. I cut, you sew, and making smaller stitches prease. Too big your sewing! Like sugar bag.'

Though they argued all the time about the size of the pieces and the placement of colours, Harriet enjoyed working with him.

At first she'd worked on the veranda, with a cane table in front of her and materials dumped about on chairs, but Tom Ling had brought some system to her endeavours, insisting she use a smooth lacquered table for cutting, and keep the pieces on his ornamental trays and materials ready in wicker baskets. While she worked at her table, he sat cross-legged on the floor, long pigtail hanging down his back, carefully studying and sorting pieces. And chattering the whole time, mostly to himself, of the worth of cloths to be honoured by inclusion in Number Two quilt.

On this day, when they were both busily occupied, Billy Chinn came out to view the proceedings and remind Tom Ling that the master would be home for lunch any minute. Tom put his work away carefully and sped inside.

For a while there, Harriet had been able to forget that nasty letter from old Maudie Hamilton, which she still hadn't mentioned to her husband and probably never would, but when he stormed in the front door, standing glaring at her, Mrs Hamilton was her first thought. He'd found out.

'In my study, madam,' he snapped, and strode through ahead of her.

Nervously, Harriet put down the section of Number One quilt she'd been working on, repacked her sewing box and followed him down the passage to his study on the other side of the house, tiptoeing on the polished floors as if by clattering across them she would make too much noise and upset him even further.

'My study, madam!' He'd never called her madam before, and certainly never ordered her to jump to attention like a servant. Regardless of that needling guilt, Harriet resented his rudeness, but she supposed it would be better to calm him down rather than make the situation worse. Whatever it was.

Furnished from his station homestead, William's study with its roll-top desk, heavy leather easy chairs, worn box ottoman and plain tallboys, was the only room in the house not furnished in oriental style, and Harriet now found it stuffy, smelling of stale cigars.

He was already sitting at his desk. 'Close the door.'

She did so, and walked over to him.

'Now, madam. What have you been up to? What possessed you to write a description of Darwin to the newspapers?'

Harriet stood gaping at him. 'To what?'

William could contain himself no longer. 'You bloody fool of a woman. Did you write this?'

He hurled some pages at her and she had to scrabble on the floor to pick them up. 'What is this?'

'You tell me.'

Harriet squinted at it, focused her eyes on the heading and began to read. She could feel the blood draining from her face and glanced over at William. His own usually tanned face was flaring red with anger and his white hair seemed to be almost standing on end. He was breathing in such angry gulps she thought he was about to have a heart attack.

Her voice came out a scream. 'No! God, no! I didn't do this. Who did this? William, no!' She began reading again, all the familiar words striking blow after blow. 'Oh my God! This was in the paper? What paper?'

'The *West Australian*,' he gritted. 'The leading Perth newspaper, as well you know.'

'But I didn't do this, William. Believe me, I did not.'

Harriet was crying but he had no sympathy for her.

'Your name is on that article. A Letter from the Far North, by Mrs William Oatley. Are you trying to tell me that you didn't pen that rubbish?'

'No,' she wept. 'I mean yes. But I wrote it to my mother, not to a newspaper. My God, William. I wouldn't do that. It was a private letter. To my mother. I'm sorry, I'm so sorry. Do you think anyone up here will see it?'

'They already have. Your stupidity has cost us a lucrative deal with that American firm; not just us, you and I, please note, but the Territory and a lot of people who needed employment. Not to mention your hurling insults willy-nilly . . .'

Harriet sank into a chair, cringing from his rage and from the obvious ramifications of her letter, taking refuge in a welter of tears.

Tom Ling knocked on the door. 'Billy say lunch on table, please.'

'Later!' William shouted. 'You wrote all that tripe to your mother?'

'Yes,' she whispered. 'But it was my business. My business!'

'There's a letter here for you. From her. It came this morning. By the feel of it, she's also sending the clipping. As have other people in Perth,' he added nastily. 'Some even giving advance notice by telegram, including Mrs Mollard's mother.'

'Oh, dear God,' Harriet whimpered, thinking of Maudie Hamilton. That was how she'd heard about the hat business. And she obviously had yet to read the rest. 'What does my mother say?'

'It's your letter, you read it.'

William passed the letter over to her and Harriet tore it open. Sure enough, the clipping fell out on to her skirt. Harriet didn't even bother to retrieve it. She looked up and appealed to William.

'It was a private letter. I swear. Someone must have got hold of it and put it in the paper.'

'There is no mention of it being a private letter, madam. The paper states it is an article, a newspaper piece, written by you.'

But Harriet was busy scanning the letter from her mother. 'Oh no! She did it! William, she says the letter was so interesting she showed it to the editor of the *West Australian* who said it was a . . . Oh God, I'm sorry . . . a rare insight into everyday life in the far north, and . . .'

'Go on,' William said icily.

'She was so thrilled she gave permission for him to publish it.'

'Let me see.'

William almost snatched the letter from her. Read it. Got up. Went to the door. Jerked it open. Yelled at Tom Ling to bring him a whisky. Sat down again. Read it again. Amazed.

'Your ridiculous mother seems to think we'll be proud as Punch to see your literary efforts in print.'

'Yes,' Harriet winced.

'And what's more, her friend the editor would be willing to pay for further contributions on the Far North front, from you, the correspondent.'

Harriet nodded. 'But I wouldn't, William. I wouldn't dream of it.'

'You wouldn't bloody want to,' he said savagely. 'Have you the faintest idea of the trouble you've caused?'

'I didn't mean to. It's not my fault. It was a private letter.'

'Private? What about *my* privacy? How dare you write, to anyone, that I have ambitions to become Resident of the Territory? I do not and never have and here it is in bloody print.'

'I just got carried away, William. That's all. I do believe you'd do a better job.'

'Aren't you listening? I never aspired to that job. Never!'

Tom Ling knocked and shuffled in, plainly nervous, with a small decanter of whisky, a covered jug of water, some tiny biscuits and two crystal glasses. He placed the tray on the top of the desk and turned away, hurrying out, not before casting a sorrowful glance towards Harriet, who was looking so distraught. Far from embarrassing her, Tom's unexpected solicitude gave her heart, told her that someone cared. Even if it was a servant. And she began to fight back.

'How many times do I have to tell you, William? I am sorrier than I can ever say that this has happened. I am abjectly and totally humiliated. Isn't that enough for you?'

'No, it's not. How can I explain that the ambition here is yours, not mine?'

'What do you mean?'

'You're ambitious and I never realised that before. You wanted me to be Resident so that you could find yourself at the top of the social heap here. And that accounts for your attacks on Mollard and his wife.'

'That's not true,' she shouted, watching as he poured himself a drink. 'And if you don't mind, I'd like a drink too. I'm thirsty. With whisky in it.'

'You don't drink whisky.'

'I'll have one now. Why shouldn't I?'

'By all means.' He gave her the whisky and water and though the sour taste surprised her, she gulped it down, refusing to react. Instead she turned on him.

'I still insist that my letter was private, but you know perfectly well that what I said about the Mollards was only repeating local talk. You don't like them, I know you don't.'

'But I have to deal with them. I do not go about publicly insulting them. On the other hand, I am reading between the lines. I can plainly see your ambitions, which unfortunately will be attributed to me. Because of your foolishness, and your mother's foolishness, I am now in a position of having to defend myself. And I am not sure how to go about this.'

'Why do you have to bother?' she asked angrily. 'You don't owe the Mollards anything. And if they find out about this—'

'Then what?' he charged her. 'Since they already know. They have known for quite a while, and are in possession of this newspaper clipping.' He picked it up and waved it at her.

Harriet crumpled. 'Oh William, I'm so sorry.'

But he continued, 'Your punishment began with your exclusion from the tennis club; mine is ongoing . . .'

Harriet couldn't stand it any longer. She jumped up and ran out of the room, back through the sitting room and out on to the veranda, where she stood for a minute, uncertain where to go. Then she fled out of the house, down the steps and across the road to the Esplanade park. She didn't stop until she was across the wiry grass, shoving through tea trees to the sand, where she fell down, weeping under a tall palm. Desperately sorry she'd ever written that letter, furious with her mother, appalled by William's lack of sympathy for her embarrassing situation. She felt violated, shockingly put upon, through no fault of her own, and through her sobs, she wondered how on earth she could ever face people again. At that thought she could feel a burning flush rising from her neck to overtake her face in the most awful blush she'd ever experienced. Even the back of her hands, usually so white and smooth, had taken on lumpy red blotches.

Miserably, Harriet looked out over the harbour at that cool, inviting blue sea. What a relief it would be to just plunge down there, to throw herself into the warm waters and swim out to the welcoming deep, to keep going and going until she could sink into oblivion.

For a long time she sat under the stiff, unbending palm that proffered little shade, with no hat to protect her from the sun, under a sky of relentless blue. No pity there for the forlorn woman; no pity anywhere.

Perspiration damped her armpits and trickled uncomfortably between her breasts, and her head ached. She would probably end up with sunstroke, she sighed, with a deep sob, but what did that matter? Still, she couldn't stay there forever. She had to do something. Go down to the sea or go home. Nowhere else to go. No one to turn to. She had no friends of her own. No one her own age. Only William's friends, and when they read that letter, how would they react? Maudie Hamilton was a good indication, that cranky old woman.

Determined now, Harriet took off her shoes and stockings – at least she was cooler, rid of them – and stood, looking over that lovely sea, but then fear grasped at her. Not fear of drowning, but of monsters. Hadn't she been told there were crocodiles in those waters? Salties, they were called, because they inhabited saltwater and were considered more dangerous than the freshwater animals. Harriet shuddered and sat down with a thump.

Tom Ling found her there. Tom Ling, agitated, fluttering about, full of concern for her, picking up the shoes and stockings.

'You come on home, missy. No good stay here. Mosquitoes, they bite, too many here. Make you sick. Bad joss this. You come on home.'

'What's the time?' she asked wearily.

'Lunch all over now but you never mind. Billy, he keep nice soup for you, plenty good, you feel better then.'

'Has Mr Oatley gone back to his office?'

Tom drew in his breath as if contemplating a fib, but thought better of it.

'Master he home, gone to lie down. You come in sitting room, nicee cool there, missy.' His dark eyes pleaded. 'You come with Tom Ling, eh? No good stay here. Evert'ing be all light. You see.'

'No. I can't go back.'

But he was persuasive. He wouldn't give up and he wouldn't go away, ignoring her angry instructions to leave her alone.

Finally he lifted her to her feet, and though she was much taller than he was, gave his support and assisted her stumbling passage back to the house, without even bothering to suggest that she put on her shoes and stockings. As she crossed the street, some men riding by stared at the barefoot, hatless woman leaning on the Chinaman in his black pyjama suit, but Harriet didn't care what they thought. She didn't care about anything any more.

It was easier to have the soup than argue with Tom, and to pick at the wee chicken dumplings Billy sent in, but after that Harriet declined tea and remained ensconced in a softly cushioned wicker chair, occasionally catching a glimpse of herself in the bevelled mirror which was the centre point of the delicate Japanese cabinet across the room. She was still barefoot, her face was already glowing with unaccustomed sunburn and her hair, having fallen loose from the pins that kept it upswept, was hanging down, but she made no move to tidy up, even to ask Tom Ling to bring her a brush and comb.

She just stayed there, trying not to think of anything, trying to rest, but the contents of the letter and its ramifications defeated her, bubbling up like water from a fountain that would not be turned off, until, eventually, William came in.

He seemed not to notice her bedraggled appearance.

'Well, madam, what have you got to say for yourself?'

'Nothing,' she said miserably. 'Nothing at all. I don't want to hear any more about it.'

'Well I'm afraid you must. I've decided the best thing to do is to make a clean breast of it. Bring it all to the forefront and get it over with.'

Harriet thought it was too much in the forefront already, but he could do what he liked, just leave her be. She listened dully as he outlined his plan.

'I shall make an appointment, insist on an appointment I suppose, with Mr and Mrs Mollard, and explain the circumstances of the publication of that letter, which was a breach of faith, beyond your control. Together we should be able to—'

'Together? You want me to go with you?'

'Of course. There's no other way. I will stand by you while you make your apologies, as I shall too.'

Harriet froze. 'I will not! It's not my fault. I will not apologise to them.'

'You will, Harriet. You must. It is unfortunate that they, and so many other people, have been made aware of the opinions you expressed. They have been publicly disparaged by your words, and it is your duty, and only good manners, for you to meet with them and apologise.'

She pushed her hair from her face and sat up defiantly. 'I will not! And what's the point? Even if I did apologise, you surely don't think they'll just simply forget about it? They'll never let me live it down.'

William drew up a chair and sat facing her. 'My point is courtesy. You owe them the courtesy of an apology no matter how difficult for you. Whatever follows is immaterial. You will have done the right thing.'

'No. I won't.'

He sighed. 'I believe you should, for the reason I have already stated. But there's another reason. Mollard has already taken the matter up with his solicitor.'

'How do you know that?' she asked anxiously.

'I know. Mollard is capable of charging you with libel. With having defamed him in print, and by your written words. I am trying to head that off, Harriet.'

'Have I defamed him, though?'

'If not, jolly close, but I'd rather not test it in court if you don't mind.'

'Court!' Harriet was shocked. 'I wouldn't have to go to court, would I?'

'I hope not. The immediate question is, will you come with me to see them? I need to arrange this as soon as possible.'

'I suppose I'll have to.'

'Good.' He patted her on the knee. 'Now you have a rest and I'll go into town and see what I can sort out.'

As he strode down the street William felt rather mean for frightening her like that, but it had been necessary. Mollard was a vindictive man, he'd want his pound of flesh, but court could be avoided. William was in no doubt that the fellow could be bought off.

★ ★ ★

For Harriet, it was the most humiliating experience of her life.

The meeting between the Oatleys and the Mollards was conducted in the drawing room at the Residency with Christy Cornford standing by, in uniform, like a sentry on guard, and the air was icy.

William was at his gracious best, even a little genial as he made his explanations, but the others were stiff and poker-faced.

When he'd finished, and had made his apologies, Mollard went to speak but his wife cut in, turning to Harriet in a fury.

'You ungrateful girl. You have been a guest in my house and this is how you repay me. I have never been so insulted. It is all very well for William to be making excuses but the damage has been done.' She raved on and on about the difficulties of administering a huge territory like this, about the personal affront to her husband, and went off on a tangent about how they had only taken this position out of the goodness of their hearts and how she missed her own family and friends and so forth until Mollard had to interrupt her.

'You haven't mentioned your ambitions, Oatley. Your wife makes it plain that you aspire to this high office.'

'That was a mistake,' Harriet tried to explain, but the Resident snapped at her:

'I was addressing your husband, madam.'

William's genial approach disappeared. 'Sir! Kindly do not use that tone to my wife. She is here out of courtesy and I expect the same from you. What was it you wanted to say, Harriet?'

Shaking, she apologised to them. Explained that it was all foolishness on her part, that she'd never meant to be unkind, and that at no time had William ever suggested he was interested in a government position of any sort. She was glad then that William had tutored her beforehand on the points to make, or she'd never have made it through this ordeal. In the end she was weeping, looking at her stony-faced hosts, hating them.

'I suppose we can put it down to immaturity,' Mrs Mollard said meanly, her pale eyes cold. 'You really ought to take a lead from your husband instead of inventing your own fanciful ideas.'

At that point Harriet saw some light on the horizon. It was clear that Mrs Mollard, for her own reasons, was not too angry with William, so she made the best of it.

'Yes, I'm so sorry. This has been extremely upsetting for William too. I hope you'll all accept my apologies.'

The Resident nodded. 'As you say. But it doesn't go far enough. I believe a letter of apology from Mrs Oatley should be published in the *West Australian* newspaper as well.'

'Not a good idea,' William drawled. 'It'll have everyone who didn't read the article scurrying to back-copies to see what the fuss is all about. It would only reflect back on you, sir, and we don't want that.'

Mollard was flustered. 'My solicitor seems to think that is the least that can be done.'

'Ah yes. But he's not a politician,' William said. 'He has no need to worry about public opinion, as do all government personages, unfortu-nately. I think the ladies have both had a miserable morning; we can have another talk about this later if you wish.' He looked to Mrs Mollard. 'Dear lady, my wife can do no more than ask for your kind acceptance of her apologies.'

Mrs Mollard shrugged. 'Very well.'

And that had to do. Christy Cornford escorted them out.

Harriet was surprised to hear Cornford, usually so priggish, remark to William that he was pleased it had all ended so calmly, and then wish her a smiling 'Good morning.'

But it didn't end there. After a private meeting with Mollard, who kept insisting that he ought to act on legal advice, William solved the problem by suggesting that the Resident might like to take a look at two fine Thoroughbred horses he was bringing to town from Weston's stud.

'A pair of beauties,' he said. 'Pedigree as long as your arm. You'd like them.'

When Mollard took possession of the horses, no money changed hands and William walked away grinning.

'That's horse-trading at its best,' he remarked to himself, well pleased with the deal.

Letters! Letters! Harriet thought she'd never write another one again after these weeks. She'd penned a scathing letter to her mother which produced a torrent of tearful apologies for the trouble she'd caused, one letter seeming insufficient, since they were still arriving. Her father, who had known nothing of the publication until it appeared in print, and was far from impressed, sent his sincerest apologies to William, and to the Resident and Mrs Mollard. He also advised William that he had reached agreement with the editor of the *West Australian* that the paper should print an apology to Mrs Oatley for publishing her letter without her permission. He enclosed a copy of the wording for William's approval before having it inserted in the paper, but William telegraphed him that it was not necessary.

'Best to forget the whole thing,' he told Harriet.

On the other hand, providing no comfort for Harriet, several towns-people, unknown to her, wrote congratulating her on her courage in giving a true account of the state of affairs in the Territory.

Lucy Hamilton, really more interested in Myles, and word of when he might be returning home, explained that Maudie Hamilton had recog-nised herself as one of the women given to wearing the old black felts. Lucy, not known for her tact, wrote that her aunt was 'as mad as a meataxe' so Harriet knew that she'd made a real enemy there. Maudie wasn't the type to be appeased by her penitence. And William still didn't know about her involvement; the bit about the hats had passed unnoticed.

As far as he was concerned everything was back to normal, his good humour restored. He even apologised for being rather hard on her, but Harriet clapped her hands over her ears.

'Apologies! Don't even mention the word. I'm sick of them.'

'This might help, then.' He produced a gold-embossed card which stated that Mrs William Oatley was an inaugural member of the Darwin Tennis Club. 'Apparently they decided to make it a mixed club since most of the lady members can't play anyway,' he laughed.

'A lot of good it will do me,' Harriet grumbled. 'I probably won't be able to find anyone to play with me.'

'Not true, my dear. Christy Cornford tells me he's delighted to hear you can play tennis, and is looking forward to seeing you on the court. He'll arrange your games.'

'Good Lord! Why would he do that?'

'I suppose he has already found it's not much fun playing with mugs.'

'Then you think I should go?'

'Of course. They're expecting you on Saturday. After that you have to start packing.'

'What for?' Harriet, still guilt-ridden, was startled.

'I have some business to do in Singapore, so I thought we might have a short holiday there as well, if you'd like to accompany me.'

'Oh, William, I'd love to.' She threw her arms about him in relief. 'You really are a wonderful man.'

'A fortunate man,' he smiled, kissing her.

Chapter Eleven

Myles Oatley resented that woman married to his father more than ever. He dreaded returning to Darwin and having to pay homage to a girl his own age as his stepmother. By the sound of his father's letters, they were still all lovey-dovey, and he cringed at the thought of staying with them and witnessing the pair of them together. An old man cavorting with a young girl. It was sickening.

But there was also his inheritance to think about. He was, or had been, the sole heir to the Oatley cattle stations and his father's very lucrative consultancy. William wrote about that all the time, pleased to keep his son informed of various property and mining deals that kept him busy, and of the success of negotiations that were netting him a fortune. Very properly too, he made sure that Myles was fully aware of his share portfolio, which was extensive, and growing in value, even seeking advice from Myles at times, and his son appreciated that. He knew it was William's way of keeping them close, and reading between the lines, a precaution in case his father fell ill, or worse, God forbid, died. He had the foresight to want to prepare his son to be able to take over in an emergency.

Surprisingly, though, in a recent letter, he had actually come out and said if anything happened to him, Myles would be well advised to carry on with the portfolio of shares but sell the agency, which was now fully established, since he was more suited to the land. And that was true. They both knew that Myles found office work boring.

But Myles wondered what had brought that on. Was the young wife wearing the old man down? Was she too much for him? Sexually and otherwise. How would he know from this distance? And even if he were there, what could he do about it? He wondered a lot of things about that woman. How much did she know about the business affairs? Did William confide in her too? And as for his inheritance, well . . . what then? Who would get what? William would never cut him out, but women like her could influence the will in their own interests.

He sighed, knowing he was in a freefall from full inheritance to a sharing that had become guesswork. He would have to go home soon. He really *wanted* to go home; life over here was beginning to pall.

At first it had been so much fun. He'd met Donald McBride from Sydney on the ship and they became firm friends, sharing rooms in Kensington and an obliging manservant who enjoyed looking after his two young bachelors. They walked about London for weeks, eager tourists, determined to see all the historic buildings they'd heard so much about, but then the invitations came rolling in, from people they'd met on the ship and as a consequence of cards they'd left on instructions from their fathers, so their routines changed from early-morning rising, to early-morning stumbling home to bed. The young bachelors were in great demand.

Myles found himself romancing Helena, a sweet English girl, but somehow, to Donald's amusement, he was 'appropriated' by Belle Symington, an urbane and madly attractive married woman who insisted on taking him under her wing, so that he should be seen in all the right places. Myles was totally smitten with her and they ended up having an affair, which lasted for months, until they bade fond farewells, since Belle was off to New York.

All this while Donald had kept on about his father's insistence that he bring home a nice Scottish girl, and it became a joke between the two of them whenever they heard a Scottish accent. Until the night he met Tess, whom he considered the fairest of them all, with her glowing red hair and ready wit. Tess was a Scottish lass from Edinburgh.

Donald and Tess fell madly in love, and Myles went with them to visit her parents, who lived in an ancient castle set in forbidding surrounds well north of the city. The family Dalgleish were welcoming but cool to the strangers their daughter had hauled home, until they learned that Donald's intentions were honourable, at which point everything changed. Donald loved the place, fascinated to find that half of the building, in need of repair, was closed down, but Myles was bored. And cold. Always cold, either in or out of the house.

Eventually he reminded Donald that they had planned to go south as the winter closed in, to roam around the shores of the Mediterranean, but Donald couldn't leave Tess, which was really no surprise to his friend. So Myles made his way back to London alone.

There he met a petite blonde actress named Shilly Shannon, who had a small part in one of Shaw's plays. Shilly, she informed him happily, was a stage name; it was really Shirley, but that was too mundane. She was eccentric, a bit mad, he thought, but excellent company and very sexy, and when the play ended she agreed to accompany him to Paris, where they had a high old time until Shilly started to talk about marriage.

When Myles wouldn't buy her the engagement ring she herself had chosen from a display in a shop window, Shilly made the most awful scene in the hotel lobby. That ended the relationship very smartly. Myles sent her up to her room, quietly paid the hotel bill, left her some money and raced off to catch a train for Marseilles.

Armed with introductions to family friends and acquaintances, he had a wonderful time travelling far south into Spain, then back to the French coast, trekking on down through Italy, at each point accepting advice on where he should go next. There was no shortage of company. English gentlemen, he found, were just as eager to travel about as he was, and

180

they knew more people than he did, in either private homes or out-of-the-way hotels. Eventually he arrived in Athens where a letter awaited him from Donald, insisting Myles return to Edinburgh for their Easter wedding and act as Donald's best man.

That duty done, Myles returned to the digs in Kensington, and though London's gaiety more than made up for the cold weather, he began to tire of the endless rounds of parties and balls, becoming thoroughly sick of constantly decking himself out in evening clothes.

'I think wandering about those French and Italian ports and cities, with something new to see all the time, has spoiled London for me,' he mused dismally.

When Donald and Tess came to London on their way home from their honeymoon, they were surprised to find he'd turned into a homebody, preferring to stay in by the fire with books and newspapers rather than make an effort to keep up with their friends on the busy social merry-go-round.

'You ought to go over to Berlin,' Donald told him. 'It's just marvellous. We had a great time there.'

But Tess disagreed. 'He ought to go home,' she said flatly. 'He's homesick.'

'I am not! I'm enjoying being here. I do go out when it suits me, especially to the theatre. I just find too many dances and soirées and stuff all rather aimless.'

'That's because you're not in the marriage market. You're missing that girl back home. What was her name? Lucy?'

'Do you still hear from her?' Donald asked.

'Of course.'

'Then I bet you're getting worried someone will snap her up while your back's turned,' Donald laughed.

'Don't be ridiculous. We have an arrangement.'

'Then I hope she's playing the field too,' Tess said sharply.

Myles grinned. 'Stop trying to make me feel guilty. It won't work. Lucy and I will marry, but we're too young yet.'

Donald whistled. 'That's a new tune. You showed me her letters; they sounded as if she'd already bought the wedding dress.'

Tess took off her shoes and warmed her feet by the fire. 'I've thought all along you were too young,' she said from her status of twenty-five years and with the benefit of her newly acquired matronly wisdom. 'But you ought to let her know.'

'Rot,' Donald said. 'He's twenty-one now. If I'd met you, my darling lassie, when I was twenty-one, I'd have married you jolly quickly in case you got away.'

'You need some fresh air, Myles,' Tess decided. 'Why don't you come back with us? You can join the hunt.'

'He'd hate it,' Donald said. 'Too constricting.'

Tess was surprised. 'You said you enjoyed it. You had a wonderful day.'

181

'I had to say that,' he laughed. 'Couldn't very well insult everyone. But it's just not our sort of riding. Myles and I were brought up on stations, where you ride for work, or to get someplace, not bowling along in little organised groups. You'll see when you come back with me. It's the distances, the wide-open spaces that are the fun.'

Myles cut short the discussion of his future plans. 'Let's go down to the Crown and Anchor. It's become my favourite pub. They serve good food there.'

Donald had hit a nerve. He refused to admit he was homesick, but he did miss the cattle station, the freedom and the excitement, and even, as Donald had said, the wide-open spaces. If he married Lucy, he'd be able to persuade his father to allow him to manage his station, Millford, and make that their home. William would never refuse the newly-weds, but as a single man he could only take his choice of working for Pop or for the present manager of Millford. Not that he'd mind either, and it was great to have a choice; he could divide his time between both stations, because one day he'd own them.

Or would he? With that Harriet person looking over his shoulder? He resented her more now; if it weren't for her, he'd be looking forward to going home.

When Donald and Tess left for Scotland, Myles felt bereft. He'd really enjoyed their company, felt comfortable with them. He considered visiting Berlin but then a bad cold kept him in for more than a week, further depressing him.

A cranky letter from Pop asking when he was coming home didn't help, and that other letter from William suggesting he sell the agency if anything happened to him was disconcerting.

He worried about Lucy, finding that absence, in his case, didn't make the heart grow fonder. Her letters no longer interested him. Maybe when he saw her again, the old, almost forgotten love they'd shared would be restored, but from here it seemed rather juvenile. Puppy love.

Nevertheless, he reminded himself, Lucy would inherit the substantial Hamilton holdings, which would offset looming losses to his new stepmother. 'The wicked stepmother,' he muttered bleakly. She was a good reason not to rush home.

He glanced at his calendar then dashed over to his writing desk to consult his diary. According to the dates they'd given him, the Flores family should be back in town by this, staying at the Savoy. That brightened his day. They were Argentinians, people he'd met first in London and again in Naples, and by chance again in Venice where they'd taken a villa and insisted he stay with them. Myles always enjoyed their company because they had so much in common; the Flores too had cattle stations, which they called *estancias* and ran big herds. The patriarch of this large group, Diego Flores, who was about seventy, had taken a shine to Myles when he discovered the Australian was in the same business, and enjoyed talking to him about his two great loves, horses and cattle, so the friendship was soon cemented.

The family group consisted of Diego's two sons and their wives, and an elderly lady, Diego's widowed sister. They were all older than Myles but they were warm, expansive people and he always felt relaxed with them.

He walked into the hushed elegance of the Savoy, London's newest and grandest hotel, intending to leave a message inviting the Flores to dine with him at the popular Russian restaurant, the Balalaika, on a date to suit their convenience, but Diego Flores came through the foyer and spotted him.

Heads turned as the tall, silver-haired man threw wide his arms. 'My boy! Myles! How good to see you! Where are you off to? You must join me for coffee! The others have all gone gallivanting.'

They adjourned to the tea room, which was awash with beautifully dressed ladies in large, gorgeous hats, and Diego beamed.

'A sight for sore eyes, this room,' he sighed. 'Always so beautiful.'

'The room?' Myles grinned.

'That too,' Diego laughed. 'Now, tell me about your travels. Where did you get to after Venice?'

They compared notes on their journeyings, and Myles remembered to extend his invitation, which was accepted enthusiastically.

'Excellent, my boy. We haven't been there yet. I believe the music is very romantic. Are we celebrating anything in particular?'

'No, not really, it's just that I will have to be wending my way home soon.'

'So will we. We've been footloose too long. I'm looking forward to going home.'

Myles wished he could say the same thing.

'Australia is so far. How do you go?'

'Down around South Africa and across the Great Southern Ocean.'

'A long way,' Diego said. 'I've got a better idea. Why don't you come with us? Via the Americas. Come to Buenos Aires, and then you can visit our ranch. You have to see Argentina, we have the best beef cattle in the world.'

'Next to ours,' Myles teased.

'You can decide. You will enjoy yourself, I promise you. Then we will put you on a ship for Sydney, down around the Cape, and you're nearly home.'

'On the wrong side of the continent.'

'But it wouldn't be difficult to get a ship to Darwin from Sydney?'

'No,' Myles agreed. He was beginning to waver. The voyage from Australia to London had been exciting but the return journey of months didn't hold out much interest for him. Why not take an alternative route? It would be marvellous to visit the Flores on their home ground and see how their cattle stations operated, since he'd heard so much about them. Why not? He was in no hurry.

'It is very kind of you to invite me, sir. But I wouldn't want to intrude.'

'Intrude? Never. You will be our guest. You have the chance to visit

183

Argentina; much easier to do so now, rather than have to go all that way another time.'

'When are you leaving?'

'About three weeks, I think. Juan is in charge of all that. I shall have him book another cabin for you.'

'There might not be one available.'

'We'll find out. So, will you come with us?'

'I would love to.'

'Good. That's settled. Now I might have another coffee.'

Diego's son, Juan, did have trouble finding a cabin for Myles on their ship, so Myles had a tentative booking on a ship leaving for Buenos Aires a few weeks later, but at the last minute Juan came rushing to his digs to tell Myles he'd managed to secure a single cabin for him, thanks to a cancellation, and so they could travel together after all. In two days' time.

For Myles it was a frantic two days, packing and farewelling friends and buying gifts to take home, wishing he hadn't left that to the last minute.

He wrote to his father, outlining his plans, cheerfully estimating that he would be home by Christmas. 'Three sea voyages,' he wrote, 'and a couple of months in South America add up to the rest of the year. You can't imagine how excited I am to have this opportunity to visit new lands on my way home.'

Completing his letter, Myles gave his next address, in Buenos Aires, and assured his father of his enduring affection, but once again made no mention of Mrs Oatley.

Three days after he sailed, an urgent cable from William arrived at his London address. The new occupant marked it as 'Person not known' and handed it back to the delivery boy.

William took a suite at Raffles Hotel this time, because he had several proposed ventures to discuss with Chinese and Malay businessmen and they would take up long hours of discussions. It would be more convenient for Harriet at the hotel and not as lonely as being left in a guest house on her own, since the hotel catered mainly for the English-speaking community, many of whom were civil servants or plantation-owners from Malaya, or local identities who liked to congregate there.

As soon as they arrived, William had a word with the manager, discovering that several people known to him were staying in the hotel. He arranged for two couples to dine with them so that he could introduce them to Harriet, asking them, on the quiet, if they would be kind enough to keep an eye on his wife, who might find herself at a loose end on her own, and they happily obliged.

Harriet was delighted to find these strangers so hospitable, especially Lena and Leslie Hopetoun, who were on leave from Malaya where Leslie was, they casually told her, secretary and right-hand man to a

Malay prince. That impressed Harriet so much, she was anxiously shy with them at first, but Lena soon overcame that, insisting on taking her shopping.

'I don't really need anything,' Harriet tried to explain. 'Darwin isn't that sort of town. I don't need much there at all.' Except boring white dresses, she thought, but never dared mention that again, even as far away as Singapore.

'Nonsense! We have to shop,' Lena, who seemed to have money to burn, insisted gaily. 'William won't mind. It's expected of us.'

So, carried along by Lena's enthusiasm, they bought baubles from street stalls, as well as more expensive pieces from the myriad jewellery stores lurking in quiet corners, proceeding on to larger stores with such magnificent displays of merchandise that they took Harriet's breath away. Then they went to lunch at a tennis club, so superbly fitted out that Harriet was ashamed to mention the club in Darwin, that had now made its home in the back room of Mechanics Hall, next door to the courts.

Leslie met them there and they joined a large table of people bent on having a good time. So much so that they made Harriet nervous. They were noisy, laughing uproariously as jokes sped around the long table, and they drank a lot even though the last course had passed by, to be replaced by requests for more cheeses and peeled fruits, and more wine. Then there were cheers when a three-piece band began playing.

Harriet was stunned to discover it was now four o'clock and a tea dance had begun, and no one looked like leaving. By this, slightly tiddly, she was enjoying herself with this smart, sophisticated crowd but was afraid to stay longer in case William had come back to the hotel and found himself faced with all those things his wife had bought and Lena had merrily ordered to be sent to their room.

In the end, she had to insist on leaving, though her new friends were calling her Cinderella, so Leslie put her in a rickshaw and sent her on her way.

William arrived at their suite just a few minutes after her, in a very good mood. His meetings had gone well and far from being put out, he was interested in seeing the results of her shopping expedition, happily assisting her with opening all the parcels. Apart from the cheap market pieces, she'd bought expensive things, blaming Lena, but he laughed as they were all spread out for his perusal. Matching gold fob watches, shaped like shells, his and hers; ruby earrings; more lengths of gorgeous silks . . .

'We've got enough here to make curtains,' Harriet moaned.

Six Fuji silk shirts for William. He liked them. Ladies' and gents' Panama hats that could be crushed and would spring back into shape. Carved animals for bookends, carved lamp bases and brilliant shades, silk embroidered footstools . . . all sorts of things.

'We can send them back,' Harriet said nervously, but William wasn't concerned.

'No. We'll keep what we want. Lena knows her onions. Everything

185

here is very good quality, worth a lot more anywhere else. The rest will serve as handy gifts, don't worry about it. I'll call a servant to pack up the heavier stuff for us, so that we can ship it home. The main thing is, did you enjoy yourself?'

'Apart from trying to buy up the town, yes. They are nice people. We went to the tennis club for lunch.'

'Did you? I've never had the time to go there. But you seem to have had a splendid day. I must thank Lena and Leslie. Jolly good of them.'

But Lena wasn't finished. Harriet had become her protégée. When she wasn't dragging her around shops, she took her to visit friends at their homes, where morning tea often meant gin concoctions which Harriet intended to decline, but it was hot, always so hot, even though most of the houses and public rooms in the hotels had punkahs, and they were thirst-quenching.

'What do you mean, you don't have punkahs?' Lena and her lady friends asked Harriet, astonished. 'Isn't it hot where you live? It has to be.'

'Yes, very hot. But it's a new town. Not too many amenities, you understand. We don't have electricity yet.'

Lena looked over to the little Malayan boy who was operating her friend's punkah. 'You don't need electricity. You have natives there, don't you?'

'Yes, but . . .'

The next night, when William came home, Harriet broke the news to him that Lena and Leslie had bought them a present. An elaborate punkah for their home, and it was already parcelled up for them in the hotel luggage room, waiting for them to collect it.

William laughed until the tears ran. 'A punkah in Darwin! Oh my dear. You mustn't hurt their feelings. I hope you accepted it graciously. I will thank them myself as well. But could you imagine Tom Ling's face if we sat him in a corner and tied his big toe to a punkah? I think he'd weep.' He turned to Harriet. 'They won't know if we give it away, though, will they?'

'Who would want it?'

'Our Resident and his missus, my dear. Are you sure it's a good one?'

'Lena said it's the very best. She uses them in Malaya.'

'Excellent,' William said with a broad grin. 'The perfect gift for their so-called Excellencies. Well done, Harriet. Well done.'

But then he broke the news to her that he would have to go north into Malaya to have talks with the representatives of a certain prince and possibly the prince himself.

'Leslie's prince?'

'Oh no. He's small-time compared to this fellow and his dad. They have wealth that fairy tales are made of and I've got them interested in investing in the copper mines that Garfield Perdoe passed on. With the sort of funds they can command, it could mean not only opening up the existing copper mines, but invaluable searches for silver and zinc and even more gold. We still have no idea what riches the Territory is hiding from us. It's barely explored.'

Harriet was at a loss. 'I don't understand. If they're so wealthy, why would they bother? Haven't they got enough already?'

'More than enough. Billions of pounds, in our money. But what do you do with it? You don't fritter it away. You have your descendants to think of, they have to have thrones of solid gold, and armies of servants and harems full of the most beautiful women in the world . . .'

'What?'

'Oh yes. That's why protocol means you stay here, if you don't mind. I'm invited to stay in the palace of our Sun King but told by my English advisers not to take my wife because women don't rate too highly.'

'You mean I'd be in the way?'

'Extremely so,' he said.

'What a shame. I'd love to see how they live.'

'Few European women ever do. I hope you don't mind waiting here for me. I'll tell you all about it when I get back.'

'No. I'm disappointed, naturally, but I wouldn't want to cause an incident.'

'Well, I really am sorry about this, Harriet, but their investments are important, even though I'm led to believe any big outlays will come through a London bank, and the company name will be British.'

'Why?'

'Who knows what complicated avenues these fellows choose to follow, but the crux of it is, the source is right there in Prince Abu Selong's palace and I have the opportunity to put my small case. They invest worldwide, by the million, so I'm not asking a lot, and I have facts and figures on my side.'

'Why can't I stay somewhere nearby, and just come to the palace for a quick visit?'

'Not possible, I'd lose face. And if you stayed at the palace – which they would never refuse, by the way – you'd be shoved off behind veils and run the risk of insulting a palace favourite by not knowing the rules. My Chinese friends, brokers, are advising me very carefully here, so I have to watch my step.'

'I see,' Harriet said tartly. 'And that probably means your prince will be trotting out dancing girls for your amusement while you're there.'

'Now don't be silly,' William said. 'I'll be there on business.'

'I was only joking. You go, I'll be quite all right here. I might even manage to do a little exploring on my own, without being dragged into shops.'

'Yes, but don't go too far into the native quarters and only take rickshaws provided by the hotel.'

Harriet had two quiet days to herself before Lena came looking for her, apologising for her absence, explaining with shrieks of laughter that they'd been to a dinner party that had lasted two whole days.

187

Harriet blinked. 'How could that be?'

'Simple. It was at the Sinclairs'. Everyone was having such fun that no one got around to leaving. It just went on and on.'

Harriet was beginning to realise that William didn't really know these people well at all.

'But now,' Lena said, 'we have got to get serious. How do you like my new suit?'

Harriet had already been admiring the pale blue tailored suit with its embroidered jacket over a neat blouse and long gored skirt. 'It's beautiful. Unusual. Is that the latest fashion?'

'For day wear, yes. I've found the most marvellous dressmaker and that's where we're going this morning.'

'What are you having made?'

'I'm not having anything made. You are. You simply can't go about in those heavy draped skirts any more, and darling, I have to tell you, those balloon sleeves you wear are quite out.'

'I thought they were very fashionable. They were back home in Darwin.'

'Oh no. All you need is a little puff of a sleeve like this one, for softness. And no more gatherings and overskirts over the hips. Slim styles are in, and bell skirts. It's all to do with the waist, you see. Wasp waists they call them. You have to tighten up your corset to look right.'

Soon Harriet found herself at the mercy of the dressmaker, a French woman named Mimi who had a half-dozen little Chinese ladies sewing busily in an alcove at the rear of her shop. The way she and Lena talked about Harriet's taste in clothes, as if she were not present, intimidated Harriet to such an extent that she ended up ordering a completely new wardrobe, lawns and linens and silks in lovely pastel shades, and oceans of lace.

'The clothes she wears are too ageing. So out of date,' Lena said, approving now. 'These are much smarter – very chic!'

'Yes. Out of date, those dark colours,' Mimi agreed. 'Madam is so tall, so beautiful, these colours will be magnificent on her. But that hair . . . too much hair.'

Harriet's pleasure at the compliments gave her confidence. 'That can't be helped, it's very long.'

'Too long, madam. All rolled up like that makes you look too matronly. Those fat rolls give you a little face. You have fine features buried there. You must cut your hair.'

'She's right!' Lena cried, pulling off her hat to demonstrate that her own soft blonde hair was really only shoulder length, pinned up into curls.

'But my hair is straight,' Harriet wailed. 'I wouldn't know what to do with short hair.'

'Then you have it smooth,' Lena told her brightly, 'just not as thick as a bird's nest. Or you could tong it. My maid often tongs my hair for me.'

Harriet didn't dare tell these smart women that she didn't have a maid, nor could she argue, for fear of hearing more about being so old-fashioned, when they hustled her off to a ladies' hair stylist. Such a person was nonexistent in Darwin. They only had a barber.

Harriet almost wept as her waist-long hair was shorn to shoulder length and strewn about the floor until a servant rushed in and swept it away, her lovely shiny hair, as if it were just so much trash. Then the woman dressing her hair took to it with a brush and comb and those sharp scissors again, flicking it into place so that it was smoothly parted at the front and drawn up into rolls at the crown.

'Good thick hair, easy to do now,' the hairstylist said, admiring her work. 'You come back to me, madam, before you go home so that I can show you how to do this. It isn't much different from your other style except you no longer have that heavy roll at the front.'

But Harriet was staring in the mirror. She'd only ever had two hairstyles – plaits, and the 'matronly' full style that her mother wore; now she looked a different person, fresher, brighter, and her eyes seemed larger. She smiled, delighted.

'I told you so,' Lena crowed. 'Just marvellous. You're a new person.' She grabbed a hat from a stand nearby, a white lace confection, boater style, with pink feathers, and placed it on Harriet's head.

'Now isn't that just lovely? You'd never have been able to fit it on your head on top of all that other hair.'

'It's beautiful,' Harriet said, amazed.

'Is it for sale?' Lena asked.

'Yes, madam.'

'Then she'll have it. It'll be superb with her pink silk afternoon dress. Send it to Mrs Oatley at Raffles.'

Harriet was dazed as they strolled back to the hotel, ashamed of her old-fashioned bulky taffeta but thrilled with the new hairstyle hidden underneath her large hat.

'Isn't this fun?' Lena said. 'Tomorrow we'll buy you some new hats.'

Three days later the dresses arrived and Lena had to call the maid to string Harriet into the new corsets that, of course, Lena had insisted she buy.

But the gowns were breathtaking: one tailored suit, not unlike Lena's but even smarter, Harriet thought, trying it on; one beautiful evening dress in yellow embroidered silk with a softly flowing skirt that flared out at the hem, and a shawl to match; while the others, eminently suitable for any occasion in the tropics except for the really formal, were a dream of style, softened by romantic flounces and not a white gown among them.

The maid was in awe. 'Madam, I've never seen such pretty dresses.'

'Neither have I,' Harriet admitted.

Lena and Leslie took her to the races, another first for Harriet, and when Leslie saw her, he was astonished.

'My, you do look lovely, Harriet.'

She thought he'd been tutored by his wife to say that, but at the Turf

Club she found herself the centre of attention, with young gentlemen eager to squire her about and explain the intricacies of betting. Two of them even asked if they could escort her about Singapore, or perhaps take her to dine, possibly not noticing her wedding ring. Blushing, she refused politely, noticing Lena giggling in the background.

No one bothered to change; she was simply swept along by Lena and her 'crowd' after the races to a party at someone's house on a beach. More drinks were served, and an informal buffet dinner set in the dining room, while floor rugs were rolled up in another room to allow for dancing to music provided by a pianist at a grand piano and an enthusiastic violinist.

Harriet had never encountered such informality, nor a party as gay as this, nor such friendly people, and she had a wonderful time. This was a far cry from the Singapore she'd come to know on her honeymoon – the quiet house, the stiff Chinese banquets. And a world away from dull old Darwin.

William was furious. The new afternoon dress she was wearing was of no interest to him.

As soon as he'd walked in the door he'd taken her in his arms, happy to be back with her again.

'I've missed you so much, my dear, and I've had such difficulty with our clients. Those fellows are hard to deal with . . . But what about you? Have you had a nice time?'

He stood back, looking at her. 'You look different. You seem to have . . .' He reached out and touched her hair at the crown.

'What's happened here?' he asked, bewildered. 'Your hair?'

'I had it cut,' she smiled, turning about so he could admire the new style. 'Doesn't it look nice? And it's so much cooler.'

'You what?' He took her by the shoulders, holding her still. 'You've cut off your beautiful hair! How could you do such a thing without asking me? Your lovely hair. Why on earth would you do that?'

'Because it looks much better now,' she said, disappointed.

'It doesn't look better. You look like a schoolgirl. Undo it, let me see what's left.'

She unpinned her hair nervously and he stared.

'Ah no, your crowning glory. It's nothing now and it used to look so lovely when it was down, spreading over your shoulders.'

'Well it's done now,' she said, in an attempt at cheerfulness.

'So I see. But ruined, you mean. A damned stupid thing to do.'

'The hair stylist said I looked too matronly with that old style,' she wailed.

'And what's wrong with that? You're a married woman, not some tizzy vamp.'

'I am not a tizzy vamp! And since when do I have to ask permission to cut my own hair? My hair, not yours. You've just come home in a bad mood and you're taking it out on me. Everyone says it looks charming.'

'Do they? And who are these flatterers?'

'Oh, never mind. It's cut and that's that. We have to dress for dinner.'

'We do not, we will dine up here. I have to get used to this. How long will it take to grow back?'

'Not in time for breakfast,' she snapped and rushed into the bedroom, slamming the door behind her.

It had never occurred to her that he would object, nor that he would find the style unbecoming. She tried to see his point of view, but could not. So he loved long hair, and was disappointed that she'd cut it, but that was no reason to fly off the handle and insult her.

She stared at herself in the mirror, lifting the loose strands up again. It did look good. That woman had shown her how to tong it if she wanted curls, and also advised her to keep the 'mouse', the rope of fake hair that she'd used to pin the heavier hair into place, to give extra thickness to upswept shorter hair, and she could manage it now in several styles. She was no longer stuck with that big wide hairdo, like wearing a hat all the time, or having to pull her hair into a fat bun, the alternative style for matronly women.

Matronly! she thought nastily. Of course. He doesn't want me to look my age, he wants me to look older, closer to his age. That's what this is about. His ego. And he was the flatterer, telling me how nice I always looked in that funny hairstyle and those frumpy dresses. Like a mountain. No wonder she'd felt so out of place with those petite Chinese ladies on their first trip to Singapore. She wished she'd met Lena and her smart friends then. The gowns she had now, and would continue to have made, were so slim and elegant, she couldn't wait to show them off.

In Darwin?

Oh God. The gorgeous sari silks she'd bought on their honeymoon were still in the camphor chest, untouched, because she'd never been able to imagine designs for them, and now they were no use. Wasted. Too bright. And her new gowns, though marvellously fashionable, wouldn't look right in Darwin either.

Harriet pouted at the mirror. 'Who cares? I'll wear whatever I choose. I'm sick of being bossed around. And he'll get over the haircut. He'll have to.'

Maggie Mollard was thrilled with the punkah, though not necessarily with the gift-givers, but they had to be tolerated.

'That doesn't mean I'll ever forgive that woman,' she warned her husband. 'We got along so well with William until she turned up on the scene.'

'You did,' Lawrence muttered from behind his newspaper. Oatley had always been a pain in the neck, like the rest of those rich cattlemen out there, wielding power like axe handles, barely able to accept that real power resided right here. Not for one minute had Mollard believed the excuse that Oatley's girlie wife had invented the bit about Oatley's ambition to run the Territory, to get his feet under this table, but diplomacy had urged acceptance of their pathetic apologies. Lawrence prided himself on his diplomatic skills. And, he mused, they surely paid off. Brought Oatley to his knees with the peace offering of those horses. It must have hurt him to part with a fine pair like that . . .

'I still think she married him for his money,' Maggie was saying. 'No fool like an old fool. They say he's mad about her, but I can't see why. I find her dull really. They're coming tonight, you know.'

'Who are?'

'The Oatleys. That's why I had to get the punkah up rather than give them something else to complain about. But it does look fine in the drawing room and I've found a black kid to keep it in motion.'

'If he doesn't fall asleep.'

'I've warned him it's the whip if that happens. But it really does create a breeze. What a pity the ceiling is too high in the great hall. Are you sure you couldn't have some put in there?'

But Lawrence was glaring at a small piece in the paper mentioning news of the reopening of negotiations regarding certain large copper deposits in the Territory.

'. . . The Minister for Mines, in Adelaide, yesterday announced that the British exploration company Ungers and Stockdale had applied for mining rights and were planning considerable investment in the area . . .'

He threw down the paper and shouted for Christy.

'What's this about copper mining? Did you read that?'

'Yes, sir.'

'Why wasn't I informed? Who are these Ungers and Stockdale? Never heard of them. Send a wire to the Minister immediately requiring an explanation. No, send him my greetings and request further advice. Remind him that I am particularly well informed on the subject of copper deposits in this area. That will do for now. Get on it right away.'

As usual with William, when his temper got the better of him he erupted but soon calmed down, and he never dwelled on the matter. He did apologise to Harriet, explaining that his surprise and disappointment at finding she had cut her lovely hair had caused him to overreact, but often now she saw him looking mournfully at her shortened hair, when it was down, and that really irritated her, but she said nothing, rather than start the row again.

They had been invited to a soirée at the Residency, and though William wasn't very interested, Harriet was excited. This would give her a chance to show off her smart new clothes. But first, she decided, rather than push her luck, it would be better not to surprise him.

First she brought out the lace hat with the pink feathers.

'It's very pretty,' he smiled. 'Very pretty.'

Then came the soft georgette, nipped in at the waist, with a low-cut satin-edged frill across the bodice and deep flounces at the hem.

'Do you like this gown?'

He nodded approval. 'Oh yes, indeed. It's very feminine, dear.'

192

She had to call him to help her with her corset.

'Pull the strings tighter.'

'It seems to be tight already,' he worried. 'Do you think it's too small for you?'

'No. It has to be tight to stay firm. I don't want it slipping about,' she told him, trying not to gasp.

'All right, if you say so.' He was laughing by the time he finished, his large hands finding it difficult to tie the final bow. But as she turned, he raised his eyebrows appreciatively.

'My word, it certainly thrusts up the bosoms, doesn't it? They're looking splendid right now. I can't resist . . .'

Harriet was delighted at the effect this was having on him as he kissed the full breasts that were almost toppling out of the corset.

When she was dressed, the pretty hat perched sweetly on her curled hair, she presented herself to him, and William sighed.

'You do look lovely, my darling. The dress suits you.'

'Even though it's pink?'

'What?'

'Most ladies up here stick to white for coolness.'

William grinned, admiring her. 'So I believe. But your dress looks as cool as ice to me. An absolute picture, ideal for a hot evening like this.'

Mrs Mollard saw the hat from her drawing room window, glimpsed it coming down the path through the greenery. Saw it again in the crowds milling around on the terrace, waiting their turn for admittance to the Residency soirée, and loved it. Feathery fine lace, almost sheer, shaped like a wide-brimmed boater.

As she welcomed her guests she wondered idly how lace could be kept so stiff. Fine wire, probably. But the pink feathers, gracefully fluffed by the crown, gave it just the right finishing touch, real style. Rare for here. The owner must be one of the English ladies connected with the gentlemen from the Cable Company. Maggie adored hats, and she simply had to have one like it. She would enquire as to its origin.

But then she was confronted by it. Affronted, as she greeted Harriet Oatley, her smile freezing to a thin, cold line. Where had that horsy girl found a hat like that?

William was smiling. 'Ah, Mrs Mollard, the punkah! You found a use for it. Is it working all right?'

'Yes. Thank you. Quite satisfactory.' She followed his gaze to the black boy in livery who was gazing with awe at the finery of her guests, forgetting to keep the thing moving, and jerked her head to Christy Cornford to remind him of his duty.

The Resident himself was also distracted from his duty by having to welcome that snake-in-the-grass Oatley, whom he now knew was at the back of plans by Ungers and Stockdale to develop those copper mines. And not only plans; apparently they'd already concluded an agreement for a substantial government subsidy and deposited ten thousand pounds

193

in the Bank of Adelaide as an expression of good faith. Mining would start with no reference to him at all. A bloody outrage.

Sourly he nodded, with one word of acknowledgement to his guest. 'Oatley.'

But there were others in the line watching, and he couldn't afford any more adverse gossip, so he tried to redeem himself by turning to the wife, genuinely surprised that the tall girl did look rather fetching in a pretty hat and sweet dress.

'My dear. How charming you look this evening.'

'Thank you, sir,' she responded as they passed on into the drawing room.

Maggie almost choked at that. 'Did you see what she's got on?' she hissed.

'What?'

'That dress,' she whispered. 'It's pink!'

'What? Eh?'

'Oh, never mind,' she snorted.

Behind their fans, Maggie and her lady friends glared at Harriet Oatley.

'She simply doesn't know the form, never will.'

'But that dress, it belongs in the bedroom!'

'I call it suggestive, what there is of it. More flounce than gown.'

'You ought to have a word with her, Maggie.'

'Why should I? Let her make a fool of herself. I'm not her keeper. But pink? What next? Lightning blue? Grass green?'

Mina Forrest, wife of the Resident's solicitor, held her tongue. She couldn't get over the transformation of dowdy Harriet Oatley. She looked so elegant and self-assured. And that lovely gown wasn't suggestive, as these women were saying, it was stylish. She wondered why Darwin women were so set on wearing white. Mina had a lovely ice-green dress her mother had sent her from Sydney, that she'd never dared wear here, but now . . . why not?

She wished she had the courage to go over and talk to Harriet. Some other time perhaps, when she wasn't so conspicuous. Not that Harriet was isolated. The older men, including William Oatley, had gravitated to a corner to discuss their own interests, but the young men were circulating, mostly around Harriet.

Christy Cornford, too, was surprised. And impressed. The young Mrs Oatley was really stepping out in style this evening. He'd be willing to bet she'd caught up with the smart set in Singapore, which Christy knew well, and learned a few things. How many? he wondered knowingly. Singapore, the closest city to Darwin, was his only respite from this God-awful town. He closed in on Harriet, his excellent tennis partner, with a new resolve. He had already been surprised to notice that though she was shy, she could also reveal flashes of quick wit, but now the girl was reinventing herself.

Well done, he mused. Now we see bosoms like cream and a waist I could encircle with my hands. And the uniform bushy hair has been disposed of. Looks a picture, she does.

194

Christy was never obvious like the raw youths gaping at the décolletage and engaging her in small talk. He simply hovered, respectfully, finding a quiet time to tell her how charming she looked, enjoying her grateful smile, noting that the new-found stylishness could not really hide her insecurity. What was she doing married to old Oatley anyway? Money, they said. And why not?

He caught sight of himself in a mirror and flicked a strand of blond hair from his forehead. He was thirty and he kept himself in good nick. That made him a damn sight better proposition for this lady than the old man. Except for money. He guided her over to meet the latest arrivals in town, a fellow called Cochrane and his wife. Cochrane was a bookkeeper for the Cable Company, brought in to replace someone who'd gone on leave. They both looked so hot and uncomfortable, he couldn't resist telling them, casually, that this was winter. The Cable Company had trouble keeping staff in this place.

He glanced across at Oatley, over there drinking whisky with his mates, seemingly unconcerned about his wife. Very sure of himself, Christy mused. The self-assurance born of wealth.

Arriving to take up this appointment, Christy had soon discovered to his amazement that there were families living out the back of beyond, as he called it, of great wealth.

He'd given this matter a lot of thought. A man marrying into one of these families would also be marrying into a network of fortunes back east. The colonial aristocracy. Such as it was.

But it was easier said than done. Christy, a widower after only four years of marriage, and childless, had only taken this appointment in desperation, finding little else on offer in the way of a respectable situation. He had slipped into the job as aide to the Resident with ease, finding his duties undemanding, though his employers were lacking in civility.

He had put his best foot forward to win favour with the pastoralists, in their company a charming gentleman and amiable guest, and though he had visited several stations with Mollard, and come to know several families as well, he'd never had a chance to form friendships with any of the eligible daughters he'd met. The families were close-knit – worse than Italians, he'd decided – keeping the girls under paternal wings, off limits to acquaintances like the Resident's aide. Except for summer holidays, he reminded himself, when the girls were in town looking for company. This year he really ought to take more notice of them.

He sighed, rallying to find a chair for Mrs Oatley, who had decided to sit with the Cochranes. But Mrs Mollard was glaring at him, beckoning him in that imperious way of hers as if he were the boots, so he hurried over to her.

'You are not employed to fuss over that hussy. The punch bowl is empty, get it refilled.'

'Certainly, madam.'

★ ★ ★

Harriet liked to think back on that evening. She had really enjoyed herself, and William had been proud of her, telling her how some of his gentlemen friends had commented on how pretty she looked. The fuss over her hair had been put to rest, but she hadn't gained any new friends. If anything, the ladies were even more standoffish. It was flattering, though, to find that Christy Cornford approved of her new image.

He was quite gallant with her at the tennis club, always finding somewhere for her to sit between games, chatting with her and bringing her refreshments, but then Harriet knew he liked to win. He partnered her in the mixed doubles and their names had been at the top of the ladder for weeks. So there was probably a bit of self-interest in his attentions; not that Harriet minded.

They had something else in common besides tennis. Harriet loved to talk to him about Singapore; he knew the hotels and the clubs and the fashionable eateries.

He seemed a rather lonely man – a widower, she discovered – and she thought she should invite him to dine with them. He'd be pleasantly surprised by her table, since Billy Chinn was such a superb chef, and he often complained that the food served by the cooks at the Residency was barely edible. But William didn't seem to like him much, so there was no point in even mentioning the idea.

Besides, now that the dry season was well under way and travel in the outback was simpler, if not easier, he was talking about taking her out to visit the family stations. At last! Since she had no idea how one arranged such journeys, Harriet concentrated on the clothes she would need for a six-week safari, leaving the travel details to her husband.

She was really excited about this adventure. They would go by train to Pine Creek, then travel in a wagon of some sort accompanied by horsemen, whom he said would act as 'guards, cooks, and bottlewashers'.

'Guards?' she'd asked nervously.

'I'm only joking. We'll have to camp out quite a bit. No inns out there, my love. So we'll need extra horses, and extra hands to set up the tents and prepare our meals. But I want to show you the beauty of the outback. There are some picturesque springs where we can swim.'

'Swim? Are you sure? How marvellous.'

'Yes. Cool us down after long hours on the track. I'll take you through Campbell's Gorge, which is magnificent, then we'll head far south to Millford, my station. It's about time I took a look at it, to see how the manager is getting on. Then, after you've had a good rest, we'll come back, north-west, to Pop's station. Stay there for a while and come on home.'

'It sounds wonderful.'

'Yes, I'll do my best to make the journey comfortable for you. I hope it won't be too tiring.'

'Never! I can't wait to go, William.'

But then came the blow. William had news that Pop had suffered a heart attack and he was needed at Warrawee station as soon as possible. His father was in a serious condition and the doctor urged him to hurry.

196

'Oh my dear, I'm so sorry,' Harriet said. 'We'll leave straight away.'

He stared. 'Harriet. You can't come. I'll be riding. It'll be too much for you.'

'No it won't. I can ride.'

'Not distances like that, Harriet. It'd be too hard. You're not used to it.'

'I'll be all right. I'll manage.'

'You don't understand. I'm not taking equipment, I'll be sleeping rough. That means on the ground, with a blanket. There'll only be one man with me, no tents, no frills, nothing.'

'I won't mind,' she begged.

'Harriet, it's impossible. You'd slow me up. Pop might die. I can't waste a minute. I'll be leaving in the morning. I've sent a cable to Myles in London, to come home right away.' He slumped into a chair. 'It'll take him months to get here. Pray God that Pop survives this. Myles would be heartbroken if he didn't get back in time. He'll be taking the first ship he can find from England, I'm sure.'

Harriet was truly offended. She resented being excluded from a family crisis, that was bad enough; but for William to refuse to allow her to ride with him, as if she were a weakling, a sissy city girl . . . Not like those station women, she sulked. Not like the first Mrs Oatley, a fine horse-woman by all accounts.

She glared at the portrait of Emily May that sat among other family photographs on the sideboard.

'Looks like one too,' she muttered.

When she'd first discovered who this stern-faced woman was, Harriet thought the presence of the photograph was an oversight, but it remained in place and she decided to leave it there rather than upset her husband, since he, obviously, had cared deeply for his first wife.

Now, though, it annoyed her. She went in search of William.

'I don't see why I can't go with you. I used to ride, back home.'

He shook his head. 'Riding for leisure around the quiet streets of Perth is a different thing altogether, my dear. I can't take you with me and that's that.'

Harriet gave up. 'All right then. What time does the train leave?'

'There's no train for two days. We're riding all the way.'

They were all up before dawn, with Billy Chinn and Tom fussing about, and a rangy fellow, whom William introduced as Sweeney, waiting at the gate with two horses.

'Won't they tire, travelling that fast all the way?' Harriet asked acidly, but William strapping on packs and rifles, didn't seem to notice her tone.

'No. We can get fresh horses along the way.'

He kissed her goodbye. 'Now you take care of yourself, my dear, and if you need anything at all, just go down to the office and ask Leo. He'll look after you.'

They swung on to the horses and then they were gone in a cloud of dust as light began to filter over the deserted street.

Chapter Twelve

William had been gone for weeks and Harriet made almost daily calls on Leo for someone to talk to, since life had become very boring. She hadn't realised until now how much she relied on her husband. In his absence, invitations had dried up, and she pondered what it must be like to be widowed, remembering Anna, her mother's friend, complaining that women without partners were socially unacceptable. Except, of course, at the dear Cunningham household.

Time and again, though, people stopped her in the street to enquire after Pop Oatley, but she was only able to say that he was still poorly, pneumonia having set in while he was still struggling to recover from the heart attack, which had been serious.

Leo was worried about Myles, because he still hadn't been able to locate him. When there was no response to the cable, or to a second one he'd sent, Leo cabled the London bank for information as to Mr Oatley's present address, only to hear that Myles had closed his account.

'He's probably on the Continent somewhere,' Leo said, 'but he should have left a forwarding address. William is very angry with him. He was only supposed to stay away a year. At this rate, whatever happens, he'll be lucky to be home before the wet season.'

'Oh well. He's not to know that Pop is ill. Obviously he didn't receive the cables. Is he needed in the business . . . here?'

'No. And fortunately it's a quiet time for us. William doesn't need to be here. I keep him informed by mail of our proceedings, even if he does get several of my letters at the same time.'

William wrote to Harriet every few days also, though his letters contained little in the way of news. But she wasn't impressed by Leo's remark that William wasn't needed here. What about his wife? Didn't she count?

She still went to tennis, the only break in long, dull weeks, but was beginning to tire of that too. It wasn't much fun listening to the others talk about functions that didn't include her.

Then she had a bright idea. She would have a dinner party. Just a small one. But who to invite? William's business friends – bankers, stock and station agents, government officials – were older and really only acquaintances as far as Harriet was concerned, so she looked about for people of her own age and her eyes landed on the Cochranes. Maybe they'd like to come.

To her surprise, when approached at the tennis club, Amy Cochrane was delighted.

'Why, Harriet! We'd love to come. When?'

'Next Saturday night. Nothing formal really, just a meal and a chat. About seven, it's cooler then.'

While they were talking, Christy joined them. 'What are you ladies plotting this fine day?'

Harriet was pleased with herself. Normally it was William who issued the invitations. 'A dinner party,' she said gaily. 'At my place next Saturday night. Would you like to join us?'

As soon as those words spilled out, Harriet knew it was a mistake, but too late now . . .

He bowed. 'Thank you. It would be my pleasure.'

Next Harriet though of Mina and Judah Forrest. The young lawyer and his wife would be ideal; a party of six, that was enough. Just right, in fact.

While she waited for Judah to come off the court – Mina must have already gone home – Harriet dismissed the worry about inviting Christy. It was a party of six after all, and if William complained she would simply tell the truth. That she hadn't meant to invite him, it had just slipped out. She could hardly retract.

Judah was a handsome man, tall, black-bearded, with piercing blue eyes, quite a heart-throb in the town and also, Harriet reminded herself, somehow related to the famous Forrest family in Perth.

Respectfully he took off his cap when she spoke to him, but when he'd heard her out he simply shook his head.

'Thank you, Mrs Oatley, but I think not.'

Harriet was shocked. A polite refusal with an excuse, a reason, would have sufficed. But this blunt rejection was appalling. The height of rudeness. Humiliated, feeling the heat of a blush which she knew left her red-faced, she rushed away to collect her racquet. She bustled it into its cover, then, keeping her straw hat low on her forehead, grabbed her basket and left without even bothering to change from her canvas shoes. The man was a pig, not worthy of his great name. One day she'd get her own back on him.

As she rushed almost blindly down the street, Mina Forrest came towards her, pushing a pram.

'Hello, Harriet,' she said cheerfully. 'You played well today.'

Harriet jerked to a stop. 'Your husband,' she said, 'has the manners of a wild boar. I pity you.' And she stamped away as well as she could in the rubber-soled shoes.

But that was the end of her excursion into invitations; she couldn't bring herself to even consider anyone else, for fear of another rebuff.

Now there would only be four. But so what? she kept telling herself. Four would be fun. Less effort than six conversation-wise, when one considered that Mr Forrest, being such a boar, and a bore, would have put a damper on everything. Who needed a sour wretch like him at table?

Forgetting that she'd told Amy the dinner would be informal, Harriet decided on a Chinese banquet, knowing that Billy Chinn adored presenting banquets, and that all the speciality dishes he cooked would impress her guests. He was disappointed that there were only four of them, but she explained that with the master away on such a sad mission, it was 'proper' to keep the numbers down.

'Just friends,' she told him.

But then, not to be outdone, Tom Ling took a hand. A banquet had to have the best wines and the best crystal glasses, along with their best little china dishes and bowls, and there had to be flowers and lanterns because the room must be in keeping. His enthusiasm thrilled Harriet. Their banquets had always been a huge success but she'd forgotten that her two Chinese servants went to so much trouble, probably because the events were held on special occasions with so many people about.

'It doesn't matter,' she shrugged. 'They've got nothing else to do but wait on me. They must get tired of serving one person. And I'm sick of eating alone.'

On the night, the dining room glittered and glowed. So as not to spoil the effect, the large sprawling sitting room with its comfy cane chairs looked much the same. Sherry was already decanted by a tray of glasses and plates of Billy's tiny pastries.

Christy was the first to arrive, and Harriet immediately saw Tom Ling's frown, which she returned in full force as soon as she had a chance. But Christy was an easy guest, admiring the Oriental furnishings:

'So much more appropriate in this climate than the heavy stuff people cling to up here.'

He gloried in the aroma from her kitchen which he said a king would die for. He drank two sherries while Harriet sipped at hers, and lounged across the room from her, chatting amiably, until at last there was a knock at the front door. The Cochranes were a little late.

Tom Ling returned, crestfallen. 'Message come, missy. Mr and Mrs Cockane, they no can't come.'

'What?' Harriet almost fainted, but Christy was out of his chair to interrogate Tom.

'Who was the messenger?'

Tom Ling kow-towed. 'Servant, sir.'

'Why can't they come? What did he say?'

'Velly solly. Missus Cockane, she sick. Can't come. Solly.'

All three stood staring, until Christy spoke up.

'Perhaps I'd better leave too. Looks like a postponement, if you would be so kind, Harriet.'

Tom Ling disappeared. Harriet was numb. Christy was being correct in offering to leave, but what a disappointment! Her lovely dinner party all over before it started.

She heard angry voices coming from her kitchen. 'Excuse me, Christy, while I see what that's about. Do pour yourself a drink. You don't have to go just yet.'

'What's this?' she demanded of the pair, who were shouting at each other in Chinese.

'He say my dinner all off,' Billy yelled angrily.

'Not proper,' Tom whined, backing away. 'Not proper, missus with man. That man. Boss no like him.'

'Rubbish!' Harriet snapped. 'He's the Resident's aide. I'll look a fool if I send him back unfed.'

'No more people coming?' Billy asked hopefully.

'No.' Harriet looked about the kitchen. 'What an awful waste.'

'I tell him go?' Tom urged, and Billy yelled at him again, then turned back to Harriet.

'Banquet just as good for two. You see. I make you nice time, missus. Tom, he stupid. What you do? Eat the lot on your only alone again? No. You take in gentleman. No waste.' He brandished a heavy spoon at Tom, who skidded out of his kitchen.

'Oh, why not?' Harriet said miserably. 'You're right, Billy. The food's here and I'm sure it'll be delicious.'

She hurried back out to Christy. 'Could I impose on you to stay for dinner after all? Otherwise my cook may kill himself.'

Christy gave a shout of laughter. 'Well, if it's that serious then I must. But it's no imposition.'

Still pouting, Tom Ling led them through to the dining room where, to Harriet's delight, Christy stood back in astonishment.

'Look at this! How marvellous! And what a shame the Cochranes couldn't make it. They're missing a treat just to see this room.'

Tom Ling even managed a proud grin.

The banquet was a success, their mood hilarious, as Tom brought dish after dish, far too much for two people. Fortunately Christy had a healthy appetite, accepting generous servings with obvious pleasure.

'The food is delicious,' he said enthusiastically. 'No slacking there, Harriet. We can't let the side down.'

They laughed, drank more wine, discussed each dish as it came to the table, groaned when Billy Chinn's *pièce de résistance* of glazed duck was presented to them but dared not refuse.

'What a feast!' Christy said when Billy appeared at the door. 'Truly delectable! Magnificent!'

So everyone was well satisfied.

When Christy left, Harriet sank with relief into a chair. She had drunk too much and felt a little tipsy, but she'd been saved from disaster by that kind man, and had made a point of telling him.

'Don't thank me,' he'd said. 'I had the time of my life. Mean of me, but I won't be able to resist telling the Cochranes what they missed.'

Harriet liked that. All evening she'd wondered whether Mrs Cochrane really was ill, or whether they'd just decided to pull out for some reason. But there was a way to find out, she thought darkly.

In the morning she sent Tom Ling to their house with a prettily wrapped tin of biscuits, and a note wishing Mrs Cochrane a speedy recovery.

'While you're there,' she said, 'talk to the servants, Tom. Find out if she really is ill. Or if she was only pretending to get out of coming here last night.'

'Ha! She do that?' Tom scowled, mightily offended.

'I don't know, you find out.'

'Ha! Yes, missy, I find out.'

The news was unfortunate for Mrs Cochrane but consolation for Harriet. The lady had gone down with the fever.

William was back, worried and upset. Pop was still very weak but he had flatly refused to leave his station, either for the Darwin hospital, which wasn't much of a place anyway, or for William's home, where he would be closer to medical care.

'If I'm going to kick the bucket,' he wheezed, 'I'll do it right here under my own roof.'

'You're not going to kick the bucket,' William said.

'Then what are you making such a fuss about? You go on home and tell Myles to get out here.'

'Can't find the bugger.'

'He'll turn up,' Pop said sadly. He was missing his grandson, probably afraid that he mightn't last until Myles got home, and that upset William even more.

He talked to the station overseer, rode for miles in all directions, inspecting the stock and the state of the countryside, distressed to find it drying up, desperately in need of rain, hoping the next wet season would be early or that the land might be blessed with a few random storms in the meantime.

'Not much hope of that, though,' he said to himself, staring at the relentless blue skies.

Eventually he returned to Darwin, aware that another telegram from Warrawee station could call him back to his father's side at any time.

Then, at long last, came a letter from Myles. Obviously he had not received the cables. He was leaving England for Argentina, of all places, to visit cattle stations owned by friends, and could be contacted through the Bank of England in Buenos Aires.

'God almighty!' William exploded. 'He's in Argentina! Where exactly is that, Leo?'

They studied a map of the world.

'Here. He's on his way home. Good lad.'

'The hell he is. He intends to dig in with new chums for a while.'

'But he's crossed the Atlantic,' Leo said. 'One ocean closer to home.'

'Dammit. If he'd got that cable he'd be here by now. Let's hope he gets this one. Send it to that bank. Don't know if it will make any difference, but mark it urgent anyway.'

While Leo was away he tried to figure out how long it would take Myles to reach Darwin from Argentina, sailing down around the Horn; and that worried him too. The Horn was a notoriously dangerous passage for ships.

With a sigh, he turned to his mail, sorting quickly, picking up a thin square envelope and slitting it open with the ivory letter-opener that Harriet had bought him.

Reading the note inside, he shook his head sadly.

And that reminded him . . . He waited for Leo to return.

'Sent?'

'Yes. That gave them a turn. Argentina. Everyone in town will know Myles is there now.'

'Good. I've got a new rule, Leo. We don't do business with Judah Forrest any more.'

'We don't do much anyway. We use Sinclair.'

'I know. But other people do when it comes to conveyancing and contracts and things. In future, anything that arrives from Forrest is to be returned forthwith. We do not deal with him, we do not recognise any correspondence from him. If his clients want to deal with me they'll have to find another lawyer.'

Leo whistled, surprised. 'That'll make it awkward for him. Why? What's up?'

'He insulted my wife. Cut her dead when she addressed him at that tennis club, in front of the crowd.'

'Oh. I see.' Leo nodded. He went back to his desk, pondering on the ramifications of William's edict in this small town. Word would soon get out that Oatley had lowered the boom on Forrest, for reasons not stated. That in itself would cause speculation, wild gossip, leaving the rumour mill to churn out its own answers, anything from overcharging to corruption, or worse, and William wouldn't have said a word.

He grinned. Forrest could end up with His Highness the Resident as his only client. Leo could empathise with Harriet's discomfort and hurt. He'd been on the receiving end of Forrest's cold stares himself; the bastard always treated him like dirt, refusing to discuss business with a lowly clerk, even when Leo had been acting under William's specific instructions. He'd often complained about him to William, to no effect.

'You picked the wrong one this time, mate,' he smiled, turning to his ledgers.

William showed the note to Harriet after dinner that evening, and she flushed scarlet as she read the spidery handwriting.

Dear Mr Oatley,
    While you were away that wife of yours has been playing up. She and Captain Cornford are a real scandal. She has been sneaking him into your house of a night and indulging in orgies with him.

It was signed: 'A friend.'

'It's not true,' Harriet cried. 'You know it's not true. I told you exactly what happened with my dinner party, William. I was lonely. It was just something to do. And Billy Chinn and Tom Ling were here all the time.

204

Christy didn't even stay for coffee. He left immediately after dinner.'

William smiled. 'When you'd managed to eat enough to make Billy happy, as I recall.'

'That's right. Who wrote this awful thing?'

'I've no idea. I don't suppose you recognise the handwriting?'

'No.'

He lit a match and burned the offensive note. 'We'll forget it, but I thought you should know about it. Ladies have to be careful about their reputations, especially with the likes of Cornford, who is known to be a bit of a rake.'

'Surely not? He's always been extremely courteous with me.'

'Nevertheless, Harriet, he's not a trustworthy person. Not in business, and that's a fact. On the other hand, he may have innocently boasted about the fine dinner he enjoyed here . . .'

'And what's wrong with that?' she flared. 'Billy and Tom went to so much trouble.'

'Nothing, except people are apt to put two and two together and make five, as you yourself worried about at the time. And he does partner you quite a lot at tennis, you say?'

'Yes.'

'Well, you never know, someone, anyone, might be jealous. Small towns can be quite a horror at times.'

'As I'm finding. You should have taken me with you to Warrawee.'

'Had I known I'd have to remain out there so long I would have arranged for someone to escort you. I'm sorry, my dear.'

Harriet shrugged. 'Never mind. I really am glad you're home, though. And what a relief to have located Myles at last. I am so looking forward to seeing him again.'

Her husband wished she hadn't said that. It only reminded him of another looming problem. He lit his pipe and strolled out into the front garden, worrying about Myles, who still hadn't, in any of his letters, acknowledged Harriet. He would have to be pulled into line as soon as he arrived. Face facts. Accord Harriet proper respect and friendship. Or else.

Or else what? he wondered. He could send Myles straight out to Warrawee, out of the way, but this was his son. He had missed him so much, more than he'd told Harriet, and he could hardly wait for him to come home, to be able to sit about and talk to him, to just be with him. They had years ahead of them. A split between father and son was unthinkable. No. There could be no 'or else'. He would appeal to him, beg him if necessary, to accept his father's wife. He'd do that when he saw the happiness in this household, how they got along so well, and how they both rejoiced in his homecoming. William sighed. There were only three people in the world he loved almost to distraction: his pop, who was teetering on the edge of life; his son, who was unnerving him with his determined antagonism towards his wife; and Harriet herself.

He put the pipe aside and sniffed the night air. It was clear, with an ocean of stars above, but the damp was there, wisps of muggy sea breeze. Somewhere out there over the East Indies the monsoons were forming, gathering force for the southern run, winding up into rainstorms that would slam across this coast. He hoped they had enough force in them to carry rain out to the parched land beyond. Last year the rains had been poor, not enough to sustain nine months of a dry winter.

With a jolt, he realised that it was nearly October. He should have insisted on bringing Pop in. What was he thinking of? Getting old, you fool. Worrying about his family instead of watching the weather, smelling it. All roads out of Darwin would be cut off once the wet set in. What then? Cripes! He ought to go back now and get Pop. But it would be a waste of time. Pop wouldn't care if the rivers ran high and the plains flooded as long as his stock were safe. Many a time the Oatley family had opted to sit out the isolation of the wet season for some reason or another. They coped. Holidaying in Darwin was a recent innovation. Years ago the village of Darwin wasn't worth the trouble; their own homesteads were far more comfortable.

Far to the north William saw a glow of lightning. No thunder. Just a glow that lit up concealed clouds for a few minutes. That didn't mean much, but the waiting had begun and William had an ominous feeling about the coming wet season.

'Waiting for the thunder,' he muttered, turning away. It always put people on edge, waiting for the thunder.

'What's this I hear about you romancing Mrs Oatley?' Mollard grinned. 'You're a sly dog, Christy.'

'Not at all,' his aide said stiffly. 'I was invited to dine to make up the numbers. Unfortunately Mrs Cochrane was ill, so they were unable to attend—'

'So you stayed to console the grass widow.'

'Hardly,' Christy said evenly, not wanting to aggravate the boss, nor to add fuel to the gossip. He had told Bill Cochrane that he'd enjoyed the evening immensely, and of course a few of his friends, and it was no surprise to him that there'd been talk. The same thing would have happened even if the Cochranes had been present. Harriet would have known that when she invited him, so he wasn't concerned.

'As a matter of fact, lacking the propriety of the other invited guests,' he continued, 'and finding ourselves alone, Mrs Oatley and I decided it would be best if I left. And being a gentleman,' he emphasised, 'I was about to leave when her chef threw a tantrum.'

'He did?'

'Oh yes,' Christy laughed. 'Screamed blue murder. The banquet he'd prepared with such care, headed for the bin. You should have heard the racket. So there I was, a hand on the door at the same time as smelling that food, wondering where I'd find a meal at that hour, hungry as a dog, with the beleaguered hostess running around in circles. What would you have done, sir?'

'By God, I'd have stayed.'

'Exactly, rather than be thrown out into the night on an empty stomach. So I offered to remain and I thought the poor woman would faint with relief.'

'But you still got to dine tête-à-tête with the lady!' Mollard leered.

'If you could call it that. Under the nose of the houseboy, who never turned his back. He acted the waiter, rushing in and out with an endless supply of dishes meant for four people.

'A rather difficult situation all round,' Christy lied. 'Trying to make conversation and eat as much as possible to placate the chef. Quite the reverse of normal dining. I kept hoping Mrs Cochrane would be miraculously cured and bring her husband to the door, or someone would call by. But that did not eventuate, so I just kept on eating.'

'What a fiasco!' Mollard said, highly amused. 'But then what?'

Christy appeared not to understand the implication of the question. 'What then? Sir, I bolted after dessert. I rather think the poor woman was relieved. After all, I could hardly retire for port and cigars on my own.'

'Good Lord. What a spot to be in. You simply left?'

'Disappeared into the mists, as one might say.'

'She has no idea how to conduct herself, that woman. They say she drinks?' Mollard asked, raising a furry eyebrow.

'A glass or two of wine,' Christy said vaguely. 'But I made up for it. Nothing like a good claret to wash down a hefty meal.'

Mollard was chortling away at the story as Christy recalled the two bottles of wine that he and Harriet had demolished with that very excuse. He had had a wonderful time in her company; she was a bright, entertaining woman, and Christy had come to know her better with the barriers of company removed. Under no circumstances would he have been stupid enough to frighten Harriet off, that night, by flirting with her. Even though he knew well that she'd had enough wine to admit a little more warmth as he left, away from the prying eyes of Tom Ling.

But Mollard had had his fun. Now it was time for Christy to turn the knife.

'I practically staggered away down the street after that,' he said. 'Almost ashamed that I had eaten so much in company. But sir, I have to tell you this. That fellow can cook. When the Chinese can cook, they're good. And I'm not talking about those station cooks; this fellow is a genius. Each course – and there had to be a dozen – absolutely delicious and carefully planned to complement the next. Fish, pork, soup, vegetables, beef, all with delicate sauces, and the duck, roasted, glazed and sliced . . . If ever I got invited to that house again I'd be on the doorstep in a shot.'

'You don't say?' Mollard stared greedily. Here was a man who loved his food, even the sludge served up by the Residency cooks. 'What's his name?'

'Billy Chinn.'

'I wonder what they pay him.'

'Nobody pays a Chinaman much.'

207

'That's what I was thinking. If we had a fellow who could serve up banquets like that—'

'Mrs Mollard would be spared a lot of worry,' Christy added.

'My word, yes. You have a talk to him. The man is obviously wasting his talents in a private home. To work here would be a step up for him. Look into it, Christy.'

'I certainly will, sir.'

As he left the Resident's study, he laughed. 'Fat chance.' Over dinner with Harriet, he'd learned that Billy Chinn and Tom Ling were Oatley family retainers. He'd even learned that Harriet had got rid of them when she'd first arrived, not being accustomed to manservants, but soon called them back. He'd learned a lot that night. About the son too. Her age. Who was due home from overseas shortly. Harriet and her husband were excited about his return. Looking forward to it.

Christy wondered if the son was equally thrilled. Why would he be? The old man marrying a young girl in his absence. Not such a charming scenario, in Christy's experience. You never knew, one of these days Harriet might need a friend.

The old man was back home now, and Harriet had suddenly stopped turning up at the tennis club. Not hard to figure out why, with that gossip doing the rounds.

Christy kept an eye out for Harriet and soon came across her in the street.

'Harriet, my dear, how are you?'

'I'm very well, thank you, Christy,' she said nervously.

'We miss you at tennis.'

She drew him aside. 'I really can't come any more. Someone sent an awful anonymous letter to William. Quite scandalous.'

'What about?'

She blushed. 'I'm sorry, Christy. I'm so embarrassed to have to say this, but it was about you and me. I mean, there's nothing, but it was written, and I'm so sorry. I owe you an apology. I meant to write to you but I didn't know what to say.' She heaved a sigh. 'But there it is. I hope you'll forgive me.'

He paled. Gossip was one thing, but anonymous letters to the husband, to William Oatley, he could do without that.

'Harriet! You don't have to apologise. People get up to all sorts of mischief in this town, but you are above reproach. I can't believe anyone would do such a wicked thing. I hope Mr Oatley rejected it.' He prayed that Mr Oatley had.

'Oh yes, he did. William didn't believe it for a minute. He showed me the thing and burned it to prove his point. But I've thought it better not to come to the tennis club for the time being. At least until this ridiculous talk dies down. It's really upsetting, Christy. Why can't people just live normal lives without this nonsense?'

'Nothing better to do,' he murmured. 'Anyway, the tennis club is closing down for the summer months. We wouldn't be able to play without waders.'

She smiled, that lovely broad smile of hers, totally without guile. It seemed to Christy that every time he saw Harriet she looked more attractive, so he wasn't about to allow this opportunity to slide by.

'If I have compromised you in any foolish way, Harriet, I'm the one to apologise, but I don't have many friends here and you have been very kind to me. Of course it comes down to the plain old jealousies. You outshine all the ladies in this town and therein lies the problem.'

Her cheeks tinged pink. 'Really, Christy, you do go on. You know that's not true.'

Well, not exactly, he admitted to himself as he watched her walk away, but right of centre. She was smarter these days, better groomed, and though not a raving beauty, definitely a sexy lady, he mused. He'd heard Mrs Mollard comment nastily on Harriet's height, but then that lady couldn't be expected to notice the shapely figure that went with it. Pity it was wasted on old Oatley.

Interesting that Oatley had taken that infernal anonymous letter so coolly. Christy wondered if he should call by his office to pass the time of day, showing that he had no reason to duck a meeting with him, but thought better of it. Oatley was a clever old coot; best to follow his example and ignore the whole business.

Myles was having the time of his life in Argentina. Buenos Aires was a gay and colourful city and he enjoyed exploring and socialising there, but he'd really come alive in the back country, staying with the Flores family on one of the great cattle properties where the pastoralists were known as ranchers or *estancieros*. The homestead was Spanish style, and very gracious, and the hospitality of his hosts was overwhelming. It had been a long time since he'd been able to ride free as he could here, made all the more exciting by the challenges thrown down by the gauchos. They were wild men who in no way resembled the laconic stockmen back home, but they could ride equally well, and with less care for their necks.

He met some attractive young ladies, but even as a respected guest, Myles never found himself alone with any single girls. There was plenty of entertainment – formal and informal dining, music and dancing – but always the dark-eyed chaperones were on the job. Smiling sentinels.

He wrote to his father that he and a party of friends had decided to mount an expedition to explore the great rivers and falls they'd heard so much about.

But no sooner was the letter sent than a cable arrived from William, via the bank in Buenos Aires:

'Pop seriously ill. Urgent you return home as soon as possible. William.'

A week later, in Buenos Aires, he boarded the *Ohio* bound for Sydney via the Horn.

When at last he reached Sydney, after a miserable voyage in the discomfort of a merchant ship and made worse by the heavy seas in the

Tasman, the last leg of the journey between New Zealand and the haven of Sydney harbour, Myles wasted no time. He soon found a coastal steamer headed for Darwin and managed to scramble aboard with his luggage only minutes before it left the quay.

Myles Oatley was out on deck as the ship sailed across the familiar Darwin harbour, and as it approached the small port, he noticed it was high tide, making disembarking an easier prospect than having to wade ashore as he'd done so often over the years.

The longboat left the ship, delivering passengers to the jetty, and Myles was home, unannounced. He was excited now, looking forward to surprising his father, trying not to worry about Pop, and the wife almost forgotten.

He ran up the jetty, found a Chinese coolie with a handcart and paid him a shilling to collect his luggage and deliver it to the Oatley house on the Esplanade.

He hurried up the hill, ignoring townspeople who'd come down to greet other passengers, dashed across the road, narrowly avoiding three bearded riders cantering past trailing a packhorse, who yelled at him to watch where he was going, and rushed over to William's office. It was almost noon, he should be there.

The office was closed. Myles, confused, stared at the door and then looked about him and realised it was Sunday.

With a shrug, he turned back towards the Esplanade. Towards the new house that William was so proud of, now that it was completed.

He slowed, walking along the Esplanade, pleased to be home at last, pleased to belong, to know every stick of this town. He noticed the palm trees had grown along the front, doubled in size since he'd left, and the shrubs were more orderly, learning how to behave in a garden setting, but the huge old fig tree was still there, defying the axe. Two black cockatoos suddenly burst clattering from the trees, disturbing a group of wallabies that had been grazing quietly on the thin grass. They peered over at Myles, soft eyes contemplating him, and he smiled, nodding, as if to old friends.

He almost passed the house, fenced now and surrounded by a young garden of neat palms and native shrubs. William's house was exactly as he'd planned it, even to the bamboo shutters that enclosed the wrap-around verandas. The slats were open now, welcoming what little breeze might come by on this glaring hot day. He marched along the path and up the steps to the solid front door, deciding to knock – for fun.

Tom Ling answered the door. Tom Ling, just the same in his black pyjama suit and the little round cap from which, it always seemed to Myles, the long pigtail sprouted.

He stared, and then gave a shout. 'Mister Myles! That you? That you! Ah! You come home.' He threw back the door, grinning and bowing. 'Come in! Come in! You bigger boy now. Lookee you.'

He was so excited his voice was shrill. 'Missy, come see. Come see, missy. Mister Myles home! Mister Myles home!'

She answered his call. She came running, slippered feet dancing up the hall in eager anticipation. A rush of pale blue muslin. Hair shining, a sort of chestnut colour, tied up, French style, with delicate blue ribbons. The face unblemished, brown eyes aglow under finely arched eyebrows, the mouth curved into an O of delight. Dismayed, he saw she was better looking than he recalled, much better looking.

Tom Ling was jabbering. 'Your room, Mr Myles. You come see. All kept special for you. You never see it yet . . .'

She was talking over him. 'Myles! How wonderful to see you. When did you arrive? I'm so sorry, I should have gone down to meet you. I didn't know a ship was in. But how marvellous to have you home at last.'

She was reaching out to him, his stepmother, as if to hug him or maybe plant a motherly kiss on his brow, this woman who had seduced his elderly father.

Appalled, he turned on his heel to Tom Ling. 'Where is my father?'

'He away, Mr Myles. Out fishin' on Chinee boat.' Tom Ling giggled. 'He be back, one, two day. Soon, you see. He get pretty big surprise, eh?'

Myles nodded. 'Very well. You may show me to my room. My luggage will be along shortly.'

Harriet stood, transfixed by the snub, blushing, bewildered. Hardly believing that he had cut her. But he had. Deliberately. Hot tears welled, but she blinked them away. Was he just cross because his father was not home to greet him? Disappointed? But how could he expect William to be here without any proper notice? It was so unreasonable. She could hear their voices from his room and was a little jealous that she was missing out on the pleasure of introducing him to it. William had set aside a suite of two rooms for Myles and Pop. He was very proud of their inclusion and had furnished them with an eye to their needs, making sure that Tom Ling kept them well aired. Harriet herself had seen to it that all of Myles's things were looked after with great care – his books, his clothes, and all the oddments that young men collect – so that when he did come home everything would be in tiptop order, as if he'd only been away a few days.

Uncertain what to do now, she retreated to the sitting room and picked up a newspaper, but then decided Myles might like morning tea, so she made for the kitchen, tiptoeing, as if she might be creating a disturbance, only to hear Billy Chinn's excited voice coming from the bedroom too.

Feeling miserable and excluded, she sighed and fell back on her original plan, posting herself in the sitting room trying to concentrate on a week-old Perth newspaper, trying to curb her rising resentment. He looked older, as if the puppy fat of his personality had fallen away, and his voice was more mature. Plummier, she thought crankily, straining to hear him talking to the servants, in the dining room now. Her dining room. He sounded so very English, strutting about in there.

211

'Damn cheek,' she muttered. 'Who does he think he is?'

And that, she pondered, was a good question. Who does he think he is, barging into my home and cutting me as if I don't exist? Disappointment or not, there's no excuse for such behaviour. How dare he ignore me? She felt like doing some barging of her own. Barging back there and asking him point blank if it were a new fashion to ignore one's hostess. Something like that. But she couldn't decide on the right words, and besides, he might yet come in and apologise. Wait a while.

She waited. Heard the bustle and chink of a tea tray, heard the jolly voices, then his luggage arrived, coolies jabbering, handcarts squeaking as they hurried down the side of the house to the back door, Tom Ling a distant voice giving orders.

Harriet could just see her guest, sitting in state in her dining room, sipping tea, nibbling biscuits, while her servant, Tom Ling, unpacked for him. The house was very quiet. Ominously quiet. And it was hot, stifling, humidity almost dripping about her. She hoped he found it uncomfortable after the chill of England and those other countries he'd graced with his presence. Harriet fumed. Why did William have to pick now to go off on that fishing trip? Why wasn't he here to make sense of this? To tell that prig of a son to behave himself. To save her the trouble.

But then caution took a hand. She might be overreacting. He could be sitting in there waiting for her to join him. And another thing. William loved Myles. He was the apple of his eye. Common sense told her to avoid trouble here at all costs.

The decision made, Harriet stood and checked her appearance in the mirror, fingering her hair, dabbing with her handkerchief at the little beads of perspiration settling on her forehead. She was relieved that she'd chosen to wear this day dress on this particular morning; it was pretty and cool. How awful it would have been if he'd caught her still in her dressing gown. Suddenly she remembered that this was Sunday. Too late now. God would forgive her absence; she had family matters to consider.

He was still at the table, a magazine propped up on the sugar pot, and Harriet entered with determination.

'You being looked after, Myles?'

He nodded, barely lifting his eyes. 'Thank you, yes.'

'William will be thrilled that you're home at last, safe and sound. He's been worrying about you.'

'There was no need. I came as soon as I could.'

'Yes. Of course. What are you reading?'

'I would have thought it was obvious. *The Countryman's Gazette*. I have some catching-up to do.'

Harriet didn't flinch. 'I imagine you do. Pop is much better. He was so ill for a long time but fortunately he seems to have got over the worst.'

'Yes. Tom Ling told me.' He rose from the table, pushing up unbuttoned shirtsleeves that she noticed were poorly laundered. 'Would you excuse me? I want to see where Tom Ling is shoving my effects.'

'Oh, don't worry. He won't have a shred out of place.' Harriet clung on. 'What do you think of the house?'

He replaced his chair neatly. Firmly. 'Larger than I had imagined. But suitable for Darwin.'

Now Harriet was trying to ingratiate herself. 'Yes, I believe your mother designed it.'

'My late mother. Yes. But I doubt she envisaged an Asiatic décor.'

She felt that this man, standing there in her house, still looking the dandy only in a shirt and well-tailored trousers, was trying to provoke her. As his hostess, she had not given him permission to take off his jacket. To loll about her house, his hair unbrushed, shirt buttons undone at the throat as if, as the son of the father, he did not need to observe proprieties. Then again, as the wife of the father, Harriet knew she had to avoid unpleasantness.

'I suppose you're right,' she said quietly. 'But it seems these days that Orientals are more accustomed to dealing with excessive heat than we are, hence the lighter furnishings in the house.' She smiled. 'It might be an illusion, but the cane and bamboo seems cooler than the old and tried mahoganies.'

Myles shrugged. 'I imagine it boils down to taste. My late mother had excellent taste. And she was born in the Territory. We don't need lessons on how to cope with the heat. Now, if you would *please* excuse me, I do want to see to my things.'

Harriet dreaded Sunday dinner with him, and though the table was set for one, she still expected him and instructed Tom Ling to set another place.

'No, no, missy. Mr Myles gone out.' He winked. 'Young man. His town. He gotta see people!'

His stepmother was relieved. And furious.

Myles knew exactly where he was going. The Hamiltons would be in town. Lucy would be there. He sprinted down the road to Doctor's Gully, where quite a few of the station people had built their holiday houses – rebuilt, he recalled, after a cyclone had wiped out the town years ago.

The sight of the Hamilton house cheered him, dismissing the world-weariness that seemed to have descended on him. Probably caused by having to confront that woman, he snorted to himself as he paced along.

The house was more of a high-set cottage with rooms pasted on and wide verandas guarded by flapping canvas blinds, but it was their beach house and they liked it that way. No fuss. Myles had fond memories of summers at this place: bare boards, bare feet, sand in everything; the damp smell of the sea, of fish feasts, and cigars; people wandering freely, laughter and lethargic sweltering afternoons; and Lucy, always there, sunny, smiling, organising games, bossing everyone about, even as a little girl . . . He stopped. The house was unusually quiet.

213

Tea tree bushes scattered about the unfenced block made way for a sandy path, but Myles had no need to follow it. The doors were all closed, doors that were always left open when the Hamiltons were in residence. There was no one home. Confused, he considered the date. It was October, wasn't it? They should be here by now. Dammit. Where were they? This was some homecoming.

He strode across the road to Sweeney's stables and found a young fellow hosing out the stalls.

'Have you seen the Hamiltons about?'

'No. They're not in yet.'

'This is late for them, isn't it?'

'Yeah, most of the bushies are in town by this.' He turned off the hose and picked up a squeegee. 'Zack had a spot of trouble.'

'What sort of trouble?'

'I heard he got speared by a blackfeller. That must have slowed him up.'

'Is he all right now?'

'So they say. I dunno. I reckon they must be stayin' home this summer.'

Myles made his way back into the town, avoiding the Esplanade, disappointed and irritated, especially since people were strolling about now and several recognised him, forcing him to stand in the street and make polite conversation. It took him the best part of an hour to run the gauntlet of their surprise and hearty questions, but eventually he found himself outside the Victoria Hotel, which was closed, naturally. But Myles knew better. He tramped around the back and banged on a door, soon to be admitted happily to what was known as the Catholic Hour, when certain locals, including police, gathered in the closed bar.

This time, with a cold beer in his hand, Myles didn't mind being the centre of attention. He laughed when a couple of his old mates nodded to him across the counter with laconic grins:

'You're late, Oatley.'

By five o'clock that afternoon Myles and his friends were around at Charlie Wong's café, roaring drunk.

Myles was home at last, relaxed, happy.

She heard him come in at some ungodly hour, crashing about, drunk, but she stayed in bed, ignoring him, trying to go back to sleep with anger constantly nagging her awake.

The day was endless. He slept; Harriet wandered about fidgeting, unable to concentrate on anything, his presence so large, so invasive she felt as if she had a whale in her house.

When he finally did get up, he breakfasted in the kitchen on whatever Billy Chinn provided for this young prince. Harriet didn't know and didn't care. Later she heard him go into his father's study, and there he stayed. She could smell the aroma of William's cigars.

★ ★ ★

Myles was filling in time, nursing a hangover that had largely been dispersed by Billy Chinn's insistence that he have a good feed of steak and eggs and sausages before setting off to call on Leo at the Mercantile Company office and then meet up with his mates again for a celebratory dinner at the Victoria.

He pottered about the study, poring over magazines and scrap books, reading reports from the Millford station and Pop's letters from Warrawee, opening drawers and generally fishing about, knowing that his father wouldn't mind. He looked through a box of newspaper cuttings, mainly of stud horses and cattle – pictures, pedigree and prices – but one page from a Perth newspaper seemed incongruous. He had almost flicked by it when the name caught his eye, so he began to read. It was a letter to the newspaper from her. Mrs William Oatley.

As he read, his eyes widened, and then he began to laugh. He laughed until the tears ran. It was an outrageous letter, and she'd had it published! For God's sake, was she mad? No, not exactly. It was spot-on, this letter. The worst send-up of the silliness and snobbery of some of the ratbags in this town. Or the best, he laughed. She'd got them right. He wondered if this clipping had ever seen the light of day in the port of Darwin.

He was still amused after he'd dressed to face what was left of the day, and as he passed the parlour where she was sitting, sewing, he called to her.

'Excuse me. I won't be in for dinner.'

She jumped up as if bitten. 'Thank you very much for letting me know,' she said sarcastically. 'But it is of no consequence to me. Perhaps you would prefer to stay at the hotel.'

Myles was taken aback. Several sharp retorts surfaced but he thought better of it and left without a word. The cheek of her! She'd look damned stupid if he did. William might not appreciate his son being chucked out.

He was still in the office talking to Leo, telling another eager listener tales of his travels, when a buggy pulled up and his father jumped down, carrying a string of fish.

Myles hardly recognised him. He was wearing baggy old fishing duds and a squashed felt hat, but even so, Myles could see he had lost weight, shed the portliness he'd acquired as an office johnny after all his years on the land. He looked younger now, fitter, as he strode to the door, an expectant grin on his face meant for Leo. The fisherman home from the sea with his catch.

'Ho, me hearty,' he called as he shoved open the door. 'Here's a feed and a half for you.'

Then he stopped, squinting in the transition from glare to the dim office, squinting at the other man in there.

'Well I'll be blessed! You're home! Good God, he's back!'

William tossed the fish to Leo and threw his arms about his son, hugging him, laughing. 'Well, this is a great day, this is.' He pushed him back. 'Let me look at you. Yes, you don't look any worse for wear. Does

215

he, Leo? By God, it's good to see you, son. When did you get in?'

'On Sunday, in that old hulk sitting in the bay. You're looking pretty good yourself. We weren't expecting you until tomorrow.'

'There's a storm building up. We decided to run home ahead of it. You've been to the house of course?'

'Yes.'

'Harriet looking after you?'

'Certainly,' he lied. 'With Tom and Billy spinning around like tops. You never saw such excitement.'

'Good. But I missed it all. Damn! Why didn't you let me know you were on your way?'

'Didn't have time. I had to run to catch the ship. But the Hamiltons aren't home either. Where are they?'

'They're late, that's all. Zack got speared by a renegade black but he pulled through. Just got to rest up a bit now. But you needn't worry,' he grinned, 'I had a message from Lucy; she's coming on ahead with Maudie.'

He turned to Leo. 'No more work today. Shut up the shop, we've got some celebrating to do. Come on, Myles.'

'I didn't think you'd be home tonight. I arranged to meet some of the lads for dinner at the Victoria. I'd better go over and cancel.'

'No fear,' his father said. 'I have to get home and clean up and deliver the rest of my catch to the cook. Sweeney's waiting out there in the buggy, he'll drop us home. Then we'll all go to the Victoria. You too, Leo. Bring your wife. We have to welcome home the prodigal son. By God, it's good to see you, Myles, and I want to hear all about your travels from go to whoa.'

'Tell you what,' Myles said. 'You go home and put on your dancing pumps and I'll go on over to the Vic and tell them the party has grown.'

'All right. You do that. But come outside now and say hello to Sweeney.'

Harriet didn't fool him for a minute. She was delighted that he was home a day early, pleased that the fishing trip had been a success, but he saw her relief, and he knew things had not gone well, even though she declared it was a wonderful surprise to have Myles arrive so suddenly.

He should have been here. He was angry with himself for failing them, knowing Myles's attitude to the marriage. She was still unaware of that, thanks to all the good wishes he'd invented. He wondered what had happened.

'A spontaneous welcome home party!' she said. 'What a good idea. It will be fun. Who else is coming?'

'Just a few of the lads, and probably now some girls, since it has just changed from a bucks' night, and Leo and his wife, and anyone else around, I suppose. Later on we'll have a real welcome-home party with all the trimmings, eh?'

'Yes. That'll be marvellous!'

Her voice was enthusiastic. Her eyes were not.

While she was dressing, he took Tom Ling by the ear, down into the back yard, and got the story out of him. Myles had been 'no speaks' to the missy at all. He had not been in for meals. They'd had no conversation. So Myles had snubbed her, William reflected. This would have to stop. Then Tom, cringing, did recall their 'one speak, one time.'

'What did they say?'

'Too fast. Too much quick talk. Missy yell at him. Then he go.'

William smiled. Good for her. But they'd both have to be called to order. They were family and they had to get on.

He was sorry Lucy Hamilton hadn't been able to make it to town in time to welcome Myles. She'd be hugely disappointed. But then it would please her to hear that Myles called at their Darwin house, on his first day home. Some little consolation.

William was relieved to have learned that Zack was recovering from the spear wound but he was more concerned for Sibell. She had written to thank him for sending Zack a supply of bridles that were sorely needed and hard to find, but had upset him by adding that she found station life too difficult now and the sooner she could get away, the better. She was relocating to Perth! The tone of that letter had been so final, William was quick to respond, asking her what 'really' was wrong. One didn't just up and leave a station like that. Were they selling? Or leasing? Hard to imagine Zack leaving Black Wattle.

But he hadn't heard from her again. It seemed to him that the sooner all the Hamiltons came to town, the better.

Chapter Thirteen

Word was out that Myles Oatley was home and his dad was 'turning it on' at the Victoria, so friends and acquaintances, and not a few complete strangers, converged on the hotel, some even bearing hastily assembled gifts in sincere appreciation of this momentous occasion.

The bar was already full of men, and Mrs Ryan was at her wits' end trying to cope with the constant stream of guests accompanied by their wives and daughters – especially daughters, she noted with a wry smile. After all, Myles was the most eligible young man in the district. As they crowded into her dining room, she appealed to William.

'Are these all your guests?'

'It seems so,' he laughed.

'Then would you mind if I just set up a buffet? Let them help themselves? It will be a bunfight, but the best I can do.'

'Not at all. I'm sorry if this has caused you any inconvenience.'

'Darlin', if you're payin' I'll not be inconvenienced!' She turned to Harriet. 'And might I say you're lookin' beautiful tonight, Mrs Oatley? That surely is a lovely dress. Now come on through, I've got a family table reserved for you.'

Harriet thanked her. She was astonished that so many people had arrived, but immensely relieved. She'd been dreading an intimate family group with Myles across the table from her, sour-faced, snubbing her.

Christy appeared beside them. 'I say, I'm rather confused. I was intending to dine here this evening, but is this a private party?'

Harriet looked to William, who was at his heartiest best.

'It was,' he said, 'but it seems to have grown. You're welcome to join us, Christy.'

Harriet squeezed his arm. 'You are the nicest man,' she whispered, as Christy followed them through the crush and took a seat at their table beside Leo and his wife. Myles and his friends were still in the bar. She hoped they'd stay there.

Mrs Ryan, they all admitted, knew her business. There was a banner up over the stage with the message WELCOME HOME MYLES, and three musicians hurriedly took their places beneath it. She soon had the dining room guests sorted out and there didn't seem so many after all, once they were placed at their tables.

Eventually William left the table to fetch Myles from the bar, and Harriet surveyed the room. She couldn't resist remarking to Christy that

Mr and Mrs Cochrane were present. And Judah Forrest and his wife.

'They dare not stay away,' he grinned.

'Though uninvited?' she asked.

'It's a very small town. I gather by this that your husband issued an open invitation.'

'Yes, he did. It's not unusual here, they say. Especially when a digger strikes gold. The sky's the limit. Mrs Ryan loves nights like this; she has them down to a fine art, as you may note.' She paused. 'But still, Judah refused my invitation. To dinner that night.'

'Did he? Well, I imagine that explains why he has lost Mr Oatley's business.'

'Really? I didn't know that. But the Cochranes have never invited me back. After leaving me in the lurch. Us,' she added with a giggle. She took yet another glass of champagne. 'I think I'll go over and welcome them.'

'Why not?' he laughed.

With her husband safely out of the way, and Myles still in the bar, Harriet assumed the role of hostess, as was her right. She went from table to table, chatting with people, charming them, eventually coming upon the Forrests and the Cochranes, who were sitting together.

'It's a lovely night,' she said to them enthusiastically.

Judah Forrest agreed. 'Very pleasant indeed. Though I fear we may get drenched on the way home. We're in for a storm.'

They were all talking to her at once, all smiles, Amy Cochrane complimenting her on her gown.

'I'm so glad you're all enjoying yourselves,' Harriet said. 'I fear we are intruding on your evening. Whose party are you with?'

The two gentlemen were still standing; they looked to each other, thunderstruck, for a response. Their ladies gaped, but another voice at another table was calling to Harriet, so she moved on serenely, as if enlightenment was of no interest to her.

William was not just on an errand to bring the guest of honour to his table; he sent his son's pals on ahead and managed to sideline Myles into the quiet of Mrs Ryan's office.

'I need a word with you, son.'

'By all means. Anything wrong?'

'There is and you know it. I need to have my say before you get any more drink in you. It's about Harriet.'

'What about her?'

'She is my wife. I know you disapprove. I have mentioned this too many times in my letters but you have kept ignoring me. Now you have to face it. I love Harriet, she is my wife and you will treat her with respect.'

'What am I supposed to do? Call her Mummy?'

William stood, affronted. 'Were it not that you have already swallowed enough drink, I would knock you down for that.'

'I'm sorry. You're right. That was uncalled for. But you have to understand, the situation is difficult for me.'

'It is not difficult for you at all. The difficulty is of your own making.' William stood back, looking out through the half-open door at Mrs Ryan, who was telling her staff it was time to close the bar. 'Your life is all mapped out for you, Myles,' he said sadly, 'and I pray it will remain so, but you can't run other people's for them. You just have to get on with your own and hope for the best. I want you to let us live our lives. You are my son and my best friend. The least you can do is regard my wife as a friend too. A good friend. Family.'

He watched Myles fumble for a cigarette from a silver case.

'Are you hearing me?'

'Yes, sir. I suppose so.'

'Good. And her name is Harriet. That's not too hard, is it?'

'No, sir.'

William laughed, relieved. 'The "sir" bit is new. Bit of English there, eh? Why couldn't I have banged that into you when you were a kid? Did I tell you I'm overjoyed to see you after such a long time?'

Myles grinned. 'Yes, Dad, you did.'

'Then let's go join the company, and tomorrow I want to hear all about your travels and those Argentinian cattle.'

Arm in arm, father and son walked into the dining room to a standing ovation as the little band struck up with 'For He's a Jolly Good Fellow'.

Myles looked over to Harriet, who was laughing uproariously with Christy Cornford, the Resident's aide, and felt a sting of jealousy. On behalf of his father. If William loved her so much, this young, attractive woman, he shouldn't let down his guard to the likes of Christy.

As the table was being rearranged to accommodate the newcomers, Myles saw to it that Christy was moved away from her.

By the time Myles arrived at the table, Harriet didn't care. She was having a wonderful time. She danced the first dance with William, and the last. She managed to notice that Myles had addressed her several times quite politely, but it was of no moment. He made a speech too, somewhere along the line. Everyone applauded. She danced with Myles's friends, and with Christy, and joined in the community singing that William organised after the dinner was cleared away. It was all such fun.

When it came time to leave, she needed the assistance of both father and son as they all stumbled down the Esplanade in the teeming rain, the warm, healing rain, splashing through widening puddles like children, tossing care to the steaming tropical night. Laughing when Tom Ling opened the door to them in a great fuss to find them soaked to the skin, missy's hat and good dress ruined, their suits sodden.

The camaraderie of that homeward romp didn't last. Harriet knew that Myles's change of heart was only skin deep; the courtesies were there, even conversation, to please his father, but glimmers of resentment remained when William wasn't around. Or in the background as Myles witnessed the love they shared. But, she decided, that was good enough for now. He wouldn't be living with them forever. After the holidays he'd go out to one of the stations. Probably Warrawee, to help Pop. In the meantime, though, Myles could be excellent company when it suited him, keeping them entertained with tales of his travels which William loved to hear.

Then, at long last, Lucy Hamilton arrived on the doorstep, just as they were sitting down to dinner. Myles jumped up to greet her as she came running through the house to throw herself into his arms, weeping, laughing, so thrilled to have him home again.

William was overjoyed. He invited her to join them but they both declined, so, tactfully, he sent them off to the parlour.

'You two lovebirds will have plenty to talk about. Don't worry about us . . . off you go.'

When they'd left, he turned to Harriet. 'I think wedding bells are in the air. You know, my dear, I was always worried that he might find another lady, come waltzing home with a bride on his arm.'

'Yes. I thought that could have been a possibility too. But all's well that ends well.'

'I wanted to ask her about Zack and Sibell. Whether they're coming in. I hope Zack is fit enough to travel.' He sighed happily. 'But my questions can wait.'

Zack had refused to travel by wagon. 'I'm riding, Sibell, and that's that. Bumping about in a wagon would be worse than horseback. I'm comfortable on a horse.'

'Very well,' she said. 'I'll ride too.'

'Are you sure you feel up to it?'

'I'm as up to it as you are.'

The men who had escorted Maudie and Lucy to Pine Creek came back, reporting no incidents except for a problem with the wagon in the gorge when the wheel came off.

'We got it fixed, though,' they laughed, 'with Maudie spitting fire at the delay.'

'No trouble with landslides?' Zack asked, and they shook their heads. 'None. We saw the results, though. That's why we had trouble with the wagon . . . where it got narrower.'

It was agreed then that Casey and another stockman would accompany the boss and his wife to Pine Creek and eventually they were on their way.

Sibell felt as if she were in a little heaven. It had been a long time since she and Zack had taken on this long trek without a wagon slowing them up and it was exhilarating to be riding with him again. And comforting, just to be with him like this, like old times. A lovely memory to take with her.

They rode freely across the miles of Black Wattle land and turned on to the track, just cantering along; no one was in a hurry. Even when it rained she wasn't bothered, strapping on an oilskin and pushing back her hat to allow the water to cool her face.

Zack showed them the waterhole where the attack had occurred, but it was deserted. No sign of any Aborigine presence at all.

They camped some miles further on, and Sibell was content, sitting around the campfire with the men before settling down for the night, until she remembered to ask them about the lad Yorkey.

'I can't believe he just ran off. Why would he do that?'

'No idea. Probably just gone walkabout.'

'He wouldn't do that. I heard him talking to you, Zack. He wasn't tribal. He was new to this district. They only go walkabout to their own sacred places, in their own lands. He didn't belong to the local clans at all.'

'Maybe he felt he didn't belong at Black Wattle either. He's a drover. They like the road. He'll probably be back some day.'

When Sibell was in their tent, stretched out on a bedroll, Zack came back to talk to Casey.

His overseer, too, had thought it odd that Yorkey had just upped and left without a word, and he'd questioned everyone on the staff until he came to Dodds, and that led him on to Mrs Dodds.

'What did he talk to you about?' he asked her.

'He wanted to know all sorts of things. He wanted to know about Jimmy Moon.'

'Who's he?'

'Ah, before your time. Your brother was here then. They hung Jimmy Moon.'

Casey was indignant. 'My brother Joe never hung anyone.'

'No, not him. A posse. A pack of roughs.'

'Why?'

Mrs Dodds launched into her story again, and Casey took it in, though it left him no closer to finding out why Yorkey had left so suddenly.

'Last seen he was yarning with Ma Dodds about the old days and a blackfeller called Jimmy Moon,' he told Zack.

'Jimmy Moon?'

'Yes. Do you remember him?'

Zack groaned. 'I wasn't here at the time. Never met him. But Sibell collapsed when she heard they'd hung him. He was a friend of hers.'

'So Ma Dodds said.'

'Yes, but there's more to it now, I think. When Sibell first saw Yorkey, she mistook him for Jimmy Moon. It gave her quite a start. Do you suppose Yorkey is a relative of Moon's? Why else would he be snooping about, asking about him? He's a hard little bugger, got a chip on his shoulder too, I can tell you that.'

'But it's all history now.'

'Maybe not to Moon's family. Not that there's anything to be done now. It's over, long past. Except for . . . Wait a minute, Casey. Did she say who was in that posse, the bullyboys who hung Moon, an innocent man?'

'Yes. She reckoned Syd Walsh was one of them.'

'And now Yorkey knows.' He took off his hat and wiped his damp forehead with the back of his hand. 'Supposing we're adding this up right, where would you reckon our friend Yorkey has gone?'

'Glenelg station,' Casey said grimly.

'Let's hope we're wrong. Yorkey's no match for Walsh and his gang.'

She slept so well, a bonus for her, that the men already had bacon sizzling in the pan when she emerged from the tent to a fine morning. The little soak, nestled by a bench of vivid layered rock, had gained some water overnight and black cockatoos, flashing their red tails, swooped about screeching noisily as if to alert the world to their find. In the distance, a big monitor lizard reared sharply on its hind legs to survey the scene, and Sibell laughed. Where once she'd thought this land a vast emptiness with thin horizons like the end of the world, time had taught her it was far from empty, and the strange flora and fauna were a source of wonder. Although lately she seemed to have lost interest, this morning colour was back in her life. She picked a yellow flower from a gum tree, stuck it in her hair and went to join the men.

They were in luck. They arrived at Pine Creek only hours before the train was due to leave, avoiding the necessity to camp by the river until it decided to chug into the station.

Zack unloaded their canvas travel bags from the packhorse and put them on board and Sibell took the opportunity to rest, lying along an empty leather seat before the passengers began piling in. It was stifling in the carriage but more comfortable than sitting outside on the hard benches.

Zack looked in on her later and was pleased to see her fast asleep. He returned to the station platform to yarn with fellow passengers.

Eventually the whistle blew and there was a last-minute scramble to board and sort out the seating, which was always first come first served. Sibell was awake, reserving a seat for him, but Zack had spotted Casey on the platform, beckoning to him. He pushed back to the carriage door.

'What's up?'

'I've seen Yorkey.'

'Where?'

'In the guard's van,' Casey rushed to tell him. 'He's under arrest.'

'What the hell for?'

'I think you were right,' Casey grinned. 'He's in a heap of trouble. He burned down Syd Walsh's house. But that's not all.' The train was already grinding its wheels to move out. 'Two of Syd's men are on their way to Fannie Bay jail as well. Cattle duffing. The police caught 'em altering brands.'

'Whose cattle did they have?'

'I don't know yet,' Casey yelled, as the train gathered momentum, leaving him far behind.

'Well I'll be damned,' Zack said. Then he remembered Yorkey.

'Silly bugger. Why didn't he leave well enough alone?'

There were always crowds at the Darwin station to meet the train, if only to watch the comings and goings, for not much else happened in this lovely port. Zack handed Sibell down from the carriage, and some other ladies went back for the bags.

Sibell saw heads turning towards a commotion down near the guard's van, and curiosity took her in the same direction.

Before the train left Pine Creek, Sergeant Riley saw to it that the three prisoners were secured in the guard's van with Constable Smith in charge, then he sent a telegram to the Darwin police advising them that Smith was bringing in three prisoners and would need an escort to the Fannie Bay jail. His duty done. Riley retired to the tiny Pine Creek pub where Constable Grimm was waiting.

Smith too saw that the prisoners were secured, all chained to iron loops on the walls kept there for that very reason, but he didn't feel it was necessary to stay in the van, sitting on the floor for the entire journey, since the guard occupied the only seat by his high desk. He waited until the guard took out his flag to wave all clear to the engine driver's partner, and then announced that he'd duck into the second-class carriage next up.

The guard shrugged. 'Please yourself. Those blokes are staying put, they can't get away.'

Smith wavered for a minute, looking at his pack, his rifle and the heavy keys to the prisoners' chains. He decided to leave his pack, take the rifle, and hang the keys by the door alongside tagged keys needed by the railway men.

As soon as the constable was safely aboard the next carriage, the guard waved the all clear and began sliding the van door closed. But not quickly enough. Two men running to catch the train pushed against it, forcing it open so they could clamber aboard at the last minute.

The guard was annoyed. Tramps were always pulling this stunt to get out of paying their fares. 'You blokes can jump right off again, while the goin's good. No one's allowed to ride in here, against the rules.'

'Too late,' they grinned. 'We're on and we're stayin.'

'Well by Jeez, you'll pay at the other end or I'll put you on a charge. There's coppers on the train.'

'Whatever you say, mate.'

Grumpily the guard rolled his flag and slid it into the rack on the far wall, but while his back was turned the nearest man struck him a crushing blow across the back of his head. As soon as he crashed to the floor, one of the chained men yelled to them, 'The keys! On the hook by the door.'

225

Swiftly the two white men were freed, and one of the newcomers turned to Yorkey. 'What about the nigger? Will I let him go too?'

'No bloody fear, Andy, he's the bastard burned Syd's house, and he snitched on us, sent the coppers to check the cattle.'

'This bloke?'

'Yeah.' The man steadied himself in the rocking van and kicked Yorkey again and again, then he took to him once more, lashing at him with the discarded chains until the battered prisoner was lying barely conscious, blood streaming from his wounds.

They dragged the guard over, chuckling as they placed him in chains, then threw the keys down to the other end of the van, among the parcels.

Yorkey lay very still, hands clutching the back of his bloodied head, curled up tight to ward off any more blows. He knew some of his fingers had to be broken under the onslaught, but he dared not move them yet.

But the men were soon on their way. He heard them standing at the open door, charging each other to jump before the train got real speed up, and then they were gone and he could hear only the rattle-tat of the wheels beneath him. Slowly, painfully, he tried to edge himself upright but thought better of it. His left arm, closest to that vicious boot, wouldn't work for him and he realised it was broken. Strangely, his fingers hurt more.

Ribs broken too, he thought, big ones, hard to breathe. He felt he was passing out and tried to fight against it . . .

The guard woke to find himself chained beside the blackfeller, who had taken a hell of a hiding. His own head was splitting, he felt, from the pain of the blow, but that poor bugger was in real trouble. The other prisoners had gone of course, rescued by mates obviously, and here he was, not even close enough to offer the young black some assistance.

'Are you all right?' he called, but there was no answer. He looked at the blood seeping over the boards and wondered if he was already dead. Wouldn't be surprised.

Uniformed police were there, shouting angrily. The train driver pushed through the gathering crowd to join them. Men were helping the guard down from his van and a young policeman rushed forward to assist, but the guard abused him in such terms there was a shocked hiss from the crowd. Then they were lifting down another man, a blackfeller, his clothes drenched in blood.

'Is he dead?' people asked in awful whispers.

'Looks like it,' a voice replied.

They were careful with him, lifting him bodily to waiting hands, then they placed him on a long railway barrow and Sibell, standing nearby, saw it was Yorkey.

Zack heard her screaming. He was running towards her. He heard voices saying it was too much, that the police should not inflict such sights on ladies. Another woman fainted. He grabbed Sibell from the solicitous bystanders and hugged her to him, shushing her. 'It's all right, Sibell. Quieten down. It's all right.'

'They've killed him!' she wept. 'They've killed Yorkey too!'

'No, no, missus,' a woman said. 'I saw him close. He ain't dead.'

A man said, 'That's right, madam. He's not dead. No need to go on so.'

Zack led her away. They sat on a bench as the station emptied out, the drama over. Recognising them, the stationmaster brought Sibell a glass of water, which she sipped shakily.

'I'm sorry you had to see that,' Zack said to her. 'But you heard what people said; he's not dead, Sibell. They're taking him to hospital.'

She pulled away from him. 'They won't take a black man to the hospital, Zack, you have to follow this up.'

'All right, but let's get home first.'

Normally they would walk from the station, there being no such thing as horse cabs in Darwin, but Sibell wouldn't allow Zack to carry their packs, so he solved the problem by stepping out of the station and hailing the first gig that came past. Anyone would give them a lift.

The gig happened to be driven by Reverend Walters, who was only too happy to oblige. On the short ride to their beach house he asked if Zack would put in a good word for him with his friend William Oatley.

'What about William?' Sibell asked.

'He's objecting to the building of our church on the Esplanade, next door to his house. As if a church would be any bother! He really is causing me immense difficulty.'

'Did you say next door to his house?' Sibell echoed.

'Yes. I find his attitude appalling. You will speak to him, won't you, Zack?'

'I'll look into it.' He pointed ahead. 'Up there, Reverend. On the left. The house is half hidden by the trees.'

Maudie was delighted to see them, but still concerned for Zack. 'How are you? Is he all right, Sibell? You didn't let him strain himself, did you? You ought to have a rest now, Zack. I'll put the kettle on. We'll have a nice afternoon tea.'

He grinned. 'I'm fine, Maudie. I just have to keep away from spears for a while. You make Sibell a cup of tea, I have to go out. I won't be long.'

'Go out? You just got here. And you haven't heard my news.'

'What news?'

'Myles Oatley is home at last. No need to ask where your daughter is.'

'That is good news.' He kissed Sibell. 'But I have to run, the Reverend is waiting outside.'

'What's he doing out there?' Maudie wanted to know.

'He brought us from the station,' Sibell said. 'You go along, Zack, but do be careful. You've been doing well up till now, you don't need to tire yourself.'

'Where's he going?' Maudie persisted, as Zack left.

'To find Yorkey. Just let me get out of these hot clothes and I'll explain. A cup of tea would be heaven right now; that train is dreadful.'

As Walters drove Zack out to Fannie Bay jail, he heard the story about the blackfeller who had suffered a beating, but he was appalled when Zack expected him to accompany him into the jail.

'As a man of the cloth, you'll carry much more clout than me, Reverend. I have to see what has happened to Yorkey. He saved my life.'

'But you told me yourself, the man's a criminal.'

'That doesn't give anyone the right to bash him. He's in a very serious condition.'

'This is not my business, Zack. I can't intrude.'

'As a Christian you *can* intrude. You can demand to see him.'

'Even then, what could I do?'

'We'll take one step at a time.'

'I'm afraid not, Zack. I've done my best for you. I'll drop you here.'

'The hell you will. Don't you know who owns the block at the rear of the site you've chosen for your church? The one with two cottages on it?'

'Yes. Two families live there, billeted by the Telegraph Company.'

'Right. But the Company leases the land from me. I own it, Reverend. One hand shakes another up here, so you'd better get off your Christian high-horse while the going's good.'

'I find your attitude threatening, sir.'

'Dead right, Reverend. Are you coming with me or not?'

They found Yorkey lying in the squalor of the blacks' compound. As soon as they were allowed in, the other prisoners started shouting at them for help, for someone to attend to this poor 'pfella' who had been thrown in among them 'to die'.

The warders blamed the visitors for causing a minor riot, demanding they leave immediately. But Zack was on his knees beside Yorkey, furious that no effort had been made to care for him, except for the pathetic bid by fellow prisoners to set his broken arm with torn pieces of dirty cloth.

He jumped up and abused the warders, demanding to see their boss, not a little surprised to hear Walters backing him up. It occurred to Zack that the Reverend had never been inside Fannie Bay before – so much for his Christian parish – but the man was genuinely shocked now. As he should be. The filth, the stench was overpowering, and left there, in that unattended state, Yorkey would die.

The chief warden came down, a fat, blathering blowhard, as Zack called him, complaining to these two well-known local identities that he had problems with the conditions, with funding, with space, and that the infirmary, such as it was, was only for white prisoners.

'Then he has to have a doctor,' Zack shouted.

'Doctors won't come for blackfellers,' the warden sniffed.

'Yes he will. I'll get him. You stay here, Reverend, and see they don't murder him while I'm gone.'

Walters jumped up in fright, but then he looked over to the young blackfeller lying gasping in the corner, his body stinking of dried blood, and found pity.

'A doctor can't see him in this state,' he told the warden, 'or you'll be answering for it. Bring some soap and hot water and I'll get these two prisoners who are minding him to clean him up. Do it, sir!'

The doctor, a friend of Zack's, came willingly after hearing that Yorkey had saved Zack's life. He had Yorkey removed to the infirmary, to a filthy row of lice-ridden bare mattresses, set the broken arm and fingers, worried about his ribs, dressed his wounds and shook his head. 'I don't like his chances. He's got internal injuries. With all that bruising, I think his kidneys are bashed. Can you pee, boy? No, I didn't think so. He's distended here . . . he needs proper nursing.'

That wasn't good enough for Zack. He saw the warder's cold eyes. If the nigger died during the night, that bastard would have an end to these interferences. He needed to get Yorkey out of this place. He took the Reverend's gig again and drove into town. A white man could get bail. Why not Yorkey? he thought, seeing this as the only way of rescuing him. He would have to appeal to the chief magistrate but he didn't know him very well. So who did?

William Oatley. Of course.

The hours had passed unnoticed. Zack's heart sank when he realised it was almost nine o'clock, but William was still up, though his wife had retired.

'This is a surprise, Zack! I didn't even know you were in town. Come on in. Did you know Myles is home?'

'Yes, I heard. How is he?'

'Very well. Didn't Lucy tell you? He's taking her to the fancy-dress ball this evening.'

'No. We only got in this afternoon and I've been busy. Very busy, you could say. That's why I've come to talk to you.'

'Nothing wrong, I hope?'

'There is, I'm afraid. It's rather urgent, William, I need your help.'

'By all means. Come through. What about a whisky?'

'Wouldn't say no.'

They settled in the parlour and William poured the drinks. 'Here's to you, Zack. It's good to see you again. That spear wound giving you any trouble?'

'You've heard about it? No, it's still a bit sore, that's all. But I wanted to talk to you about a bloke who's in Fannie Bay jail. He's been beaten up and is in a real mess. I'm trying to get him out of there on bail.'

'Tonight?'

'If I don't he may not survive the night.'

'Good heavens! Who are we talking about?'

'A blackfeller called Yorkey Moon. I didn't know his surname until I heard it in the jail today.'

William gasped. 'Did you say Moon? Not a common name, Zack.'

'Don't I bloody know it.'

'Is he any relation to *that* Moon? Jimmy?'

'I'm not sure. I think so. And what's more, Sibell is getting very upset about things lately. The violence, she says. She saw them carry him, all beat up, off the train, and nearly threw a fit.'

'Oh dear!'

'I'd better start from the beginning. He's the chap who rescued me after I got speared, found me by the side of the track.'

'He just happened along?'

'It seemed so at first, but now I'm not sure.' Zack shrugged, wincing at the strain on his shoulder muscles. 'Sounds as if I'm not sure about a lot of things but I'll sort it out eventually.'

He outlined the story as quickly as possible. William was sympathetic but did not know what he could do to help.

Zack leaned forward. 'Your mate. Patsy Vickery. He's the chief magistrate. He could set bail, I reckon. For a mate.'

William digested this. 'Hard to say. Rum thing to ask at this hour. Shouldn't we get a lawyer on to it in the morning? Make a reasoned plea?'

'No. I have to make a reasoned plea now. Yorkey is suffering from multiple injuries, I can't leave him alone in that filth, with no one to look after him.'

'All right, we'll give it a go,' William said. 'Patsy's partial to schnapps, and I have a bottle of the best here. I'd better bring it along. Christmas and all that.'

Patsy was still roaming his house, not averse to visitors at this hour. 'Can't sleep in this bloody soppin' heat. I pray for winter, lads. Cold bloody Irish winter and rain to chill your bones, not this stuff that steams the life out of you. I'll be goin' home one day, you mark my words.'

'Get out with you,' William laughed. 'You've been going home as long as I've known you. You'd shrivel up and die over there.' He handed over the bottle and Patsy beamed.

'Schnapps is it you've got for me, William? You're kindness itself. I can't remember when I last saw a darlin' bottle of this stuff.'

'My pleasure,' William said.

'And God almighty, Zack! Didn't know you were in town. Heard you turned your back on a wild man. Thought you knew better.'

Zack laughed. 'I didn't see him in time, Patsy.'

'Well there you go. And to what do I owe the honour of youse company? Is it cards you're thinkin' of, to get us through the night?' He peered at them from under dark beetling eyebrows, his sharp green eyes taking their measure.

'No, I think not,' he decided. 'What is it you want of me?'

The chief magistrate heard them out. 'Are you mad?' he asked eventually. 'Mollard would have me socks giving blackfellers bail.'

'He doesn't have to know about it,' William said.

They argued the case until Zack said, 'He saved my life, Patsy. I owe him. And he got beaten up while he was in police care. That could cause trouble. Half the town saw him bleeding and barely conscious at the station.'

But Patsy was able to offer more information on Yorkey's case.

'The men who roughed up your nigger were under arrest for cattle duffing. Over at Glenelg. The police thought they had them cold, but they pulled an escape before the train left Pine Creek. Some of their mates jumped into the guard's van and set them free, after bashing the guard. They also bashed your nigger, Zack.'

'Why?'

'Twofold, according to the constable in charge. He set fire to Syd Walsh's homestead, but then he dobbed them in to the police for cattle thieving. I hear they gave him a good going-over.'

The liquor was mellowing all concerned. They talked over the situation, and the weather, while Zack curbed his impatience. Bail was agreed upon. After all, who gave a damn about Syd Walsh; no one liked him anyway. A cattle thief. Everyone knew that. And if somebody burned down his house, he must have had a good reason.

The papers were drawn up, signed and witnessed. The hour noted.

Armed with Yorkey's right to temporary freedom, William and Zack piled into the Reverend's gig.

'We can get him out,' William said. 'But where do we take him? He can't go to the hospital.'

'My place,' Zack said grimly.

Then he stiffened, as the horse plunged on. 'Oh no. I'd rather not. Maudie will raise hell, and Sibell . . . Well, things aren't too good with us right now.'

'You and Sibell? I don't believe it,' William said tactfully, remembering her letter.

'I'm hoping to sort it out while we're in town. But for now, what do I do with Yorkey?'

William didn't hesitate. 'We'll get him out and take him to my place. There's a storeroom at the back, next door to where Tom Ling and Billy Chinn live. Stop a minute at my house and I'll tell them to get it ready for a sick man.'

They arrived at Fannie Bay jail to find the Reverend still waiting – though very cross because he'd been vomiting for the last half-hour, unable to stomach his surrounds any longer – and Yorkey conscious, grateful for their help.

Zack noticed the warden hardly looked at the bail notice; he was only too pleased to be rid of them all.

★ ★ ★

231

Both Harriet and Myles were stunned next morning to hear of the events of the previous night, while she slept and he was out with Lucy. As soon as William explained the situation, Harriet rushed down to take care of the patient. Myles looked in on him, out of curiosity, but came away distressed to see the poor fellow so battered.

'Is there anything I can do?' he asked his father. 'He looks as if he's been trampled by a mob of bullocks.'

'By a mob of bastards more like it,' William growled. 'I'm staying home today. Why don't you go into the office and help Leo.'

'Yes. Sure.'

He met Zack Hamilton at the gate. His future father-in-law. The last person he wanted to see right now, but Zack was delighted. He shook Myles's hand, clapped him on the shoulder, apologising that he'd been so involved with Yorkey's welfare that he hadn't been home to see Myles last night.

'How is Yorkey this morning?' he asked.

'He doesn't look too good,' Myles told him. 'My father is expecting the doctor any minute. Harriet and Tom Ling are looking after him.'

'Good. But Myles, it's great to see you again after all this time. You're looking well. I'll catch up with you later on and we'll have a good old yarn. Oh . . . and how did the ball go last night? Lucy was still asleep when I left.'

'The ball? We had a wonderful time, Zack. It was such fun.'

'Good on you,' Zack beamed. 'Good on you.'

What a lie, Myles thought to himself as he opened the gate and left for the office. What a bloody lie. But what else could I say to him? To a nice bloke like Zack Hamilton.

Chapter Fourteen

Myles had always hated fancy-dress balls: burly men galumphing about dressed as women; girls embracing the curious gender switch as pirates, highwaymen and convicts; lumpy women coy as shepherdesses; their wretched daughters in limp netting contriving to represent fairies and coquettes, or maybe Queen of the May – he didn't care enough to enquire. And there was Lucy, looking ridiculous as a painted doll, her hair tonged to a frizz, red spots on her cheeks, wearing a spangled little-girl dress and shoes frosted silver. And as usual, men barged through the throng causing more shrieks of laughter at their impersonations of natives, skins darkened haphazardly with burnt cork or shoe polish, bodies covered for decency, in lengths of sheeting, feet bare, waving spears and growling fit to fear the giggling maidens. As he sat back at the overcrowded trestle table amid the debris of balloons and bunting, Myles wondered how long he'd have to endure this raucous ugliness.

Supper was over but there was no chance of dragging Lucy away. She was enjoying herself in a taut, determined manner because she was cross with him. Cross because he hadn't wanted to attend in the first place, and then, relenting, had refused to wear fancy dress.

'But you have to,' she'd insisted.

'I don't have to. I'm wearing a dinner suit. You know I hate dressing up in stupid outfits.'

'They don't have to be stupid. Maudie said you can go as a Chinaman. She'll get the material from the Chink shop and make you a pyjama suit like they wear, and you can put on a long droopy moustache. It'll be fun.'

'I'm wearing a dinner suit, Lucy.' And I'm not about to be dictated to by your battleaxe of an aunt, he added to himself. He couldn't stand Maudie Hamilton, never could, but more so lately since she'd begun to make snide remarks about the 'lovebirds' and Lucy's popularity in the district with other young gentlemen, all aimed, he knew, at nudging him into setting a date for the wedding, or at least announcing their engagement. But he just wasn't ready for that yet.

Lucy hadn't changed, she was still a very nice girl and, if anything, better looking than he recalled. He'd met a Swedish girl in London who was the image of Lucy, with platinum-blonde hair and lovely tanned skin, and was so taken with her that he'd gone out of his way to renew the acquaintance, only to discover that she spoke little English. The short time he'd spent with her had been awkward.

In much the same way, he felt awkward with Lucy after the first few days, after the first flush of love and chatter and excited kissing and cuddling. It wasn't as if they ran out of conversation; they always had things to talk about – families, people, the stations, the same old subjects – but after a while Myles found these topics dull. Repetitive. Miserably, he realised he was finding Lucy dull. Boring. He knew she was expecting an engagement ring but couldn't bring himself to take that step, yet. He understood her fits of petulance, which often developed into rows, like the one over the dinner suit. But he could hardly tell her that. Bring the subject out into the open. Because he didn't know where it would lead. No doubt he would marry Lucy in time. He supposed. But he needed time.

He'd thought of escaping. Going out to see Pop. After all, it was his grandfather's illness that had brought him rushing home, but when he'd mentioned that idea to William, his father wouldn't have it.

'Pop's a lot better. You can't desert us now, with Christmas only weeks away, and Lucy would be upset.'

Later he'd overheard William talking to the wife. 'When do you think Myles will make the announcement? Maudie says it's a strain on Lucy not knowing what's happening, when she should order the wedding dress, that sort of thing.'

He'd been surprised by the wife's response. And a little comforted, he had to admit. Coming from her, the enemy, quite a turnabout.

'Maudie Hamilton should mind her own business,' she'd retorted crossly. 'Women like that can only create embarrassment. These things should go at their own pace. Myles is probably waiting for Zack and Sibell to come to town.'

That had given him some respite. But Zack and Sibell were in town now. Myles was fond of Zack and he adored Sibell. She was vague, admittedly, but the sweetest woman. He remembered, at his mother's funeral, when everyone else was giving him the manly handshake and the be-brave hug, she had taken him in her arms and wept with him. And she'd written to him, quiet, private letters, talking about his mother, her love for him, all the good times, while everyone else had been avoiding mentioning her name for fear of upsetting him. Myles had never shown anyone her letters.

How could he disappoint Sibell now?

Lucy was back at the table, after joining in a wild, swinging array called the Alberts, but she was still sulking.

'Everyone thinks you're being snobbish, not dressing up,' she hissed.

'That's interesting. I wasn't a snob before I went away when I wouldn't get into stupid costumes, but now I am.'

'Well, you know what I mean.'

'No I don't.'

'Everyone else in town simply adores fancy-dress balls.'

'No they don't. They stay home. Like I wanted to do. My father and his wife preferred not to attend for the same reason.'

'Oh, I see. She's making the rules now, is she?'

'Who?'

'Harriet. The town clothes-horse. She wouldn't be seen dressing up like the common herd.'

'Not a bad description,' Myles drawled, looking at the general air of dishevelment about them as wigs and weird getups began to succumb to frailty and fall awry. 'Are you ready to leave?'

'No I am not.' She clung to him. 'Oh Myles, please, darling. Be nice. There are only three dances to go, and we always have the last dance together.'

He considered nipping across to the pub to join the thirsty gentlemen needing a break from the dry ball, but remembered they'd nearly all be drunk by now, so he might as well stay.

He might as well.

William was searching his study for the title deeds to one of his properties, rifling through drawers and cupboards.

'It has to be here somewhere,' he muttered. 'See if you can find it, Myles. I give up.'

'I'm surprised you can find anything in here. Have you ever thrown out a piece of paper in your life? Every niche is stuffed to overflowing.'

'Yes, I'd better get a chest of drawers in here.'

Myles laughed. 'There's no need for a chest of drawers. Look, why don't you let me go through everything and sort them into some semblance of order? You just can't go on shoving things in drawers willy-nilly. That way I'm bound to find the title if it's in here.'

'Would you do that? It might take some time.'

'You don't need me in the office. I've nothing else to do.'

'That would be a big help, but don't throw anything out. It could be something important.'

'I'll get a box and put in it every scrap I think should be dumped, and you can go through it when you come home. Final decision, so to speak,' he grinned.

'All right, I'll leave you to it.'

Myles worked patiently, shaking his head at the confusion until he began to devise a system. He attacked one drawer at a time, placing papers in separate heaps on the floor, according to subject matter. The box was winning, though; the discards even included used envelopes, cigar tins, advertisements, out-of-date stock market reports, as well as myriad trivia that couldn't possibly have relevance now, but dutifully he dropped them in the box. He found the title deed his father had been searching for and placed it with several others he'd been accumulating, interested to see that his father hadn't kept all his eggs in the one basket; apart from properties in the Territory that he'd known William owned, he'd also invested in land in and around Perth. A good move. Myles nodded agreement.

Then he came across that letter again, the one the wife had written to the Perth newspaper. Before placing it on a heap of papers he'd decided to call 'personal', he read it again, still amused. He saw her walk past the open door and his curiosity got the better of him.

'Harriet,' he called.

She came back. 'Yes?' Already on the defensive.

'Could I ask you something?'

'What?' She hung back from the door like a deer sensing danger.

'I'm not going to bite you,' he said, unable to get the grin from his face. 'I just wanted to ask you about this.'

He held up the page.

She recognised it immediately. 'Oh Lord. Has he still got that? Throw it out.'

'Sorry. Can't. I'm under orders not to throw anything out. Did you really write this?'

She was blushing. 'It's none of your business!'

'I suppose not, but I enjoyed it. Did anyone else up here read it?'

'Anyone?' She shuddered. 'Try everyone. It was a nightmare.'

'But you must have known that when you wrote it. They get the Perth papers up here eventually.'

'I didn't write it for the papers.'

Tom Ling appeared beside her. 'Morning tea, missy. You want me bring your tea here, Mr Myles?' He peered into the study, appalled. 'Crikey. What mess you make!'

'It's all right. I'll clean it up. Where do you have morning tea, Harriet?'

'In the sitting room.'

'Do you mind if I join you?'

Her shrug was by no means welcoming, but he persisted. 'I have to get to the bottom of this mystery of who wrote what and why.'

Over tea and hot scones he prised the rest of the story out of her, though she saw no humour in it.

'It was ghastly. I had to apologise to the Mollards, thanks to my mother's interference. It caused no end of trouble. And poor William, he was furious at first, understandably. Then he had to defend me when they were singularly unpleasant as I tried to apologise.'

'I wonder why,' he grinned.

'All very well for you to laugh,' she said miserably. 'Mollard was so offended, he snatched a business deal away from your father, giving some American investors the impression that William was not reliable.'

'Oh come on. Mollard would do that anyway, and Dad would survive. But I loved the bit about William becoming the next Resident. You're absolutely right. He'd be ideal for the job.'

'He doesn't want the job but the Mollards didn't believe him, I'm sure. It was just awful. And I got blackballed from the tennis club.'

As if to compensate, she spooned some extra whipped cream on to a scone while Myles laughed.

'Well, the Darwin Tennis Club isn't exactly the royal enclosure.'

'They think it is.' Harriet smiled nervously. 'To be honest, this is the first time I've ever been able to talk about that time, or even think about it without nearly dying of embarrassment. I was just about ready to drown myself. Throw myself into the sea until my hat floated.'

She began to laugh. 'Only I was scared that sharks might get me first. Or crocodiles. And it got worse. I had a dinner party and no one came . . . a Chinese banquet. It was awful!' She was giggling now. 'I was lonely. I mean, only Christy Cornford came, and we had all this food, because I wanted to impress people! And we had to keep eating so as not to offend Tom and Billy . . .'

Tom Ling was in the garden when Lucy arrived. He was attending to the half-dozen staghorn ferns he'd attached to the trellis beside the front steps, feeding them banana skins, which he insisted they liked to eat.

He beamed on Mr Myles's fiancée and sent her on up the steps through the open front door. She was a regular visitor, she knew her way about.

Lucy heard them laughing. Just the two of them. Scotching all the rumours she'd heard – not to mention Myles's own caustic comments – that William's young wife and his son did not get on. She froze, standing on the enclosed veranda right by the main door to the house, listening. She couldn't grasp what they were saying, but the tone was enough. William would be at his office. these two had the house to themselves. And they were in there, having a jolly good time.

She strode through to the sitting room.

'Is this a private joke or can anyone join in?'

Myles wrote to Pop, as he did every few days, to help him feel part of the looming Christmas celebrations in town and to let him know that his grandson was thinking of him. It was probable that Pop would get a handful of letters at a time, but that didn't matter; later, maybe into January or February, he wouldn't be able to receive any mail at all, once the rivers banked up. So far the rains had been consistent, with the monsoons building but nothing spectacular, and the old-timers had differing opinions, always mulled over by the populace. Some said the rains this year would be no good, not enough to satisfy the desperate thirst of the outback; others warned they were only amassing out there somewhere, like a dam ready to break its banks, and would come down on the north like an avalanche. In fact, as Myles wrote moodily to his grandfather, no one knew. He just hoped they'd be good rains and not too much.

His letters to Pop were becoming despairing as he tried to sidestep the reason why he had not announced his engagement, discussing everything but. The old man was already pointing out that any decision on which station Myles should go to – his own, Warrawee, or Millford – after the wet season, should be shared with Lucy. He was right, of course; she was entitled to that courtesy if they were to marry. If. The possibility was becoming ever more remote as long, difficult days passed.

Her rudeness to Harriet that day was uncalled for, and it had annoyed him having to explain to Lucy that it was an innocent, and rare, friendly occasion. Then he'd had to apologise to Harriet . . . all too ridiculous and embarrassing.

He lit a cheroot. Lucy was actually jealous of Harriet. And for no reason at all.

Or was there? he wondered. Before he'd left for London, he'd have said that Lucy was by far the better-looking of the two, but not any more. Harriet outclassed her now . . . she was quite lovely . . . so stylish and, well, he had to admit, sexy. Marriage had certainly changed the dull suburban girl into a very attractive woman.

It irritated him to think that his father, an elderly man, had anything to do with this transformation, preferring his guess that her shopping expeditions in Singapore had more to do with it. William had often written to him of their enjoyable visits to Singapore, and that annoyed him even more now. God knows what people there thought of him, married to a girl young enough to be his daughter.

His thoughts strayed back to Harriet. She was sexy now, tall and bosomy with slim hips and a neat waist. He recalled Belle Symington, his London paramour with fondness.

That night he dreamed of Belle, a sensuous, voluptuous dream, so passionate that he tried to hold on to it when it was fading into his awakening. Then he realised that it wasn't Belle, it was Harriet in that dream with him, but it didn't matter, drowsily he willed himself to drift back to that exquisite pleasure.

In the morning Myles experienced no embarrassment, no regret, rather a tingling of excitement when he met Harriet in the passageway as she was returning from her bath, gown wrapped about her, hair damp and that soft skin smelling so sweetly of delicate perfumes.

She blushed as they met and he grinned, wondering why she would be blushing. Unless she'd had the same dream. But then, he laughed, if so, the lady would be blushing from the tips of her toes to the tip of her nose.

He resisted the temptation to pat her on the bottom as she passed, to tease her. After all, they'd spent the night together.

But then he spent the rest of the day thinking about her. The dream gave him no rest.

Over breakfast Sibell heard of the previous night's events and was impressed by Zack's efforts.

'That's marvellous. Well done! And how kind of William to take Yorkey in. I hope it doesn't inconvenience Harriet.'

'Why should it?' Maudie asked. 'She's got those two Chinamen to look after him. Will he be all right now?'

'I hope so.'

'I'd like to visit him,' Sibell said, but Zack shook his head.

'Better to leave him be for a couple of days. Until he's a bit stronger and more aware of his surroundings.'

He looked outside. The clouds were low but the rain had ceased for a while. 'Let's go for a walk on the beach, Sibell. See if we can pick up a breeze.' He wanted to talk to her in private without Maudie hovering about.

They left their shoes on the grassy verge and walked along in the shallows, discussing Lucy and Myles, since Zack hadn't seen either of them yet. Lucy was still in bed.

'Our paths haven't crossed,' he laughed. 'But I presume all's well?'

'Oh yes. You were sound asleep, you didn't even hear Lucy come in, but she said she had a good time. And last night, did you say there was more to tell about Yorkey? I should think being arrested for burning down the Walsh homestead and then being bashed by his men was quite enough. I can't imagine why he'd do such a thing. While I have no sympathy for Syd, it's hard on Mrs Walsh. A terrible thing to lose your house.'

'That's what I wanted to talk to you about. Here's a surprise. Yorkey's full name is Yorkey Moon.'

'It's what?'

'You heard me. Maybe you were on the right track thinking he looked like Jimmy Moon.'

'Good lord! Are you sure? How do you know?'

'Police records at the jail. It's a fact.'

Sibell stopped to stare at him. 'Do you think he's a relation?'

'I don't know. And look out, your dress is getting wet.'

She shrugged. 'It doesn't matter. It's only cotton. It will dry out. But Zack . . . why didn't he tell us?'

'I don't know. Maybe that throws some light on why he burned down that particular house.'

'What do you mean? Payback? Surely not after all these years.'

'Food for thought.'

'Then we have to ask him. For heaven's sake! Yorkey Moon! It is an unusual name.'

'Yes. Perhaps you ought to have a chat with him when he's feeling better. He might open up to you since you knew Jimmy and I didn't.'

'I will. I'm bursting with curiosity.'

They walked across the beach to take a rest on the grass under a pandanus tree, and Zack turned to the real reason for the walk.

'I wanted to ask you, Sibell. Are you still set on leaving?'

'Yes, Zack,' she said softly. 'I'm sorry, but yes.'

'Well tell me this. Are these happenings – my run-in with a spear, Yorkey's bashing – are they adding to your grievances? I mean, is this the violence you talk about?'

She frowned. 'Not you too, Zack! I wish Lucy hadn't repeated that. I didn't mean it that way. Not at the time, but now I'm not so sure. So many things can go wrong in the bush.'

'They can go wrong anywhere. I could get thrown from a horse right here in Darwin,' he said harshly. 'Plenty of tombstones in the local

239

cemetery tell that tale. No one is immune from accidents, no matter where they are. It's no excuse for leaving your home.'

'That's true, Zack. We're both making too much of that side of station life.'

'I'm not. I'm only trying to understand what this is about. Running away doesn't solve anything. You have to tell me what's wrong.'

'Please. I have told you over and over, I just want to live in a town from now on. I can't see why that is so hard to understand. I'm miserable and depressed all the time. I can't cope any more. I have to get away.'

'And to do that you're leaving me? If it was over between us I might be able to accept this. Why don't you tell me the truth. Just say so and we'll get this sorted out once and for all.'

'I can't say that. I do love you. But you have your station, that's your life. I know I'm being selfish, but I don't know what else to do.'

He got to his feet, glaring down at her. 'You are being selfish. Bloody selfish. And stupid! Please yourself what you do!'

He stormed across the beach and Sibell let him go. She was shaken. His anger, rare until she'd first broached this subject, upset her. She wondered if her decision was worth all this trouble, but then she had made up her mind. She had to go before this depression got any worse.

Harriet took Sibell down to see Yorkey. 'He's rather impatient,' she said. 'Obviously not used to being laid up.'

'What man is?' Sibell said. 'They regard the sickbed as a prison. How is he?'

'Coming along. His arm's in plaster, he's lost a front tooth, and his face is still swollen with all that bruising, but don't take fright. The doctor says he looks worse than he is now. I think he said his kidney had taken a beating too, which is why he wants him to stay in bed. Rest being the cure, I believe.'

Sibell was pleased to see that someone had made the effort to spruce up the shed that was now Yorkey's sickroom. There was a large mat on the floor, a blind on the window and a table beside his bed with a water jug and medicines covered by a net throwover. But Harriet was right about Yorkey; he did look a mess, though an improvement on the state he'd been in at the station.

'Look who's here,' Harriet said brightly, and Yorkey, who'd been lying flat on the bed, turned his head painfully. He winced, recognising Sibell. 'Sorry, missus.'

'What for?' she asked.

'Running off,' Yorkey mouthed through swollen lips.

'Here, take this chair, Sibell,' Harriet said. 'I'll leave you to keep Yorkey company.'

'Thank you,' Sibell said, settling herself as Harriet departed. 'No need to apologise for leaving, Yorkey. I thought you were being sorry for burning down that house.'

The lips closed firmly. He had nothing to say to that.

'I'm interested in your name, Yorkey,' she went on. 'And I hope you won't mind my asking, but I was wondering if you were any relation to a man called Jimmy Moon. He was a friend of mine. He died a long time ago.'

'They hung him,' Yorkey growled.

'Yes. That was a terrible thing. I'm guessing that he was a relation of yours.'

'My father.'

Sibell saw the hurt in his eyes and nodded. 'I thought so. You should have told us, Yorkey, saved yourself a lot of trouble. I suppose you found out about Syd Walsh being part of that posse?'

'Yes.'

'I see. But Yorkey, you wouldn't be old enough to remember your father. Who told you about him? Your mother?'

'Some.'

Sibell didn't want to tire him, so she asked one more question, an important question, because as far as she knew, Jimmy Moon had been a single man when he'd died.

'Where did your mother live?'

'Black Wattle station,' he said firmly.

Despite her good intentions, Sibell had to disagree. 'Oh no! That couldn't be right. Our station? I'd have known her, Yorkey.'

He eased himself on to his side, facing her. 'You did, missus. She worked for you. Don't you remember Netta?'

Sibell sat back in surprise. 'Netta! For heaven's sake! I knew Netta. Of course, she was there then. It was a terrible time for all of us. And Netta is your mother?'

'Gone now.'

'I'm sorry to hear that, Yorkey. I remember Netta left about that time. She left with a drover, married him they say.'

He shook his head. 'He dumped her, missus, when he found out she was having a baby. Not his. Jimmy Moon's baby.'

'Oh dear. That is sad too. But she had a fine son, I see, so we won't talk about it any more today. Another time maybe?'

He nodded, and then managed a smile. 'She said he was a fine man, Jimmy Moon.'

'Yes, he was. A good man. Now you get some rest, Yorkey.'

She came other times too, and Yorkey looked forward to her visits. They had good yarns about the old times, because she wanted to hear all about Netta and what had become of her. And Zack came. Standing there, hands on hips, grinning at him.

'So you're Netta's son, eh? What do you know about that? I suppose now I'll have to try harder to see if I can get you off that charge. Don't forget, you can't leave town, Yorkey, you're only out on bail.'

'He's hardly well enough to do that,' Mrs Hamilton said.

'I know. I'm just warning him. Is there anything you need, Yorkey?'

There was. Yorkey had been brooding about it for a long time now. 'My horse and saddle. Those blokes at Glenelg station, they've got them.'

Zack laughed. 'You have to be joking. You'll never see them again.'

'But they're mine.'

'Yes. Well, you see, crime doesn't pay. And don't think you can go back there and get them. Glenelg is out of bounds for you, for life. Do you hear me?'

Grudgingly Yorkey agreed. But that meant he had no horse, and no money. And no job. Even if he did manage to stay out of jail. A drover without a horse!

He had other visitors. The Oatleys came down to check on him every so often, but it was the mad Chinamen who kept him entertained. They were always arguing about something in their own lingo, especially when it came to looking after him. Tom Ling was forever plastering the bruises with ointments which he claimed would cure him, but Billy Chinn reckoned he had better stuff. Sometimes he was stuck with two lots of potions slapped on his face, feeling as if he was in full warpaint, but they assured him they were colourless. Whether they were doing any good or not, he couldn't tell. He would rather just wash his face, but there was no arguing with that pair. They were the experts at that.

They stuck him in an armchair when he felt better, swaddled up like an old grandma, refusing to let him walk about much, making him rest until the doctor told him his 'middle' was in good shape again. He presumed that was his kidneys, since those bastards had sunk the boots hard there. He was still sore but he could pee and he gathered that was a good sign.

It was strange, though, when suddenly the Chinamen stopped arguing. They became cold and silent and there were a lot of peeved glances going from one to the other. It worried Yorkey so much he asked them if he had done anything wrong.

'No, no. You good chap. You be better soon,' Tom Ling said.

'Then what is wrong?'

'Nothing!' Tom cried. 'No thing at all! Everyt'ing excellence!'

Like hell, Yorkey thought.

But then one day Mrs Oatley came in to see him, and shortly after, she was followed by young Mr Oatley. Myles. They joked about the oversupply of visitors in the little room, which only had one chair, but neither of them stayed, so it didn't matter. Yorkey laughed with them, trying to think of something to say, but then Tom Ling dodged in with his tea, and Yorkey was surprised to see the quick glare Tom gave the visitors. It was gone in a second, but Yorkey thought if looks could kill, they'd both be dead on the floor.

Still chatting, neither of them noticed. When Tom left, Mrs Oatley got up to leave too, and it was then that Yorkey saw something. He saw her hand brush over young Mr Oatley's hand, and the smile she got from him in return was all wrong.

Did they think he was blind? Because he was a blackfeller or something? That touch and that smile. Not good at all. They'd been, for that minute, like a courting couple, and Yorkey was shocked.

Afterwards he tried to tell himself that he'd imagined it. And if not, so what? They were family. Fondness existed. But he'd also tuned in on the atmosphere in the room. He'd been around! He wasn't so naïve as to miss what that was about. God almighty! What were they up to? Mr Oatley's wife and son! He drank his tea in a gulp.

Tom Ling came back in to collect the cup and saucer, snapping peevishly, but Yorkey made no comment. Yes, he'd been around, so he was aware there were things better not to know about. And he bet the two hawk-eyed Chinamen were on to it too. That would account for their recent whisperings.

The two men were playing chess on the veranda. Neither of them looked up as Harriet wandered through the sitting room. She was restless, unable to think what to do to occupy herself. The night was so steamy, even the walls in this room were sweating, thin brown stains dribbling down the plaster. She shrugged and dropped into an armchair, reaching for a fan. There was not enough air in this room. A design fault, Myles had said. Most of the rooms had French windows opening on to the veranda, others had windows, ordinary windows, but the sitting room had no outer walls, just two doorways from the passages on either side. Harriet hadn't noticed before, but of course he was right; inner rooms were a mistake in this climate.

Contrarily she stayed, sighing, wielding the fan with languid strokes. She picked up the beautifully illustrated book on London that Myles had brought home for his father, opened it and gazed at a picture of the Tower, so cold and gloomy and comforting. She thought of snow. Harriet had never seen snow, but Myles had. It had snowed in London while he was there, and he'd said it was just wonderful, so soft and quiet and white.

'And cold,' Harriet murmured enviously.

She heard a shout. Then laughter. One of them had outmanoeuvred the other. William was the better player but Myles was improving; he'd won the game on Sunday night and had been crowing about it ever since.

Harriet dropped the fan, and trembled as she retrieved it. How had this happened? They certainly hadn't wanted it to happen. Good Lord, it had not occurred to her in those early days that they could even be friends, let alone . . .

Oh God! Oh Lord!

In a way, Harriet thought defensively, we're sort of innocents. How were we to know, when we were thrown together so much, that a mutual attraction lay ahead? When we were both relieved that we could find common ground without having to pretend, and so please William. Humour had started it. Innocent laughter that had allowed them to relax in each other's company, and then seek it out, for neither of them had much to do while William was at work. Often now, Harriet wondered how she had occupied these stormy, sultry days before Myles had come along. And then there was that night when he'd stood back to allow her to pass through a narrow doorway, and she'd felt it, that sudden bolt like an electrical current. Harriet had never experienced anything like that in her life before. Myles had felt it too. They'd stared at one another for a second. Gaped really, and Harriet had run, cheeks blazing.

Then had come the avoidance. The embarrassment. Even a return of mild hostility, until that night at the Cable Company ball, when he'd finally danced with her. And then only because they were the last two left at the table. A waltz, and he'd held her in his arms. They hadn't wanted this, this attraction. Neither of them had set out to flirt. It was never like that. But she was in his arms and he was saying, 'You're avoiding me again,' and she was denying it, and he said she was beautiful and she said, 'No, no, don't say that,' and he said they had to talk about this and she said, 'Talk about what?' and in the end she'd agreed because as he said, they couldn't go on dodging one another. Behaving oddly.

They met in the gardens, by the swollen boab tree. Harriet was there first, pacing along the path between a row of florid hibiscus, glancing up at the restless grey skies, praying for them to send down a deluge and give her an excuse to run because she was so nervous. What did they have to talk about? What was she doing there? Praying that he'd forget. Maybe he'd had too much to drink.

But Myles came. And there was joy, and the heady perfume of frangipani, and they were in each other's arms before a word was said. That was how it happened, she thought miserably, guiltily. That was how romance came into their lives. Bittersweet, she thought tenderly. Bittersweet. Because she did love William, and Myles did love his father, but the love that took hold that day was too strong. And the furtive touching, kissing in dark corners took on a life of its own, of frustration and guilt. Always that guilt.

They tried. She tried. Harriet was on the defensive again, recalling the morning when they were alone in the house and she'd gone to him to tell him that it had to stop. To his room, knocking gently, afraid even then that someone might intrude.

'It can't stop,' he'd said to her. 'My love for you is ferocious. Ferocious, Harriet! I don't want it to stop, and neither do you. You can't.'

They made love in his bed, urgent, engrossing love, new, exciting lovemaking that both bound them together and made their lives even more frustrating. That had Myles hanging about the house as often as he could, sending the servants off on errands. That left Harriet like this, restless, wandering about her own home like a stranger, not knowing what to do with herself when left alone. Lonely.

She kept up appearances with William. She allowed him to make love to her, but there was no love any more, only duty, and thankfully he didn't seem to notice any difference. And thankfully too, Myles didn't enquire about that side of her life.

Besides, William had his own problems. He was worried about Sibell Hamilton and her threat to leave Zack. 'Astonishing,' Myles had said. And about Yorkey's looming court case. Yorkey was better now, but still living in the servants' quarters.

Harriet found it a slight irritation that Sibell called on Yorkey every so often. Zack had insisted his wife had no wish to bother Harriet, and she used the side entrance, avoiding the main house, but Harriet was bothered. Her afternoons were no longer private in case Sibell did decide to call on her, and often, just to be sociable, Harriet felt obliged to invite her to afternoon tea, even though Sibell rarely accepted.

Myles said he thought his father was half in love with Sibell, which caused Harriet to sulk a little; unreasonable she supposed, but that remark had implied that William was not totally in love with her.

Whatever was to become of them? she worried, discarding the fan and the book and unbuttoning her blouse down from the collar for some respite from the heat. William was becoming more and more impatient with Myles about Lucy Hamilton. Kindly, but insistent. Myles had a battery of excuses, sometimes blaming Lucy for being too ill-tempered, while his father thought the answer would be for Myles and Lucy to have a good talk.

We all need to have a good talk, Harriet thought, but who's going to bell the cat? At one stage Myles had suggested to her that he would go out and take over management of the Millford station, which had belonged to his mother's parents originally, and that once he got settled, Harriet could leave William and come to join him. They could go bush, go to Millford, away from everyone, and take up their own lives.

'But doesn't your father own Millford?' Harriet had reminded him.

No point in taking that any further. The hard fact remained that Myles without his father was penniless. With his father and Lucy, and of course Pop, he would be, in time, a millionaire several times over.

Harriet's hands were damp. Ferocious though his love might be, she wondered how long it could survive against odds like that. But dear Lord, how she did love Myles, despite this awful guilt. She wished they could just run away, not to Millford but to London. To the cold and the big log fires and strangers; to anonymity, with just their love to sustain them.

She went to bed depressed, leaving them to their game, or another game, feeling that, in all this, she would end up the loser. But she was too much in love with Myles now to want to look too far ahead.

The letter was clearly marked PRIVATE, so Leo had left it unopened on William's desk.

He slit it open, unhurried, his eyes still on the list of interesting horses to be offered at the forthcoming yearling sales, and then glanced at it expecting yet another invitation to the interminable round of end-of-the-year parties organised by local businessmen; boring affairs, always the same people, the same format, boozy dinners that often ended in rows. He had dodged several of them this year.

But this was not an invitation. He felt his face redden as he read the first few words.

Dear William,
    I am only writing because I feel you ought to know about this matter, something I cannot bring myself to mention to you in person because it is too upsetting. To come straight to the point, I believe your wife and your son are having an affair. You should know too that other people are voicing their suspicions. I feel this is also my business because my niece is involved and is suffering bewilderment at the hands of your son . . .

He couldn't read any more. Sadly he screwed up the letter and dropped it in the waste-paper basket; then he stared, unseeing, out of the window.

'I know, Maudie, I know,' he whispered miserably. 'I just hoped that no one else knew.'

He'd known for some time. How could I not have known . . . noticed? he worried. At first I kept telling myself I was just being a jealous old man. I wanted them to be friends. I threw them together, maybe it was my fault. But what else could I do? I never expected this. It didn't occur to me that this could happen. I love them both so much and they've let me down. Myles had been so much against the marriage, William wondered if he had deliberately seduced Harriet. Then he shook his head. It takes two, it takes two. For that matter he couldn't be sure how far this affair had gone. Were they just flirting, or was it already worse than that?

In his heart, William already knew the answer. He'd seen the fondness, the furtive glances, all the wretched rigmarole of an affair. And he'd begun to watch the servants. Their attitude to Harriet and Myles bordered on hostility, beneath those smiling Chinese faces and their seemingly pleasant chatter. They were keeping up appearances for his benefit, out of loyalty to him, just as he had been keeping up appearances, hiding the anger that was boiling up inside him.

'Damn them!' he exploded, glad that Leo was out of the office. 'Bloody bastards! Ingrates!'

All this time he'd been keeping himself under control, hiding his anger and his desolation, hoping he was wrong, that this thing between them would go away, trying not to face the fact that they were breaking his heart. That was the worst of it. Lucy might be suffering bewilderment, but whatever happened, she was young, she would get over it. For him, though, it was grief, all over again, as painful as the time he'd lost his beloved Emily May. And he found himself grieving for her again. Emily May would never have turned against him so cruelly.

But now, since Maudie knew, and others were suspicious, their disgraceful behaviour would be common knowledge, and he, the cuckold, would have to do something. Do what? Confront them? What if they denied it?

What if they did not.

'Oh Jesus!' he cried, close to tears. He was afraid that he would make a fool of himself if he did confront them. That his already shattered nerves would reduce him to a blubbering mess. He opened the deep drawer in his desk and took out the whisky bottle, but then quickly shoved it back.

'I can't start that again. I dare not. I'll just have to work this through. Damn them.'

Rage was easier. More satisfying. He began to roam through possibilities. Rage would fend off embarrassing blubbering. He could go home and order Myles out of his house. Her too. Why not? Then he'd have a grip on things. Even give them voice. Hear their sorry tale. Then what? Watch them leave together? Leave the sorry old man to his empty house and empty life.

The walls of his office seemed to be closing in on him. He was breathing heavily; he needed air. He grabbed his hat and stormed out of the office with no particular destination in mind; he just wanted to walk and never stop. But as he passed the church, the Reverend Walters came dashing out to accost him.

'Mr Oatley! Just a minute! I was wondering if Zack Hamilton has had a word with you?'

'No. What about?' William asked abruptly. He was in no mood for this fellow. This man who preached goodness at Harriet Oatley every Sunday. At a hypocritical woman who pretended to be a good Christian. Wasting time, the lot of them.

'About that block next to your place. We were hoping you'd reconsider your appeals against our plans to build the new church.'

William stared at him, hardly registering what he was on about for a few minutes, then, suddenly, none of that mattered.

'Do what you like!' he snapped. 'Build anything you like. I'm selling that house.'

Walters' thanks gushed, but William strode on, ignoring him. He had surprised himself with that statement, but now it seemed a good idea. He'd never be happy there again. They'd defiled it, spoiled it. Spurred on by the realisation that he was at last making a move of some sort, William hurried back to the office to have a talk with Leo.

His clerk was stunned. 'You're selling your house? Why?'

'Because I'm retiring.'

'What? From the business? The agency?'

'Yes, but don't worry, I'll not leave you in the lurch. I thought you might like to take over.'

'In what capacity? Manager or owner?'

'Up to you.'

Leo leaned forward in his chair and stared across the desk at his boss. 'Are you serious?'

'I certainly am.'

247

'Where does Myles fit in?'

William looked about him. 'I don't see Myles. Do you?'

'No, but . . .'

'But nothing. Myles has no interest in this firm beyond putting in a few days when he has nothing better to do.'

Leo nodded cautiously. It was true, Myles hadn't spent much time in the office since he came home, and his rare appearances had been a source of irritation to Leo, who felt he was only there to lord it over him, and quiz him about the finances. Nevertheless, Myles was the son and heir, and this was an odd turn of events. Out of character for William Oatley to make sudden decisions like this. He wondered if William had heard the rumours going about the town about Myles and Harriet, rumours that Leo had hotly denied.

He stalled for time, searching for his pipe and lighting it, as figures danced about in his head. He couldn't risk taking over as manager with Myles in the wings. Their dislike was mutual. The son could interfere at any time. And what if, God forbid, something happened to William? Leo knew he'd be out on his ear overnight.

'How much are you asking?' he said, totting up his assets and his not inconsiderable share portfolio.

'You're better at that than me,' William smiled. 'I guess I'm selling goodwill, unless you want to buy these three blocks as well. The office doesn't have to be located here.'

'But they're a good investment,' Leo said. 'If you have no use for them, I'd like to include them in the package. If it's all right with you, William. But are you sure you want me to list the house for sale?'

'Yes. No point me hanging about Darwin if I've nothing to do.'

'Where will you go?' Leo noted he'd said 'No point in me . . .' not 'us', and that made him nervous. There was trouble in the Oatley household. Such a shame. William and Harriet had been so happy until that little rat came home.

He sighed. William was now talking about returning to his own station, Millford.

'I miss the bush,' he said quietly. 'It'll be good to go back.'

'Don't get carried away,' Leo warned. 'It's late and they still haven't had enough rain out there to make the grass grow. They've only got a few months left for good rains, and if they miss out they're in for a drought year.'

'Listen to you,' William grinned. 'You're the numbers man. I'm the bushie. It's cyclical, the weather. You get the good and the bad. Anyway, for what it's worth, I'm betting we'll get plenty of rain this season. It's late, that's all. Now, do you want first ask on the business, lock, stock and contracts?'

'It's good of you to give me the chance, William. I'll work out a fair figure based on our profit margin. But I might have to take out a loan to cover part of my offer.'

William stood up. He seemed anxious to be away. 'It's a deal then,' he said, reaching out to shake Leo's hand. 'Congratulations to the new owner of the Oatley Mercantile Company. And if you need a loan to reach the sale price, my friend, I'll cover it. I'm in no hurry for cash.'

Now for home. William had no regrets about relinquishing the business or the house. He felt he was stripping himself for battle, even though he knew his efforts were tinged with bravado. And he had also come to accept that his failure to put a stop to the mischief in his house was sheer cowardice. Another man, a better man would have gone at the problem with a stockwhip. So why couldn't he? Maybe the better man didn't have to deal with love. He adored Harriet, he still did. And how could you stop loving your only son? Basically, he knew, he was afraid of losing them. The hurt, the grief was bad enough now, his stomach churning, his bones aching, his mind obsessed by the unfair challenge of youth. William felt old before them.

That evening there were fireworks in the sky. Fiery bolts of lightning struck at the earth with deafening cracks; zigzag bolts raced across the sky, searching for targets, and sheet lightning took its turn in transposing night into bright brittle daylight, while the thunder rolled and crashed in a frenzy, encouraging this intimidating display as if to remind earthlings of their impotence against the forces of nature.

Harriet was terrified. Her mother used to cover mirrors against lightning, but no one bothered up here; the summer storms were too frequent. She wouldn't sit on the veranda where it was cooler, so William joined her in the parlour before dinner.

'It's no use worrying about the lightning,' he told her. 'Unless you're standing under a tree. Anyway, that storm is out to sea. Count the seconds between the lightning and the bang and you'll know how far off it is.'

'But what if there's no time in between?' she asked nervously.

'Then it has just hit this house or nearby,' he grinned. William had already been served three whiskies, building up to the question. Finally it had come down to the weakest of all his considerations.

'Harriet. My dear. I have to ask. Is there anything you want to tell me?'

She jumped as if she had been jabbed with a pin. 'What about?'

Already William felt deflated. 'I don't know. Are you happy? You seem so distant these days. Is everything all right?'

'Of course it is. It's just this weather, it's so depressing. It wasn't like this last year; the rain really swept in, almost taking us by surprise, but this year it has been dragging on and these storms are the end. They're too terrible, and still not enough rain to clear the air.'

'Rain doesn't clear the air up here,' he muttered. 'It just adds to the humidity and discomfort. It's at the end of the rain when the sun dries everything that the air becomes clear.'

Harriet snapped a response. 'Very well. Whatever you say.'

'I was thinking,' he added, 'that you don't appear to be sleeping too well these nights. If the heat is bothering you, perhaps you'd prefer for me to sleep in the spare room?'

She was surprised, but then agreed.

'Oh William, would you? It would be so much easier for us. I mean, we both add to the heat, and one does perspire far too much, no wonder it is so difficult to get to sleep.'

He nodded, not appreciating her enthusiasm. 'Have Tom Ling move my things if you think it's for the best, for the time being.'

Before she could rush off, he had another question. 'By the way, what's happening with Myles and Lucy? I hear the Hamilton family is becoming agitated.'

'Really? Then they should ask Lucy. She's going out with Christy Cornford. They're quite a twosome.'

This was news. Not good news. No wonder Maudie had taken up the cudgels. Cornford's credentials were no match for young Oatley in her eyes. Bugger Cornford. Why did he have to stick his bib in now? Lucy had been William's last chance to separate this pair. But if one faced the truth, for Lucy's sake, Christy was probably a better proposition than Myles Oatley and his despicable behaviour. At least Christy was up front with the ladies, making no bones about the fact he was looking for a suitable wife. The Hamiltons just might approve of him to spare Lucy the humiliation of Myles's seeming disinterest.

Myles didn't make it home for dinner, but when he finally came in, his father was waiting. Unfortunately William had drunk several more whiskies to fill in the time. He was sitting on the veranda when Myles came in the front door.

'There you are! I thought you must have moved out. I rarely see you lately.'

'I'm never far away.'

'Did you have a good time tonight?'

'Oh yes. I suppose so. The company in Darwin is hardly exhilarating.'

'Then perhaps you ought to leave.'

'To be honest, I wish I could. I've got my heart set on taking over Millford station. I can't get there fast enough.'

'Then why don't you go now?'

Myles dropped his coat on a chair. 'Have you been drinking, Father? Playing up?' He was amused.

'Not much,' his father said amiably. 'I asked why you don't go now?'

Myles dropped into a cane chair. 'Jesus, Father, what's got into you? In the first place, I'd like to stay for Christmas, and secondly, the roads are washed out. I'd never make it to Millford at this time of year.'

'The roads aren't washed out. There hasn't been enough rain out there to drown a snail as yet.'

'All right, but what about Christmas? I was looking forward to a family Christmas.'

'What? You, me and Harriet?'

'And all of our friends.'

'I see. But it seems to me that you are running out of friends here.'

'What do you mean by that?'

Tom Ling popped his head round the door. William had never seen him so distressed. 'Your room ready, master. Not good you drink no more, you come to bed now.'

'Get out,' Myles slung at him, and he disappeared.

'Lucy,' William said, trying to concentrate on his son rather than Tom Ling, for the minute.

'Oh, you've heard. Lucy has a new admirer.'

'So you blame her for the break-up of your relationship?'

'No, I don't, Dad. We grew apart, that's all. I'm sorry if we didn't match up to all your plans, and the Hamilton plans, but that's the way things happen.'

'So there's no lady in your life now? No one.'

'Correct.'

'Can I tell Harriet that?'

'What?' Myles almost shouted at him.

'You heard,' William said evenly. Marvelling at the steadying influence of alcohol.

'Are you accusing me . . .?'

'No. I need to know the truth. Are you having an affair with Harriet?'

Myles sprang to his feet. 'What a vicious thing to say. Are you mad? Or just a jealous, besotted old fool. I'm going to bed and I'll expect an apology in the morning. When you're sober.'

Tom Ling witnessed the performance from the other end of the veranda. When Myles charged away, incensed, he came down to William. 'I make you nice hot tea, master, and sweetie biscuits. You come along now.'

'Thank you,' William said wearily, allowing Tom to help him to his feet. The alcohol had turned on him now with a cruel headache.

Tom brought the tea and biscuits, and a headache powder in flimsy wrapping, but before he left he turned back to his master, tears in his eyes.

'He lies,' he whispered, and bowing apologetically, shuffled out the door.

The sun was blazing merrily again as if the wet had been and gone, as if it were now time to be about the housekeeping, drying out loitering clouds, mopping up the damp countryside, beaming down on the great blue harbour; in all doing little but creating a mischief.

To fend off the glare, Leo lowered the wide canvas blind.

'Doesn't look too good,' he said. 'You wouldn't like to take a bet on this season's rainfall, would you? I reckon we'll only get half our quota, if that.'

William shook his head. 'You'd lose. It'll come.'

'Always the optimist,' Leo grinned.

251

As they turned back to sorting files prior to Leo's takeover of the firm, William had never felt less optimistic. He and Leo had come to an amicable agreement for the transfer of ownership of the Oatley Mercantile Company, but that was minor compared to the dark clouds looming on his home front. He had expected Myles to come forward this morning and demand that apology, but instead he was missing. Gone out early, Billy Chinn had told him. And Harriet, she'd been overly cheerful at breakfast – in quite a dither, as a matter of fact – but William had been too depressed to comment. He'd been glad to get out of the house himself.

Later in the morning he looked up to see Yorkey standing shyly in the open doorway.

William sat back. 'Come in, Yorkey. Good to see you up and about. What can I do for you?'

'I come to say goodbye, boss. And to thank you for puttin' me up. Zack says the police they don't want me no more.'

'You were lucky Syd's wife didn't prefer charges. She's had enough of Syd herself; she's pulling out.'

'Is she selling the station?' Leo asked, eyes lighting up.

'Yes. I forgot to tell you,' William said. 'She's divorcing that bastard. I heard she's staying at the Victoria.' He winked. 'Maybe you'd better get around there and strike while the iron's hot. Those Brisbane graziers are still looking for a property up here, aren't they?'

Leo was up, reaching for his hat, then he hesitated. 'You wouldn't like to come with me?'

'No. You're on your own now, mate.'

When he'd left, William turned to Yorkey. 'And where are you off to, Yorkey?'

'Ah . . . I thought I'd go on down the track. Maybe Pine Creek. Or on to Katherine. Have a look about. Zack Hamilton, he give me a horse.'

'Good. Now you keep away from Syd Walsh and don't go burning any more houses.'

'Yeah, boss.' Having done his duty, the shy Aborigine was edging out, but William told him to wait. He was fishing in his pocket to give the lad a couple of pounds to see him on his way, but an idea came to him. He handed over the notes, insisting that Yorkey take them, and then asked when he was leaving.

'Today good as any,' Yorkey shrugged.

'Could you hold on until tomorrow?'

'Yeah.'

'I was thinking I might go out and see my father. He hasn't been well. He owns Warrawee station. Do you know it?'

'Can't say I do.'

'Well, that doesn't matter, but I'd be glad of company. Do you want to come with me?'

'That'd be good, boss. Somethin' to do. Yeah.'

'Right. We leave in the morning. Bright and early. I'll get supplies organised this afternoon. You go on home and tell Tom Ling to come and see me, he can pick up everything we need.'

William sighed. 'I could do with a good long ride to clear my head. It's still dry enough for us to get through.'

Yorkey nodded. 'Rains late this year.'

Harriet dressed slowly, watching for Myles. As soon as he appeared she put on a large sun hat and hurried down to the gate to meet him as if by chance, as she was leaving for her walk.

'He has moved out of our bedroom,' she told him urgently.

'I know. He practically threw me out of the house last night.'

'Oh God! Does he know?'

'Not really. He thinks he does, that's all.'

'That's all! What did he say?'

'It doesn't matter. We just have to be more careful.'

Harriet smiled radiantly at some passers-by and Myles turned to acknowledge them, and then looked back at her.

'You look beautiful this morning. It must be the luxury of getting him out of your bed. Pity I couldn't join you.'

'Oh don't, Myles, please,' she whispered. 'What are we going to do? I can't stand this much longer. Why don't you go and have a quiet talk with your father and we'll get this over with.'

'About what?'

She was becoming cross. 'Don't be obtuse. William has to know sooner or later. You can break it to him gently.'

'The hell I can. He'd throw us both out.'

'I know. It will be terrible. But we could go out to Millford station. You're always talking about that. Why don't we just go now? I feel sorry for William, so guilty—'

'And you think that will help? You don't listen, Harriet. That station is presently leased to the manager and his wife. I can go out there, but if I took you with me, I can assure you we'd get a very nasty reception. I checked the lease contract; they've got another six months to go.'

'Six months! No! I can't go on like this for another six months, Myles. I can't bear it.' She was close to tears but still managing to give the impression that she and Myles were simply engaging in amiable conversation.

'Then what's the alternative? Do you want me to go now? I love you. I want to stay with you as long as possible.'

'I don't know,' she said wretchedly. 'Perhaps it would be for the best.'

'So that you can get all lovey-dovey with him in the meantime and forget all about me,' he snapped. 'Have I become an inconvenience?'

'No! No. Of course not.'

'Then stop worrying. I have a good excuse to stay until after the wet season. Then I'll be the dutiful son and work out there, learning the ropes, until I take over officially. I'll have the lease. You can join me and no one can do a thing about it. I'll insist on a five-year lease, and by that time the fuss will have died down.'

'Are you sure?'

'Yes. Now, if you're going into town you'd better get going. We can't stand here all day.'

He watched her walk up the street, wishing he could have taken her in his arms then and there. She was beautiful and she had the most marvellous body. Why hadn't he paid more attention to her back there in Perth? But then she was just the dowdy daughter of a bank manager. She had matured magnificently. He envied his father, and resented him now. Resented the unfairness that an old bloke like William had her, could bed her night after night while he had to wait for the rare chance. Only three days ago they'd made love in a lonely, secluded corner of the Botanic gardens, heavy with tropical growth, and she'd groaned with pleasure at his hard, fit body. He wondered if she'd ever been so abandoned with William in that stuffy bedroom.

But the situation wasn't as simple as he'd told her. Whichever way he looked, William held the purse strings. He could work at Millford station, but would his father give him the lease? Despite his bravado of the night before, for the first time in his life Myles had seen a flint-eyed William Oatley, and it had unnerved him. Which was why he'd disappeared to the Chinese café for breakfast and moved on to the billiard room, keeping out of sight until William had gone to the office.

What to do? There were plenty of easy options, all of which meant giving up Harriet. William had had an easy run all his life; everything, including a happy marriage to Mother, had been handed to him on a plate. But his son had fallen for Harriet. He was mad about her, desperately in love with her. Just once couldn't William fail? Would it hurt him that much? How could a man expect to be so permanently lucky? If it hadn't been him, Myles thought meanly, who was to say Harriet wouldn't have fallen for another man, a younger man. She was ripe for the taking, as he'd found.

In the end he decided to do nothing. They would have to be more careful. Come to think of it, why place his financial prospects at risk? Harriet was pliable; no matter what happened there was no reason to end his affair with her. Rather than look for trouble by having her leave William, and thereby costing him a fortune, why not keep things as they were? It would be rather delicious to know that Harriet was always there for him, no matter how often or for how long they were separated. He could even marry; plenty of married men had mistresses.

Finally Myles had settled the matter. He and Harriet would always be lovers, on the quiet. No need to discuss his solution with her; it would simply evolve in time.

And maybe he ought to call on Lucy again, ease out that upstart Christy Cornford.

His visit to the Hamilton household was short-lived.

Maudie saw him coming up the path and hurried down the steps from the front veranda to meet him. To head him off, as it turned out.

'You are not welcome in this house, Myles Oatley.'

'I beg your pardon!'

'You ought to beg your father's pardon. And the Lord's!' she flung at him. 'And while you're about it, has no one informed you that our public gardens are not bedrooms? Now get out of here!'

She turned on her heel and stamped back to the house, but Myles was already rushing away, horrified. He hadn't seen a soul on that garden tryst. It had been in the afternoon, the hottest time of the day, when most people were indoors. But someone had seen them. Who? Maybe someone had been following them, spying on them. And who else knew? Oh, Jesus! Was this why William had confronted him?

He was shattered. The enormity of the situation only just beginning to dawn on him. Harriet should have reminded him about the narrow-minded country town gossips. He'd been away too long. In London, everyone seemed to be having affairs, especially marrieds, and everyone else looked the other way. But here, nothing was private. Angrily he realised that even if he and Harriet hadn't been involved in their love affair, the local gossips would have invented a relationship. Both young, both living under the same roof! So . . . there was only one thing to do now. Stand their ground. Deny it, strongly and defiantly. Play the innocents, wrongly accused, if it came up. He prayed to God it would not come up, because from now on, Harriet would have to keep away from him, at least for the time being, until he had things worked out; no more meetings, or even walks together, no more sweet minutes in the house . . .

He took refuge in the billiard room for the rest of the afternoon, making up his mind to be punctual for dinner this evening, and all other meals, instead of avoiding a threesome as often as possible. There was nothing to worry about now. Temporarily, the affair was over. The gossip would peter out.

William knew he was taking the coward's way out by running away, but even his attempts at anger and retaliation could not stem the grief he was suffering. The pain was physical, and he felt old, unable to match their youth. He was losing his wife and son and he had become so shamed he couldn't cope. And all the time there was this itch to reach for the bottle, drown his sorrows in a drunken haze. He couldn't let that happen again. He must not. Going bush was the answer; five days out on the track with Yorkey was just what the doctor would order, five days of good healthy living again. Then he'd stay with Pop for a while and not mention a word of this. Peace beckoned. He refused to look further into the future.

He told them at dinner that he'd be leaving for Warrawee station in the morning and countered their expected questions by claiming that he was worried about Pop.

'I'll come with you then,' Myles said, and sadly William noted his wife's surprised reaction.

'No. I'm going with Yorkey. You stay in town. I don't want you to miss the festivities of the season.'

'But I haven't seen Pop yet. I'd like to come.'

'And leave Harriet here on her own? No. I'll only be away a couple of weeks. I'll be back in time for Christmas.'

'Why don't we all go?' she said.

'No. It's too difficult with a wagon this time of year, it would take too long keeping out of bogs, with the creeks starting to run.'

She turned to Myles. 'In all this time I've never been out to any of the stations. We've always been too busy.'

'Or taking off for Singapore,' William reminded her.

'But I wouldn't need a wagon. I could ride.'

'No you couldn't,' Myles snapped. 'Not in this heat. You're not an experienced rider.'

'And whose fault is that?' she demanded of William.

He sighed. 'No more arguments. I'm leaving in the morning with Yorkey, and that's that.'

As soon as he found a minute to speak to her alone, Myles whispered, 'It's a trap, you know. He probably won't go far at all. Then turn up here suddenly hoping to catch us out.'

'Oh no! Do you think so?'

'I'm sure.'

They were both up early to see them off; William looking pleased, Yorkey grinning broadly, and the two Chinamen fussing over the supplies and equipment on the packhorse.

'You didn't take a packhorse last time,' Harriet said to William.

'No. That was urgent. This time I'm not in such a rush and we might get held up looking for crossings.'

Myles looked at him curiously. 'You'd travel a lot faster without the packhorse.'

'Maybe I'd like a bit of comfort this time. And I have it on good authority that Yorkey is a damn fine cook.'

'You bet!' Yorkey grinned.

After they'd left, Myles went straight to his room to pack.

'What are you doing?' Harriet asked him.

'I told you. This is a trap. I'm moving into the Victoria Hotel.'

'But he wanted you to stay here. To keep me company,' she added archly.

'Don't be so bloody stupid! If I stay here alone with you we'll be looking for trouble. It'll cause talk.'

'Your father didn't seem to think so.'

'I don't know what he's bloody thinking. Going off like this is mad. Now tell Tom Ling to bring me some fresh shirts.'

256

PART THREE

December 1900

Chapter Fifteen

Numinga didn't appreciate any of Mimimiadie's plans to rescue his son, mainly because they involved him and, naturally, put him at risk. His former colleague had taken for granted that Numinga would gladly go forth into the white world, find Boomi and bring him back to his heartbroken father, and was astonished at his reticence.

'Have you checked the stations hereabouts?' Numinga asked. 'The police probably dumped him on the nearest white woman they came across. It would be easy to grab him back.'

'Don't you think I've done that?' Mimimiadie growled. 'I've had everyone looking, watching for him. All you have to do is go into Pine Creek and ask. White people know everything, they've got their message wires, the ticktack machines.'

'And then what? I take you in and hand you over in exchange for Boomi?'

'Never! They'd kill me and keep Boomi. You find out where he is and come back and tell me and we'll raid the place. Kill them all.'

Numinga appealed to the stony-faced elders sitting round the campfire. 'Can't you see this is impossible? The police know me. If they spot me I'll be back in jail, no use to anyone. I'm sorry about Boomi, I wish I could help, but it's too difficult. You should turn to the spirits for better advice. But I do thank you for freeing me from that jail.'

'We could put you back,' Mimimiadie growled. 'They say it is shut down now. They wouldn't find you until after the rains.'

Numinga's stomach reeled in fear but he put on a brave front. 'Would that bring Boomi back?' he snapped.

'Make no difference,' Mimimiadie shrugged, and Numinga knew the threat was real. Even more menacing than the clear instructions of these old magic men that he was to co-operate or face punishment by the spirits; in other words, one of them would point the bone at him so he would wither and die. Much the same thing, he pondered, as Mimimiadie's punishment.

'I will need better clothings,' he said finally, and they were immediately produced. A red checked shirt, dungarees, large boots, a rawhide hat, even a stockwhip.

'And a horse.'

'Horse coming,' Garradji, the spokesman for the council of elders, told him.

'Not much use without a saddle and bridle,' he retorted, but a few days later, there it was. A horse, fully equipped, with a stockman's battered saddle and an ancient bridle, the reins as thin as string.

'I have to think about the best way to go about this,' Numinga countered, but that had been taken care of too.

A woman appeared to cut off his long, grey-flecked beard and shave his skin raw with sap soap and a rubbing stone. She trimmed his eyebrows too, and cut his long hair to ear length. Numinga thought he saw rare laughter in Garradji's rheumy eyes as he nodded to her to keep going.

Chewing and spitting, she made a paste in a gourd and applied it to his hair.

'What are you doing?' he asked.

'Making you young fella. No more old hair,' she grinned, and looking down at the black paste he realised she was dyeing the grey in his hair. Pitching it black again, something only effeminate men did.

Mimimiadie was delighted. 'You look different now. I wouldn't have known you my own self, maybe. Now we go.'

'Where to?'

'The gorge. Make camp there. Same place. Gopiny is waiting. Garradji is coming too. To make sure you don't scare off.'

Numinga felt his smooth face, wondering what he looked like. He'd worn a beard all his life, just as his father had done, and this felt very strange. He turned to Garradji.

'This now makes me a new man. You ask the spirits to give me wisdom to carry out this difficult duty, for I am just a feeble man.'

'You are more than that,' Garradji said tonelessly. 'You are new to me but I have been watching. You have the spirits in you, and the wisdom.' He turned to Mimimiadie. 'You are wrong. You told me this man was a warrior.'

'He killed a white man. I learned that as a true fact.'

'From justice, I think. You two are mismatched, but we must proceed now. That boy must be found. They have taken too many of our children. This one is one too many.'

Only then did Numinga understand that Mimimiadie wasn't in charge of this operation at all, despite all the aggressive plans that had been discussed and eliminated. These old men were making a stand. His stomach turned over again. He was caught in the middle.

Wandering about in the savage heat of the little settlement at Pine Creek, Numinga wondered why the white people brought this on themselves. Admittedly, it was a rail station, a telegraph office and civilisation for men still digging futilely for gold, on the outskirts, but they huddled together in this miserable place when there were much kinder camping areas not too far away. Over to the east of this barren town there was such coolness and beauty in the quiet reaches and pools of natural springs that it was beyond him to understand why they all stayed here. Then again, he

260

decided, as he trudged along ugly Railway Street, it was just as well. The water, earth and bird spirits would probably have convulsions if white folk built their awful timber and iron houses out there.

So he kept wandering about, not having the faintest idea what to do or who to ask, peering into every house and building like a starving dog, hoping to spot Boomi, or for that matter any child of his age who could fit the picture. But there were none. He was able to question the Aborigines hanging about the town, putting the fear of spirits into them, demanding they search the place for the famous Mimimiadie's son, but none had seen him. Not one, no matter how hard they tried, could bring him back any news.

He had no money. They didn't think of that, did they? So he had to rely on his own folk, poor as they were, to keep him fed until he got a job for a few pence cleaning stables. But one good thing emerged. He passed Constable Smith in the street and the silly young fool didn't recognise him. That gave Numinga more confidence. With the money he earned, he hung about the next level of Aboriginal social standing, the stockmen who were permitted to buy drinks out the back doors of the pubs. Some of them had heard about the kidnapping of Mimimiadie's son, and were sympathetic, but could not help.

In the end Numinga sent a man he trusted out to the gorge to tell Mimimiadie that Boomi was not in Pine Creek, so he had gone south to Katherine, to search there. Katherine was the headquarters of police in this area. He hoped he could find the child, or learn something there without being apprehended.

His beard kept growing at an alarming rate, and Numinga spent irritating mornings at each of his lonely camps shaving with a rusty razor and broken mirror that one of the women had found for him. She was very dark and very sweet, and she'd taken a whitefeller name, Lulu, so a man could hardly forget that. It had a nice ring to it.

But Katherine, though a bigger town, had no answer. There he even contacted Aborigine folk connected with the dreaded mission settlements where a lot of their kids were held, but not Boomi. There was no sign of him anywhere. Until one night an Aborigine girl came to him with her story. She was a floozy, she said, better paid than black or white trash, because she could sing and dance as well as being a good bed slut, so she had a better class of customers in her own hut behind the George Hotel. She even had policemen customers, she told Numinga proudly, so she had quizzed them about the famous Mimimiadie renegade, who had become as well known as the white bushrangers. She even heard about the man – a captain, she assured Numinga – who had actually snatched Mimimiadie's kid.

They were still waiting for Mimimiadie to give himself up in exchange for his kid, but they didn't think he'd have the guts, since he was known as a cowardly ambusher and murderer. And that was true, they said, because they hadn't heard a word from Mimimiadie. No message. No nothing.

'But where's the kid? Where's Boomi?' he'd asked.

'I'm coming to that. They're not going to give him back whatever happens. They got orders to shoot Mimimiadie on sight. They reckon the kid's going to be brought up proper. Speaking English. Growing up a real good boy, not like us, livin' in dumps on the edge of nothin'.'

'You don't believe that?'

'Too right I do. We're finished, Numinga. Nothin' left for us no more. Us a dead people. Them whites too strong with their guns and all.'

'It's not true, pretty girl. Not true. We have been here since monsters stalked the earth thousands of years ago. There have been other crises like this, there have been. The songs tell you this. All life is change, we will survive this new change.'

'Yeah. So the songs say. But I dunno how. Anyway, I won't starve. I'll cut my throat when I get too ugly.'

'Oh no,' he mourned. 'Oh no.'

'Didn't you want to know about the kid?'

'Yes,' he said absently, too grief-stricken about her attitude to concentrate.

'They've taken him to Darwin. To a mission school. The best in the Territory, they say. He'll be all right. You tell Mimimiadie not to worry about him no more. He going to be pretty good off.'

Numinga rested the horse at an isolated cattle station for a few days and then began the long ride back, travelling cross-country, not looking forward to delivering this bad news. As he left the open country studded with eucalyptus and bedraggled wattle, he was pleased to see tiny green shoots peeping out across the land and hoped there'd be quick rain again before they withered and died. Here were the beginnings of fresh pastures at last, to save some of the poor gaunt cattle he'd seen gazing about in despair.

He knew that Mimimiadie and his mates would have seen him approaching from their lookout high above the gorge, so he was not surprised, as he negotiated the rocky terrain leading to the entrance, when Mimimiadie and Gopiny suddenly appeared in front of him, but his horse took fright. It reared, squealing, almost dislodging its rider.

Unconcerned, Mimimiadie was already shouting the question.

'You find Boomi?'

Numinga made him wait. He calmed the horse. Gave it a chunk of apple. Gave Mimimiadie the other half, hoping to calm him too. 'We will sit and talk,' he told the two men.

Mimimiadie crunched the apple in a couple of bites, his dark eyes wary, but he listened without interruption as Numinga explained the situation.

'We can't raid any place in Darwin,' he said. 'It's a big town, plenty people, plenty police. I never been there but this I hear. Big jail too, full of blackfellers.' He had no wish to take part in a raid of any sort.

Mimimiadie seemed pleased, though; at least now he had some

knowledge of his son's whereabouts. He decided to climb back up and confer with Garradji.

While they climbed, Numinga took a roundabout route of miles before he found a way to lead the horse up to the plateau, but it was worth the effort. Rain had fallen in the heights, bushes had sprung into life, patches of green littered the thin soil and rocky hollows were filled with crystal-clear water. The horse drank greedily.

A meeting was in progress, and when all eyes looked to the newcomer expectantly, Numinga had the sinking feeling that another plan involving him had been decided upon.

Gopiny explained this one to him. He was to go into Darwin at night, on foot, go straight to the mission house, which could be identified by the cross sign they always displayed, kill the missionary men if necessary, grab Boomi and hurry out of the town with him to where Gopiny and the two other warriors who had already joined them would be waiting by the long track.

It took ages to explain that Darwin was not like Pine Creek. It had lots of streets, and far too many people.

'Even if we get Boomi out,' Numinga said, with the emphasis on the 'we', 'we'd have a posse of horsemen after us; they'd run us down, they'd have guns—'

Mimimiadie stood. 'Wait. Enough of this plan. It leaves too much to chance. It could place my boy in danger. I have the answer. I should have thought of it ages ago.'

He walked to the rim of the plateau and looked down into the gorge. 'They will bring my son to me,' he said savagely. 'They will bring him to me.'

'What are you up to now?' Numinga asked. 'More landslides?'

'No. I just have to do what they do. We wait and watch.'

For days they waited and watched. They saw a half-dozen horsemen go through the gorge together. A party of Aborigines meandered through, then a day later a couple in a spring cart escorted by several outriders came from the other direction, headed for Pine Creek. There weren't many travellers out this way now.

They all looked curiously at Mimimiadie, who would not divulge his plan; he simply required a daylight vigil and information on any folk coming from either direction.

Eventually Gopiny spotted two horsemen coming from the east, from the direction of Pine Creek.

'Them!' Mimimiadie shouted. 'I want them.'

'Are we killing them?' Gopiny asked nervously.

'No, you stupid lump. We catch them and keep them.'

While their chief was shouting orders for them to get moving, Numinga guessed what he was up to. Keep them. Keep two white men in exchange for Boomi. All very well in the first part, if their intended victims didn't get shot in the ambush, but after that, what? Something

263

told him he would have a further part to play, the only one of them who spoke English. He wished those men riding steadily across the lonely plains with their packhorse would turn back, suddenly change their minds about heading for the gorge, go somewhere else. Anywhere. Numinga had a bad feeling about all of this.

Never mind. He was allotted a lower lookout while Mimimiadie and three followers ran swiftly down to the ground level and positioned themselves, spears at the ready, either side of the track. Garradji was watching from above in case more travellers appeared on the horizon to upset their plans.

Nothing like the wind in your face to clear away the cobwebs, William told himself as they put their horses to the gallop on the third day of their long ride to Warrawee. He was almost content, refusing to think about Harriet and Myles, determined to enjoy himself. Yorkey was an excellent companion, a typical drover; he didn't talk much, and when he did it was to observe the seasonal changes, or maybe the sudden eruption of bird life in the area, which boded well for good rains, eventually. Never anything personal, for which William was grateful. Had he travelled with a friend, or his son, he'd have been carrying his troubles with him.

Yorkey was fast and efficient in making camp, and indeed a jolly good cook, which helped. They yarned a little after sundown as the campfire drooped, but so did William's eyelids after a long day in the saddle and he soon stretched out on his bedroll under the stars and dozed, each night knowing that Yorkey would check the horses, wander about a while, sit and have a smoke . . . In all, William felt good, really relaxed at last, and he slept well.

They were headed for the gorge, with not a care in the world, when it happened. They were both armed with rifles, but the attack by four tribal blacks was so sudden, and so appalling, that they were taken by surprise.

Numinga watched as the riders drew near, realising that one of them was a blackfeller, which would complicate this kidnapping plan but for now was beside the point. Mimimiadie and his three men were well hidden in a tumble of boulders either side of the track, and when the riders were almost upon them, they rose up and spears flew.

For a second Numinga was stunned! Mimimiadie had said they would keep the two riders, not kill them, but then he saw what had happened. They hadn't speared the riders; they'd plunged their spears into the horses! Killed them.

'Ah no,' he cried as the animals crashed to the ground, screaming. Numinga was very fond of horses and thought this was unnecessarily cruel, but it had the desired effect. Both riders plunged down too, leaping free of their mounts to avoid being crushed, and by then they didn't have a chance. The black stockman was fast, though, and nimble; he was already dragging at his rifle and fumbling for ammunition as the four tribal men swooped with waddies and rawhide ropes. He tried to fight

264

them off but took a battering for his trouble, while the white man, an older bloke, seemed dazed by the fall. In the meantime, the packhorse had bolted, swerving around rocks to gallop on into the gorge. Soon the two riders, more or less unhurt, though the white man had a limp, were bound and hobbled.

Only then did Numinga go down. He saw Gopiny running off into the gorge after the packhorse, and shouted to him to stop.

Gopiny halted. 'What?'

'Get the food, strip the horse and hide the rig, then let it go.'

'What?'

'Do what he said!' Mimimiadie thundered, and Gopiny ran.

'What the hell is this all about?' Yorkey shouted as he suddenly came face to face with his former cellmate. 'Why did they kill our horses?'

'You know him?' black-bearded Mimimiadie growled, and Numinga felt his face. His beard was growing again, a rough stubble, but Yorkey had recognised him.

'He was in jail with me,' he retorted.

'You know them?' William shouted.

'No. Only him,' replied Yorkey. 'The one speaking English. I don't know what's going on.'

Mimimiadie was concerned about the horses. They were dead. He gave instructions to his two offsiders to drag them away, dispose of them, burn them, frustrated by the necessity to tell them what to do and why.

'What's going on?' Yorkey asked again.

'Never mind,' Numinga said, rather than interpret.

'Who's he then?' Yorkey asked, jerking his head at Mimimiadie.

'He's the boss. Be careful.'

'Is he going to kill us?'

'No. Not if you shut up. Big fella this. Plenty trouble.' Numinga was relieved that the white man had the sense to stay quiet and let Yorkey do the talking. He hadn't said a word but he was watching Mimimiadie warily, as if not knowing who to trust, outnumbered by black men five to one. Six when we get up top, Numinga remembered.

Mimimiadie ordered him to get the prisoners moving quickly.

'They can't climb hobbled and tied. It will take too long.'

The chief strode back and stared at his prisoners. The white man stood straight; he equalled him in height. Mimimiadie solved this by belting the man across the shoulders with his waddy until he dropped to his knees. Then he grinned.

'Hands stay. Cut the hobbles.'

Numinga cut their ankles loose. 'Do as him say,' he warned.

It was a long, hard climb. Yorkey managed, but the older man had trouble and this pleased Numinga a little. He figured this bloke – whose name was William, he now knew – was about his own age, but for all his good whitefeller food and succour, he lacked the muscle and wiry strength of Numinga, and he was sweating like a fat woman.

Garradji was waiting, delighted with the outcome. Though Numinga was nervous of the ancient with the hoary face and the string of crocodile teeth that hung round his sunken chest, the more he saw of Garradji, the less he liked him. Garradji spat on the white man and poked at Yorkey, who swore at him in English then resorted to the worst attempt at the Waray language that Numinga had ever heard.

'What's he saying?' Garradji asked Numinga.

'He says he is ancient Waray,' Numinga lied gleefully. 'He says you are too young to understand his dialect. He is of the gorge people, of the Dreamtime, and if you harm him, his ancients will throw you over that gorge right there.'

The story didn't seem to impress Garradji, but he kept away from Yorkey after that, seemingly more interested in the white man.

'Ask who he is.'

'They want to know who William is,' Numinga interpreted. 'They say he look like a bossman. Important.'

'No,' Yorkey said. 'He's just a stockman.'

'He's dressed up pretty for a stockman.'

'I know. He's just been to a wedding in Pine Creek. In his best duds.'

'A wedding?' Numinga couldn't place that word.

'You know. Marry. Big celebration.'

'He rich? Horses, grub?'

'No fear. You look in my pocket. I got two pounds meself.'

Numinga remembered then. 'Why aren't you in jail still? You burned down a whitefeller house. They hang you for that.'

'True. And thanks for nothing. You escaped and left me there, you bastard.'

'It wasn't my fault.'

'Yeah, like this isn't, you slimy weed.'

'How did you get out of jail?' Numinga persisted suspiciously.

'This feller, William. He helped me escape. Now we're just going bush. Looking for a safe place and you bastards attack us.'

When Numinga left them shoved into the back of a cave stinking of bats, William had his say.

'I'd be careful of him. I think he'd like to help us but he's up against a chief and a magic man, Yorkey. Don't get him offside by calling him names. Since they're not planning to kill us, then I think we must be hostages.'

'What? Why?'

'That's for you to find out. Stop talking to Numinga. Demand to talk to the boss through him. And listen hard to what they say. You're trying to talk Waray and they understand that lingo as well, the next-door tribe, but they're not Waray. Numinga's a ring-in, maybe because he speaks English and various dialects, but the rest of them are Victoria River mob.'

'Oh, Jesus! Do you reckon?'

'I know they are. I know that mob better than I know you. They're very dangerous, but they're a long way from home ground, so there has to be a reason. I want you to speak to the bossman with the utmost respect, and so will I. No more backchat. Do you understand?'

'Yeah,' Yorkey breathed. He had heard frightful stories of the ferocity of the clans that went under the white man's name of the Victoria River mob because most of them still lived wild along those shores, refusing to bow to white rule, but he had never expected to meet any of them, and certainly not as a prisoner. Until now he hadn't really been concerned – these captors were his own folk, blood brothers, something like that, and he hadn't thought they would really harm him – but going on this information, he was lined up with the enemy. They wouldn't give a shit about him. Like the horses.

He was right. After a good feed from the whitefeller's packs – tinned beans and peaches, corned beef, bread, golden syrup, potatoes and chops – the captors luxuriated in the joys of fine tobacco before Mimimiadie began to outline the next move. It was very simple.

Numinga was to go to Pine Creek. Go to the police station. Announce that black men had captured a whitefeller and unless Boomi was brought to him, the white man would be killed and another one taken. Numinga was to organise the exchange. The white man for Boomi; after which there would be peace.

'What about that other blackfeller?' Garradji asked. 'He no use.'

'That's true,' Mimimiadie said carelessly. 'You go in the morning, Numinga.'

'They'd grab me and put me in jail. I'm a wanted man. Then what happens? Nothing. You sit here forever.' Having guessed what his role would be, Numinga had a different plan. 'I say we send the blackfeller Yorkey.'

'So he can bring back police and troopers,' Garradji scowled.

'And condemn his friend to death? I don't think so.'

After endless argument, Numinga was sent to bring out Yorkey, filling him in on the situation before they left the cave.

When they sat down, Numinga began to talk to Yorkey again, explaining what was wanted of him, but Yorkey surprised him, holding up his hand and pointing to Mimimiadie.

'Him bossman. I only talk to him.'

'But he doesn't talk the English.'

'He'll figure it out. You translate.'

Cunning old Garradji grinned toothily and spoke to Mimimiadie, who beamed, pointing to himself.

'Bossman me!'

'That's right, chief.' Yorkey nodded, figuring that the old bloke knew a lot more English than he was pretending.

Pointing again, Yorkey made it plain that Numinga could interpret, but he was talking to the bossman, who was more important and entitled to respect.

So began the conversation about the kidnapped son, Boomi. Yorkey expressed shock and great sadness, with sincerity. Then he was told that the wife of this chief, mother of the stolen child, had been murdered and mutilated by white men.

Yorkey was truly sorry for this fellow, truly upset about the woman. He meant it and said so. No wonder the poor bugger was fighting for his kid. He offered to help. He told them his own father had been hanged by white men.

Mimimiadie believed him but the ancient was suspicious.

'He wants to know why you live like them then,' Numinga said.

'Because I grew up among them without my Dreaming, just like Boomi will do if we don't get him back.'

That shut old Garradji up and Yorkey plunged on. 'I will help you. I will never tell anyone where you are, but let the white man come with me. He is a very important man. He will get Boomi for you if you ask him.'

This was too much for Numinga, who had already reported to the group that William was only a stockman. Enraged, he started shouting at Yorkey that he was making a fool of him. Creating dangers.

Mimimiadie took offence at this break in the order of translation. He shouted at Numinga: 'Me bossman!' And slammed a punch into his face that sent the interpreter flying.

Order was restored, no notice taken of the blood seeping from Numinga's mouth, and Yorkey addressed the chief directly, eye to eye, talking slowly, giving Numinga time to translate. He explained that he had lied because he hadn't wanted them to know that they had an important man in their clutches, not knowing what was happening, but now that he understood, William's importance was of immense value to them.

'He is a big boss. He owns cattle stations. You know Warrawee station? And Millford, further south? You know these places?'

They talked among themselves, nodding.

'What feller name him?' Garradji asked.

'Oatley. William Oatley.'

At that Mimimiadie grinned, saying something to Garradji.

'He says we got a big fish here true 'nuff,' Numinga said.

Nothing would persuade them to let William go. Yorkey had to go alone.

'Then untie him. Make him more comfortable.'

On Mimimiadie's orders, William's hands were freed, but instead he was placed further back into the dank cave and tethered to the wall by his neck. When Yorkey complained, the chief smilingly offered to dangle William over the gorge by ropes until he returned.

'I'll be all right,' William told him. 'See if you can get me a bedroll, though. This rock base is hard on the bones.'

'Can't, I'm sorry; they chucked all our stuff away except the grub and the guns. They're happy with the guns, they can defend themselves well up here.'

'Yes,' William sighed. 'Now listen. Don't go to the police in Pine Creek. You've got money. Take my wallet as well. Buy yourself on to the train somehow,' he said, knowing it was difficult for Aborigines to get tickets, 'and go straight to Darwin.'

'That'll take time.'

'It'll be faster in the long run. If you go to the police in Pine Creek they'll telegraph Darwin for instructions and you won't get the child, you'll get troopers. Bypass the police in Darwin too. Go straight to Zack Hamilton. Tell him he has to find the child. What's this fellow's name anyway?'

'Mimimiadie.'

'Who?' William was stunned. 'Christ, he's famous! Bloody bad news. We're lucky we're still alive. But if he wants his child back, we've got a chance.'

Numinga was listening. Gopiny had told them that the police were offering to exchange the kid for his father; better that Yorkey not know that side of the picture. He was impressed that William suggested keeping the police out of it. These important white men would get the boy themselves on Yorkey's instructions. This was great news to report to Mimimiadie. The plan was very clever and it was actually working. He was so impressed he almost gushed his admiration for Mimimiadie, who nodded serenely, accepting praise from his followers.

'Now,' Yorkey said to Mimimiadie through the interpreter, 'no rough stuff. You look after Mr Oatley. You feed him too, because if he gets hurt you'll have all the police in the Territory after you and your people.'

Mimimiadie shrugged his response. 'Tell him if they try any tricks they'll find Mr William Oatley down the bottom of the gorge.'

'This could take time,' Yorkey worried.

Mimimiadie spat a reply and Numinga translated.

'Too much time and he kills the white man and gets another one. You take my horse and go. Rains comen'.'

And they were. As they watched Yorkey ride away, sweeping rains came in from the north and it teemed all day. Numinga expected to be able to wait up here, but he was given another duty. He was sent to make camp on his own at dingo-howling-place, a rocky outcrop far to the east, high above the track between Pine Creek and the gorge. It was a place often used for smoke signals in the old days, smoke signals that could easily be seen from the plateau. There he would have to stay until given permission by Mimimiadie to leave, because it would be his job to keep vigilant and warn of any approaching riders, especially police or troopers. The rain was a good thing, though. Soon the gorge pools would swell and overflow with the run-off from above and it would become impassable. They should not expect visitors.

Numinga was hardly thrilled by this isolation, but at least he wasn't in jail and he was free from Mimimiadie's bullying. Not so bad after all; time to sit and dwell on things.

Zack Hamilton was outraged. 'Where have they got him?'

'I can't tell you that,' Yorkey said. 'My job is to get the boy, give him to his dad and get Mr William.'

'But you must know where they are!'

Yorkey's silence was rock hard.

'Mr William has been very good to you,' Zack warned.

'And Yorkey is trying to protect him,' Sibell said. 'You're wasting time, Zack. We have to find that child right away and let Yorkey take him to his father. Obviously the poor man is desperate to get his son back or he wouldn't have gone to such extreme measures. He wouldn't really hurt William, would he?'

The question was addressed to Yorkey, who squirmed inwardly. He would hardly call that hulking brute a 'poor man', but he didn't want to stir up too much trouble.

'He wants the kid,' he said firmly.

'What's this bastard's name?' Zack asked.

'Don't know. He never said.'

'You'd better not be lying. Did William recognise any of them?'

'No.'

'And you didn't know any of them either.'

'No. I don't know that country too good. First time out your way. I just know the kid is Boomi. Gone to the mission in Darwin.'

'How do they know that?'

'Oh, for heaven's sake, Zack! How do the Aborigines know anything?' Sibell cried. 'They have their ways of finding out things. We have to find Reverend Walters, see if he can help. I've sent Lucy to tell Myles. He'll be distraught.'

Harriet saw Lucy almost running up the street, and immediately mistook urgency for a looming confrontation, especially since Lucy flew in the front gate, raced up the steps and hammered on the veranda door. Harriet drew back from the open louvre windows, hoping Lucy hadn't seen her, cursing that Tom Ling was out on errands. She considered not answering the door but decided to face her. After all, as Myles had said, all they had to do was to deny everything, for the time being anyway. Nevertheless she was nervous when she did go to the door.

'Where's Myles?' Lucy demanded.

'He's not in.'

'Maybe he is and you don't want me to see him.'

'I told you. He's not in.'

'Then where is he?'

'I don't know.' Why should she tell her?

'Harriet, this is urgent. His father is in danger. Where is he?'

'What? Has something happened to William?'

'A lot you'd care, but yes. He's been taken by a mob of blacks. Now where's Myles?'

270

'He's staying at the Victoria Hotel,' Harriet said with a rush. 'With his father away, we thought—'

'Oh never mind!' Lucy turned away.

'Wait! What can I do?' Harriet called to her.

'Stay home and shut up. We don't want the world knowing about this.'

Lucy was gone, running towards the town. Harriet stood in the doorway, shocked. What did she mean, taken by blacks? What was going on?

Myles decided that this morning, with his father out of town, he ought to spend some time in the office, keep an eye on Leo, that upstart of a clerk.

He strode briskly into the office, saw Leo pottering about in the back room and settled in at William's desk, picking up a folder to read that the Walsh property was on the market. He was studying the description of the station when Leo came quietly in.

'Are we in competition with the stock and station agents now?' Myles asked. 'Dealing in cattle stations.'

'We always have been to a certain extent,' Leo said. 'Now, what can I do for you, Myles?'

'Nothing right now. What does Walsh want for his station?'

'It hasn't been decided. Mrs Walsh is waiting for my clients to make an offer.'

Myles picked that up. He grinned. 'I see, and who are our clients?'

'That's private, Myles, and if you don't mind, you're sitting in my chair.'

'Oh ho! While the cat's away, eh? But I'll be needing this desk in his absence. I have quite a bit of correspondence to catch up on.'

'Myles. Didn't your father tell you? He has sold the business. This business.'

'He has what?' Myles jerked upright in the chair. 'Since when?'

'Before he left. It is sold.'

'I don't believe you. What sort of game are you playing?'

'No game. This is my office now.'

'Are you trying to tell me you're running this place for the new owners?'

'No. I'm sorry if this is a shock for you. But I am the new owner. I bought the business from your father. He has retired.'

'I don't believe this. I want to see the paperwork.'

Leo waited patiently. 'If you'll forgive me, Myles, the contracts are private. I am not obliged to give you access to them.'

'What did you pay for the business?'

'I think you'd better ask your father that.'

'Dammit! He's not here. How can I?'

'There's no hurry. I'm sure he'll inform you when he returns.'

'I'll see about this,' Myles sneered as he slammed out of the office. 'You'll be hearing from me.'

'I doubt it,' Leo shrugged as he took his place at his desk.

Myles was angry and confused, storming down the street, well aware that he'd made a fool of himself. No, William had made a fool out of him. How dare he do this without a word! And why? Then it dawned on him. Oh, Jesus! Was this the beginning of payback? Was William shutting him out? Myles had been making for the hotel, with nowhere much else to go, worrying about the suddenness of this action, but now he turned towards the Esplanade. He had to tell Harriet about this. Let her know that William, by his silence on this matter, was definitely up to something. Selling out. Leaving them on their own. What was the old bugger up to?

But then he saw Lucy Hamilton running towards him, calling out to him. Dammit. The last person he wanted to see right now was Lucy.

'Myles! I'm so glad I found you. Your father's in trouble.'

She was puffing, upset, almost in tears, and he had to quieten her to get the story straight.

'Come on,' she said eventually. 'Dad's waiting for you.'

'Does he really think my father is in danger?'

'Of course he does. They're not station blacks, they're tribal blokes. That much we know. And they want that kid back. Bloody quick too, or else . . .'

'Or else what?'

'They say they'll kill him.'

'How do you know this?'

'Come on, Myles. Dad will explain.'

'I still say we ought to call the police,' Maudie was insisting as they arrived. She scowled at Myles but made no objection to his presence. 'Get a posse of police and troopers to flush the buggers out and rescue William before it is too late.'

'We don't know where they are,' Zack said, exasperated.

'He knows,' she retorted, pointing at Yorkey.

Myles shoved forward and grabbed Yorkey by the shirt, shaking him. 'Where's my father, you bastard? Tell us where he is or I'll get the whip to you!'

Zack pushed him away. 'Stop it, Myles. You and I are going down to see Reverend Walters, to see if they've got a six-year-old kid called Boomi in the mission school. Right now!'

'I'm coming too,' Sibell said.

'No. You stay here with Yorkey.' He glared at Maudie. 'And you stay here too, do you hear me?'

On the way, Zack gave Myles his instructions. 'You keep quiet, let me do the talking. The kid may not even be there. No mention of your father. We'll just make quiet enquiries.'

'Then what? If he isn't there?'

'We'll have to find out where he is.'

'And if he is there? We can't just take him.'

'Christ! I don't know. One thing at a time.'

272

★ ★ ★

The Reverend was delighted to see them. He shook hands eagerly, confusing Zack by thanking him for putting in a good word with William, which Zack hadn't done; he'd forgotten that promise. But Myles came in for the warmest handshake.

'I can't tell you, sir, how relieved I am that your father has withdrawn his objections to the construction of our church.'

'Since when?' Myles asked almost angrily, but a glare from Zack reminded him to tread carefully.

'A few days ago,' Walters said airily. 'Good of him. The Lord will bless him.'

'Reverend,' Zack said, 'we've come about a little boy. An Aborigine boy called Boomi. Is he here at the mission?'

'Yes,' Walters said sadly. 'Not settling in too well yet. Tribal, you know. They take time. But he'll be all right eventually. Do you know him?'

'No, not really. We know of him. You see, his father is fretting for him and would like to see him.'

'Ah! So he's given himself up, has he?'

'Who?'

'His father. That renegade Mimimiadie. Nasty piece of work, that one. I never thought he'd come in, even for the child. But since he has, he must love the boy. Even heathens like him have a little goodness in them.'

'*Who* is his father?' Zack asked, and even as Walters repeated the name, Myles saw fear in Zack's eyes.

'Do you know him?' he demanded.

'I know of him,' Zack said carefully.

'Oh yes. He's well known,' Walters said. 'Victoria River mob. A murderer, that one. Even his own people are afeared of him. Where have they got him? In Fannie Bay jail? I would be willing to take the child to visit him.'

'Good of you,' Zack said coolly, 'but not a word about this just yet; they're keeping it very quiet for a while. Just thought I'd give you the tipoff. Good day to you, sir.'

He had to nudge Myles away, but when they turned the corner Myles exploded. 'What's this about Mimi-whatever-his-name-is? Is he the one who's got my father captive?'

'Sounds like it. And it sounds as if the police have told Mimimiadie that if he gives himself up they'll let his kid go. Or rather that was the bait. They won't let the kid go back to his tribe, no way, and I'll bet Mimimiadie knows that. So he grabbed a white man as a hostage, turning the tables.'

'Didn't Yorkey tell you this?'

'No,' Zack growled.

'So my father is in the clutches of a killer and you won't go to the police. Well, I will, right away.'

273

Zack grabbed his arm. 'No you don't. Your father sent Yorkey to me, remember? I'll figure it out. We have to get that kid.'

'How? Snatch him? Walters would raise the alarm in seconds. Why don't we go back and tell Walters the situation, and ask him to hand over the kid? He'll understand.'

'The hell he will. The child is a hostage too. He'd check with the authorities and find out that Mimimiadie is still on the loose. He's got his claws into another convert now anyway; he won't help.'

'Even to save my father?'

'He can't. He works by the rules. We couldn't trust him. As soon as we turned our backs he'd bolt for the police station, for instructions. Shut up and let me think.'

By the time they got back to the Hamilton house, they still hadn't figured out how to get their hands on Boomi, and they were furious with Yorkey for only telling them half the story.

'I didn't know that stuff,' Yorkey argued. 'I knew his name, though, but I didn't want to panic you.'

'And you didn't know Mimimiadie was wanted by the police?'

'Not exactly. I didn't know nothing about the police offer. Neither did Mr William, but he told me to treat him with respect.'

'Respect? Why the hell should you?' Myles shouted.

Yorkey looked about him nervously. 'Because.'

'Because William knew he was dangerous,' Zack snapped. 'In other words, he's not some ordinary blackfeller fretting for this kid.'

'No. But I didn't want you worrying too much. William said bring back the kid soon, so he can get free. Simple as that.'

'Like hell,' Myles said. 'My father is probably already dead. We just hand over the kid and wave those bastards goodbye.'

'We haven't got the kid,' Zack said gloomily. 'We may have to get permission from the police after all.'

Sibell had been sitting listening to them. 'No you won't. The mission school will close down for the holidays any day. They billet out the children. A couple of years ago we took two little girls for a fortnight over Christmas. Don't you remember, Zack?'

'Yes, but—'

'My dear, I'll visit Reverend Walters and offer to take another child this year. Two if he's short of takers. But I'll make sure Boomi is one of them. Leave it to me.'

On the way home Myles threw caution to the winds and called on Harriet. This was an emergency.

They held a whispered conversation in the far corner of the front veranda, and when Tom Ling intruded, his face furrowed in a frown to ask if they wanted lunch, Myles shouted at him to buzz off.

'Why all this secrecy?' Harriet asked finally. 'This is a police matter, Myles. It's your father who's being held captive. My husband. I demand you go to the police.'

'I know. Zack thinks he's got it all worked out. He's too trusting. We don't know where they're holding Dad, but Yorkey says he has to go back to Pine Creek with the kid, so that's a start. I won't say anything until we get there, then I'll alert the police. I don't believe a word that Yorkey is saying. I reckon he's in with them. What's to stop him taking the kid to the father and keeping on going with them? He doesn't give a hoot about William. Why should he? He's on their side. The blacks stick together.

'And there's another thing. Dad has sold the business.'

'What business?'

'For God's sake, Harriet. The bloody agency, here in town. Sold it to his clerk.'

'Why?'

'You tell me. Why would he do that without mentioning it to us? Leo says he's retiring. And what's more, your dear husband, who claims to be anti-religion, has agreed to let those idiots build their church next door.'

'Never!'

'He has, I tell you.'

'Why would he do that?'

'How the bloody hell would I know?'

Harriet was silent for a few minutes and then she said: 'Something strange happened today. A man came to the door. He said he believed the house was up for sale, and wanted to look through, but I chased him away. I mean, I had enough to worry about without people asking silly questions. Do you think that would have anything to do with William relenting on the church plans?'

'I don't know. How would I bloody know what he's doing? Including this dopey idea of going bush for a few weeks. Well, that's fallen flat, hasn't it? He's walked himself into real trouble. Now we've got to get the old fool out.'

'Would those blackfellers really harm him?'

'I'd say it's a certainty. Kid or no kid.'

'Myles! How could you!'

'How could I what? I didn't invent this situation. Zack wouldn't say so but he knows as well as I do that they've probably got the old man trussed up in the bush somewhere. Feeding him burnt rats if anything. He'll be lucky to survive.'

Harriet looked at him warily, wondering what she was hearing. Obviously William was rearranging his life in some way, and given the circumstances, if you thought about it, this wasn't so surprising. If he knew about their affair he'd be terribly hurt, and angry, and would have to react in some way. Maybe he had decided to sell the house as well as the business. You couldn't blame him. She wished she could talk to him. Somehow soften the blow. He had always been very good to her.

Myles kissed her passionately. 'I have to go. Don't you be worrying. It's not our fault he's got himself into this mess.'

275

She didn't respond. She was afraid to. Afraid to say what she was thinking. That Myles in his heart did not want his father to survive. It was not in what he said, but in the deadness of it, the inflections. If William didn't survive this terrible captivity, their problems would be solved. But would they? Harriet found herself objecting to Myles's attitude. When he left, her coldness stayed and she shivered. Was it the money? Or was it her? Was that what they'd come to? Forsaking the man who had loved them both so much? Wishing him dead?

'No!' she cried. Oh no. This was all wrong. She'd seen a side of Myles that repelled her. She wished she had someone to talk to, but no one came. The world had forgotten her.

That night she dreamed that she was standing on a cliff, high above the world, and an eagle was swooping at her, taking pieces of her, clumps of hair, fingers, one by one, an arm. It didn't hurt but terror had her screaming soundlessly, and then there was William; he could see she had to jump to cast away that ferocious eagle and he was running towards her, calling her name, shouting, 'Wait! Wait!'

She awoke in a bath of perspiration, in the bed alone, and she wanted to run to the other room to tell him something but she couldn't recall what it was. And anyway, he wasn't there. He was somewhere out in the bush in terrible danger.

The translator had gone so William had to communicate as best he could with the others. It had been a shock to learn that the chief was Mimimiadie. Certainly not encouraging. He'd heard enough about this rascal to be even more wary of him, so he went to more trouble to be respectful. When the others refused him food and water he demanded to see the boss, who enjoyed countermanding their decisions.

Being tied up so long he fouled his trousers but refused to allow this to get to him. Instead he called to the boss for permission to strip and wash in the rain, and this, too, was eventually allowed. So he stood nude, ignoring them, grateful for the warm, cleansing rain, taking as much time as he could scrubbing his shirt and pants in a rock pool. He ate the food they gave him, once a day at odd hours, with cold deliberation. It was only scraps of wallaby, or reptile meat, leftovers, barely singed by fire; or berries and the occasional half-eaten yam, but food was food. He closed his eyes and chewed on, knowing he'd soon be racked by the pains of diarrhoea, which would give him another excuse to ask to be taken out of his cave to clean up.

After one cleansing outing, he put on his wet pants, knowing they'd soon dry out in the humid air, and used pointing signals to request permission to sit with Mimimiadie for a while, guessing that he would also be under strain, waiting hopefully for the return of his son.

With the help of pidgin English and his smattering of Victoria River dialects and Mimimiadie's bits of English, they laboured to fill in time, making conversation. He told the great man that he too had a son, hoping for pity, but when Mimimiadie asked how old and if he was a good son,

William gave Myles's age and found himself admitting: 'No.'

He was astonished that he should do that, but after four days in captivity he reasoned it was down to physical and mental weakness, and anyway, what the hell?

Mimimiadie frowned. 'You beat him?'

William shook his head. 'No. But I should. I suppose.'

The great man banged the ground with his waddy. 'Beat him. Break his head.'

William didn't have to be told that Mimimiadie was a diehard – a patriot if you preferred, determined not to give in to the whites – and he tried to talk to him about peace. Mimimiadie understood but he shook his head.

'Die first.'

'But what about your boy? Boomi? If there's peace he will be safe.'

Garradji helped here. 'He says to that, maybe. New time. First he get home to river. Then see.'

'You kill me?' William asked the bossman directly.

He shrugged. 'No Boomi, no white boss.'

William needed to know that, to put his thoughts in order. He wasn't afraid of dying. Just the manner of it. Death in the bush had a habit of suddenness: snake bite, falls from horses; you could get gored by a bull, trampled by cattle, drown, starve, die of exposure in the heat; here today, gone tomorrow. He'd lived an easy life in Darwin; now he was in home territory but facing the prospect of imminent death. No suddenness here – no such luxury. He didn't believe for one minute that the authorities would hand over Mimimiadie's son. By this he'd learned the rest of the story, that he was only half of the hostage arrangements.

Mimimiadie was fighting for his son. William hoped that when the boy grew up he'd discover how much this determined warrior, living in the past, had loved him. And he hoped that his own son was now working hard for his release. Moving heaven and earth to gain his freedom, as he would have done for Myles.

In the darkness, harnessed by his neck, being assailed by irritated bats, cramped and sore on his rocky bed, William tried to think more kindly of Harriet and Myles. He saw his reckless selling out of the business and the house as trivial, unimportant. His dash into the country equally irrelevant. Look at me, he pondered, all dignity gone. He scraped some bat droppings from his hair and face. So what price now those hurt feelings, the indignity of their behaviour? Precious little. He didn't want to die unforgiving of two people he'd loved so dearly. Still loved, in his own way.

But the grief persisted, so he tried to think of better times, lying there in the ruins of his life.

Gopiny had to crouch to reach the rear of the cave. He brought the prisoner some fresh water, stared at him bleakly, shrugged, and left him to the shadows.

★　★　★

Reverend Walters was greatly relieved that the Hamiltons would foster the child, Boomi, over the holidays, because they understood the situation. He had been concerned about foisting another kid on little Mrs Branigan, who had already agreed to take two others, but until now he'd had no alternative.

Sibell and Zack met the boy. He was a sturdy little fellow, very dark-skinned, with a cap of clipped curly hair. He seemed very shy, cringing away from them, but when he looked up, his big dark eyes blazed in defiance.

'He's a darling,' Sibell said, reaching out to him, without success.

'Don't be taken in by the heathen cherub looks, Mrs Hamilton. He's far from a darling; he bites, scratches and kicks. Zack will need a firm hand with him.'

'We'll see to that,' Zack said. 'Don't worry about him. We've had plenty experience with these kids. He'll be all right. Sweets and jinker rides work wonders. As a matter of fact, while we're here, we might as well take him with us. I don't suppose he has much to pack.'

'Oh no, he can't go today. I've got christenings this afternoon; he has to stay to be christened.' The Reverend patted the squirming child on the head. 'You'll have a new name tomorrow. A new holy life ahead of you. Your name will be Elijah.'

No amount of gentle persuasion would convince Walters to hand over the child, and rather than make an issue of it, Sibell sweetly agreed to call back the following day.

'Don't you realise time is against us?' Zack said to her, but he had to agree they had no choice.

'There's time,' she said. 'We'll pick him up tomorrow and get the train the next day. Yorkey can take him on from Pine Creek.'

'You're not concerned about tricking Walters?'

'Not under these circumstances. We have no choice. Keep in mind the child was kidnapped too, Zack.'

'They call it saving him.'

'Not this time. There was an offer to return him if his father gave himself up. We're giving him back, that's all. Why? Are you having doubts about this?'

'No. But you're the one so fed up with the violence up here. You keep saying you don't want any part of our life in the Territory any more. Taking the child is an act of violence in itself, some would say. There could be trouble afterwards.'

Sibell hugged her shawl about her as they walked down the windy street.

'Well?' he demanded.

'William's life is at stake. Since you brought it up, yes, you could say the violence is too much for me.' She sighed. 'But Boomi, he's only a little boy, caught up in this miserable adult game. He has a right to go home to his family. To be left in peace. I'll look after him until we send him on to his father.'

278

'And then? What happens when this is all over?'

'I haven't changed my mind, Zack. I'm leaving after Christmas. Living in the bush has drained me, I feel old and tired.'

'You don't look it,' he said sadly, but his wife had nothing more to say. They'd been over this too many times.

Chapter Sixteen

The train heaved into Pine Creek, steam hissing into the rainswept darkness as if offended by the competition, and alighting passengers ran for shelter past the swaying lanterns and through the small gate to disappear into the night.

Zack left them huddled under the station awning while he ran across the road to the shanty hotel, pushing through the crowd of drinkers to locate the owner, one Scotty McCabe.

'How many of you?' Scotty asked.

'My wife and I, and two men.'

'I only got a cabin out the back, but you're welcome to it, Zack. You and the missus. There are bunks on the veranda for the men. Might be a bit damp by this.'

'It'll do. We'd be grateful for the shelter. Any chance of getting a feed?'

'Yeah. My missus is in the kitchen. She'll slap you on a few steaks. Just give her a hoy.'

They hurried Sibell and Boomi into a cabin with an iron roof and canvas flaps over the windows in place of glass. The only furniture was an ancient double bed and a bare bench that supported a kerosene lamp.

'This is disgusting,' Myles said.

Sibell laughed. 'It's about the best in town.'

'Have you stayed here before?'

'No. We either camp or stay with friends, but we can't do either tonight.'

'Where should I sleep?'

'You and Yorkey get the veranda,' Zack grinned. 'And don't start whinging or we won't get anything to eat. Mrs McCabe won't abide critics.'

Sibell was settling the weary child into the bed. 'I think he's too tired to eat, but we'll see.'

Contrary to Walter's warning, Boomi was very well behaved.

When she'd bathed him back at the house, Sibell had been shocked to see light weals across his back and legs. They'd beaten him. No wonder the child was truculent. She gathered him up in her arms, fussed over him, put food in front of him and let him help himself. At least he had a good appetite. She didn't demur when he chose jelly and a banana, a chop and bread and jam, and she found some chocolates for him as she

281

put him to bed. When he cried out in his sleep, she was sitting by him so she picked him up and held him, reassuring him with the movement of her rocking chair.

The next morning, when he heard he was to have a ride on the great train again, he was too excited to be upset. Taking one day at a time, she did not tell him that he was to be reunited with his father and forbade the others to speak of it, in case something went wrong.

All the way to Pine Creek he clambered over the three men, Yorkey, Zack and Myles, to look out of the windows at the passing countryside, until he tired and fell asleep on Sibell's lap.

In the morning, the men went with Yorkey to retrieve his horse from the stables, and Zack bought two of the best mounts he could find.

'What are you doing?' Yorkey asked anxiously. 'Why two horses? My horse is here. I only need a spare for William.'

'I'm coming with you. Part of the way at least.'

'You can't. I said I'd come back with Boomi, alone.'

'No. You need backup. It's essential.'

'I don't like it.'

Neither did Myles. 'If anyone goes it should be me. I'm going with him.'

'No you're not,' Zack snapped. He told the stablehand to saddle up the horses and went back to break the news to Sibell. He'd been dreading this disclosure, but he couldn't put it off any longer.

He closed the flimsy door, leaving Myles outside, and put his arms about his wife.

'I have to go with Yorkey.'

'What? You do not! Let Yorkey go on his own as he planned to do.'

'Too risky. I have to back him up.'

'Oh yes, of course. Good old Zack. You have to be the hero, don't you? What do you care that there are wild blacks out there? Renegades who'd stick a spear in you for spite, no matter what you did for them. See, there's no end to this. You'll never make old bones, Zack Hamilton, and neither will I if I put up with this terrible place any longer. You can't go. Send Myles. It's *his* father.'

'No! That would be a mistake. He's too hot-headed. William knew what he was doing asking for me.'

'Rubbish. If you go I won't be here when you get back. If you get back. And I mean it, Zack.'

Eavesdropping, Myles grinned. Good for you, Sibell. This is my business.

Zack came out with a rush. Obviously Sibell had lost the argument.

'I have to get some supplies.'

Myles fell into step beside him. 'How do you know what to buy? You don't know how far you're going, or where.'

'I'll just get some essentials.'

As her husband charged away, with Myles in tow, Sibell was standing angrily by the door when she heard a whisper behind her.

'Missus. It's me.'

She pushed a piece of tattered canvas aside to find Yorkey waiting at the rear of the cabin.

'Please, missus. Quick. Give me Boomi. I have to go alone for Mr William's sake.'

Sibell agreed. She'd felt all along that Yorkey knew best what to do. She picked up the child. 'You're going for a horsey ride with Yorkey!' she said brightly, and rushed to the window with him, kissing him goodbye. In a second they were gone.

She sat on the bed and prayed for them, for safe passage for all concerned.

Myles watched as Zack loaded the supplies into a pack.

'How do you know how much you'll need?' he asked.

'Not hard to work out. Pop's station is four days' ride from here, but they didn't make it all the way. That's obvious. Yorkey won't say where they were ambushed but it has to be somewhere in between. They probably then veered off the main track to a lair somewhere, but I'm betting it won't be too far.'

Myles was listening carefully, storing the information.

As they approached the cabin, he made his stand. 'Sibell doesn't want you to go, Zack. I'm sorry but I couldn't help overhearing. I'll go with Yorkey.'

'I told you no! And leave Sibell out of this.'

'I'm sorry, I have to insist—'

'You can insist all you like. You're staying here.'

'In which case I'll go straight to the police station and ask for an escort. Mimimiadie is out there, don't forget. They'll jump at the chance to go after him and rescue my father at the same time. I'm not sure we shouldn't do that anyway. This is police business.'

Zack grabbed him by the arm and twisted him about. 'You little weasel. We've got the chance to get William back without any trouble. You're gonna stay here and shut your mouth.'

'I'm sorry, I can't do that. I go with Yorkey or I go to the police.' He grinned. Zack was beaten and he knew it. 'What's it to be?'

'All right, you can go. But by God, you be bloody careful. Don't antagonise them no matter what you see. No matter what state William is in. Just keep cool. Let them take Boomi, and the less said the better.'

'I don't need all this. Just let me get the kid and get going.'

Sibell was sitting on the bed, alone. They stared about them. 'Where's Boomi?'

'Yorkey collected him.'

'Good,' Myles said. 'You'll be pleased to know Zack has decided I should go with them. I'll take that pack of supplies if you don't mind, Zack.'

'I'll come over to the stables with you,' Zack growled.

Sibell made no comment. At least Yorkey had a start. And only Yorkey knew exactly where he was going.

Yorkey had been prowling round the pub before dawn. He was waiting when Mrs McCabe came into the kitchen to light the stove. He gave her a whistle and put two shillings on the windowsill to buy leftovers, blackfeller food. She was in a cheery mood, buoyed up by the rain, which she said had come just in time to save her vegetable garden, since they'd been running short of water. As she talked, she shoved some tea, bread and cooked meat into a sugarbag for him, and some stale cake.

That'll do for now, he decided, thanking her.

By the time he picked up Boomi, he had the two horses ready and waiting behind a shed. Then he was off, the boy sitting in front; him leading the extra mount that was needed to bring William back.

He might have a head start, but he knew Zack would soon overtake him, since he couldn't travel fast burdened by Boomi and another horse, so as soon as he quit town he fled the western road and detoured into the bush, making for the maze of stock routes that serviced station properties.

Soon they were travelling steadily, Boomi enjoying himself but wanting to know why he couldn't ride the other horse.

'Later,' Yorkey laughed. 'You hang on and be a good boy and I'll give you some cake when we stop for a rest.'

But it wasn't Zack, it was Myles Oatley who pounded out on to the worn road, heading west, convinced he'd catch up with Yorkey in no time. And he'd give the bugger a good dressing-down too. Bloody upstart Abo! Who did he think he was? Sneaking out like that. And who was to say this blackfeller wasn't mixed up in the whole thing? Well, he'd soon find out who was in charge here.

He'd been riding fast for a good hour, without sighting Yorkey, and he began to worry. Where had he got to? He had to be on this route. Unless he was trying to shake him.

'Well it won't work. I'll find you. There are only two roads through the hills; one goes via the gorge, the other one, for when the gorge is impassable, takes an extra two days. You won't take that one, so sooner or later you'll come back to the gorge road and I'll be waiting for you.'

Because they were dealing with men from the Victoria River mob, it hadn't occurred to him that these renegade blacks would be anywhere other than near their own territory, which bordered Pop's station. And Yorkey had flatly refused to give any indication of where the ambush had taken place. Riding down this lonely road, Myles began to wonder if they'd roam closer to civilisation, looking for a likely victim. They could be even closer than he'd thought. Yorkey had taken off without any supplies. He wasn't a bush black. He wouldn't find it easy to live off the land. Besides, it would slow him up.

As the shadows drew long, and there was still no sign of Yorkey,

Myles knew he would have to make camp soon. Night birds swooped, a dingo ran soundlessly across the track, reminding him that wild blacks could attack without a sound. He was nervous at the thought of having to dismount and find shelter, with no one to keep watch, but it had to be done.

By this he was wishing he'd let Zack take on this duty. For all he knew, Yorkey could be in league with those bastards, and they could capture him too.

It was the longest night of his life. He was afraid to light a fire and draw attention to himself, so he chewed on the food, straight from the pack, watered the horse, and sat upright against a tree wrapped in his bedroll, battling sleep. Every squeak and sound emanating from the all-enveloping darkness startled him, and he clung on to the loaded rifle across his lap. He remembered that Zack had been speared in the back on his way home, much closer to the gorge than Pop's place. Warrawee station was more than seventy miles on from the Hamilton property, Black Wattle. Fear fired his imagination. He thought he saw painted black figures lurking in the scrub around him, so he fired the rifle, reloaded, fired again, fumbling, peering uselessly into a forest of ghost gums.

Then the rain swept in. Myles knew that with the weather so unsettled he should have made a shelter from foliage, but his bush sense had deserted him. He sat in the mud, praying for the dawn to deliver him.

Flies woke him, hordes of flies, and as he brushed them aside he touched a huge spider burrowing into his collar. He flung it aside and jumped up, the heat of the morning coming at him like a hammer. It had been a long time since Myles had slept hard, as it was called, without a softener under his bones or a roof overhead, and he was paying for it now. He was stiff and sore and hungry, and the warm, misty rain denied him any chance of a hot breakfast. Still unnerved by the night fears, he allowed his horse to graze while repeating his meal regimen, unpacking some bread, beef and cheese, and hard biscuits that tasted like cow dung.

By the time he was out on the road again, tired and uncomfortable in damp clothes, Myles wondered what he was doing here anyway. He'd taken umbrage right from the start at Zack's attitude . . . as if he were the boss, and William's son only an onlooker. But more to the point, at William's deliberate slight. He had sent Yorkey to Zack for help. Not to his son. The Hamiltons had all glossed over this, as if it were perfectly normal, but what were they saying behind his back? What was William telling them? That he had no faith in his son? Who knew these roads as well as any of them. Who had grown up in the Territory!

Daylight restored his confidence and by mid afternoon he had covered about forty miles. The very fact that he was out here had checkmated Zack's attempts to play the hero, but since he still couldn't find Yorkey there didn't seem to be much point in going on. He figured that he was within reach of the gorge now, and once through, into more dangerous territory, what could he do on his own? Keep going down the track and get speared as Zack had been? Or ride about searching for Yorkey? Worse, ride about searching for trouble. Yorkey had said Mimimiadie had five wild blacks with him. Six against one, with Yorkey an unknown quantity. What the hell was he doing out here? It would be madness to go on past the gorge unescorted, with tribal blacks out there on the rampage.

As he pushed on down a road soggy with red mud, Myles saw dingo tracks and remembered there was a lookout away to the right from there, a huge rocky outcrop. He'd climbed it with his father years ago. The Aborigines called it something like dingo-howling-place, but to Myles and his friends it was always known as the Dingo Lookout. He decided he'd head there, climb up and have a look around.

The plan made him feel better. From there you could see anything that moved on the plains below, and as far as the bulky hills that hid the gorge. With luck he could spot Yorkey, and any other travellers on the road who might help him. He knew he should have brought the police in on this. Mimimiadie had a fearsome reputation. It was madness to even think of trusting him. Once he had his kid back, there'd be no reason for him to keep his word.

The skies were low, the colour of smoke, rolling clouds parting every so often to allow the sun to blaze through, turning up the heat. Myles wiped his sweating face with a handkerchief and drank the rest of the water from the canvas waterbag, and as he replaced it he thought he saw movement in the trees at the bend of the road. Horses, he was sure he'd seen horses! He raced madly down the road, crashing into the scrub, only to find several bullocks standing glaring at him, their bulk a wall of power, daring him to attempt to dislodge them from their shelter. He slowed the horse and turned carefully away from those lowered horns, but kept on through the bush, watching for the rock formation that loomed high above the treetops.

Numinga saw the two horses coming, not along the main road but along a track that was headed his way, just a faint ribbon of red soil, barely discernible against the grey-green of the bush. And he was certain one of the horses was riderless. It would have to be Yorkey, bringing a spare horse for Oatley. But did he have the boy with him? Mimimiadie's boy? Was it possible? He hoped so. By this he was convinced that the white men would have beaten Yorkey to a pulp and got Mimimiadie's where-abouts out of him. No one cared about black kids. Or the likes of Yorkey, for that matter.

He scrambled down to get a better look as the horses came closer, and jigged about in delight to see Yorkey riding quietly along with the boy propped in front of him. He wanted to shout out to him, to welcome him, but there was time enough for that later. He was the lookout. For all he knew, Yorkey and the boy could be bait, to catch Mimimiadie. The bossman had impressed that on him with threats that were hard to ignore. White men could be trailing Yorkey, with or without his knowledge. Police, a posse, all armed. He had to keep watch.

Reluctantly he climbed back up and lit a fire, adding damp leaves when it was going well. He protected it from the breeze with a flat piece of bark, sitting back, pleased with himself as he saw the spiral of smoke lifting lazily into a sooty curl. They would be watching too. They would see it. And they would know he was sending news; the long, uninterrupted curl of smoke was peaceful, a friend. So far, so good.

Myles was out of condition. Another thing he'd forgotten in his rush to assert his authority. Though he still had the long, lean figure of a countryman, nearly two years of the good life had taken its toll. Where once he'd spent days on horseback, mustering cattle, long, hard days, he now climbed down from his horse almost bandy-legged with aches and pains after covering only about eighty miles in a couple of days. He felt like one of those new chums he'd laughed at when he'd lived and worked on the stations. And this climb, in a temperature which he knew would be around a hundred and four degrees among these rocks, was already wearing him down. He was sweating like a pig, but there was plenty of water in shallow rock pools, thank God. In this heat a man could dehydrate very quickly without water. He'd filled the waterbag and brought it with him, stopping to drink every fifteen minutes or so.

Not that it was a hard climb, it was just a matter of wending one's way onwards and upwards around these great boulders that had been left to wear down on the stump of an ancient mountain. William had said it was probably the remains of a volcano, which would account for the presence of all these boulders, some as big as huts. Something like that, anyway, he pondered crossly as he dragged on. They seemed to him to have come straight out of a bloody volcano, they were so hot to the touch. He hoped his father would appreciate what he was going through on his behalf.

He was almost at the top when he saw Yorkey, far below, riding east, not towards the gorge road but off, north, on the long detour road.

'Bloody hell!' he spat. 'I missed the bastard. That's him all right, with the spare horse. Bugger him! Where the hell is he going? And why is he bypassing the gorge?' There hadn't been enough rain yet to fill that narrow pass. Or had there been? Up top on the plateau was known as a catchment area. Maybe they'd had good rains out here, enough to send a heap of it cascading over the sides. But if so, how would Yorkey know that? Unless he'd already had contact with them. No. He was following a planned route. Suddenly Myles knew he was already closer to his goal than he'd expected to be.

Myles was no longer confused about his role. He would follow Yorkey, see what was happening and keep them in his sights. Abos weren't armed and he had plenty of ammunition. At the crucial time he would step in. There was no question of capturing Mimimiadie; he was wanted dead or alive. That'd be something! Even if his father was still alive, there was no reason to spare his captor.

As he turned to go back down, he saw something above him. Smoke. A campfire? No. Not an ordinary campfire. Myles had lived in close contact with Aborigines all his life. He knew exactly what it was. A smoke signal. It was too contrived to emanate from a spluttering bushman's fire. So who was sending smoke signals, and why?

One of them! What white bushmen called a cockatoo. A lookout. Quietly he took the rifle slung across his back and loaded it. Then he discarded the waterbag, his boots and his hat and slid easily up through the last of the rocks to see a blackfeller, sitting cross-legged with his back to him, drop a piece of bark on to his fire, letting it blaze into ash, the signal finished, completed.

Myles thought of dashing forward to club the bugger, but that was a dangerous thing to do with a loaded rifle, and he had no other weapon. Besides, it wasn't all that smart to try to sneak up on an Abo. So he took aim with quiet care, and shot him in his bony hip.

The Abo gave a shout of pain and fell forward, almost toppling into the fire.

Calmly Myles walked over and wrenched him on to his back.

'You speak English?' he asked, squatting down beside him.

Groaning in pain, the Abo rolled about, clutching a bare hip that was now running blood.

'Yes,' he muttered. 'Yes, boss.'

'Good. Who were you signalling to?'

The process took a while. Admittedly the fellow was in pain and losing a lot of blood, but there wasn't much Myles could do about that. Nothing really. And this brute wasn't about to give any information at all, which made Myles even more suspicious.

'Mimimiadie?' he asked, and after a few hard kicks, he achieved the welcome nod.

'Ha! And do you know Yorkey?'

'Yes, boss.' He was a middle-aged, miserable-looking bloke with odd-coloured waxy curls, the front part flecked with grey, the back jet black.

Myles laughed. If this was a sample of Mimimiadie's feared warriors, then the whole episode was a joke.

'Where's my father?' he asked.

The man cringed into himself. 'I dunno.'

'My father. Mr Oatley? Is he alive? You'd better tell me or I'll put a bullet in the other hip.'

'Yes, boss. Him there.'

'Where?'

'In the gorge now.'

'You're a liar!' Myles kicked him several times, forcing him to roll over again. 'I saw Yorkey riding out there. He isn't going towards the gorge, he's riding away from it with the kid. Now you talk to me, you bastard. And get it right this time.'

Numinga knew his time had come. It was very sad really. He'd die like that boy, with no kin to take up the crying. Not even an acquaintance to sing him on to the spirits. No one. Then he remembered that this was the dingo-howling-place. And his kin, almost forgotten in his travels, his mother's kin that is, were dingo totem. Perhaps this was right after all. But he had to deal with this whitefeller first, this brave warrior with his gun.

He had told the truth. They were waiting for Yorkey in the gorge. They'd all come down, so they could make a quick getaway. Mimimiadie had planned the end of this business well. He was very smart.

Yorkey was to bring the boy to the gorge. Oatley would be there for the exchange. But Mimimiadie didn't trust white men and he had guns. Two guns, ammunition as well, taken from Yorkey and Oatley when they were captured. His two warriors had been shown how to use the guns and they would remain hidden, to protect them.

Everyone had been very impressed at this cunning plan. Even old Garradji, who was in charge of the prisoner.

But no one had told Yorkey about it, naturally. In case he spilled it to the enemy. Just in case. He was still headed for the plateau.

There was no one left up top on the plateau except Gopiny, whose job it was to watch for Numinga's signal, already given, that Yorkey was on his way with Boomi. Gopiny would have time to come down, head Yorkey off and redirect him to the gorge itself. Unless he saw another signal indicating trouble. Danger.

Numinga hugged his shattered hip, trying to set it back in place. He knew that he couldn't survive this injury. He was now a wounded animal, unable to walk, let alone run. Defenceless. Sad to think he'd miss the big wet now, and all the colour it painted on the land. And the roar of the rivers . . .

What a futile conversation this was to be having with yourself, he pondered, enduring more brutal kicks. Tell this vicious fellow, the son of Oatley, what he wanted to know! It occurred to Numinga that the father Oatley was the better man. A gentleman. Fathers and sons! He hoped Boomi would turn out a better man than his father . . . wiser. Smart was fleeting.

I might have survived too, he mused, if I'd been a bit wiser, but it's too late now.

He looked up at Oatley's son and spoke, firmly he hoped, but it came out a wretched croak.

'I lied, boss. Don't hurt me no more. They not in the gorge. They got your daddy up top, them blokes. Mimimiadie, him too. Right up on the plateau. You know what I say?'

'Yes, I know. I've been up there. So Yorkey's not detouring round the plateau, through the swamps. He's going up top. Is that the meeting place?'

Numinga nodded. 'Up there. Yes, boss. Good looking spot from up there.'

'Yes, it would be,' the son said. 'Yes. Ideal. And how many men has Mimimiadie got?' He laughed. 'Not counting an old goat like you.'

'Four he got. Good old fellers,' Numinga breathed, taking exception to the insult, thinking of Garradji.

'Older than you?'

'Magic men, them fellers,' he managed to say, before he was shoved aside.

'And you were signalling to them that Yorkey was on his way? Is that what you were up to?'

'Yeah,' Numinga said. His jaw was stiff from the blows and he had to struggle to speak; he had more to say. 'I tell them everything all right.'

'All's well, eh? We'll see about that.'

But Numinga had collapsed, face down by some fresh sprigs of grass that had found new life between the rocks. There was even a tiny white flower blinking at him. He smiled and lay there, expecting to be shot, now that he'd outlived his usefulness, his body tensed, waiting for the final blow, the shot the white men used on wounded and dying animals. But it didn't come.

After a while he realised that the son of Oatley had gone. Left him to die.

He dragged himself back to the cooling embers of his fire, gathering leaves and twigs thrown about from last night's storm. As he worked, he blotted out the pain, concentrating on one last effort.

His elbows were red raw. He was leaving trails of blood that brought biting ants crawling all over him, but still he persisted. He searched for bark but none was to be found at this level, so he broke a leafy branch from a bush. Not the accepted practice, but it would do. He breathed the embers of the fire into life with twigs and more twigs, determined to get this one thing right, to outwit the son of Oatley if it was the last thing he could do. Admitting the point grimly.

'I'll teach you to shoot me, you bastard,' he said quite clearly, in their language.

The smoke signal that went up was jerky, intermittent, jerky, ongoing, scads of smoke, urgent, puffy, on and on until there was no fire any more and no breath left in the lungs of a lonely Aborigine known on police records as Neddy.

Gopiny was jubilant. He had hated being left up top here with all the action happening below. Once they'd thought it would have been a great place to sit out the wet, but it was not, and he could tell them that. It was the wettest place he'd ever been in his life. The rain seemed endless; it was like living in a cloud up here. The rocks were slippery; water filled every crevice and plunged into the caves. Cascades that didn't just trickle to the edges of the cliff, but rushed at it, making him terrified of going anywhere near the cliff face, and yet he was expected to stay at a high point and watch for Numinga's signal.

But then it came! At last something was happening!

Ever since they'd moved down to the gorge there'd been problems. As the rock pools at the base filled up and flooded, and more water splashed down from above, the residents, reptiles and small animals, began to take their leave for safer surrounds, and Mimimiadie was irritated to find no food within easy reach. They didn't have any women to forage for them, so he had to order his two warriors to leave the guns and get out on the hunt. They argued, reluctant to leave the precious rifles, but he forbade them that luxury.

So far he'd only allowed them to shoot one bullet each, that being their one and only lesson in marksmanship. He hoped that if necessary they might be able to hit an enemy, or at least scare him off, but he knew full well that they'd never hit a moving target like a kangaroo or an emu. It would be a waste of ammunition so he sent them off with their spears.

This left him pacing about with only Garradji for company, and the whitefeller Oatley, whom he kept hidden in a cleft between some rocks, his hands bound and the halter still on his neck so they could lead him about.

Then some riders came from the other direction, and all three had to keep out of sight until they'd splashed on through.

Days later they had all resumed their positions at the mouth of the gorge, watching and waiting as planned, but for Mimimiadie time had started to drag. He wasn't accustomed to tension or this forced inertia, and he became more and more restless and frustrated. He wished he'd set a time limit. This waiting was bad and getting worse. Where was that Yorkey who'd said he'd get his son? What was taking so long? He had a horse. Men on horses could travel like the wind. He'd said he'd pick up Boomi from that big town. What was so hard about that? But what if he'd just run off? Why would he worry about the whitefeller?

His impatience turned to anger and he harassed Oatley with questions, threatening him with a bashing if Yorkey didn't get back soon, but Oatley seemed confident, more interested in teaching him English words. Mimimiadie didn't mind that. Something to do. But his men were getting heartily sick of their duty, or non-duty, just standing about nursing their guns, and they began to wander, exploring deep into the gorge until he roared at them to stay on watch.

More days passed and Mimimiadie decided he was fed up with the gorge, they'd be better off up top, so they all moved out, dragging Oatley, who had become weak in the legs. They skirted the rocky terrain outside the gorge and moved into the flat forest area that they had to traverse before beginning the climb, but then Mimimiadie changed his mind again. He announced that they'd stay tight there, with the tilt of the foothills that led to the plateau at their backs.

Garradji was full of complaints. He felt safer in the gorge. They were too exposed out here, with nowhere to run, and that annoyed Mimimiadie, especially since he realised that the old man was right.

'If we stay in there we'll be up to our knees in water soon, you old fool, so shut up,' he blustered.

He worried that maybe they should all go up top again, but not yet. He was the boss. He was the only one to say where to go and when. If that Yorkey ever got back, he would have to come this way, Gopiny would send him this way. He made big talk with his two men about the best positions to take up, ready to defend themselves if necessary. They liked that, and it created a welcome diversion. But that night the skies opened and it teemed. There were hiding places here, among the rocks and trees, but no shelter, so they simply had to put up with it.

In the morning the men demanded to go back up top to where Gopiny waited, safe and dry in a cave, but Garradji refused, claiming the climb was too hard on his old legs.

The men grumbled. Garradji was no use anyway. Just another mouth to feed, and to placate them, Mimimiadie agreed. He was nervous, though, of offending a magic man, so forcing a voice of kindness, he told the old man he was free to go if he wished.

That brought screams of rage from Garradji.

'You ungrateful rat. You needed me, to make the search for Numinga; now you cast me aside. You dare expel me and I'll have worms eat your heart out.'

'No, no, no. I thought it was your wish to leave. I am honoured to have you here. Your advice is invaluable. There are scrub turkeys in this forest, I will have the lads catch one just for you. See, the sun is out now, it will be pleasant here.'

But Garradji wasn't listening. His weathered old face blanched to grey and his jaw dropped open. Frantically he scrabbled in the ground for a handful of red mud, and slapped it on his tongue, coughing and spluttering as some went down his throat in his haste.

Mimimiadie stared. 'What are you doing?'

'Making amends,' he muttered, spitting and slapping more on his forehead and cheeks, leaving it caked there like a mask.

'For what?'

'For saying the name of the English-speaking one.'

'You mean—'

Garradji lurched at him, clapping his hand over Mimimiadie's mouth. 'Don't speak! Don't say it. He is dead, that one. Even now he is on his way into the Dreaming.'

He let his eyes droop and lapsed into a meditative state, sitting cross-legged as usual but head held high as he chanted softly, mournfully.

Mimimiadie knew it well, that age-old singing, with its familiar rhythm, a crying song for the dead. Not for a moment did he disbelieve what he'd been told. He jumped up, grabbed Oatley's harness rope and led him away.

'What was that about?' Oatley asked as Mimimiadie, troubled, searched about for somewhere to place him. He looked up and saw a slim gum tree sprouting from a ledge just above them. Nodding grimly, he dragged Oatley up the incline, tested the tree, found it firmly rooted, and tied his prisoner to it, leaving him fully exposed to the weather and anyone who came by.

'What the hell are you doing?' Oatley demanded. 'You can't leave me here. It's too hot.'

Mimimiadie ignored him. He ran down and looked up at Oatley, forced to stand in front of the slim tree. He assessed the distance. Yes, failing a bullet, a spear could easily finish him from here.

He didn't know what had happened to Numinga, but he was certain he hadn't died of natural causes. Now, if they were attacked, he thought furiously, this one wouldn't die of natural causes either. He'd be the first to die. Thoroughly rattled, he gave up hope of getting his son back, this time, but the warrior in him raged. No more the grieving, hopeful father, Mimimiadie was ready for a fight. Payback! He picked up one of his spears and ran swiftly down to alert his two men. As soon as they heard that the other one was dead, they armed themselves with spears, as well as the rifles, and kept their eyes on the thin track leading to the main gorge road. At last, some action.

Everyone in Pine Creek was there for a purpose – railway workers, Cable Company staff, maintenance men and telegraph operators, a few wives, a couple of policemen – and all looked forward to the day when they'd be relieved of duty in this wretch of a town. The general store sold everything from supplies to saddles, depending on availability, and the same man owned the stables. He was also the blacksmith, and his wife proudly held the title of postmistress. The pace was so slow it was said the crows flew backwards over Pine Creek. The only respite was the pub, a shanty, but it was a meeting place. The bar had a short, stubby counter but you didn't have to sit inside; you could hang about the veranda or sit on the wooden steps or take up a posse under a patch of shady trees inhabited by screeching parrots, and from there watch the world go by . . . the world being mainly station folk, or the long bullock trains that hauled heavy goods from the port of Darwin to all points of the compass.

The station folk were inspected and identified. High-living cattlemen like Zack Hamilton and his kin, who came through on their fine horses; station hands with their sturdy stockhorses; drovers, their mobs cooling their heels outside the town under the watchful eye of outriders. But none of them hung about. They were in and out, maybe to catch the train or just to use a few hours to quench hard thirsts, but then gone. No one actually came to Pine Creek, it was said, they just passed through.

And that was why the mystery had the town talking.

What was Zack Hamilton doing here holed up in one of Scotty's old cabins? He'd been here for days, just hanging about, taking his meals with Scotty and his missus, calling in at the bar for a couple of pints, but doing nothing in particular, day in and day out.

They speculated about this. Maybe something big was about to happen in the town. Zack had the dough. A new pub? Nah. He wouldn't do that to Scotty without telling him first, not Zack, and as it turned out, Scotty was just as much in the dark as the rest, though he'd thrown out hints. A real post office? Nah. That was the Govmint. A café? A real eating place, a restorint? That was on the cards. That'd be something. Mrs McCabe only served counter grub when she was in the mood, for the average blokes, not big-timers like Zack, who ate in their kitchen.

So what was he doing in that crumby old cabin? He had a few mates here, mates who'd offered to put him up in their houses. They weren't mansions, that was for sure, but they didn't leak. He'd thanked them, though, and stayed put. Why?

The story was mulled over from go to whoa. He'd come by train with his missus, a young fellow, a black stockman and a black kid. Right? Now the black stockman had taken the kid wherever blackfellers go. To home camp somewhere. Nothing unusual about that. As for the other bloke, someone had recognised him. Myles Oatley. Hadn't been seen about these parts for a year, maybe more. Well, he'd ridden west, hell for leather, and why wouldn't he? His grandpa, old Pop Oatley was out that way at Warrawee station. Myles would know he'd have to put some speed on to get out there before the wet set in. So that left Zack and his missus. But what do you know? Mrs Hamilton gets on the train the next day, high-tailing it back to Darwin, with Zack standing there waving her off.

That left Zack, wandering about like a pup looking for his tail. Bloody strange.

Zack knew all this. He knew tongues would be wagging, but he said nothing, ignoring barely disguised questions and even the straight-out enquiry from Sergeant Murphy at the pub.

'Zack! Good to see you. What are you up to here?'

'Just looking around.'

'What for? Thinking of investing here?'

'I'm a cattleman, Jim. Not a townie.'

'Well let me tell you, Zack. If your mates in the Govmint are thinking of spending a few quid here – and not before time, I say – we bloody need a proper police station. I'm working out of a shed, and a poddy calf could bust out of my lockup. It's time they did something useful for us.'

'I'll keep it in mind.'

He meant he'd try. He had a lot on his mind, not least Sibell. He should have gone back with her, he'd wanted to, but he couldn't leave here just yet. She understood that, but it didn't alter the fact that she was intent on leaving him. Zack found it hard to express his feelings. A man could only say, 'Don't go. Don't leave me. Leave us.' He couldn't beg. He was still so numbed by the thought of Sibell leaving him that he'd become tongue-tied, intimidated by her arguments, by the litany of woes that she'd unburdened on him. By the fact that she'd been unhappy for so long and he'd never noticed.

'Don't you know I love you?' he'd said that morning in the cabin, before she left.

'Zack, we've been over this so often, it's only words now. Of course you love me, and I love you. I always will. But I can't live out there any more, and that's final.'

'What do you want me to do?'

'Nothing. Black Wattle is your life. You love the place and all the people out there. It's just not mine any more. I don't think I was ever cut out to live like that, isolated from the world.'

'And it took you twenty years or more to find out? Nice bloody time to tell me.'

'There you go getting angry again. We can't even discuss this—'

'What is there to discuss? The station has been good to us. You've never wanted for anything—'

'Oh spare me! Living out there, how could I want for anything? Like normal weather. Clean water. People. Shops. Civilisation. All we've got is your damned money, which you keep ploughing back into the station to keep thousands of cattle happy. No, we can't discuss it because you haven't the faintest idea what I'm talking about.'

Now he sat alone in the cabin, leafing through old magazines and newspapers, miserable as hell in this dump, which an army of fleas had just discovered was occupied by a tasty human.

But he had one thing in his favour. Sibell wouldn't leave Darwin until she heard news of her old friend William Oatley. She wouldn't do that.

And what of William and the rest of them? Zack was nervous, anxiety churning in the pit of his stomach. Had he done the right thing not reporting this whole episode to the police? Thinking he could handle it himself. Only to be shunted aside by Myles, who did have a right to take part in the rescue of his father after all. Unless . . .

Zack hated gossip. He'd heard the tale about Myles and Harriet Oatley and didn't believe it for a minute. Sibell found it hard to accept it too, but Lucy and Maudie were adamant. Possibly they'd used the story, rumour, as defence. Maudie was so fond of Lucy, she was outraged that Myles Oatley seemed to have lost interest in her. Lucy, he knew, was very upset, but he'd heard Sibell talking to her, explaining that it was better to find out now than later, like after the official engagement, or even the wedding.

She could talk! Try twenty years, Sibell. It hits even harder then. It smashes your whole world apart, it makes you wonder why you worked so hard all these years. He'd offered to take Sibell on a sea voyage back to England, back to the little town where she'd grown up, to the bright lights of London, and even to Paris, but she'd refused.

'No, it won't do, Zack. I was shipwrecked, remember? My parents were drowned at sea. I was lucky to survive. I'll never consider it! This coastline is far enough for me. There being no other way of getting out of here.'

Later, he'd apologised. Coming in late one cold night to find her sitting on the veranda, huddled in a blanket, enveloped by the darkness and her own thoughts.

'I'm sorry. I did remember, Sibell. How could I forget that? I just thought you might be over it and like to go back.'

'That's all right, Zack. It was a good idea. I'd love to see London again but I'm too frightened of those big oceans. You don't have to apologise. But you see, that would only postpone the problem. I still don't want to live in the bush. I'm tired of it.'

Maybe she was just tired of him.

Sergeant Murphy worried him too. Murphy was nobody's fool, and he was still very curious about Zack Hamilton hanging around Pine Creek. He'd bust a boiler if he really knew.

And what was going on out there? This waiting was the most godawful strain, with nothing to do to help fill in the hours, days. There would come a time, Zack knew, when he might have to call on Murphy for help. If they didn't return. If they did come back but without William. But how long should he allow this to go on? And where the hell was Mimimiadie hiding, waiting for the boy?

He should have knocked Myles down. Stopped him. Taken over himself.

To have Myles come charging out there with the cavalry? Hell, no!

Jesus, this waiting was killing him. He felt like strapping on a couple of guns and going out there after them. To make a fool of himself trying to find them.

But if the worst came to the worst and no one showed, he'd have to go to Murphy and there'd be hell to pay. But when?

When Sibell arrived back in Darwin, she wasted no time in calling on Harriet Oatley. The poor girl was in a state, naturally, worried about William, and Sibell was astonished that no one had remembered to enlighten her as to what was happening. Not even Myles, which Sibell thought was rather a poor show. He had only told her that her husband had been captured by wild blacks, but not to mention a word of it to anyone. So now here she was, afraid to venture out of the house, just waiting for news.

Sadly there was nothing Sibell could tell her, nothing much except that Myles and Yorkey had gone to talk to the Aborigines who were holding William.

'But why?' Harriet asked. 'What is it? Do they want money?'

'Something like that,' Sibell said, for now. Too soon to mention the child. 'I'm confident they'll bring William back safely.'

'Oh Lord, I hope so. I feel so useless not being able to do anything to help.' She looked terrible, her hair uncombed, her face pale and drawn, and Sibell realised she was tipsy.

'Can I do anything for you?' she asked. 'Could I get one of your friends to come and stay with you?'

'What friends? I don't have any friends. They're William's friends, not mine.'

'I'm sure that's not true, my dear. Keep in mind that no one outside of our families knows that William is in difficulty.'

She felt guilty that she couldn't invite the girl back to her own house, as one should in these circumstances, but Harriet wouldn't get much sympathy from Maudie and Lucy. Rather the opposite. Sibell wondered about that nasty story. Could it be true? Maudie seemed to think that was why William had upped and left town so abruptly. Certainly an odd thing to do with Christmas only a few weeks away. William was a great celebrator; he loved the festive season.

Harriet sighed. 'Do you really think he'll come home safely?'

'Yes, of course. But now, dear, if you'll forgive me, I don't recommend alcohol at this time.'

'What?' For a minute it seemed that Harriet would deny it, but then she shrugged. 'Why not? A little gin in the afternoon is good for the constitution in this heat. I've got nothing else to do.' Her voice rose. 'I never have anything to do in this horrible town. Look out there! It's so grey and depressing, miserable drizzling rain all the time, it's getting on my nerves.'

'You'll feel better when the weather breaks.'

Harriet stared at her. 'Breaks? What the hell is this, then? I've forgotten what sunlight looks like.'

'This is just the overture. When the monsoon really descends on us, the storms have us jumping, and the rain is so heavy you can't hear yourself think. And yet, somehow, it's a tremendous relief.' She stopped, and looked at Harriet. 'But you know that. You were here last year. I remember you saying the tropical downpours didn't worry you at all.'

'Last year it was different,' Harriet sulked.

'Of course it was. William was here and you were having a good time. He'll be back soon; don't let this waiting get you down.'

Harriet shook her head. 'I really need a drink.' She rang a tiny silver bell and replaced it on a carved occasional table by her chair.

Tom Ling appeared in an instant. 'Yes, missy?'

'I'll have a gin and lemon,' she said defiantly. 'What would you like, Sibell?'

'Lemonade, please.'

The drinks were prettily served on a silver salver with sparkling linen and tiny wafer biscuits. Sibell thanked Tom Ling and sipped the lemonade, which was delicious, but Harriet gulped her gin.

'Anyway,' she said sadly, 'if William gets back—'

'What do you mean, *if* he gets back? I told you, he will be back, Harriet. You're just depressed.'

She burst into tears. 'You don't know! You just don't know!'

'What don't I know?'

'Oh leave it, for God's sake. I'm not feeling very well. I think I'll lie down.'

'Yes, I think that's a good idea.'

On her way home, Sibell pondered the conversation. She wished she hadn't interrupted when Harriet had said, 'If William gets back . . .'

What did she have in mind? What did she intend to do when William got back? Maybe it was best not to know. Whatever it would be, it hadn't sounded too cheerful. What was really going on in that household?

297

Next she had to deal with Lucy, who was in a mood. She'd had an argument with Maudie about Christy Cornford.

'He's really sweet, Mother. And he's just marvellous to me. And he's so handsome!'

'She's fallen in love with that popinjay,' Maudie growled. 'I keep telling her it's only rebound. Not to take him seriously.'

'How dare you call him a popinjay,' Lucy retorted. 'He's a gentleman. Not that you'd know one if you fell over one.'

'There you are, Sibell,' Maudie crowed. 'Listen to that. If you don't pull her into line you'll have that ever-so-elegant Mr Cornford planting himself with you at Black Wattle. He's on a good wicket, shining up to Lucy, and she's too silly to notice.'

'That's enough from both of you,' Sibell said firmly. 'Leave her alone, Maudie. Just because Mr Cornford is Lucy's latest escort, it doesn't mean she wants to marry him.'

'And why not?' Lucy flared. 'You've kept me believing Myles was my beau all this time and he turned out to be a rotter. So much for your opinions. I won't ever listen to you again.'

Maudie sat back in her chair. 'See! I told you so! She only has to crook her finger and Cornford will come running with a wedding ring. You'll be a nice foursome out at the station. Does he know a steer from a heifer?'

Sibell hesitated. She was worried about Harriet. And William. And she had a horrible feeling that the rumour about Harriet and her stepson could be true. She could still see Harriet's fear, definitely fear. If William came back? What was she trying to say?

It struck her suddenly. What if? What if Myles preferred that his father didn't get back? Leaving the coast clear. Surely not? 'You don't know! You just don't know!' Harriet had cried.

Surely not! And Sibell had insisted that Myles rather than Zack go to rescue William. Oh God! Was that why William had turned to Zack for help? Not Myles?

She ought to go back and force the truth out of Harriet. Find out what Myles intended to do. But what was the point? It was too late now. Zack was waiting in Pine Creek. Myles had gone after Yorkey and the child.

'Oh God,' she said eventually, and Lucy misinterpreted her attitude.

'What do you care?' she shouted. 'You won't be there. You don't give a damn about me or Daddy. You wouldn't care if I married a chimney sweep!'

'That's not true,' Sibell tried, but Maudie intervened.

'What's this, then? What do you mean, she won't be there?'

'Oh didn't you know?' Lucy said tartly. 'My mother is still leaving us. Leaving Daddy. She is bored with station life. She's leaving for fresher fields.'

Maudie was stunned. 'What? I thought that nonsense was all forgotten.'

'Oh no. Tell her, Mother. Tell her you're leaving. Any day now. Tell her you're breaking Daddy's heart and he won't lift a finger to stop you.'

'You're not?' Maudie said, deflated.

Sibell walked away from them. 'I don't want to talk about it. Not now. I'm tired.'

But Maudie was on her feet, following her to her room, genuinely distressed. 'Sibell, please. Talk to me. What is wrong? I thought you and Zack were so happy.'

'Please, Maudie. Will you leave me be?'

'No. Not until you answer me. Is it true?'

'Yes! Are you satisfied now?'

Maudie wandered back to the wide country kitchen that doubled as a dining room in the beach house. She glared at Lucy, who was still sitting moodily at the table.

'Jesus!' she said. 'What's the matter with all you people? We come to town to have a good time and all I get is woe. And you, you brat,' she snorted at Lucy, 'are you enjoying yourself abusing your mum? If she's a mind to take off, you're not helping.'

'What am I supposed to do?' Lucy complained.

'Keep out of it.'

'Oh yes. That's a good one coming from you!'

Chapter Seventeen

Gopiny stood watching Numinga's signal, relieved that all was well. He ran back to the cave, grabbed his spears and began the descent. If everything was going according to plan, this should be Yorkey coming. With the boy. With Mimimiadie's son! What great celebrations there would be back in home country when they returned, triumphant. They'd shown the whitefellers that others could play at their games. They'd be heroes!

A little way down the road he stopped, staring out over the sparsely wooded land, searching for a rider. It had to be Yorkey. No one else would get Numinga's approval. What a great day this was! He settled down, eyes skimming the landscape for movement, or the glint of metal from the sun's reflection on a horse's harness.

Eventually there it was, that flash of silver appearing and disappearing through the trees, but moving this way. Moving steadily, in no apparent hurry. Or the best pace Yorkey could go with the boy on board, he pondered happily.

Still, Gopiny waited. He couldn't afford to lose sight of Yorkey; he had to redirect him to the gorge. Mimimiadie would be furious if he missed him.

When he did spot the rider moving across a clearing he was startled. Not one horse but two. This was not right. Who else would be travelling with Yorkey? A policeman, maybe. Come to arrest Mimimiadie. Gopiny was confused. He had his instructions. Two riders weren't expected. He was at a loss to know how to deal with this. Frantically he watched for another clearing, to get a better view, and then he sat back, relieved. The other horse was riderless! Yorkey was bringing a horse for the prisoner. He'd need a horse to get back from here. That was, if Mimimiadie really meant to let him go. Gopiny didn't care one way or another. That wasn't his business. His job right now was to move down to the slopes, keeping Yorkey in view until he could intercept him.

But it wasn't over yet. He had to pay heed to Numinga, up there on the lookout, to make sure Yorkey wasn't up to any tricks, that he didn't have a posse trailing him, ready to pounce as soon as Yorkey located Mimimiadie. In his excitement he'd almost forgotten that duty. He glanced to the west and almost fell back in shock. Numinga was signalling. No calm swirl this time; thick puffs of smoke spoke urgently to him. What? What was wrong? They went on and on. And Yorkey was getting closer.

Gopiny stood, panicking. There were no other travellers in view, no movement out there at all. And the smoke signal had stopped.

But Numinga had sent a deliberate signal. Warning. Gopiny forced himself to wait. There was still plenty of time to get down to Yorkey with his important instructions.

Then he picked up the glint of metal again, moving fast. Fast. He stood very still lest his eyes wavered. He mustn't lose this rider. Yes, one rider, not several. One rider, that wasn't so bad, but Numinga had made it plain that this man wasn't welcome. And it was obvious to Gopiny already that the rider was tracking Yorkey. Not a good sign. No one else had been invited to this important meeting. No one.

He had to go. He jumped and slid down the slopes, over boulders and slippery streams emanating from the watery plateau, and raced across the flats, through the trees to call to Yorkey.

Little Boomi was sitting up front of him, grinning like this was a joyride, and Yorkey was smiling too. He didn't know that someone was tracking him. Or did he? Gopiny had to move them on quickly. He had a plan of his own.

He pointed Yorkey towards the gorge but Yorkey disagreed, pointing up to the heights, arguing.

Gopiny couldn't speak his language, but he stamped his foot, jammed his spear firmly in the ground and made it plain to Yorkey that he had to go the other way, and fast.

'Mimimiadie!' he whispered, pointing urgently, and to his great relief Yorkey understood, turning the horses in the other direction.

Gopiny studied the heavily rutted track. Even a whitefeller could follow the tracks of two horses in this damp soil. The rider would be coming this way very soon. And Gopiny would deal with him himself. Hadn't Mimimiadie shown them how to do it, when they'd captured both Yorkey and the white boss? Too easy. They'd all be proud of him. He wouldn't allow anybody to interfere now that the boy was back. They only had to take him and leave; it was a long trek back to their own country.

He positioned himself by the track, well hidden behind a rocky outcrop, testing his spear for the throw.

Myles Oatley saw the tracks of the horses as a gift as he ploughed along, hot on Yorkey's trail. He'd soon catch up with him, before he had time to communicate with the bastards holding his father up there. They knew Yorkey was coming; all the better. He'd be right beside him, and they'd have the kid for protection.

No funny business. Hardly likely, though, guns against spears.

The main thing was to find William. He sidelined considerations about the situation with Harriet, or William's attitude for that matter, simply because he couldn't make up his own mind on how to sort out the mess without losing Harriet, or his share of the family finances. It was bloody annoying, he pondered darkly, to think that William, with all his wealth, had never put a thing in his son's name, not a share in a property or even some of his stocks and bonds, not a penny. Some of the lads he knew had received title deeds to large holdings on their eighteenth birthdays, but not Myles Oatley; he was kept under the thumb. Totally beholden to Daddy, who had better be grateful to his son for making this huge effort to rescue him.

But what if William had not survived weeks of ill-treatment by this bastard Mimimiadie? Or if he'd already been killed? Had he written a new will before he went raging into the bush? Cutting them both out? But if not, how much would Harriet get? That was a dismal thought.

Suddenly, and for the first time on this rash expedition, Myles wondered what he and Yorkey would do if this promise of an exchange of hostages wasn't real. If Mimimiadie had never had any intention of keeping his side of the bargain. If his father wasn't here at all. If he'd already been slain.

What would they do? Hand over the kid anyway?

Myles had no idea. And a small thought lodged once again. That he really didn't know what he was doing out here. He'd have to rely on Yorkey for protection if push came to shove.

The great bulk of the plateau loomed ahead of him, a red-brown mass that had lurched skywards in yet another of the convulsions sustained by this ancient land. The sides were worn, he knew, weathered down into rocky foothills, but it would take another million years to have any effect on the plateau itself, even though it had been split asunder, creating the gorge. Campbell's Gorge.

The sight of the plateau, and the knowledge that wild blacks were sitting comfortably up top, thinking they'd won this game, made him nervous. What if some of them were down below, hoping for an ambush? He studied the tracks of Yorkey's horses. They were steady, no change of pace, and no indication that he'd halted the horses at any time. Nevertheless, he decided, it was time to take care. He slowed his horse to a trot while he loaded his rifle.

Gopiny was waiting, almost bursting with excitement. He could do this on his own. And he'd get it right this time. That other whitefeller he'd speared had got away. Not this one. He knew the procedure now. Spear the horse and then the man before he had time to grab for a weapon, too busy trying to save himself from being crushed by the collapse of the great animal. He wished he'd brought a waddy, most probably a better weapon at close range than a spear, but the second spear would do. If he said so himself, he had a strong arm, one of the best, and he was fast. He moved the second spear closer to him with his toes.

A noise caught his attention and he glanced away, his eyes resting on the unmistakable brilliant blue feathers of a sacred kingfisher making a nest in a tall termite mound, punching its way into the central chamber with its beak. He grinned. Clever birds, those kingfishers, but sometimes they came undone, taking on mounds that were too hard, risking

303

breaking their beaks. But this fellow was getting through, head ducking into the hole . . . tap, tap, tap . . .

Then there was that other sound. Hooves plunging, harness jiggling. 'Oh-oh!' Gopiny grabbed his spear frantically; the rider was here! He could smell that horse, that strange, musty smell.

He rose up, spear raised, and dashed out . . . dashed out! But something went wrong. A force of wind in his chest threw him like a little slight leaf and he was blown back into the trees, drifting down ever so gently into the tall grasses, settling there, a leaf come to rest . . .

Myles stared at him, shocked. He didn't dismount, he couldn't spare the time, but he rode over, peering down at the attacker. Not an old bloke at all; that one on the lookout had lied. This fellow was in his twenties. Was. His eyes, flat and dead, were wide open in the black-bearded face, and blood was spreading across his shiny black chest where the bullet had struck him.

'Jesus! That was close. Just as well my rifle was loaded! The bastard was planted there ready to kill me! Jesus! I knew we couldn't trust them!'

He did halt his horse then, unwilling to go on. Afraid to go on. How many others were in this scrub with their spears? He felt a prickling down the nape of his neck and looked furtively about him, expecting a hail of spears. His horse too was spooked; it was straining, anxious to get away from this frightening scene, so Myles gave it its head. Riding fast after Yorkey. Figuring he'd be safer with Yorkey than in this dangerous scrub.

He saw the trampled soil where Yorkey had stopped his horses before moving on again, and he followed those tracks. They weren't going off to the right, but towards the gorge. Myles didn't care which way as long as he could stick with Yorkey, who must have decided it was safer to make for the gorge.

They all heard the shot. The crack seemed to linger, suspended in the thick, humid air, until it snapped off into a hostile silence.

Instinctively, Yorkey veered the horses into the shelter of trees, clutching Boomi, hushing him, waiting. Who would be shooting? And why? Mimimiadie had guns, Yorkey's own and William's, but what would he be shooting at? Yorkey couldn't tell where the shot had come from, so he decided it would be best to sit awhile. See what happened. He had no doubt that Gopiny, having sent him on to the right track, would already be taking a short cut across the rocky terrain to tell his boss the good news. He'd been so excited, with good reason; he'd skip over that rough country as fast as any agile little wallaby, but the horses had to detour.

Mimimiadie knew exactly where the shot had come from. His ears were trained to hear and locate bush noises however slight, all part of the armoury of a hunter, so pinpointing the area was no effort. For a few hopeful minutes he thought it could be Yorkey, firing a shot to announce his presence, but why would he do that? Gopiny was there. And why would he be firing a gun if he had Boomi with him? Boomi was terrified of guns. Maybe it was just some white man, hunting tucker. He really had no reason to believe that Yorkey was even on his way back yet. Though he should be. He should be, if everything was going to plan. But Mimimiadie had a sinking feeling in his gut that something was wrong. No use thinking up excuses; he was a survivor of countless raids, countless dangers, and his gut was rarely wrong. He turned to Garradji, to judge his reaction, and was astonished to see the ancient darting away, scampering uphill as fast as his skinny old legs would take him, without even a backward glance. Suddenly the wizened frame was having no trouble making for the plateau, for safety . . . the rat. He knew something bad was up, but what was it this time?

He wrenched a gun from one of the sentries who had taken cover and was waving it about uselessly anyway.

'Get down there and see who it is! Move!' He gave him a kick in the rear to emphasise the need for speed.

Then he too waited in the long afternoon shadows as the sun began its dip behind the plateau. He looked up at Oatley who had managed to slip down to a sitting position, his back to the tree, head hanging down. He ought to consider himself lucky that this boss had allowed Garradji to remove the neck halter so he could tip some water into him. Well, his minder had gone now, and for the time being, no one else had time to attend to his troubles.

More waiting. A terrible thing that a grown man should have to be hanging about here, doing nothing all this time, just living on scraps. It was nearly as bad as being in prison. Mimimiadie would never come back to this place again. Never.

Nothing happened. Yorkey wondered if Zack was trailing him. Wouldn't put it past him. But why would he fire a gun? To have him wait? He'd know that wasn't on.

In the end he decided he might as well keep moving. He pulled out on to the track again, worrying about Boomi, who was very tired, his head lolling back against Yorkey's chest.

'Not long now,' he murmured. 'I hope.'

He'd only gone about half a mile when he heard a horse pounding after him, and turned, exasperated, expecting Zack. But it wasn't Zack; it was Oatley's son, Myles. That two-faced wife-stealer. No friend to his own father.

'What are you doing here?' he shouted. 'Get the hell out of here!'

'Thought you were smart, didn't you? I don't trust you, Yorkey. I reckon you're in cahoots with this mob.'

'Don't be bloody stupid! You turn about right now. I know what I'm doing.'

'I bet you do. How come you sailed past that blackfeller down the road and he attacked me? Why did he attack me if this is just an innocent exchange? What are you trying to hide?'

'Who attacked you? Gopiny?'

'Of course, you know their names, don't you? Mates, are they?'

'What happened? Where's Gopiny? That shot? Oh, Jesus! Was that you?'

Myles grinned. 'Yeah. He came off second best.'

'You killed him?'

'Stone motherless dead, the bastard. It was him or me.'

Yorkey looked about him nervously. He had what he called a healthy fear of tribal men of his own race, on the warpath, and he also harboured a very real respect for the 'secret business', engendered in him by his mother. A lot of them were mystics; they knew things, had powers beyond the scope of the uninitiated. He wondered if they knew Gopiny was dead. Heard it on the wind, on this hot wind blowing from the north. A shudder went through him as he dismounted, lifting Boomi down, and planted him on his hip, afraid he might run off.

'You get out of here,' he barked at Myles. 'Go back. I'm not leaving here with you. I don't want anything to do with you.'

'Then we'll camp here. You make camp. I'll hold the kid.' Myles dismounted too.

'Keep away from him! You lay a hand on him and I'll put a bullet in you.'

Yorkey wasn't sure what to do now. Mimimiadie would know he was close, Gopiny would have . . . No! What was he thinking of? Gopiny was dead. They wouldn't know he was coming. Unless they had other lookouts, which was on the cards. And soon they'd miss Gopiny. Come looking for him. If they found his body, it would be all over. None of them would get back to town.

He found himself staring at Myles's trousers. He was thinking of Numinga. He wasn't a bad bloke. He would intercede for them. Boomi was back safe, no more trouble, please. No need, no more. But he was still staring at those dungarees. Expensive cloth. Light-coloured . . .

Yorkey put the boy down. 'You want cake? You sit here.'

The child grinned, nodding. He loved cake.

Quietly Yorkey turned to Myles. 'You shot him from your horse?'

'Sure did. Plugged him, dead on.'

'Then what's that on your trousers? On both legs?'

Myles was startled. He looked down and stared for a minute, then he shrugged. 'Mud.'

'That's not mud, it's blood!' Now Yorkey was beginning to panic. 'What blood? How did that get there?'

Myles blinked, then he stammered, 'Oh for God's sake, I cut myself. What of it?'

Yorkey grabbed him, shaking him. 'You're lying. Show me the cut! You've got blood splattered all over your pants. Down there at the ankles. That couldn't be from a cut.'

Myles tried to shake him off. 'Leave go of me. I'll report you for this!'

'Who to? What about that blood?'

'Ah, Jesus, if you must know, I was protecting your back. There was another one. Up on the dingo rocks. He was watching you. Signalling.'

'So you killed him? You didn't kill him?'

'I had to make him talk,' Myles whined. 'To protect you. Can't you understand that?'

Yorkey's head was in a whirl of fright. A signal. Of course.

So they would know he and Boomi were on their way. And they'd be waiting, on the alert. The word 'understand' thrust into his mind.

'Understand? You made him talk. But how come you understood him?' The answer was terrifyingly clear.

'He spoke English good enough,' Myles said smugly.

Numinga! He'd killed Numinga. Their only friend in that mob. Yorkey lashed out, punching Myles in the face, sending him sprawling, then pulled him up by the shirt and punched him again, leaving him lying there dazed while Boomi watched, fascinated.

Yorkey realised he'd have to get to Mimimiadie quickly, before the bad news of the two deaths reached him. It was now or never. He grabbed Boomi and leapt on to his horse, pulling the spare mount towards him. As an afterthought, he manoeuvred both horses about until he was close to Myles's animal. He leaned forward, grabbed Myles's rifle, then smashed the butt over his knee, throwing it down to its owner in disgust.

He took the two horses back on to the track and, setting their noses for the gorge, took off as fast as he could safely allow the horses to travel. Boomi was crying. He wanted his cake.

The messenger saw them. Heard them shouting at each other. He couldn't understand a word, but it was of no moment. They had Boomi. Boomi was here. He'd never really believed that the whitefellers would ever hand him over, but there he was. He skittled back, shouting the good news.

'Boomi is back! He's here! We go get him quick.'

Mimimiadie reacted the same way, throwing his arms to the sky in jubilation until caution slowed him down.

'How did he seem? Is he bound? Is he with Yorkey? Where are they?'

'He is not bound. He sits the horse in front of Yorkey. Down this track. Another man there too. He was arguing with Yorkey about something. Yorkey bash him good.'

'What?' Mimimiadie was angry. 'What other man? White man?'

'Yes.'

'I said for Yorkey to come alone. What tricks now? And what's he doing on this track? Coming this way?'

'You told Gopiny to send him this way, remember?'

'Of course I remember. So where is Gopiny now? Didn't you see him?'

'No.' He looked back. Obviously Gopiny had redirected Yorkey or he would be heading up to the plateau with Boomi, as he'd originally been told to do. And having completed his task, Gopiny would have plenty of time to join them. Plenty of time. He remembered that shot, and stood unhappily before Mimimiadie. 'No. I didn't see him anywhere.'

'And the English-speaking one on the dingo lookout. He hasn't come in either,' Mimimiadie said harshly. 'Why is this?'

'You said he was dead.'

'So I did. But I did not say how this might have happened. I only have the word of the old man. Who has now run away on us. I should drag him back, but there's no time.' He handed back the gun and picked up his spear. 'First we get Boomi, then we see.'

Yorkey guessed he was only a mile or so from the gorge now, which was just as well, since the horses were tiring. He looked back but there was no sign of Myles. Not yet anyway. Without a rifle, he mightn't be so brave. But he'd probably follow rather than be left out there on his own. Dammit, why couldn't he have kept out of this? Jesus! He'd killed two of Mimimiadie's men. If he found out . . .

God almighty! He jerked the horse to a halt. Mimimiadie was standing in the middle of the track, his spear on the ground, held between his toes, Yorkey was not taken in by this apparently peaceful overture. He knew full well that Mimimiadie could have that spear into his hands in seconds. But as soon as he saw Boomi he forgot the spear, running forward, grasping the boy from the saddle, holding him up joyfully. He clutched the delighted child to his chest, the relief on his rugged face a rare sight.

Smiling, Yorkey climbed down from his horse, wearily rubbing his rear. At the same time he noticed that Mimimiadie's two warriors, now armed with guns, had not been able to control their excitement. They popped up from their cover to witness the reunion, and then suddenly disappeared again. They were still suspicious and Yorkey knew that with Myles in the background, this wasn't going to be easy. Especially with no one to translate.

He shook hands with Mimimiadie. Patted Boomi on the head, and talked. Some of it would get through.

'Boomi's a good boy. One of the best,' he beamed. 'But he's tired. Sleep. Need rest now. We all go quick. Where is Oatley? I take him now. All good fellers us. This all right?'

Mimimiadie beckoned for him to follow him, so Yorkey tethered the horses and headed with him into a tumble of rocks. At the same time, Mimimiadie shouted instructions to his two men, who instantly jumped up and started loping back down the track. Were they looking for Gopiny? Yorkey worried. Or did they already know Myles wasn't far back there?

He pretended not to be concerned. 'Where's Oatley, boss?'

Mimimiadie jerked his head and Yorkey looked up, shocked to see William slumped there, tied to a tree.

'Oh no! What are you doing to him? William!' he shouted. 'You all right?'

He saw the grey head lift up, peering down, then slump again.

'I'm bringing him down!' Yorkey told Mimimiadie, who shrugged approval. Yorkey was surprised, but he didn't waste any time. He was up the cliff in minutes, cutting Oatley loose.

'William, I'm sorry. Can you get up? Can you walk? Oh, Jesus. You look like hell.'

'The gun,' William croaked. 'Your rifle. He's got it.'

Yorkey looked down to see Mimimiadie standing beside his horse. Holding up his rifle. Laughing at him, waving it at him.

'Never mind,' he said to William. 'With a bit of luck we won't need it. Don't worry, we're getting out of here double quick. I've brought a horse for you.'

Together they stumbled down the hill and, determined not to waste any time, Yorkey half carried William over to the horses.

'You're not walking too good,' he said. 'But I reckon you can ride. Can you do that?'

'Yes,' William muttered shakily. He was barely recognisable, thin and gaunt and filthy. His clothes stank. His hair was dirty and matted, his face and arms peeling with severe sunburn, but there was life in those eyes. Yorkey knew he'd battle on. He daren't tell him that his stupid son was out there somewhere, ruining, or trying to ruin, what should have been a simple exchange.

'We have to hurry,' he said, preparing to lift William into the saddle, but Mimimiadie stepped forward, the rifle trained on them. 'No go.'

'What are you talking about?' Yorkey shouted, surprised. 'It's over. You got Boomi. I take him.'

'No go. Waitings.'

'What for? No! We go.'

But it was no use. Yorkey settled William on the ground by his horse and turned back, demanding that they be allowed to leave. Trying to ignore that rifle in the hands of an excitable black boss.

Myles was angry and afraid. He'd have Yorkey, the black bastard, up for assault when he got back. But what to do now? He certainly couldn't go on unarmed. And what a fool he'd look just having to turn about and go back on his own. Zack would laugh his head off. He wondered what was happening up ahead. Maybe he could stay under cover. Stick to the bush and get a look at what was going on. But the thought of the two dead Aborigines now began to weigh on him. They were Mimimiadie's men. He might miss them, ask about them. So what? Yorkey wouldn't give him up, putting himself in danger too. Or for that matter he could blame Yorkey. That was better. Blame Yorkey. Then again, given that thought, it might be better to just get the hell out of here after all. Disappear, let Yorkey talk his way out of it.

But what about William? Well, if Yorkey hadn't smashed his rifle, deliberately, he'd have been on hand to help his father. He wouldn't be forced to hang back, or even to turn back.

But the decision wasn't left to him. Something struck him from behind as he walked over to his horse, and he pitched forward. Before he'd even grasped what had happened, two fierce-looking Aborigines were dragging him to his feet.

Myles yelled at them: 'Let me go! I'll have the law on you! Don't you know who I am? I'm a bossman. Big bossman. Plenty soldiers chase you for this. Bang! Bang!'

Their stolid faces were expressionless as they jerked him about and bound his hands so tightly the cords cut like wire. Then with a shock he saw them pick up rifles, good rifles, so he altered his tone, becoming more conciliatory.

'Why are you doing this? I'm a friend. Not doing any harm here. I'm just waiting for Yorkey. To help him. Understand? You savvy?'

But now they had his horse and were pushing him out on to the track, taking him down there after Yorkey. And they were in a hurry. One of them, suddenly finding humour, grinned at him and leapt on to his horse, kneeing it forward. The other man, dragging Myles behind him, began to jog to keep up with the trotting horse, and Myles stumbled. A vicious kick in his rear had him up again, running awkwardly, sweat pouring down his face. Fear and exertion taking their toll. His legs had the weight of lead.

He almost wept with relief when he saw Yorkey standing freely beside the two horses, and his father resting in the wiry grass nearby. William looked terrible but at least he was alive.

Myles shouted to them: 'Tell them to let me go! Tell them who I am. This is outrageous!'

A large blackfeller suddenly appeared. A huge man, with thick, matted curls and an iron-hard face. He stood imperiously ahead of Myles, holding a tall spear. He didn't move, he just waited, hawk-like eyes unblinking until Myles was thrown at his feet. Myles didn't have to be told that this was the famous Mimimiadie, and he almost grovelled in terror. The man's chest was covered in cicatrices, from battles or initiations, one couldn't tell, but they spelled out the wilderness whence this fiend had emerged.

'Tell him to free me,' Myles shouted to his father.

William nodded. 'It's all right, Myles. Stay calm. Just be quiet.' He struggled to his feet, leaning on Yorkey. 'This good feller, boss. Your son Boomi. This feller my son Myles. Right?'

Yorkey joined in, using sign language to explain, but William turned to him wearily. 'He knows some English now. I taught him. Nothing else to do.'

'Good. You speak English now, boss?' Yorkey said to Mimimiadie, admiration in his voice. 'Pretty good, eh?'

'Him son of Oatley,' Mimimiadie announced proudly.

'True,' Yorkey said. 'Him good feller all right. You let him go. We all go. Boomi all right. No trouble now, eh?'

Mimimiadie held up one finger to silence them. 'First I say where Gopiny?'

Myles tried to get up but a hard foot shoved him down again.

'Where Gopiny?' Mimimiadie snarled.

'I don't know!' he cried. 'Who Gopiny?'

Mimimiadie turned to Yorkey with the same question, and Yorkey answered him strongly. 'Me, I saw Gopiny back there. Gopiny send me to you. Right? Where he gone? Maybe up top now.' He pointed. 'Maybe up top.'

Mimimiadie was anxious to get away now that he had his boy. All this talk was annoying him, but something had happened to Numinga and maybe Gopiny too. So he should kill two of these fellers now and be done with it, to save face in front of his kin. But that would bring the wrath of the whites out in force. He was certain that the whole white world back there knew of his bold plan to rescue his son in exchange for this white boss. Yorkey had said William was an important man. They'd all be poised like an army of spear-throwers, waiting for the outcome. Waiting to see if he kept his promise. And how long would they wait?

He called Yorkey aside. 'You good feller, look after my boy. Now you tell me true. Where Gopiny?'

'I don't know, boss. True. I don't know.'

'What say him?' Mimimiadie watched carefully as Yorkey put the question to Oatley's son, and he saw fear in that smooth face as he shook his head again and again, spitting out a stream of words. Why fear? What did he know? Then again, it could be fear of Mimimiadie himself, he thought smugly. Not a bad thing to see these smart white men grovel for a change. His men were watching, figuring out what was going on, so Mimimiadie gave the son another kick for good measure. That pleased them.

But he had to get out of here. Stop this messing about. There wasn't time to instigate a search for his two men. They ought to have been able to look after themselves, they weren't babies. All he'd asked them to do was keep watch. Now they were a nuisance, messing up his great plan.

He turned to his men. 'We have to get out of here now. We can't hang about any longer.'

They agreed wholeheartedly. It had been a long, boring wait already.

'I don't know where is Gopiny,' he told them. 'And we don't have time to search. Maybe this feller hurt or kill him.' He shoved Myles with his foot. 'I don't know. I think maybe I hurt or kill him for payback. But that will bring big posses after us and we don't want that, do we? Not when I have won. With your help. We have won! What a great story we will take back. If we get back,' he added darkly.

They are only young bucks, he pondered, hanging on my every word, so I still have to make some payback, for my honour. But what?

Suddenly he had a great idea. His hard face split into a wide, mean grin. He turned to the man holding the son's horse.

'The animal is yours. You can ride him back, as far as you like.'

Delight lit the young man's face, and he pranced about, patting the

311

horse, thanking his chief for this marvellous gift. He was ready to take off this very minute. Mimimiadie nodded solemnly. Problem solved.

He ignored the son and walked over to Yorkey. 'You go now. Take Oatley. Take son. Go.'

Yorkey was delighted. He shook Mimimiadie's hand. 'You good feller. You keep promise, eh? You look after Boomi now. Thank you, boss.'

But when Yorkey made for the horses, Mimimiadie took a rifle and bailed him up, ordering his men to grab the horses.

That done, he said calmly, 'You allsame go. No horses. You all walk.'

But Yorkey wouldn't have that. He started to argue angrily, and Oatley joined in. They claimed they needed horses to get back, but Mimimiadie insisted that if black men could walk that distance, white men could too. He was adamant.

Yorkey was furious. He gave up trying to sweet-talk this brute, and shouted at him: 'You promised we'd get back safe. You can't do this. No! No go. We need the horses. You don't.'

In the end he turned his arguments into a plea for Oatley's life. 'Look at him. He sick. No walk, I say. No. He die. Posses come after you, all the longa time, all longa Victoria River. You hear? You hear me now. Big bad trouble him die.'

Finally they struck a bargain. One horse. No more. Having given one away, Mimimiadie knew he couldn't retract, and he needed one for himself. To carry him and Boomi to safety. It was the best idea he'd ever had.

One horse, he allowed. Only one. One horse between three, which still left him two horses between three. A good bargain. He chose the black horse; it looked a good strong beast.

He ordered Yorkey to put Oatley on his horse, and sent the other two animals away; then, with the gun encouraging them to move on, he watched Yorkey lift Oatley's son to his feet.

As they set off, the son was shouting at Yorkey, blaming him for leaving the horses, Mimimiadie guessed, but it was of no consequence. He forgot about them. He had his boy and a horse, and it would be dark soon. At least they would be able to get through the gorge by nightfall, and then they'd be free to go home at last. He'd won. His son would be proud of him.

'Where are you going?' Myles asked, trailing behind them.

'I'm cutting out to the gorge road,' Yorkey said. 'More chance of finding help.'

'If you hadn't given in to that bastard we wouldn't need help. What do they want with horses?'

'Same as us.' Yorkey was fed up with his constant whining already. This was going to be a long, hard march, but at least they had a horse for William. 'If you hadn't killed his men we wouldn't even be in this mess.'

William peered down at Yorkey, who was leading his horse. 'What men? Who did he kill?'

'Gopiny and Numinga.'

'Oh dear God!'

Hearing them, Myles ran forward. 'I had to, Dad, they attacked me!'

'Gopiny did, so he says. I dunno about Numinga,' Yorkey said. 'He's been a great help, I don't think.'

'Well, you two had better stop bickering. Stop talking,' William said weakly. 'We'll need all our strength. Have we got any supplies?'

'Yes. He took my horse but he missed the spare pack on that one.'

'I haven't got any,' Myles wailed. 'You let them take my horse and my saddle pack.'

'So I did!' Yorkey snapped, disgusted with him.

They pushed on until the light gave out and camped near the gorge road. Yorkey lit a fire and made them a meal, while Myles looked after the horse. After they'd finished eating, Yorkey turned to William.

'Do you feel like riding some more?'

William looked up at the full moon. It was almost as clear as day. 'I was just thinking the same thing. We'll be much cooler travelling at night. I'm sorry I'm such a burden.'

Yorkey smiled. 'You're not a burden as long as you stay on that there horse.'

He nudged Myles, who was dozing by the fire. 'Come on. We're on our way.'

They padded along beside the horse, trotting at times, and dropping back into a walk to catch their breath, but Yorkey worried that they weren't making good time. Added to which, Myles's fancy riding boots were not built for a trek. The soles were already wearing thin and he was complaining of blisters. Yorkey didn't have any sympathy for him but he couldn't afford Myles to slow them up.

'Take your dad's boots. They're broken in and he doesn't need them.'

By the second night, even after resting most of the day it had become a forced march, trying to trudge on all through the night, so with William's approval Yorkey changed the schedule.

'We'll have two rest times, and to make up for it we'll walk in the mornings as far as we can, and then start again in the evenings.'

For once, Myles didn't argue; he was too tired to care. They all knew that they had at least eighty miles to go at this snail's pace, because in keeping with the terrain, this road wasn't simply a straight line. Of necessity it wound around natural obstacles, like low hills and the inevitable rocky steeples, and then chased after the easiest creek cross-ings. At least the creeks, now beginning to run well, provided them with plenty of water. Yorkey thought they'd probably do better to cut cross-country, shorten the march, but that would mean giving up the chance of meeting travellers who could help.

'What travellers?' he asked himself. 'We haven't seen a soul. Who would take a chance on this road when any day a real downpour would fill that gorge like a bucket?' But he kept plodding on and kept hoping. The morning sun was murderous, blazing down on this shadeless track, so he gave his hat to Myles, who'd lost his in the altercation with Mimimiadie's men and was now suffering from sunburn. The last thing he needed was for Myles to get what white folk called 'a touch of the sun', an understatement if ever there was one. It sent them mad. Delirious. They seemed to think that Aborigines were immune to that ailment. Yorkey hoped they were right, though his face and hair were wet with sweat.

By the fifth morning he was yearning for rain to put them out of their misery, to give them some respite from the relentless sun, from the cruel, blinding light.

It was only mid morning when William called a halt. Made them stop. Take cover in the trees, such cover as they did offer, those skinny gums. He was worried about them, convinced he could walk now, insisting they take their turns on the horse, but when Yorkey let him try he was too weak and wobbly to go more than a hundred yards. He belonged in a hospital, not out here in this furnace. His guts were shot with watery diarrhoea.

Yorkey's prayers were answered. Mercilessly. All afternoon he'd been watching the clouds moving in from the north, and he'd seen to it that they made camp and got a fire going before the storm hit. This time it was the real thing. The monsoons had come in with a vengeance. Lightning hurtled overhead, thunder crashed, the trees all about them seemed to cringe and down came the rain, in torrents.

They were soaked to the skin. Not a great problem in this heat, but the track was a bog of slippery mud. The floor of the skimpy forest wasn't much better, awash with slimy leaves, the residue of six months' or more shedding.

Yorkey hadn't bargained on having to walk back. Supplies had just about run out, and he had no weapon to shoot one of those little birds or animals fossicking about them.

'You're an Abo,' Myles snapped at him. 'Get us some of your tucker. Your mob don't need guns.'

William, huddled beside them in the teeming rain, managed a smile. 'You wouldn't like it, Myles, believe me. We'll just have to be patient and sit out this deluge.'

'We'll sit here for a week. Let me take the horse and go for help.'

'No,' Yorkey said firmly. 'No.'

Neither of them suggested the alternative, that *he* should go, and Yorkey pondered this. Not that he would go off and leave them. It was better that they stayed together and kept pushing on, helping each other. Was there no trust left between them? Hard to say. And not his business anyway.

Next morning, though it was still raining, they had to keep going, preferring the muddy track to the vagaries of the forest bed with its hidden hollows and snags. The horse had become all-important; they could not afford to risk a fall.

But then Myles fell, floundering in the mud, weeping, apologising, telling them to go on without him.

'It's all right, mate,' Yorkey said. 'We'll just rest awhile. Your pins need help. I'll give them a good massage like I do for your dad. You'll be all right in a while.'

They drank the last of the tea and William joked, 'Water's better for us anyway.'

He must have known that the supply pack was empty – it was as flat as a pan – but he didn't let on.

Myles hugged his mug of tea and looked plaintively at his father. 'I'm sorry. I've buggered everything up, haven't I?'

'No you haven't,' Yorkey said kindly. 'William's right. He knows we just have to take a break when we need it. Then we go again. That's all we have to do. We'll get there. What's the hurry?'

Myles ignored him. 'I've buggered everything, haven't I?' he said again to his father. 'Not just this. The rest too, with Harriet.'

Yorkey froze. This was not the time to introduce family feuds. Especially about women. But Myles kept on.

'I don't know how it happened. I can only say I'm terribly sorry. I wanted to hate her, meant to, taking Mother's place . . .'

William tried to quieten him. 'Not now, son. You rest. You're worn out. Yorkey will burrow down here for you. Dig out a dry patch.'

But Myles remained seated by the damp, spitting fire Yorkey had managed to encourage under a small canopy of bracken.

'No. I can't go on,' he said. He dragged off his soggy boots, his face twisting painfully, to reveal spongy, blood-soaked feet. 'I think I stayed in London too long,' he said wryly. 'Bit out of practice, what?'

'Oh, Jesus!' Yorkey said. 'I'll make some bandages for you.'

William shook his head. 'Do that, Yorkey, but he'll still have to ride. We'll double.'

While Yorkey stripped his shirt into bandages, Myles shrugged. 'I don't think they'll help much, and I won't get on that horse. It has to get my father home. Not me. Anyway, as I was saying, Father . . . I wish you wouldn't interrupt.'

As Yorkey bandaged the bloodied feet, he knew that Myles could wear the bandages or the boots. Not both. Blood was seeping through the flannel and his feet were probably already infected. Yorkey couldn't tell now. He'd have another look in the morning. Even then he could only clean them; he had no stuff to ward off the poison. Bloody hell! What now?

What now was Myles's insistence on talking to his father.

'You see, as it turned out, I didn't hate her. I found her quite beautiful, and that annoyed me too. But she was easy to talk to, when I made the effort. I had to, remember? I read that mad letter she wrote to the Perth paper. Do you remember that?'

William nodded.

'I laughed. I thought it was hilarious. Really giving it to the Resident and his wife and all the rest, and she saw me laughing at it and she, Harriet, was mortified. Embarrassed. Anyway,' he said wearily, 'I don't

315

know why I'm getting on to that. Having a bit of trouble concentrating, what?'

'Myles, please . . .' William reached out to him but his son shook him off.

'No. Don't do that. I have to tell you, it wasn't Harriet's fault. I fell for her. That's all. Who she was didn't come into it, I swear to you. And Harriet . . . well . . .'

William turned his head away. He obviously didn't want to hear this.

'Don't blame her. I was madly in love with this woman and I made it plain to her that I adored her. Flattery, I don't know. But why go on? While I have the chance I want to say to you now that I'm terribly sorry to have caused you such pain. And her too. She might have loved me for a while. Don't frown. But she was torn, terribly worried about you . . .'

'That will do, Myles,' William said sternly.

'No it won't. Can you ever forgive me? I need to know that.'

Yorkey was stunned by the reply. He'd always found William such a gentle man.

'Because you think you're on your deathbed? Grow up, Myles. We're all a long way from hell's gate yet. Get some sleep.'

In the morning it was William who made the running. 'Push him up on to the horse behind me, Yorkey. We'll have to double. Just cut the travelling time to spare the horse.'

Despite his avowals of the night before, Myles allowed himself to be legged up behind his father, and Yorkey plodded along beside them, trying to work out the distance. He'd lost track.

Chapter Eighteen

As he turned the corner, his umbrella thrusting into the driving rain, Reverend Walters barged into a gang of drunken louts staggering about outside the Darwin Hotel. Instead of making way for him, they blustered about him, insisting he join them for a drink. They were laughing, teasing him, and he was getting wet, though that didn't seem to bother them; all of these roughs were already soaked, paddling about in the heavy rain as if it were a child's pond.

'Join the celebrations, Pastor!' a voice bellowed at him, but he pulled away, wresting his umbrella from them.

'I don't drink,' he snapped, 'and the Lord is with me. He will strike down evil-doers who frequent places like this.'

'He can't very well do that,' a man laughed. 'He sent the rain. We're celebrating, thanking Him, Pastor.'

'The church is the place for thanksgiving,' Walters sniffed, pushing away from them.

He headed off down the Esplanade, bemoaning his lot at being stuck in an evil town like this. A town that had long held the reputation of being north of the Ten Commandments.

'And they can say that again,' he muttered as he sloshed along. He'd given up trying to convert Aborigines, unless they got them as babies, and now he knew that attempting any more conversions here was practically a waste of time. The large Chinese population had their own heathen ways; one could not even approach them. Nor was it safe to try to befriend newcomers to the town, as he'd discovered. A lot of men here did not take kindly to normal, genial questions as to where they'd come from. On too many occasions he'd been confronted by suspicion. Apparently it was not polite to ask.

He sighed. The rain was relentless. He hated it. But in the contrariness of this Sodom, it was worshipped as the purveyor of life.

Two young women, giggling like idiots, ran past him. He averted his eyes. They were whores. Disgusting. But only two of the scores of sluts that plied their vicious trade here, under the very eyes of the police. And there was nothing he could do about it. Their activities were overlooked – some even said legal – because of the shortage of women in the town. An outrageous excuse.

All this meant that he was left with the few real Christians who attended Sunday service. And until more came to live here, the numbers were static.

This bothered the new bishop in Adelaide, who had requested that Walters send him figures, statistics. He was displeased that the number of parishioners had not increased and now pointed out, quite firmly, that the Darwin parish did not warrant a new church. He wrote that the diocese had more pressing needs for the funds that Walters had so foolishly expended on that block of land on the Darwin Esplanade, some of the most expensive land in the town. He was instructed to sell it forthwith and return the funds to Adelaide.

The Reverend had been devastated at this order. Did they not realise that a church was built for the glory of God? That money shouldn't come into it? Obviously not. Nor did they care that he would have to make a humiliating about-turn. Sell the land that he'd already blessed only a week ago, with his parishioners, including Mrs William Oatley, gathered to pray with him.

Mrs Oatley. Harriet. One would think that the better types in this town would give good examples to the lower classes, one would hope . . . but not here. There was a very nasty story going the rounds about her, and he would have to look into that soon. It was his duty to save her soul.

He passed her house. He'd see to her later.

Pastor Walters shook his head in resignation.

'Wouldn't you think,' he asked himself, 'that I could rely on the Hamiltons, who seemed good, God-fearing people? Not a breath of scandal about them, which is rare, but apparently they can't be trusted either.'

In a quiet moment, talking to Cavendish, the Police Commissioner, who, though a Papist, was a reasonable fellow, he'd mentioned Mimimiadie.

'How is he behaving?'

'I don't know. Why?'

'I mean in Fannie Bay? Is he settling down? I shall bring his son to visit him when the court approves. It would be an act of charity, since I don't suppose, with his record, the fellow is long for this earth.'

Cavendish stared at him. 'I don't know what you're talking about!'

'Mimimiadie. You have him in custody.'

'The hell we do. You've got him mixed up with someone else. We haven't caught the bugger yet.'

Not caught? What was this? Chastened, he moved away to collect his thoughts, which soon gave way to the certainty that he was being made a fool of by Zack Hamilton and Oatley's son Myles, who, by recent accounts, had sunk to the lowest depths of depravity.

He bent into the wind, his pride sorely damaged, determined to require an explanation of Zack Hamilton. Why had he misled him about Boomi's father? Why had he lied to him? What mischief was afoot? Walters admitted to himself that he was hardly presentable by this, with his clothes wet and clinging, but he was a man of God; he was above such trivialities.

The two Mesdames Hamilton were on a sheltered veranda, playing cards, when he ran up the steps and burst upon them, shaking water from his umbrella.

They both jumped up to come to his aid, offering towels, and he suffered their ministrations for a few minutes, refusing to allow them to take his jacket and boots to dry them by the stove.

'Please do not fuss, ladies. If you don't mind. I am quite all right. One can hardly catch cold in this humidity. I should like a word with Mr Hamilton. Would you kindly announce me?'

'I'm sorry, Mr Walters, he's not at home,' Maudie Hamilton said quietly, but he had caught the women exchanging guarded glances, and immediately thought they were laughing at him.

'Oh. I see. When will he be home? Perhaps I can wait for him.'

'I couldn't quite say,' Maudie responded.

'And how is Boomi?'

'Quite well.'

'Where is he? I should like to see him.' This was only an excuse to linger. It was strange that neither of the women had offered him refreshments, forgetting their manners. He'd been looking forward to a nice cup of tea, having braved the weather to get here.

'I'm sorry,' Maudie said. 'Boomi isn't here either.'

'Really? Where is he on a day like this? It is hardly the weather for outings. I left him in your care, Mrs Hamilton. He should be with you. Where is the child while you sit here amusing yourself?' He glanced, frowning, at the cards, another dissolute pastime.

'He's with Zack,' Sibell Hamilton said brightly.

'And where might that be?'

'Visiting,' Maudie smiled.

'Visiting whom, might I ask?'

Her smile disappeared. She was an aggressive woman. 'No you may not.'

He settled himself into a cane armchair. 'Then perhaps I ought to wait. It is my duty to see the child is cared for.'

'Does caring for little children include beating them?' Maudie challenged. 'That child had welt marks on his legs and back. I'm thinking it may be our duty to have a look at the rest of those kids in your care.'

Sibell Hamilton reached out to quieten her sister-in-law, but there was no need; the Reverend was unconcerned by Maudie's rantings. His suspicions were aroused.

'By all means, madam, but for now I'm the one asking the questions. What's this poppycock about Boomi's father being in custody and fretting for the child?'

'I've no idea,' Maudie snapped.

'And you have no idea where the child is? Pray tell me, ladies, exactly when the child will be home so that I can return right away and satisfy myself that he is in good hands.'

'We'll let you know later,' she said, bold as brass.

'No, you'll let me know now, otherwise I shall refer the matter to Mr Cavendish. That child was, still is, under police protection. I have a duty to report this to the sergeant.'

'Please don't do that,' Sibell begged.

319

'Then you produce him.'

'I'm sorry, we can't.'

He sighed, shrugged. 'In that case I'll be on my way.'

Sibell Hamilton took no notice of Maudie's warning glance. 'Mr Walters, I apologise for causing you any concern. We do have a problem here, which I am willing to explain to you if you promise to keep quiet about it, for a few days at least. It is very serious, and we should be grateful for your support.'

That was better. Now he was getting some sense out of them. What had she done? Pushed the kid on to someone else? But why? Trouble in this household too? Ructions? Come to think of it, hadn't someone said there was a whisper that she was leaving her husband? And where had that come from? Why, of course . . . Christy Cornford's manservant. And that other scandal, Myles Oatley once again . . . jilting Lucy, who was now being courted by Christy.

He sat back, building his fingers into a steeple as he waited to be ushered in the door to the Hamilton secrets.

'Of course, my dear. You can rely on me. Now tell me, what is troubling you?'

The story appalled him but he didn't allow a glimmer of disapproval to show on his face, especially since Maudie Hamilton, now needing to win him back, took time off during the telling to rush off and return with a pot of tea and slices of what she called her early Christmas cake. It was delicious. He congratulated her.

When it was over, he took his leave gravely. 'I'm so glad you confided in me. You should have done so right from the start. I understand your predicament, dear lady. Perfectly dreadful for everyone, especially poor Mr Oatley, left in the hands of that mongrel. But don't you understand? You have deprived the Lord of that child, and you are depriving the police of their best chance of capturing a murderer. How many more lives will this rash adventure cost?'

'This was our only chance to rescue Mr Oatley,' she said. 'We all, you included, are charged with his rescue. I beg you to appreciate this. We didn't want to deceive you, nor did we wish to involve you in this situation. So it was better, for your sake, that we took the only course open to us. Please, I beg you, say nothing of this until we hear from Zack. We don't know what has happened since. Maybe nothing. Maybe he'll have to return with Boomi. But for now . . .'

The Reverend Walters stood. He couldn't get out of there fast enough. They had stolen that child from under his nose! Made a fool of him! Who did these people, with all their money, think they were? Above the law? Above the Lord? Their atrocious vanity was a sin in itself.

He listened to the gratitude, to their blatant insincerity, needing him now but not by choice, his hands clasped before him, nodding solemnly as if in prayer. Then he left, rejecting their offer of a greatcoat, walking out into the pure, cleansing rain, calling to the Lord to bear witness to his stoicism in this bed of iniquity. Except for the endless rain, he could be

Jesus, cast into the desert, surrounded by the devils of temptation, but no matter what, he would not swerve from his duty. He would accept the humiliation of losing the child, of being taken in by these people, even the anger of the police, all for the love of the Holy Father, because Cavendish had to be informed as soon as possible.

Harriet was surprised to have Reverend Walters ushered into her sitting room, and irritated by this intrusion. He looked like a sodden scarecrow. She had enough to worry about without having to entertain him. Grudgingly, she invited him to be seated.

'I'd rather stand,' he said tersely. 'I've come here on a matter of urgency, Sister Oatley, and if you think it is about your missing husband . . . I know all about that, and offer you my commiserations. Though he is not a religious man, I will pray for him, and pray that this ordeal will bring him back to God.'

She stared. 'Oh yes. Thank you. Would you like some tea, or refreshment? Lemonade, perhaps?'

'No thank you.' He took out his fob watch. Plenty of time to catch up with Cavendish and report the Hamilton transgressions. The Police Commissioner would be as outraged as he was.

'Sister Oatley, I want you to kneel and pray with me. Do you have your Bible handy?'

'Now?'

'Yes, my dear. Now.'

'Very well. It is good of you to come. I'm so worried about William, I'm nearly out of my mind.'

Hadn't she been listening? This was not about her husband's present misfortune, but the more serious one. The Reverend felt a little sympathy for William Oatley, but it soon faded. The man had turned his back on the Lord. What else could he expect?

She came back with the Bible, and he had her kneel at a long, low table to join him in prayer.

'We pray for the soul of William Oatley,' he intoned. 'May these sorrows pass from him.'

'Amen,' she murmured, head bowed.

'May he tread the fiery path into the arms of Jesus. Our Father, who art in heaven . . .'

He extended the prayer session at least fifteen minutes to punish her and remind her that God was everywhere, at the same time taking the opportunity to peer about the house. He'd never actually been inside before, only permitted as far as the veranda. And no wonder. It looked like a Chinese joss house, with its Oriental vases and dibdabs. Even this table before them was heavily carved in some heathen manner, and the large floor mat beneath it, though soft on his knees, troubled him with its unmistakable Asiatic design.

Eventually the Reverend moved smoothly back to lift himself into a nearby chair.

'Amen, sister.'

She looked up, relieved, but he asked her to remain kneeling so that she could speak to Jesus in her own words.

'You needn't worry,' she said, ignoring that request and settling herself across from him on a cane sofa. 'I've been talking nonstop to God for days.'

'What about?'

'Goodness! About my husband's safety, of course.'

'Do you think God will listen to you?'

'I hope so,' she said wearily.

'Perhaps He will, if first you ask for grace for yourself.'

'Yes. I suppose so.'

'And have you done this?'

'What? Done what?'

'Spoken to Him about your own soul. Purity in a woman is essential. Unless your soul is pure, God will turn His face from you. One might say that for an impure soul to be seeking aid from the Lord is a cheek. An abomination, in fact.'

He saw her eyes flicker, hand to her face to brush away an imaginary insect, or very real guilt.

'Well?'

'One does one's best,' she shrugged.

'Sister, could you define for me the sin of adultery?'

She sat up at that. 'Really, Mr Walters, I don't think this is an appropriate conversation.'

'Unfortunately, neither do I. Adultery is never appropriate, to use that word. And yet you, as an adulterer, think it is appropriate to address the Lord with your whimpering pleas!' He lowered his voice to a hiss.

'Tell me you are not an adulterer. Say it now, to the Lord, with this man of God as your witness!'

She stared at him, shocked. Her face went white and she burst into tears. 'Mr Walters, please,' she wept. 'I am not feeling very well, with all this worry. Would you excuse me?'

'I will not!' he thundered. 'I will not! Your sin is known to God, and worse, as one of my flock you are shaming the very congregation that has taken you to its heart. Will you sit there and deny this? Are you so far gone that you can shamelessly lie to God, making these prayers an abomination?'

'No! No!' she wept, and he sprang to his feet to close the door in case she had any ideas of running off from him.

He stood over her then, knowing he almost had her. One more blow would penetrate that shaky wall.

'Sister. I am here to help you, to pray with you and take you out on to the path of righteousness, but I can't be misled. I can't be part of this. You have to tell me truthfully. When you pray, do you want your husband to remain in harm's way, to never return so that you are free to continue this adulterous affair?'

'No! No!' she cried, clapping her hands to her ears. 'Of course not. Dear God, no!'

'Are you sure? Because if this is truly your intent, I will leave here this minute. Do you want me to leave knowing that in your heart you wish your husband dead?'

'No. Please don't think that, Mr Walters. I love William. He is very dear to me.'

He plopped back into his chair as if she was exhausting him. 'I find that very hard to believe, coming from a woman who has betrayed him.'

This was exciting. Not once had she denied his accusations. He would have it all soon.

'I know,' was all she could utter, twisting a handkerchief in shaky hands, no longer the fashionable lady about town, but just another wretched woman caught out in lust. No better than a harlot.

'You seem confused,' he said softly. 'And I have to admit you are confusing me. Perhaps Mr Oatley was cruel to you?'

'Oh no. Never.'

'Then perhaps his son – oh yes, the Lord sees all – perhaps his son took advantage of you, against your will? In the absence of his father? That, sister, is a crime against nature and the law. We could have him up on charges. The crime of rape, I'm sad to say, is not unknown in this town.'

She gaped. 'What are you saying? That I should charge Myles with rape?'

'For a man to have intimate relations with his father's wife – I find it hard even to conceive of a more obnoxious sin – that is bad enough. But if you could testify that you were not willing—'

'Stop! Please. You don't understand. It wasn't like that . . . God, no!'

'Then perhaps you can tell me how it was, how you have been brought to this sorry state, Mrs Oatley, so that together we can work out how to deal with your misery. You are distraught. I can see that. You need someone to talk to.'

'Yes,' she muttered. 'I can't cope with this any more.'

He listened. Disgusted. But he did not interrupt her self-pitying litany of lust and betrayal. And with the son! Appalling. What vicious people they were, living under the garb of respectability.

'And does your husband know of this affair?' he asked eventually.

'I think so.'

'What did he do?'

'Nothing much. He left. Went bush.'

'He did nothing?' Was vice rampant in this house?

Time now to call the wrath of God down on this woman. He harangued her, he shouted at her as God would have done. He knew the police station would be closed by now, but this situation was far more important. He'd report to the Commissioner in the morning.

He called her a whore. Worse than a whore. How many whores took father and son to their beds? Maybe she'd given herself to both men at the same time? That horror was not unknown. Had she romped with both of them? Exposing herself seductively to them until neither could resist. Running naked through the house to further her lust at all hours of the night . . . His own imagination ran riot at the thought of the debauchery that must have gone on within these walls, aided and abetted most probably by their heathen, slinking servants. Was it any wonder they had no white servants?

She was shattered. She sat hugging her knees, almost incoherent, her full bosoms on display as she leaned forward, dignity forsaken. He could see now what had led these men into the occasion of sin. Even with the tips hidden, their creamy roundness and the dim pit of the cleavage was enough to . . . Never mind. This den of iniquity had to be cleansed.

He moved to sit beside her and put an arm around her. She was shuddering uncontrollably.

'Praise the Lord, Sister Oatley, it's all over. You are back on the glory road. Amen. Say Amen to the Lord.'

'Amen,' she muttered.

'What can we do to regain grace? I ask Jesus. What can we do? Let me think . . . You can't stay here. You must not. I've been through this before. Persuading whores to leave the whorehouse. Of their own volition. Sadly, few have trust enough in God to set them free, but some summon the strength. Will you be one of them?'

She nodded, vacantly.

'Then we shall go together. We shall walk together from the darkness into the light. Are you ready, Sister Oatley? Do you have the strength to walk with me now? Leaving the den of debauchery behind you. Get behind me, Satan! Say this for me as we stand together.' He lifted her to her feet.

'Do I hear you say it?'

'Get behind me, Satan,' she echoed.

He walked her to her front door. She was as tall as he was but he supported her helplessness with a strong arm and the voice of the Lord.

A Chinese servant came running. 'Where missy going?'

'Step aside!' Walters ordered.

'Missy need her coat!'

'Mrs Oatley does not need anything from here. Give me my umbrella.'

'Rain stopped,' the Chinaman said, but he handed over the umbrella. He peered at his employer. 'You all ri', missy?'

She waved him away and stumbled out into the greyness of low cloud and fading light with the triumphant missionary.

He would take her back to the mission and hand her over to the two sisters in residence. She could share their bungalow and their frugal lives. They were novices. He was training them to be lay sisters. They would show her the path to righteousness. Sister Minto, a mature, hardy Scot, only recently come to God, would be her mentor. Mrs Oatley was a prime example of the depths these moneyed people could sink to. A woman living in the lap of luxury, taking debauchery for granted, could

324

only be saved by turning her life about. Taking her back to the basics, in the tried and true monastic style. Though the mission bungalow which served as home for the two women was hardly a monastery, their spartan lives based on prayer, penance and good works were dedicated wholly and solely to the Lord, and they welcomed the austerity he imposed on them.

She leaned on his arm as they hurried down the muddy streets. He was her crutch, her mainstay, sent by God to deliver her from the maelstrom that had engulfed her.

'Glory be to God,' he whispered to her when they reached his residence. 'Not much further now, sister, and the Lord will be waiting for you with outstretched arms. He loves you, sister.'

They passed down a long easement beside the church and on to a bush track overhung with dripping trees, and she trudged with him. Like a lamb, he thought, a lamb. All that swank and arrogance drained from her.

The solitary bungalow was an ideal retreat, barely discernible in a jungle of overgrown greenery so the women who lived here were not distracted from their chores by passers-by. Although their religious duties were paramount, the Reverend insisted the women contribute to their upkeep by making soap and candles, which were sold at the church door. The regimen that he'd set out for them left no time for idle hands.

Sister Minto, a scraggy woman in a faded black dress, came out to greet them, drying her hands on her apron.

'Good evening, Reverend, what have we here?'

'This is Sister Oatley. She wishes to join your community.'

'Not much of a community today. I was looking for you earlier. Sister Tolley has run off again. Gone back to that witless family of hers.'

He sighed. 'I'll have to talk to her. Would you take Sister Oatley inside and settle her down? She's very weary now but she'll be all right in the morning. Then I'd like a word with you.'

Noisy birds, settling for the night, chattered and screeched all about him as he waited, and some flying foxes flapped overhead. He walked round to the side of the house and banged on the iron water tank, pleased to note it was filling at last. Minto had wanted to buy water for the tank during the dry season, but he had forbidden such extravagance, instead supplying them with buckets to carry in their water from his residence.

She came out. 'What's the matter with her? She's as limp as a dummy. Just sittin' starin'.'

'Not surprising,' he said loftily. 'She's had a profound experience of Jesus, a painful experience, dragging herself from a sinful life to search for the light.'

Minto was impressed. 'You don't say? Who is she? Another whore?'

'Something like that. Even worse, one could say, without going into the sordid details, so to come here was a hard decision for her to make. Quite earth-shattering for a woman like her.'

'Oh, glory be!'

'The best thing to do is to put her to work, first thing in the morning.

You have to help her, pray with her, keep her busy, don't let the devil entice her away.'

'I couldn't stop Sister Tolley,' she said defensively.

'That's a different matter. Sister Tolley never did have true repentance. This one is very much aware of the magnitude of her sins, and is overwhelmed by remorse. She needs you in her misery, to show her the joys of God's grace.'

'Amen,' Minto said solemnly.

Tom Ling rushed down to report to Billy Chinn.

'Missy gone out with that preacher. Just gone out, no coat, no hat.' He peered over his shoulder as if someone might overhear, and whispered, 'I think she drunk.'

'Ooh ahh!' Billy responded, awed. 'What the boss say to that?'

Worried, Tom Ling raced back to inspect the black lacquered drinks cabinet, staring at the bottles and decanters, bewildered. Not a drop missing since this morning, when he'd topped up the gin decanter. Everything was in order. He wondered what sort of potion that devil preacher had given her.

All night he sat on the veranda waiting for her, but she didn't return. Not even by midday the next day, for the fresh clothes he'd put out for her.

The two loyal servants sat in the kitchen, worrying, waiting and not knowing what to do or who to turn to.

At the same time Walters was deep in conversation with an astounded Police Commissioner.

'Are you sure about this?'

'As God is my witness. They told me themselves. Your man Mimimiadie has defied you. He has Oatley, William Oatley, in his clutches, and those foolish people are trying to buy him back by offering the child Boomi to him. The child they stole from me with their dastardly lies. I want that child back, Commissioner. This can't be permitted.'

'I'd better go round and talk to Mrs Hamilton myself.'

'There is no need. I've given you all the information you require.'

'What about Mrs Oatley? What's she got to say about all this?'

'She wasn't told. They didn't want to worry her. It was Myles Oatley and Zack Hamilton, they worked out this scheme, using that blackfeller Yorkey.'

'But how do they know where to find Mimimiadie? We haven't been able to locate him.'

'It's a long story, don't make me go over it again. Yorkey knew, he's making the exchange. Zack and Myles are in Pine Creek now. I want to know what you are doing. We're wasting time sitting here talking. You have a chance of catching that fiend Mimimiadie now.'

'You're right!' The Commissioner sprang into action.

326

The townspeople of Pine Creek were in a flurry of excitement. Several telegrams had come for Sergeant Murphy from the bigwig himself, old Cavendish, demanding to know the whereabouts of Myles and William Oatley, Zack Hamilton, and a child called Boomi. The trouble was, though, that the sergeant and his sidekick, Constable Smith, were out of town, investigating a gunfight between the three partners at the Goodwin goldmine which had left one dead, the story went, one wounded, and one still standing.

When the third telegram tapped through, with more or less the same urgent message, the telegraph operator refused to accept responsibility for a reply. That wasn't his job. His mates advised him, therefore, to seek advice from Zack Hamilton, the only one of the aforesaid mentioned, they insisted, who could help.

Zack guessed that somehow the Commissioner had found out what was going on, or had an inkling, and that caused him even more concern. He was frantic with worry by this. Neither Yorkey nor Myles had returned and he was close to breaking point. Close to giving in and asking Murphy to round up a posse to search for them because they'd been gone more than a week. Surely that was enough time for Yorkey to get to his destination, wherever it was, and make it back with William. He'd discovered that Yorkey had taken supplies after all, bought them from Mrs McCabe, but only enough for a few days. They couldn't be far away.

But now Murphy was missing. No police available.

To oblige the telegraph operator, he dictated a response:

'Your officers out of town on urgent business. Nothing you can do to assist at this stage. All is being done that can be done. Zack Hamilton.'

'Jeez!' the operator said. 'That'll cost you, Zack. Do you want to cut out a word or two?'

'No,' Zack said, dropping a pound on the counter. 'Keep the change. Let me know if there are any more.'

The pub buzzed. They all knew the contents of Zack's reply. Assist in what? And what was being done about what? They stared about them. As far as they could see, Pine Creek was still a sleepy hollow. Nothing was being done about anything here, or they'd know about it. By God they would.

All eyes were now on Zack Hamilton as he strode across the wide street to the store, a swag and a rifle thrown across his shoulder. He was in there a long time, but they soon learned that he'd bought supplies and gone out the back way to the stables. Bought another horse – the man was made of money – and borrowed another for a packhorse, since there weren't any more for the cattleman to buy. And he'd ridden out on the west road like the others.

'Did he say anything to you?' they asked McCabe.

'Not a word,' he shrugged.

'Didn't even pay his bill?'

'Zack's good for it.'

327

But when another telegram came, this one addressed to Zack Hamilton, demanding that he explain himself, it was left to McCabe to respond.

His reply was short and cheap:

'Zack ain't here neither.'

The horse was lame. Yorkey wondered if anything else could go wrong. William was sick. Too frail to keep down the food Yorkey had managed to forage for them, not even the ducks he'd collared eventually, as they paddled about a muddy billabong. The poor old bloke was embarrassed, sick at both ends, telling them to go on and leave him. But there was no point in that. His son, give him his due, was battling on. He knew the horse couldn't carry both of them, so he walked, and kept walking even though he must have been in agony. He also knew that his boots had to stay on now. If he took them off they'd have to stay off, and he wouldn't be going anywhere. His legs were purpling with the infections and breaking out in sores.

Yorkey rested them and went foraging again, wishing he could remember the native food that his mother had relished, wishing he knew which berries, dangling temptingly from the odd bush, were food and which were poison. But he did watch and grab birds' eggs from hollows, and he easily caught fat lizards. These he caught and cooked well away from his two charges, presenting them only with the seared meat. But it wasn't enough and he knew it. They both needed medical help.

He tried desperately to make a decision. Should he leave them with as much of this bush food as he could muster and push on with the horse as far as it could go, to get help? He'd leave them the waterbag, but would it be enough to sustain them? The heat was intense; they'd dehydrate without a constant source of water. Jesus!

Then he had a better idea. They'd struggle on to the next creek or lagoon. No matter how shallow, they'd at least be able to hang on, keep cool, have plenty of water.

Though Yorkey hadn't stirred, Myles seemed to be aware he'd made a decision.

'You're going? Good man. Take Father. He's very ill.'

'No. The horse has to rest too. I'm gonna run on ahead until I come to water, there has to be a pond or creek somewhere up ahead. I'll come back for you and I'll plant you plumb in the middle of it so you can't dry out. See? Then I'll go for help. I reckon we're pretty close to the finishing line now anyway.'

'These plains are so dry they soak up every drop of water. You might have to run for miles.'

Yorkey grinned. 'A bloke like me, I'm supposed to be able to do that, no sweat.'

Myles shook his head. 'I wouldn't bet on it. Take the waterbag. It's still half full. You'll need it more than we will.'

But Yorkey took a last swig. 'No. You share it with your dad. And keep the shade on him.'

The road was already dry and rutted, the mud baked into clay, so Yorkey went carefully. The last thing he needed was a twisted ankle. But he could run now, as fast as his aching legs and bruised feet could carry him, freed from the necessity to allow for the others. He wondered if perhaps he should have done this before, but logic told him that it wouldn't have worked. He had to get them as close to civilisation as possible before leaving them, before his own strength ran out. So that he would have enough stamina to go the miles, without a horse that was now near to collapse.

The sun burned down on him, and contrarily he was praying for rain again. He kept breaking from the road, rushing through the bush, watching for slopes, for rocks, anything that would lead him to water, but the bloody land was flat and endless. He had heard an old stager say that you should suck on pebbles if your mouth dried out, and he tried that but spat them out. It didn't seem to work for him. And the bloody road was straight now, not a good sign, snaking out into the distance taunting him with mirages, shimmering silver, a strain on his eyes. He kept reminding himself that he still had to run back, so he slowed, puffing, to a jog, scanning the plains either side of him with their useless skinny trees.

Of all things, two emus spotted him, ran towards him, and thinking this was a race, they kept their distance while joining the contest, great flat feet slapping along in step with him until they gathered speed, showing off with a burst of speed and a flap of feathers, leaving this poor specimen far behind.

'Get away with you, you stupid bastards!' he shouted at them, realising they had made him speed up. Caught up in their game, he'd been running far too fast, using up precious energy.

Yorkey collapsed under a tree, reaching for a gum leaf, which he'd found better for his dry mouth than a damn pebble. He reached for another and chewed on it, watching the enemy above, the sun. It was noon, a bad time, but he had to get going. He'd walked Myles and William through the last hours of the night, and left them at daylight. He tried not to think of the stories about men who'd died out in the Territory, beaten by the heat on long, lonely tracks, and debated with himself whether or not he ought to chance this midday scorcher. Everyday bush know-how told him not to. Worry about the helpless men he'd left behind told him he didn't have a choice. He gave in to compromise. He would allow himself fifteen minutes to rest. Not a second longer. Then he would up and go again, fast, to make up for this indulgence.

A woman was shaking him.

He looked up. A dark face stared down at him, the features hazy against the glare. Yorkey had trouble focusing.

'What you doin' here, boy?'

Though he could see her now, an Aborigine woman, a bush of black hair streaked with grey, his mind couldn't focus on the presence of another human.

329

'You sick?' she asked.

'You got water?' he managed, and she stared at him.

'You ain't got none? You pretty bloody stupid, you.' She put a finger to her teeth and gave a shrill whistle.

There were about fourteen in the party. Mums and dads and aunties and six piccaninnies, travelling south on a walkabout. They were shocked to hear of his troubles. Mystified at his tale of privation, but ever willing to help.

Yorkey was so grateful to them, he found himself babbling. He was in such a state of euphoria when they gave him water and some blessed food that he apologised for not being able to speak to them in their language, which sent them off into fits of laughter. They were station blacks, almost as comfortable in English as in their own language.

She came too, the woman, and four men, and by nightfall, with renewed energy and the comfort of their presence, Yorkey had led them back to his pathetic little camp, where William and Myles lay waiting.

They sucked in their breath and muttered among themselves in their soft, rolling voices at the state of the white men, and set to work while Yorkey, collapsing nearby, could only watch and listen.

The woman lifted William up, cradling him in her hefty arms while she talked to him, feeling for his pains, nodding, understanding, then she laid him down again, very gently.

'You all ri', boss. That tummy o' yourn it allsame bloody empty. Skinny you out good all ri'.'

Myles was a different matter. The men removed his boots carefully and shook their heads. 'Your feet dyin' here, boss. You don' do no more walkin' or they gonna fall right off.'

They were all fed. For William only sour damper from the woman's dilly bag, which she assured him was needed to fill up the hole. But they had tea, and sugar, and dried beef to chew on, and then the woman made the precious old patty cakes that Yorkey remembered from his childhood, thin, hot and delicious it seemed now, though once he'd called them tasteless.

Then he slept.

In the morning they made a stretcher out of saplings plaited with vines for William, and put Myles on the sad lame horse, and set off down the road again. Though the woman asked him again what they were doing out here, how this could have happened, Yorkey could not explain. He could only thank her.

When they finally reached the rest of the mob, it was agreed that a detour wouldn't matter, so the whole party set off on the road to Pine Creek, which the woman, by name Naomi, a station name that she was very proud of, said was only twenty miles close.

And that was where Zack Hamilton found them, this strange troupe way out in the distance, coming through a mirage, figures elongated, blurred. He could make out a horse, only one horse. Disappointed, he realised it was only a mob of blacks coming his way, but they might be able to tell him something. This was the road William would have to take on the long journey to Pop's station. Then shock almost brought him to a halt!

A white man was riding the horse! It was Myles. Where the hell were William and Yorkey then?

They slowed as he neared them. Myles shouted to him. Dogs yapped. Some children capered forward and for a heart-stopping minute he fancied one of them was Boomi, but then he saw the stretcher, borne by two of the blackfellers. They were bringing William in.

He was so thrilled, shaking hands all round, thanking the bearers, trying to talk to Myles and William, bursting with questions, that he almost forgot the other man.

Frantically he turned about. 'Where's Yorkey? What happened to Yorkey?'

'Here, boss.' Yorkey limped forward with the aid of a home-made crutch. 'I gave him the kid. He's long gone now. But we had a bit of trouble getting back.'

'Why?'

Yorkey looked at Myles and smiled ruefully. 'Boomi's dad. He don't come cheap. We had to pay a bit more.'

'Pay what?'

'Horses.'

'He left the three of you with only one horse? Out there?' Zack looked fearfully at the hot, unforgiving land beyond, land that he knew only too well. 'Where were you?'

'At the gorge.'

'Oh, Christ.'

Myles beckoned to him. 'That Mimimiadie's a real bastard,' he said, and Zack nodded.

'So I've heard.'

'Yes, but if it hadn't been for Yorkey standing up to him, we wouldn't have had any horses. Yorkey made him hand over this one. I thought you should know that.' He seemed to sway in the saddle, and Zack steadied him.

'Are you all right, Myles?'

'Not the best, mate, not the best.'

Father and son were taken from the train straight to the Darwin hospital, but Zack was met by the Police Commissioner. They were still arguing fiercely when Sibell went off to find Harriet Oatley. She had made a point of sending a note to Harriet as soon as she'd received a telegram from Zack advising that they were all on their way home, including William, so she was surprised that she was not at the station.

A wary Tom Ling met her at the door, to tell her that the missy was not at home.

'Where is she? Mr Oatley is back, Tom Ling. He's not well. He is in the hospital.'

'Ooh aaah!' Tom Ling groaned. 'Whatta matter with him, missus?'

It was hard to explain. Too long a story, so she compromised.

'He's been lost in the bush, for a long time.' Everyone knew what that meant. Sunstroke. Malnutrition. Dehydration. Fever. Sunburn. Take your pick.

'Oh my! He need plenty good food now. I get Billy Chinn make him good soup, eh?'

'Yes, that's a good idea,' she said, 'but where is Mrs Oatley?'

'She gone.'

'Gone where?'

'Gone three day now.'

'What? Where has she gone?'

'She not tell us. No say.'

He was relieved when she left, and he rushed down to confer with Billy Chinn. They both agreed he had done the right thing, not mentioning that missy had gone off with the preacher. What a scandal that would create! They worried then if they should even mention it to the master. That would make him really angry; they both knew he hated preachers. Ooh aah! What a carry-on!

Tom Ling took the soup to the hospital and asked the lady if he could see his master. Perhaps, somehow, in a quiet and roundabout way, he might be able to whisper this bad news in between feeding him his soup, but the soup was taken from him and he was sent away. Sadly he understood that the hospital was no place for lowly persons, but at least the soup would benefit the poor master.

Matron stared at the tray a nurse brought before her. A large lacquered tray bearing an exquisite covered tureen.

'What's this?'

'It's soup for Mr Oatley. And look here, have you ever seen anything so pretty?' The accompanying bowl was of the finest porcelain, decorated with birds, and the soup spoon was silver. Beside them was a basket, formed out of the finest linen, containing thin biscuits.

'Very nice. Who sent it?'

'A Chinaman brought it to the door.'

'A Chinaman? Good God! You never know what's in it. Chuck that stuff out!'

'What will I do with the tray?'

'Leave it in the kitchen. Someone will come for it.'

In the kitchen, the nurse took a chance. The soup did smell good. It was, too. Delicious, after the miserable meals they had to eat here. And she suffered no after-effects.

William understood that the doctor meant well, keeping him here within reach of medical help in case he had a heart attack or any of the other dire consequences they were firing at him, but he'd rather be at home. Unfortunately, he was feeling too weak to argue just now, hardly strong enough to lift his arms and feed himself, but it would only be a day or so and he would be out of this place.

There was no sign of Harriet, and he was fretting for her but would not ask. On principle. And because of that, though everyone was fussing over him, he would not enquire about Myles, who was in a ward. And the awful part was that no one was mentioning either of them. Not the nursing staff, nor the doctor, not the tiring array of visitors who kept arriving at visiting hours. Was Harriet at Myles's bedside right now? Openly making her choice? Myles, who was only suffering from sore feet, as far as William could recall.

Then, late that night, outside of visiting hours, Yorkey slipped into the room.

'They don't let Abos in here,' he grinned, 'but they shouldn't leave doors open.'

William had kept up a fair share of bravado with all the others, but with Yorkey he just broke down and wept. And he was ashamed.

'I'm sorry,' he said, wiping his eyes. 'I suppose it's because I'm feeling weak. How are you, Yorkey?'

'Pretty good, boss. What's up?'

'My wife. Have you seen her?'

'No. I'm staying at the Hamiltons'.'

He forced himself to ask: 'Is she visiting Myles?'

'No. She's not visiting anyone. They don't know where she is.'

'What do you mean, they don't know?'

'It's not their fault. They think you're too sick to be worried with things. But I reckon if you can sit out Mimimiadie and that trek home, you're tough enough here' – he tapped his head – 'to know what's going on. What do you reckon?'

Instantly William's tears dried up and he realised that he'd been lying here feeling sorry for himself instead of pulling himself into shape. That grief thing again. Ducking for cover. Not wanting to know the worst. Or face it. The very attitude that had caused him to make a run for Pop's place, to hide out. What a fool he had been.

Yorkey was sitting quietly beside him, in that very still way he had, an age-old quality enjoyed by Aborigines, the capacity not to interrupt people's thoughts, with all the time in the world to wait for a response.

The matron came into the dim room and shone a torch on Yorkey. 'What are you doing in here?' she snapped.

'Get out!' William Oatley was at last asserting himself.

'But Mr Oatley—'

'Get out!'

She turned on her heel and disappeared into the passageway.

'So my wife has left the house?' he said, his voice flat, and Yorkey nodded.

'And Myles is still here, nursing sore feet?'

'More than sore. They say they're still in bad shape.'

'What did you bring him for anyway? You were told to come alone.'

'I didn't bring him, he trailed me. Trying to help.'

'And he nearly got us all killed!'

333

'Does it matter now?'

William sighed. 'I suppose not, Yorkey.'

He lay there wondering what did matter.

'They look after you good here?' Yorkey asked.

'No. The bloody bed's like iron and they're feeding me pap.'

'What's pap?'

'Bread and milk. Gruel. Kinder to my stomach, they say.'

'Don't sound too kind to me.'

'You're right. It's bloody absurd. I've had enough of this. Will you find Tom Ling and tell him to bring the gig round here early in the morning? I'm going home. I've had enough of this.'

'I'll get the gig myself,' Yorkey said. 'And I'll bring the lads to help you out.'

Despite Matron's protests, Mr Oatley left the hospital assisted by two Chinamen and climbed into a gig driven by that Aborigine fellow she'd seen in the room the night before.

'I don't know what the world's coming to,' she muttered. 'He didn't even call on his poor son before he left. Heartless, some people.'

William was back in his own bed in his own house, already feeling much better thanks to Billy Chinn's light and tasty meals. Billy understood the necessity to deal gently with malnutrition but he had more imagination than the hospital cook. At long last William was enjoying being pampered.

The rain was a comfort too, thundering down on the iron roof, restoring a sense of well-being, not only for himself but for that land out there that had once again been spared the terror of drought. At least for another year.

Sibell Hamilton was his first visitor and she was delighted to find him sitting up in his comfy old armchair, but it was an emotional reunion.

She hugged and kissed her old friend. 'We were so worried about you, William. I never thought that wretch would let you go, even if he did get Boomi back.'

'Never mind about that, how are you?'

'I'm well. Much excitement in our household at the minute. Christy Cornford has asked for Lucy's hand in marriage.'

'Christy!' William felt a twist of embarrassment. That proposal should have come from his son.

'Yes. Zack isn't too thrilled. They want to live on the station. And Christy isn't exactly ideal as a station hand. I don't think he has any idea what that life entails.'

'He sits a horse well. Then again, you didn't have any idea of what you were walking into when you married Zack either, and life was a lot harder for women in those days.'

She was quiet, and William knew he'd hit a nerve, but he pressed on. 'So what are your plans now?'

'My plans?' she said vaguely.

'Yes. Are you still planning to leave Zack?'

'Don't say that, William. Please. It's not Zack. I can't stand that life any more. I have to go. I'm sick and tired of all the crises. There's no end to it. Even lately . . . Zack gets speared. You get attacked and nearly killed by blacks . . .'

'Oh, Sibell, they were one-off problems.'

'That's what Zack said about the mice plague, about the droughts, drownings, accidents, sand blight . . . Listen, William, I went through his station journals one day and listed the crises for one year only . . . death and disaster and that bloody awful climate.'

'Did you make a list of the good things too?'

'Don't preach at me. I've made up my mind. I thought you at least would understand. You didn't take Harriet out to live in the bush. I was only nineteen when I married Zack, fresh from Perth like her. Fresh from England to make a further point of it. But I did my bit.'

'Because you loved Zack, and hard though it was, you enjoyed yourself, you often told me that.'

'I don't deny that, but it's over now. I'm dead tired of it all. I want a better lifestyle. I never want to see any more cattle or hear about their woes as long as I live.'

'And what about Zack?'

'He's staying, of course. It's his life.'

'I'm sorry to hear it.'

'Anyway, to change the subject, he's got his own problems at the minute. That wretched Walters is demanding he be charged for kidnapping Boomi. Actually, I was just as involved but he doesn't seem to think I matter.'

'What does Cavendish say?'

'He'd rather forget the whole thing, since your rescue was imperative, but Walters is hanging on like a leech and has telegraphed our beloved administrator, who is in Adelaide, for his support.'

'And has he got it?'

'Of course. You're not his favourite citizen.'

'Dammit. Is it a very serious charge?'

'Apparently. Something to do with interfering with police business, too.'

'Can't we buy off the preacher? Tell him I've changed my mind about letting him build his church next door.'

'I didn't know you'd given in to him. But that's no go. There isn't going to be a church. His bishop reneged on the cash.'

'Oh, hell! Stay and have lunch with me.'

'I'd love to.'

Sibell was glad of the invitation. There had still been no mention of Harriet. Nor of Myles. And she had to get William to open up on this subject; she was certain he wouldn't talk to anyone else. Where was Harriet anyway? Did he know?

★ ★ ★

335

William insisted on taking his place at the dining table with her, rather than have their meal on trays, and as he sat down he picked up the local newspaper, carefully set in its usual place.

'Oh no! Sibell, look at this!'

WILLIAM OATLEY KIDNAPPED BY BLACKS, ran the headline.

Sibell jumped up to read over his shoulder of the desperate rescue raid led by Myles Oatley to save his father. No mention of Yorkey or Boomi.

'Where would they have got this from?' Sibell asked, amazed.

'Bloody half-baked rubbish,' William snorted. 'Probably from the police.'

He went to throw it on the floor, but Sibell grabbed it, reading on.

'You're a hero,' she laughed. 'Standing bravely against all the fearful torture inflicted on you over weeks by the savage Aborigine chief Mimimiadie, refusing to give in. A man of our times. A true—'

'No more, please. You'll put me off my lunch.'

'You'd better get used to it. This is only a small piece. The papers will have a ball with this story for weeks. Though I don't think it'll make Cavendish too happy.'

As Tom Ling served the fish, William managed a smile. 'Maybe it won't be so bad after all. Will you ask Christy to come and see me?'

'Of course. Why?'

'Never mind why, my dear. Just tell him I'd like a word.'

After lunch they took tea on the veranda. All the shutters were firmly closed against the weather but the air was still misty and humid, rich with the fragrance of frangipani.

'This reminds me of Singapore,' William said quietly as he puffed on a forbidden cigar.

Sibell took the opening. 'And Harriet,' she added. 'So might I ask where Mrs Oatley is?'

'I've no idea.'

'What a fool I am. I thought you loved her.'

'I did. Once. And since you have not enquired until now, I presume you know the gossip.'

'Is it true?'

'So they say,' he shrugged. 'It seems she has left me, so the question becomes academic.'

'She was very worried about you, William. Terribly worried.'

'Good for her. And I suppose she was equally worried about my son.'

'Oh Lord. Why don't you ask her yourself?'

'Because she is not here, as I have already mentioned. And we have nothing to say to each other.'

'I would think there would be plenty to say. You can't just sit here and sulk.'

He shook his head. 'Don't try to provoke me, Sibell. It won't work. I've accepted the situation, so leave it be.'

★ ★ ★

336

Later, though, he wondered if he *was* sulking. In truth, he wasn't doing anything in particular. He certainly had not accepted the situation; he missed Harriet. The house was a lonely place without her. But that was just too bad. She'd gone. No use fretting about it. The future looked bleak indeed. He wondered where she was. Not with Myles, who was still recuperating in hospital. Staying in a hotel? Or with friends? What friends? Who else had she involved in this dreadful business?

He reached over and rang the little bell.

Tom Ling hurried in.

'Did you say missy left without her coat? Did you say that? I can't recall.'

'Yes. No coat. No clothes. All still here. She take nothing.'

What was she up to, taking nothing? Divesting herself of the past? Like a snake shedding its skin, he thought nastily. But still it didn't sound like Harriet; she was always so fastidious about her appearance. Unless she'd gone off and bought new outfits in preparation for her secretive departure. Maybe the wretched pair had a love nest tucked away somewhere. Well, this was a small town; he'd find her and have this out once and for all. Get it over with.

Tom Ling was still standing there.

'Did she go on her own?' William asked, rather foolishly, he thought, since Myles would have been out of town by then.

To his surprise, Tom Ling blinked, looked away and then finally stammered: 'No, master.'

'Oh? Who did she go with? Some lady friend?' That made more sense; she'd be with some silly sympathetic female.

'No, master. A gentleman.'

'What? What gentleman?'

'The preacher. In the black hat. That one. She go with him.'

'Walters?'

Tom Ling nodded miserably.

'Why didn't you tell me this before?'

'Not nice. You too sick.'

William laughed. 'I doubt she'd elope with that cold fish. He probably just escorted her someplace. Thank you, that will be all.'

As Tom Ling scuttled away, relieved, William was still smiling. Walters, that sneaky prude; he'd have a fit if he knew what the servants thought about his interference. Running off with a married lady. Then he realised he was laughing, had laughed, for the first time in ages. Something comic happening for a change. And that made it easier. He'd have no trouble finding her now.

He pushed himself out of the chair with new determination and forced his wobbly legs to take a turn around the room, hanging on to chairs for support. Then he called to Tom Ling for assistance.

'Time I got moving. We have to do plenty of exercise from now on, and you tell Billy Chinn I want bigger meals, no more half-serves.'

'Jolly good!' Tom Ling beamed.

Though the inevitable evening storm was growling and glowering in the distance, Christy Cornford dressed with care: tailored trousers, freshly laundered shirt, stiff collar, neat black tie, well-cut jacket and polished boots. He donned his military greatcoat and stood before the mirror, slicing a careful parting in his pomaded hair. A summons to visit William Oatley was not to be taken lightly. He was Zack Hamilton's best friend, and Zack had not yet given him an answer to his proposal.

Christy knew that Zack would not, as Lucy's father, stoop to ducking his responsibility, he would not ask a friend to deliver his reply, especially if in the negative, but perhaps Oatley might be conscripted to begin the process of letting Christy down lightly. In which case he would have an opportunity to talk the matter over with Oatley, who was a fair man.

He had to convince them that he did, truly, love Miss Hamilton. Make no mistake about that. He did love her; she was beautiful, a lovely, easy-going country girl with a natural charm, and Christy considered himself the luckiest man in the world that she loved him too. But there was the matter of station life. Already she'd taken it for granted that they would live at Black Wattle, accepted practice for newly-weds in those families, and he was happy about that too. But though it wasn't actually said, he could see Zack was worried. Afraid he wouldn't fit in. He had no experience of station life, didn't know anything about cattle. Zack had said they'd talk some more, and no doubt that would be the stumbling block.

But he could learn. He was willing to learn. If they'd let him. He was even willing to admit that it would be a humbling experience, but he would accept that.

'Oh well,' he shrugged, reaching for his hat. 'Let's see if I can get Oatley on my side.'

He rode past his block, where a small timber cottage was nearing completion. Though it was not much different from the other cottages further along the street, Christy was proud of it, his first house, and he would see to it that the interior reflected good taste, not the ugly, cheap stuff on sale here. He recalled showing it to Lucy.

'We could always live here if you like. I'm happy to stay on at the Residency.'

She'd nodded. 'I suppose so. But what would I do all day, Christy? I'd be bored.'

'There are always luncheons and parties and balls . . .'

'I know, but I can't pretend I'd enjoy that life. It all seems so useless. Pointless. Quite fun now, if you know what I mean, for a break, but permanently . . . I don't think so.'

Sadly, he did understand. Would she become bored with him too? A new chum in that hard bush environment, lacking even his wife's competence. Christy's confidence was ebbing away. Maybe he should give this more thought.

★ ★ ★

Oatley had lost a lot of weight but looked better for it, the tall, spare frame giving at first glance the impression of a much younger man. Christy noted the scar round his neck, since his host was wearing an open-necked shirt.

'Glad to see you back safe and sound, sir,' he offered as they shook hands.

'Yes, it was quite an experience but not as bad as that newspaper article makes out. Would you care for a whisky?'

'I would indeed.'

Oatley made small talk until they were seated in the parlour, the same room in which Harriet had entertained him, and this time he took more notice of the furnishings with his own cottage in mind, thinking some of these lighter pieces might be suitable for his place.

'You still busy at the Residency?' Oatley asked him. 'Even with the boss away?'

'Yes. There's always office business, and in the absence of Mrs Mollard I'm paymaster and unofficial butler, keeping the staff on the job.'

'And when do you expect the Mollards back?'

'Not until the New Year. January some time. I haven't been advised of the shipping arrangements.'

'Good. Would you mind telling me if you've seen any correspondence from Cavendish and Reverend Walters about Zack and the child Boomi?'

'Scads of it, I'm afraid. And a pile of telegrams from the Resident. He wants Zack prosecuted.'

'Would a fine get him out of it? I'll pay it.'

'Probably. Zack's got answers for them. Boomi wasn't officially a ward of the state, so he'll beat the kidnapping charge, as well as the rest of it. But Yorkey's in trouble.'

'Yorkey? Why?'

'He actually knew where you were. And where Mimimiadie and his mob were hiding out. He didn't tell anyone, not even Zack.'

'But I ordered him not to.'

'Yes. Zack told them that, but Cavendish is being pushed to find a scapegoat. Mr Mollard is reading all this stuff in the Adelaide newspapers, about your kidnapping, and the exchange—'

'Don't tell me they've picked it up as well.'

'Oh yes. You're all famous. But the papers are making the local police look rather stupid. Tricked by a black outlaw, and his nibs is spitting chips.'

At a nod from Oatley, the servant refilled their glasses and offered cigars, waiting to light them for the gentlemen.

'Apparently,' Christy added, drawing on the excellent cigar, 'the papers are having a field day, asking what sort of a show he's running up here, with wild blacks making fools of the police, kidnapping white men while everyone but the police knows where their hideout is.'

'But that's not true.'

Christy shrugged. 'Makes a better story. Mollard would throw the book at everyone concerned if he could.'

Oatley sat back in an easy chair. 'I see. I'm famous, am I?'

'Oh yes. And rightly so, I have to say. After what you endured. I admire your courage. Do you mind my asking . . . that scar on your neck . . . they didn't try to hang you, did they?'

Oatley grinned. 'It looks like a gallows necklace, doesn't it? I'll have it as a memento for life. But no, I was tied by the neck all the time, by a cord that felt like hot wire. A very bloody efficient restraint, believe me.'

'God almighty! And that Mimimiadie – what was he like? Were you in fear of your life?'

'I tried not to be. But he was a hard man, and moody. Anything could have happened. Several times I repented all my sins . . . but that's over. I want you to do a favour for me.'

'By all means.'

'I'd like you to advise Mollard that I am throwing my hat in the ring as administrator of the Northern Territory. Perhaps you might even warn him that in his absence, and due to recent events, I am receiving public acclaim and overwhelming support for my possible entry into public office. Lay it on thick.'

Christy was bewildered. 'I was under the impression that Mollard has had his tenure extended.'

'He wouldn't be the first of our administrators to be sacked,' William growled, and Christy had to agree.

'But I also understood that you had no wish to be administrator, sir.'

'I've changed my mind.'

'Oh. Yes. Very well.' This altered things. Oatley would make an excellent administrator, much easier to work for than the mean and penny-pinching Mollards. The Residence could become a pleasant place to work after all. Christy was a little sorry now that he was leaving. But he hadn't given his notice yet.

'Is that all?' he asked.

'Yes. I won't have any trouble rallying support in Adelaide, where the power rests. Sir David Fullarton, Minister of the Territories, is fed up with Mollard; he never liked him but he hasn't been able to settle on a replacement. Now his problem is solved.'

'Yes,' Christy gulped. 'I'm sure it would be.'

'Would you let me know Mollard's response as soon as possible?'

'Certainly.'

Christy took his leave soon afterwards. Nothing had been said about his marriage proposal. And there was no sign of Harriet Oatley, another mystery, and part of an unsolved scandal rife in Darwin. But Oatley was an important patron and Christy would do exactly as he had been instructed. Compared to Oatley, his boss, Mollard, was small fry.

★ ★ ★

When Cornford had left, William was depressed. Had he really meant to aspire to public office, his aspirations would have been dashed by the scandal brought down on him by his wife and his son. But Mollard was too far from the centre of things to know about it yet. He was banking on that. No doubt it would occur to Christy eventually, but he knew where his bread was buttered; he wouldn't inform Mollard and take the risk of offending Zack Hamilton. Not with his marriage to Lucy hanging in the balance.

He savoured another whisky, chiding himself for sinking into the miseries over something that wasn't real in the first place. Another warning that he had to keep fighting off that grief, the self-pity that hung on to him like an army of leeches. Remove one and another appeared.

'It's only a game, a ploy,' he reminded himself. 'You have no intention of seeking to be administrator. So get on with it.'

He'd let Mollard stew for a while. Let him worry about the ignominy of being sacked.

Then he'd make it plain to the Resident that unless all of these charges were dropped, William Oatley had the will, and the backing, to replace him. Not much to ask. He would send that telegram himself. With best wishes. And Happy Christmas.

Now for that preacher.

Reverend Walters pulled on his gumboots and plunged down the muddy track to the mission retreat, cursing as he snagged his umbrella on a low-hanging branch. The foliage here was growing so fast that the track was now more of a dim, boggy hollow than a lane, thanks to this incessant tropical rain. He'd have to get Minto to cut it back. In fact, he pondered crossly, he should have set the mission teacher and his aides to it before they took their Christmas leave.

As he rounded a corner he almost collided with Minto, swathed in a long cloak and barefoot, carrying a pair of raffia sandals.

'Where are you off to?' he demanded.

She looked at him guiltily, stammering, 'Nowhere. I mean, I was just going for a walk.'

'Where to, at this hour of the morning? Haven't you got work to do? And what about Sister Oatley? Are you leaving her to do your work?'

'Oh no, Reverend. I'd never do that. She's all right, I've got her cleaning the stove. I told her I wouldn't be long.' She frowned. 'Not that it will make any difference to her. I'll probably have to finish it when I get back. Most of the time she just stands and stares. Never gets anything finished.'

'Let me see.'

Sure enough, when he walked into the kitchen there she was, sitting on the floor in front of the small open stove, bucket and scrubbing brush beside her, daydreaming.

'We can't have this, Sister Oatley,' he intoned firmly. 'We all have work to do. Now get on with it.'

'Yes,' she muttered, without acknowledging him, and slopped the brush into the stove in a slow, weary movement.

'I don't reckon she's done a stroke of work in her life,' Minto complained. 'She's worse than useless, Reverend. I don't know what I'm supposed to do with her.'

'She's not here on a holiday, Sister Minto, she's here to repent her sins. Isn't that right, Sister Oatley?'

Mrs Oatley nodded but the brush moved so slowly, so tediously, he was irritated.

'Come on now. Buck up. Show her how, Sister Minto.'

With a frustrated sigh, Minto dropped down beside her, took hold of the hand with the brush and forced it to scrub energetically. Two large cockroaches scuttled from the grimy interior, and Minto went after them, squashing them with a sandal, but Harriet didn't appear to notice. She still sat there in some sort of trance, or maybe she was just sulking. Either way, she had to smarten up.

Walters turned to Minto. 'It is one thing to be deep in repentance, quite another thing to wallow in self-pity as she is doing. When I have time I'll come down and we'll pray with her. Bring those sins out into the open with you as witness, though they are so horrendous I fear they will shock you.'

'I'll pray for her,' Minto said stoutly.

'In the meantime she is no different from naughty children when they first come to the mission. They have to be taught obedience. A touch of the switch is the best course and it won't do her any harm either. Bring her down to earth.'

'Amen,' Minto said enthusiastically.

He looked at Minto's lean scrubbed face. 'And make her clean herself up. Have a wash, comb her hair. If she won't follow your good example, then you see to it yourself.'

Minto beamed at the rare compliment. 'I'll give her a good scrub.'

'Excellent. By the way, I was coming down to tell you to bring her to church tomorrow, but it is too soon. We can't take her in that state. It's better to wait. I want her to be able to stand up bravely before the congregation and repent her sins for the glory of the Lord. It will be an important day for us. I think we'll have a choir as well.'

Saturday was a busy day for the Reverend. He had house calls to make, ministering to the sick, then he had to call into the office of the *Darwin Clarion* to lodge an extract from the sermon he proposed to give on the morrow, so that it could be published on Monday morning. Always in some-out-of-the-way corner of the paper, which annoyed him, but at least he was in print.

After an argument with the clerk about the length of the extract, he proceeded to the general store to study, and then pay, his weekly bill. Typical of these Chinese shopkeepers; the prices were always exorbitant, but he kept them in line by querying every entry. The store was busy, nearing half-day-closing time, and people sheltering inside, staring out at the wind and rain battering the wide street, were muttering fearfully about the possibility of another hurricane. Ever since that massive hurricane years back, before his time, this concern came up every year and he found the discussion pointless.

'We're all in God's hands,' he announced blithely as he dived outside to his patient horse.

For a fleeting minute there he thought he saw Minto disappear around the hotel corner, but dismissed the idea. Most of the women wore long black coats and dark hats in these wet, windswept streets. It could have been any one of them.

Next he rode out to the hospital to do his rounds, and make a point of visiting a certain person. He discovered that Myles Oatley was in the only private room, previously occupied by his father, a room usually reserved for people recovering from recent operations, and there it was again. Nothing but the best for the rich. But when he peered in he saw not only two doctors, but a Catholic priest as well, and he ducked away. What bad luck. He'd have to come back another time to have a quiet word with Myles about his part in that sinful triangle.

As he left, he wondered what William Oatley, the avowed atheist, would think of a priest hanging about his son's bedside. He wouldn't be too pleased, that was certain.

Myles Oatley was a difficult patient. The doctors had called in the priest to try to talk some sense into him.

'Why? What's wrong?' the priest asked.

'We have to operate. His feet are in a bad way.'

'Then it's not my opinion you should be seeking. That's your field.'

'No. We have been hoping to save his feet and we've succeeded with the right one, but the left . . . gangrene. It will have to come off.'

'Oh, God save us! And you have told the lad?'

'Yes. But he won't give permission. He flatly refuses to have the operation.'

'The consequences? Have you told him the worst? Am I right in thinking he could die?'

'Yes.'

'Where is his family, by God? Why aren't they here?'

'There's only his father, William Oatley. You know him. It seems they've had a falling-out. He doesn't want to see him.'

The priest sighed. 'There's no accountin' for people. They stagger in from the jaws of death, so to speak, and cart with them some trivial row. But I'll talk with him if you think it'll do any good.'

But Myles only turned his head away from him, resolutely refusing to allow them permission to operate, to amputate.

'I'm sorry, Father,' he said eventually, rejecting the priest's entreaties. 'I'd rather die.'

'Now there's a strange decision to make when you're lying here, a handsome young man just down in the dumps. What if you change your mind next week and it's too late? You can't be standin' there at heaven's gate sayin', I think I made a mistake.'

Myles managed a smile. 'I'll take my chances, Father.'

'But that's the thing. It's a bad bet. Your horse is runnin' dead, if you'll pardon the pun. You can't take a chance on the leg getting better; it's not going to happen. You have to listen to the good doctors. Come on now, get it over with. You'll be smilin' in a week.'

Nothing he could say would break the lad's resolve. Before he left he heard Myles instruct the doctors not to allow any visitors in. He did not want visitors.

'Ah, poor lad,' the priest said. 'Where is his father? I'll have to find the man meself.'

Luck was with him. He met Zack and Sibell Hamilton at the entrance to the hospital, on their way to visit Myles Oatley.

'This is not a good time,' he told them, 'but you'd be doing the lad a much better service if you could locate his father and get him here if you have to hog-tie him.'

He explained the situation and they were, of course, shocked.

'We'll get him, Father,' Zack said, but as they hurried away Sibell whispered: 'I hope we don't have to hog-tie him.'

'Is it that bad between them?' Zack asked.

'I'm afraid so.'

'What about Harriet? Couldn't she talk to Myles?'

'I don't know where she is. She's left William.'

'She's what? Why didn't you tell me this before?'

Sibell was silent, pacing out beside him, and he nodded. 'I see,' he grated. 'A bit close to home, was it? Wives upping and leaving their husbands all over the place.'

'No it wasn't, Zack! She might even be back home by this. They've got a serious problem to work out between them.'

'And we haven't? I'll walk you home then I'll take the buggy and go in search of William. His son's life is at stake. I won't let him refuse to see him.'

Reverend Walters was hungry. He was looking forward to lunch. His housekeeper always made him steak and kidney pie on Saturday mornings. A thick, crusty pie with juicy gravy, and as he often said to her, the sky could fall in but it wouldn't stop him lining up for that midday meal. He had a loaf of fresh bread under his arm to go with it, as he stabled his horse and walked around to his front door.

But there was someone sitting on his front porch. William Oatley!

'I've been waiting for you, Walters,' he said, unfolding from the bench to his full height, towering over him.

'So I see. But I haven't time to talk to you now. I'm busy.'

'You'll talk to me, mister. Where's my wife?'

'I've no idea. Will you let me pass?'

'I'll ask you once more. Where is Mrs Oatley? She left my house with you. Now where did you take her?'

'She has no wish to see you. I did my duty. That is all. I presume that if Mrs Oatley wishes to see you, she will get in touch with you herself.'

'But I wish to see *her*. Now you can do your duty again and tell me where she is staying.'

'I can't discuss her address. Now kindly leave.'

Oatley took him by the arm and almost bounced him down the three steps to the porch until they were both standing, facing each other, on the muddied remnants of a lawn.

'You take your hands off me, Oatley,' the Reverend said as he steadied himself. 'Or I'll have the law on you!'

'Oh yes. You're good at that, aren't you? But let me tell you something. Before I'm finished with you I'll have you run out of town, you creeping Jesus.'

'Blasphemy won't help you, sir. Your wife doesn't want to see you and that's that. And considering the damage you Oatley men have done to that poor woman, I'm not surprised. Men like you ought to be tarred and feathered. Now get away from me.'

Furious, William decided that he might as well go; he wouldn't get any sense out of this ratbag. Not today anyway. He shoved him out of the way and Walters lost his balance, falling back into the mud, his loaf of bread flying into the air as he made a desperate attempt to save it.

William took the warm unwrapped loaf and hurled it into the road.

'I'm not finished with you!' he growled.

Zack's foul mood matched William's. He saw his friend marching along the street, stabbing the ground with his cane, and pulled the buggy in beside him.

'Get in!'

William climbed aboard, glad of the lift, but Zack's hard-set face worried him. 'What's up?'

'We're going to the hospital.'

'What for?'

'So that you can see your son.'

'Turn about. I don't want to see him.'

'I'm not interested in what you want. Myles needs you.'

'The hell he does. I told you, Zack, I don't want to see him.'

'Why not?'

'That's my business. And slow down.'

Zack slapped the reins, urging the horse to go faster. 'Well, now you've made it everyone's business, you bloody fool. Myles is in trouble. The doctors are asking for you. Wondering where the hell you are.'

'Let them wonder.'

They hurtled round a corner and William held on. 'Are you mad, Zack? You'll get us both killed.'

'No I won't. You're going to that hospital to see Myles, and help him.

His foot is gangrenous. The doctors have to amputate but he won't have it. He flatly refuses. If you want your son to live, get in there.'

He pulled the buggy up with a jerk. William's face was grey with shock. He seemed unable to move. He clutched Zack's arm.

'I don't know how to talk to him any more,' he whispered. 'Will you come with me?'

'No. This is your son, your business. You get in there and sort him out. You can't let him die.'

William hated being accosted by the doctors and the matron as he progressed down to that room. He was fighting off tears, trying to think what he would say. He was worried that Myles might ask to see Harriet; he was distraught over so many things that his voice was harsh as he ordered them to leave him be.

Myles was lying flat on the bed with a small pillow under his head, his bandaged legs resting on bolsters. His fair hair was neatly combed and the sunburn that they'd both sustained, and overcome, had left his face deeply tanned, in contrast with the whiteness of the room about him. He was wearing thin hospital-issue pyjamas, the pants cut off at the knees. He looked forlorn and lonely now.

He turned and saw his father.

'I told them I didn't want any visitors.'

'So I believe, but they didn't count me as a visitor.'

'What do you want?'

'You know perfectly well what I want. You're to have that operation.'

'What for?'

'Don't double-talk me, Myles. You don't have any say in this. Not any more. I'm in charge now. You have to have the operation; you don't have any choice. I'm sorry, really sorry, son, but it has to be.'

'Oh yes. You'd like that, wouldn't you? What a great way to get your own back! Turn me into a bloody cripple!'

William had exhausted his small supply of bravado. He had tried to be strong, to use the voice of authority to prevail against his son's stubborn-ness, but now he put his head in his hands as he sank into a chair by the bed, totally overcome with emotion. The agony that Myles was facing had suddenly shaken his confidence.

Eventually he got up and closed the door. 'I'm sorry, I didn't mean that,' he said. 'I meant I want you to tell them they can go ahead. Please, Myles. It's a terrible thing, I know that. But I beg you. I beg you . . . Oh, Jesus! I don't know what to say to you. But you can't fight them any more.'

Myles seemed to be talking to himself. He didn't look at his father; he stared up at the ceiling.

'Trouble is, I'm frightened. I'm a coward. I'm scared bloody stiff.'

William nodded. 'So would I be.'

'No you wouldn't. You'd charge on like the Light Brigade. Be the big hero.'

'The hell I would!'

346

They were both quiet. Maybe thinking things over. Maybe trying not to think.

'You haven't even asked how I'm feeling,' Myles said querulously.

'I'm sorry. How are you?'

'I'm hot. It's bloody hot in here. One leg's sore. The other is numb. The crook one, I suppose. My bum's sore. The food is shit.'

'I know. They only gave me bread and milk.'

'But you look all right now.'

'I didn't have to walk.'

'You've still got a scar round your neck.'

'Yes. I'll have to live with that.'

The rest of the time they just sat. Or rather William sat. Myles lay back dozing, occasionally scratching at the bandages on his legs, until finally he asked:

'How's Harriet?'

'I don't know,' his father said softly. 'I think she's had enough of both of us. She left. I don't know where she's staying.'

'I tried to tell you I was sorry about that.'

'It doesn't matter now.'

'Yes it does. You know I'm scared. That bloody chloroform and that operation, what if I don't come through it?'

'For God's sake, Myles, of course you will.'

He sighed. 'Stop bossing me! Let me say something, for Christ's sake. I'm sorry. Very bloody sorry. It was all my fault. I don't want you to take it out on her.'

'All right, I won't! But it's getting late. What can I tell the doctors?'

'Tell them anything you bloody like.'

William wanted to reach over and take his hand, but he was too shy. 'I'll be here, Myles. I'll be here all the time.'

'See that you are. Give them hell. Don't let them cut off the wrong one.'

William smiled. 'You can count on me to be on guard.'

The hours dragged. He walked about outside the hospital, up and down, but keeping within shouting distance of Myles's empty room. He watched visitors leave, remaining in the shadows so he wouldn't have to engage in any conversations; saw patients settling in the long veranda ward where Myles had been while his father occupied the private room, the room that was now in darkness, ominous darkness. Lamps were flickering all along the single-storied building. It was only a bush hospital, the best that poor old Darwin could afford, a wooden building in need of paint with a corrugated-iron roof to fend off the summer deluges, not very prepossessing at all, not a place to instil confidence. He hoped the doctors were up to the task.

Eventually he lit his pipe and planted himself on a low bench directly opposite that room, so that he'd know when they brought Myles back from the operating theatre. He wished he could pray, envying believers that comfort, and tried not to think about what was happening to his son. Difficult to find anywhere to place his thoughts; there were quicksands everywhere. The recent past was out of bounds. Could he ever really forgive them, despite his claim that it didn't matter now? The future was equally discomforting. Was Harriet really fed up with both of them? Or was she waiting for Myles to come to her? Wherever she was. He didn't want to think about Harriet right now. Even the thought of seeing her again made him nervous.

Overhead the high gums were swishing in the warm winds; squally winds, restless, as if impatient for him to move on, take his clamour elsewhere. Leave them be. William felt queasy. He wished he had a drink. He'd give anything for a couple of whiskies, doubles, but he dare not leave. And he dreaded having to stay.

Lucy Hamilton was appalled. Distraught.

'They can't cut his foot off! They can't!'

'I'm afraid they have to, darling,' her father said. 'He'll be all right.'

'How can you say that? How can he be all right? Myles will be devastated. It's terrible. We have to go and see him right away!'

Maudie looked up from her knitting. 'Listen to you. Last month he was the worst in the world. Now you're all teary about him.'

'He's my friend. He's still my friend! Don't be so bloody heartless. I'm going to see him if none of you will.'

Zack took her by the arm. 'No you don't. Calm down, Lucy. His father is there, I doubt they need anyone else just now. And anyway, we haven't heard how the operation went yet.'

'What do you mean, how it went? Could he die?'

'Of course not, but he'll be in shock. We can only wait now. What about getting me a cup of tea?'

'Where's Mrs Oatley?' Maudie asked caustically, but a cold glance from Zack sent her back to her knitting needles.

Harriet was alone. Minto hadn't come back and she didn't know what to do. Shakily she lit the lamp and went over to lie on her bunk. The birds were noisy, giving her a headache. She seemed to have a permanent headache these days, and that made her dizzy. She'd tried to explain to Minto that she wasn't lazy, only terribly tired, and everything seemed fuzzy, making it hard to concentrate, but Minto only got cross with her:

'Stuff and nonsense. You're bone lazy, never done a stroke of work in your life. You don't know what work is! Ladle that hot water from the copper into this bucket and be quick about it.'

Harriet was mortified. She couldn't manage even a simple job like that without spilling the precious boiling water everywhere, and she understood Minto's impatience. The woman worked hard inside and outside their little house and it must be infuriating to have someone as useless as her stumbling about trying to help. The worst job was making those horrible bars of soap. Harriet couldn't comprehend the process –

that fuzziness again – she only knew they boiled stuff and poured it into tins to set and the cold bars had to be cut into three squares. And whatever the mixture was, it smelled quite dreadful. At one stage she had mentioned to Minto that perhaps they should add some perfume. That was when Minto struck her with the wooden pole they used for stirring, telling her that she was mental. And she probably was. Being so useless.

But then they'd gone down on their knees and prayed and Minto had encouraged her to speak to Jesus, out there under His heavens, and to admit her sins, in detail.

'He knows about them,' Minto had said, 'but you have to cleanse yourself by speaking out for the love of the Lord.'

Twice a day, Harriet had cleansed herself, with only Jesus and Minto to hear her in this haven, and she'd told all . . . all about Myles. And more than that. Minto had encouraged her to release the intimacies of her marriage.

'That's where it began,' Minto said. 'That's where your degradation began. Married people, good people, don't behave like that. No wonder he brought the son into your orgies, with you so willing.'

Harriet wept. 'I don't think so. I don't know . . . I thought . . .'

'No. You didn't think anything, you poor girl. You didn't know how vicious men can be when they have an unprotected woman in their clutches, but redemption is nigh. You have to think now of Jesus and no one else, nothing else, except for reparation.'

'Yes. Reparation. How do I do that?'

'Only through work. I've told you before about idle hands. Stop gibbering about being tired, because you're not. You're a strong woman. Jesus has blessed you with a healthy body, but you've abused it.'

Gradually Harriet had become frightened of Minto. Confused. Sometimes Minto was harsh, bullying, because she didn't understand that Harriet wanted to work, it was just that she couldn't concentrate and she'd become so clumsy it was hard to get anything right. Other times she left her alone, ignored her for hours and hours, and that was frightening because Harriet didn't know what to do. She could only wander about tangled up in guilt and a web of anxieties.

When Minto went out again she tried to read her Bible but couldn't concentrate, so she lay on her bed until it was too dark to bother getting up.

In the morning she realised that Minto hadn't come back, so she stayed in bed, but the flies got so bad she had to make an effort. She found the fly swat and spent a long time hunting them down. Hungry, she found some bread and butter in the cupboard, and guiltily stole a little of Minto's jam, a nice home-made plum jam. She sat outside for a while, looking at the kerosene tins of tallow and the cold copper, and thought she should make a start, either at the candles or the soap, but she couldn't recall how it was done, so she took a bucket, filled the copper and lit it. At least there'd be plenty of hot water when Minto got back.

349

Mindful of her duty, she knelt to pray for a while, then opened the Bible to read the Psalms – which she liked best, but which Minto thought were too airy-fairy – until she dozed off in the chair. It was a very hot day and their little house was stifling, surrounded by all the greenery. Minto spent a long time each day clipping it back, but as she said, this jungle kept on coming at you like a train, and that was true enough.

By nightfall Harriet was well rested, feeling better but guilty again. Minto had probably gone to visit people. No doubt she'd said where she was going but Harriet couldn't remember. She wouldn't just go off like that, not without the Reverend's permission. But anyway, it was really lovely here now, so peaceful to be alone, to be able to commune with Jesus without the bother of Minto's interruptions.

The four-note call of the kingfishers woke her in the morning, so she shared the rest of the corned mutton in the meat safe with the gorgeous birds, delighted that they were bold enough to come within a few feet of the back steps. Her headaches had gone, but without Minto to take care of her Harriet was disoriented. She couldn't remember where she was exactly, but she knew she was safe here and that was the main thing. In a fit of pique that Minto had left her alone for so long, she took the key from the dresser drawer and opened Minto's cupboard directly below, surprised to find it full of groceries, nice things too, that Minto had never mentioned. Tea, sugar, honey, biscuits, preserves, tins of beans and sardines . . . all sorts of things.

She ate like a child, pouring honey on the biscuits and heaping sugar, previously forbidden, into her tea, then quickly locked the cupboard again and ran to curl up on her bunk, trying to think up excuses for the theft. In the afternoon she went bravely, giddily, for a walk in the bush at the back of the house, pushing aside the damp branches and tramping through the thick undergrowth in bare feet like a veteran bushie, enjoying this exploration, wondering where it would lead. She startled a dingo, as pretty as any dog she'd ever seen, and called to it, but it dashed away. She watched flocks of flashy parrots, and a few hefty lizards that reminded her that there could also be snakes here, but they kept out of sight, so she struggled on until she deemed it time to turn back.

That wasn't so easy. Harriet became worried. Minto would be home by this, and angry with her. She hurried in one direction then another, searching through the top tier of this three-dimensional forest for the sun, as if it could give her directions, as if she had some idea what the sun could tell her, but the tall canopy allowed only some light, not assistance. She was lost. The bush walk had become hideous, terrifying. Her arms and feet were bleeding from sharp grasses and thorns. Her skirt, her only skirt, was torn, and Minto's blouse, which she used when hers was in the wash, was soaked with perspiration.

Then, by accident, from out of that humid maze, Harriet stumbled into a clearing and there was the house. Their little house.

The sun was setting; she'd been spared a night in the wilderness, a certainty that had already beset her! She sank to her knees to thank Jesus before running into the dark house and curling up, defeated, on her bunk. Never again would she disobey Him. This was where He wished her to be, and this was where she would stay until He forgave her. With or without Minto.

Lucy Hamilton was praying, fiercely accosting God on behalf of her dear friend Myles Oatley, who was critically ill as a result of the most terrible operation. They had amputated his leg! Lucy hadn't really accepted that they would do such a thing to a fine young man like Myles until she actually saw him lying there in the hospital, with that space, that flat side of the bed. She'd thought, hoped, that the doctors would operate, look at the poisoned foot, find it wasn't so bad after all, remove the gangrenous part like you would an abscess, a deep abscess, and find a way to save his leg. But no. Not them. They'd amputated the leg mid-calf. You would think then, if it had to be done, it would be all over by now, but it had been three days . . . three long days, and he was still feverish, barely conscious.

Shock, they said, fever, already weakened by exposure, all sorts of excuses, and Lucy thought the doctors incompetent but she dared not say so, for fear of upsetting William even further, so she could only pray, and keep William company, though the doctors preferred no visitors in the sick room. William had been pitifully pleased to see her, and she was glad she'd come. And at least she was able to take his place, keep vigil so that William could take a break, go home for a few hours. Get a few hours' sleep.

Christy was becoming impatient with her, but that couldn't be helped. He couldn't, or wouldn't, understand that she and Myles were childhood friends, that no matter what had happened between them, she couldn't desert him now, in his hour of need. Christy had even complained about missing the annual Christmas ball at the Victoria Hotel, strictly invitation only this time, and Lucy had reacted angrily.

'How can you think of dancing? How can I, with Myles lying there like that? If you're so keen, go on your own!'

He had of course, last night, and Lucy didn't care. It was no loss missing yet another bunfight. And she'd sort Christy out as soon as she was sure that Myles would recover. A numbing fear lodged. He would recover, wouldn't he? He had to.

She sat quietly by the bed, feeling so damned helpless with Myles lying there, his eyes closed, his thin face blotched with fever. She wondered if he realised what had happened.

He shuddered and she reached for his hand, holding it gently. 'Come on, Myles. You can beat this,' she whispered. 'You've had the fevers before. Remember the snake bite? Boy, were you sick that time! They all thought you were a goner, but you wouldn't give in. You can't give in this time either, you have to get better, fight the bloody germs or whatever they are. You can wake up properly, I know you can . . .'

William came back, listened to her talking to Myles, encouraging him, and backed away, believing this was the best medicine he could have right now. That pair understood each other; she could charge him with the responsibility to recover, which was desperately needed now, far better than a father could.

He wondered how things were working out between Lucy and Christy. Zack had tried to draw him out on that subject but William considered he was singularly ill-equipped to be handing out advice about relationships, and had made no comment. When it came to Christy, he did have private reservations. Although he was the very one who had bribed the man for information, and so could hardly cast any stones, Christy's disloyalty to his employer was scarcely a plus. Even if the employer was Resident Mollard. He shrugged; these young people would have to sort out their own problems. Which reminded him. Where *was* Harriet? With Myles so very ill – it had been in the local paper – surely she should have called at the hospital or sent a note, shown some compassion, but there hadn't been a word from her.

When he returned to the room, all was quiet again. Myles was very still, his eyes closed as if he were shut off from the world.

Lucy took his hand again. 'Ah! Here's your father, Myles. Come on, wake up and talk to us. You can't lie there forever feeling sorry for yourself!'

William winced, thinking that was rather harsh, but suddenly Myles stirred, struggling to speak, startling them.

'I'm not,' he whispered, and Lucy almost whooped with joy.

'There you are! I knew you were in there listening to us all the time. How about that, William? I think he's been playing possum.' She kissed Myles on the cheek. 'You have to wake up properly now, so that we can get you out of here.'

William went around to the other side of the bed and placed a trembling hand on his son's forehead.

'He's much cooler now, Lucy. I think his temperature has gone down at last.'

But she was rushing away. 'I'll call Matron.'

Passengers were boarding the steamer *Belfast* bound for the east-coast ports of Brisbane and Sydney. Blustery winds and fretful showers hindered their progress as they battled along the pier, hanging on to hats and umbrellas, but one lady was unconcerned by the weather. Her step was determined. Her new bonnet was firmly in place, its coloured ribbons fluttering gaily. Her long navy cloak, also new, was buttoned high to the neck, and its fullness, sweeping the timbers underfoot, was adequate protection. Her gloved hands didn't need the assistance of sailors or rails as she strode up the ramp with a contented smile and without a backward glance. Minto was shot of Darwin for good and all.

Two days later William was conferring with Tom Ling before he left for the hospital. He was feeling much better now that Myles was recovering, though still mightily depressed, trying to come to terms with his son's misfortune.

'How will he be walking?' Tom Ling wailed.

'He'll have to have a wooden leg,' William said wearily.

'Ooh ahh! How can that be?'

'I have telegraphed Perth. My friends know a man who is expert in these things,' William explained. 'He will make a leg for Myles, see that it fits him, the right size and all.'

'Then he'll be walking good?'

'I think it will take some getting used to. But yes, he should be able to manage if he is patient.'

Tom Ling was still mystified, but William moved on. 'I can't understand why you haven't found Mrs Oatley yet.'

He had commissioned both his servants to search the town for her, certain that the Chinese community, given the nod, would locate her. They knew every nook and cranny of the place.

Tom Ling shook his head. 'No one know. We good lookers. We look in every place, white houses, Chinese houses, she not here no more. She gone.'

'Oh well. Maybe she has.'

'Velly solly, master.' Tom Ling bowed sadly.

'It's all right. I'll find out. In the meantime, you keep your folk watching for her.'

The thought had already occurred to him, so he'd asked Leo to check the passenger manifests of all ships leaving the port over the previous weeks. Especially ships bound for Perth, her home town. He'd considered telegraphing her parents to ask if they knew anything, but that would take some explaining, so he'd decided to leave well enough alone for the time being.

On this note he detoured into town, to call at his former office and see if Leo had any news. If she had taken passage out of town by ship, there being no other way of departing the Territory for a woman like her, what had she used for money? The housekeeping cash that he always left for her was still in his desk drawer. And her clothes! She hadn't taken a stitch, not even a coat and hat, as Tom Ling kept insisting. Had someone given her money? But who? Not Walters, that was sure. Not that penny-pinching Bible-thumper. He'd have to get after him again.

Leo was worried. 'There is no record of Harriet having sailed from here on any ship, in any direction,' he said. 'And if she can't be found in the town, then something could have happened to her, William.'

'Like what? I know Darwin has a wild reputation, but our women are safe. The rough types can get themselves into strife, with fights and arguments, but not women like Harriet. It's unheard of.'

'You never know. I don't mean to be offensive, but if, as you say, she has wandered off, not even dressed in street wear, then she might have been taken advantage of, so to speak.'

'I don't think so. I reckon Walters has placed her with some of his

God-bothering parishioners. She's holed up in someone's back room.'

'Maybe you ought to go to the police.'

'And cause a real hullabaloo? I don't know if I'm up to that right now.'

'Shouldn't your wife's safety be your first concern?'

'What if they find her and she's quite all right? I'll look a bloody fool.'

'And what if she's not all right?'

'I don't bloody know!' William snapped. 'I'll think about it. I have to go to see Myles.'

'Yes, of course. I'm glad to hear he's recovering. Say hello to him for me.'

Myles Oatley was recovering, Christy knew, but that didn't seem to make any difference to Lucy. She still saw herself as the angel of mercy, having to be by his side at the hospital, to keep his spirits up.

Christy wasn't unsympathetic, really. It was a terrible thing for any fellow to lose a leg, but Myles had got himself into that trouble. It had been blackfellers' business. He shouldn't have interfered. It had been Yorkey's job, on Oatley's specific instructions, to liaise directly with Oatley's captor, a bullish chief called Mimimiadie, to arrange the exchange. Yorkey had known what he was about; he'd even given Zack Hamilton the slip. Zack had left it at that, but not the pig-headed Myles Oatley. He'd marched out into the wilderness, unprepared and stupidly confident. Of doing what? The man was a fool.

But Lucy didn't think so. Oh no, he was a hero, valiant, unbowed. This man who'd dumped her for his own stepmother. They all seemed to have forgotten that scandalous episode in their orgy of grief over his misfortunes.

Lucy had said Christy was jealous, and damned right he was. With good reason. He could feel in his bones that she was slipping away from him, heading back to Myles Oatley. If he'd have her. There was always that possibility, thank God. When Myles came to his senses he could easily walk away from her again, as carelessly as he'd done the first time, for Harriet or someone else.

But Christy was finding it difficult to keep in contact with Lucy since she'd almost made her home at the blasted bedside. And because of that he rarely saw Zack Hamilton, who had not yet responded to his request for permission to ask Lucy to marry him. Poor show that, making him cool his heels like a peasant at the gate.

He had found an excuse to visit their house, asking to see Zack, but only Maudie Hamilton had been home, and she'd prised his message out of him, promising to pass it on to her brother-in-law. The Resident had sent instructions to the Police Commissioner that any and all charges against Zack and Yorkey be dropped, no doubt in a knee-jerk reaction to Oatley's threat to oust him from his soft spot as administrator. A copy of William's telegram to Mollard had been slipped to Christy by a friend at the Cable Company.

Maudie had been delighted. 'Good of you to let us know, Christy. Not a nice thing to have hanging over our heads. Zack didn't seem too concerned about it but I said to him: "People like us don't get mixed up with courts. We'd never live down the disgrace." I warned him about grabbing that kid. Both of them! But no one listens to me. Of course, Mrs Mollard is a friend of mine. I'll wager she had a say in putting a stop to the charges, knowing I'd be upset.'

Christy was glad to escape, claiming busy times in his office with the Resident away. In fact, though, he had little to do now, since Christmas was so close.

He strolled into town, peering into shops with their drooping Christmas decorations, half-hearted at best, and found himself in front of the Chinese pawn shop. Perhaps he could find something in there to please Lucy, a gift of some sort. Items left here were rarely recovered by the owners, so it had ended up more of a bargain basement, with boxes of oddments heaped about the floor and a counter covered in trays of jewellery ranging from trash to an assortment of more decent offerings.

'I was looking for a gift for a lady,' he said vaguely to the elderly Chinaman known as Sleepy Lee, who sat in a high cane chair behind the counter, dressed as usual in a long embroidered coat with the mandatory small round cap atop a very long pigtail. The deeply hooded eyes barely seemed to notice him, the eyes that had earned him the nickname, but everyone knew Sleepy never missed a trick and was apt to leap off his chair, screeching like a banshee, if a light-fingered customer was foolish enough to think it possible to take advantage of him.

He waved a skinny hand languidly across his counter, as if the request was of no moment to him.

'A brooch, maybe,' Christy offered, and gaining no response, he peered at trays of trinkets, moving along for something better, studying the collection. There were some opal brooches, and some set with gemstones, but nothing that took his fancy. Next to them was a large collection of wedding rings that caused him to smile. What was the story behind this lot? he wondered. It was always said that the last thing a woman lost sight of was her wedding ring. Maybe the females who'd come through this town hadn't cared about the rules.

Since he was here, he decided he might as well enquire as to the average cost of a wedding ring, for future reference. He held up a thin gold band.

'How much this one?'

'Five shillin'.' Sleepy hadn't stirred.

Christy tried the other end. He pointed to a thick gold band with rubies set in it, only small rubies; he had to squint to pick up the colour. There were several in much the same style, all still in fashion, which was good to know. Quite a few ladies of his acquaintance wore rings like this.

'How much?'

'Twenty pun.'

Twenty pounds? That was a bit hot. He'd liked to have asked Lee what

355

carat the gold was so that he could assess the costing, knowing little of these matters, but Lee wasn't a talkative man. He wasn't there to discuss the merits of gold or gems. You either bought or you didn't buy. It seemed immaterial to him.

As he glanced at a tray of dress rings, Christy had an idea. A good idea. Why not buy an engagement ring? Jump the gun. Present it to her. *A fait accompli.* That would seal their betrothal and there'd be nothing Zack could do about it.

But it would have to be something really special. Something that she would really like. Not from a pawn shop, though, that wouldn't go down very well if they found out. But he might as well start looking at prices.

Eagerly he began studying the dress rings. Some of them were attractive, diamonds and gemstones in fine settings.

Lee must have picked up on his mood. He deigned to speak.

'Best quality, sir. Gennelman like you know good quality, see. Those velly cheap, those.' He nodded benignly and sank back into silence, allowing Christy to take his time making a choice.

Christy was mostly interested in the diamonds, but a dark sapphire set between two diamonds caught his eye. It was a lovely ring but it would probably cost the earth. He picked it up to ask Lee the price but replaced it quickly. He'd seen that ring before. He was sure he had. But where? Christy prided himself that he had a good memory, but now he was irritated that he couldn't place the ring.

He couldn't ask Lee who'd pawned it. These hole-in-the-wall shops were notorious for receiving stolen goods but there was nothing much the police could do about it, if they cared, because no records were kept. Lee never dealt in paperwork; the information was safe in his head.

Christy stalled for time, feigning interest in other rings while his glance kept moving back to the elegant sapphire. He did know. He just had to force himself to recall. But then what did it matter? Maybe it wasn't stolen. Maybe the owner had just become tired of it, sold it, replaced it with something different. But who? Curiosity kept him at the counter and Lee didn't disturb him.

It was a lovely ring, though. Lucy would adore it. At least he should price it. That wouldn't do any harm. He was about to pick it up, to show it to Lee, to ask him the price, maybe beat him down on it, the Chinese loved to bargain, when it hit him!

Harriet! It was Harriet's ring. He would swear to it. Either that or an identical one. But what were the odds on that in Darwin? He stared. The two diamonds nursing the sapphire glittered at him. They were classy. Even he knew that.

But what to do now? He needed another opinion. William. He had to get him down here. But in the meantime . . . well, he couldn't buy it, nor could he leave it here for sale.

Christy picked up the ring and handed it up to Lee. 'Could you hold this one for me for a couple of hours? I want my fiancée to look at it. She'll have to make the final decision. You know me, don't you?'

356

Lee nodded as his hand closed around the ring, but the other had shot out. 'Money?'

'No. You hold it for me. We'll talk about the price later. And might I remind you that I am aide to His Excellency. It had better still be here when I return.'

William was at the hospital. So was Lucy, of course, he learned from the matron, but this time he wanted to speak privately with Mr Oatley.

'What is it, Christy?' William asked testily when he came out to the front entrance.

Christy wasted no time explaining his mission and William left with him, but by the time they reached the pawn shop they had another man with them. William had enlisted the help of Charlie Wong, owner of the big café only a few doors away.

It was Charlie who demanded to see the ring, and Lee handed it over calmly.

William identified it. 'Yes, I'm sure it's Harriet's ring. Can you find out when she sold it?'

The two men talked in their own language until Charlie turned to Christy and William to explain the conversation.

'Mr Lee does not want any trouble. He bought it from a lady only about a week ago. In good faith. It was not pawned but sold. He is anxious to help, you understand. He did not know that the ring belonged to your wife.'

'What do you mean by that?' William demanded. 'If she sold it to him, then of course it belonged to her.'

'No, no. He did not buy it from Mrs Oatley. He knows Mrs Oatley by sight. He has often seen her walking by. Sometimes she even came in to look about, but she is not a customer.'

William was confused. 'What's this? Who sold it then?'

'Mr Lee does not know the lady's name,' Charlie apologised. 'He is very sorry.'

'Sorry nothing!' Christy snapped. 'The whole population passes this door. He knows everyone. You tell him we want a name or I'll go for the police.'

Eventually, after further inquisition, Charlie had an answer, of sorts. 'It is true. He does not know her name. But he has seen her before with the preacher. With the churchman, Walters.'

'What?' William exploded.

'Just a minute,' Charlie said, as Sleepy Lee climbed down from his perch to search among the wedding rings. 'She brought another ring as well. Mr Lee wishes to extend to you his abject apologies. He had no idea the rings were stolen.'

Obviously Lee understood the conversation. He reached for a gold wedding ring and handed it over.

'Does this belong to Mrs Oatley too?' Charlie asked, and William nodded.

'Yes. That's all he can tell us? What did the woman look like?'

Charlie translated the reply. 'About forty. Skinny. Ugly.'

'I see,' William said ominously. 'And it didn't occur to him that this woman, skinny, ugly, a friend of the preacher's, wouldn't own expensive rings like this?'

Lee himself gave a spirited reply in Chinese and Charlie smiled smugly as the angry pawnbroker ranted on.

'Mr Lee says that often ladies send their servants in to sell things rather than face the disgrace of entering a pawn shop. Common practice, you see. And if you are taking the rings, he wishes to be recompensed.'

'Like hell!' William said, but Charlie disagreed. Politely.

'In fairness, you see, Mr Lee points out that you have no claim to the rings. They are his property. He has paid for them, even if to a servant girl. There is no proof that they are stolen.'

William had to end this. 'How much does he want?'

'Three hundred pounds.'

'Rubbish. I'll give him fifty.'

Lee held up two fingers and William retaliated, poking one finger at him. 'One hundred, you bloody old crook. One hundred. No more.'

The old man smiled faintly and held out his hand.

William was in no mood for niceties. He caught Walters as he was walking towards the empty church, grabbed him by the scruff of the neck and shook him violently.

'I want the truth out of you, you bastard, or you're coming to the police station with me. I'm charging you with robbery. With the theft of these rings. Do you see them, you bastard? These are my wife's rings. Sold by you in a pawn shop.'

Christy thought that was a bit harsh, since they knew that a woman had sold them, but he supposed it was a start. The woman, thief or servant, was known to the preacher.

Walters struggled, tried to argue with Oatley's rage while passers-by stopped to stare at this commotion right outside the church. William started dragging him down the street towards the police station. By this time Walters was screaming.

'I don't know anything about her rings. She had them last time I saw her. I'm not interested in her fripperies. Leave me alone! You're tearing my jacket!'

'When was the last time you saw her?' Christy shouted at him, running alongside them like a terrier.

'Three or four days ago. I forget. I demand you set me loose. I'll have the law on both of you!' He tripped and fell, but William jerked him to his feet.

'Where did you see her?'

Walters managed to stop their progress. He grabbed hold of a gatepost and clung to it. 'I'll tell you where she is. I'll tell you,' he whined. 'I don't know anything about the rings. If she sold them that's her business.

How dare you accuse me of theft! How dare you!'

'Where is she?' William demanded.

'Let go of me first. Take your hands off me, Oatley, you ruffian. I'm the one should be charging you.'

'Where is she?'

'Your wife is in good hands,' Walters began, but it was all too much for William.

'I'll break his bloody neck,' he said to Christy, who decided it was time to take over and stepped in to separate them.

Harriet was asleep. She hadn't even attempted to make the soap or candles, but she had found work for her idle hands in the vegetable garden, never-ending work since the weeds grew like beanstalks. It was pleasant, though. Quite satisfying, with no one to hurry her, and she didn't mind the rain, she could work in the rain just as easily. After all, it was only water.

Minto was still away, but God provided her with carrots and parsnips, which she ate raw because she couldn't light the stove. There wasn't any dry wood. Harriet marvelled at Minto's ability to manage all these difficult tasks, accepting that she herself really was a useless being. When Minto came back she would pay more attention, learn how to do these things. She still tired easily, though, and had a very bad habit of forgetting what she was doing, or where she'd put things.

When she came in, on this day, she couldn't find any towels, which was irritating because she was soaked. In desperation she discarded her wet blouse and skirt, meaning to put them on the line on the veranda, and climbed into one of the heavy cotton nighties that she'd inherited from that other girl who'd run off. She wandered about for a while, then, finding herself in a bedroom, in a nightie, decided to take a nap.

Loud voices woke her, and she was frightened. It was daylight, she must have slept in, missed the early prayers. She grabbed at the sheet, terrified that the Reverend would come in and find her still in bed. It was too late to go looking for her clothes, wherever they were. She heard him calling Minto and prayed that he wouldn't come into the bedroom, but suddenly the door slammed open and men crowded in, their angry voices a shocking invasion.

Harriet cringed against the wall, screaming, petrified that they were about to attack her. She pulled the sheet over her head, trying to hide from them, screams her only defence.

Christy gaped, trying to take this in. This woman in the worn old nightdress was Harriet. Though he hardly recognised the sunburned face and tangled hair. William was attempting to calm her, but she was fighting him, punching and slapping at him, while Walters was pounding about outside, shouting for someone called Minto.

As he'd led them down that track, half hidden by scrub, he'd kept insisting that Harriet was staying in the church retreat with another lady.

Staying of her own accord, he'd repeated. And she was quite all right.

Though the bungalow was only a small two-roomed wooden building, it was no different from many others in the town often erected in back yards for extra accommodation. At first glance, Christy had been reassured. The setting was quite pretty in its surrounds of native trees, some in bloom, and clumps of palms. A large stand of bamboo, rattling in the breeze, towered over the low roof by the side of the house.

Walters had barged right in without knocking, and they'd followed, only to be stunned by the disorder and the smell of the place. No harmonious retreat this, Christy noted, more like a rat's nest with that stale stink of mould.

She was quieter now. William had retreated, seating himself a little way from her bed, on a three-legged stool, talking to her.

'Harriet . . . it's me. William. There's nothing to be afraid of. What happened to you? No. No. Don't be frightened. I'm not going to touch you. You know me, surely? William? Yes, you do, I can see that. Now you just settle down and we might have a nice cup of tea.'

Not here, though, Christy thought, leaving the room to confront Walters. 'So this filthy dump is what you call a retreat, is it?'

'It shouldn't be like this! It's never like this. I don't know where that woman has got to.'

'I can guess. Harriet's not wearing her rings. I'd say your woman has lifted them and done a bunk.'

'She wouldn't do that. She's an honest, God-fearing woman. It's unthinkable.'

'Was anyone else here?'

'No. Just the two of them, leading a peaceful life of meditation.'

'Really? That only leaves you. Did you ask her to pawn the rings?'

'Certainly not!' Walters gazed about, bewildered. 'I don't know what's happened here. It's disgraceful.'

'It is all that and more. You'd better start saying your prayers for when William comes up for air. He'll need some answers. And so do I. How did Harriet get into this state? She's like a mad woman. What have you done to her?'

'I told you, nothing!' Walters bleated frantically. 'Nothing! She needed somewhere to go, to get away from them—'

'Who's them?'

Walters glared at him meanly. 'Don't pretend you don't know what those two men have done to her. Father and son together, taking advantage of the weakness of the poor woman. I know all about their orgies, so you needn't think . . .'

For a second there, Christy couldn't quite take in what was being said to him. He blinked, aghast at the appalling accusation.

It was then that Christy struck the Reverend.

William was too upset to be bothered about Walters, who was lying on the floor, dazed, nursing his jaw.

'We have to get her out of here,' he said. 'But she's not dressed. Can you find me some transport? A gig or a wagon, anything.'

Christy did better than that. He sprinted down to the Residence and ordered the coachman to harness a horse for Mollard's landau, the wet-weather vehicle well protected from the rain by shiny oilskin covers. And well protected, for Christy's present purposes, from prying eyes.

He could only take the vehicle some of the way down the track behind the preacher's house, so Harriet had to be brought out to meet it.

She was docile enough by this but not keen to leave.

'There you are!' Walters sneered, careful to remain close to the back door to avoid another attack. 'I told you she could leave of her own accord if she wished. There are no fences here.'

'Shut up,' Christy snarled. 'The poor woman doesn't know where she is.' He noticed there was no further cheek from Walters about having the law on them, even after that punch. And he was very pleased to see that his handiwork had resulted in a purplish bruise building up around Walters' right eye.

Just then Harriet appeared in the doorway, wrapped, pitifully, in an old patched sheet, looking, he thought, like death walking.

William reached out to her but she edged away from him, turning to Walters.

'What do they want?' she asked him.

The preacher's response was smug, infuriating. 'They want you to go with them, my dear.'

'But I'm not ready yet, am I?'

'I think so,' he nodded. 'I think so.'

'Oh.'

She just stood there, uncertain.

William held out his hand. 'You know me, and Christy, don't you?'

'Yes. Where's Minto?' She still kept her distance.

'She's gone.' William kept his voice very low and even. 'We'll look after you now. There's nothing to worry about. We all have to go now.'

She looked nervously at the front door. 'Where to?'

'Home. We're taking you home.'

She seemed to brighten up. 'Yes. I suppose that's best. I really haven't been much use here. I'm sorry, Mr Walters.'

'Use at what?' Christy wanted to know, a baleful eye on Walters.

'Oh, the soap-making and the candle-making. You know . . .'

'Ah yes.' He nodded. 'Can I help you down the steps, Harriet?'

'No. I can walk.' To their astonishment she sailed out the door and down the front steps as if a sheet over a nightdress was suitable outdoor attire, but they didn't make any attempt to stop her. They dared not in case she changed her mind. Thank God for the privacy of Mollard's vehicle.

She wouldn't allow either of them to touch her as she plodded up the track with them, the sheet trailing forlornly in the mud.

William turned back to look at the lonely bungalow.

361

'I wish Yorkey was here,' he said to Christy.

'Yorkey? Why?'

'I'll bet he wouldn't have any compunction in setting a match to that place.'

Once home, Harriet created even more problems. She sat on the side of the large four-poster bed, refusing to have anything to do with any of them, not even Tom Ling.

'She seems to think she's been in a nunnery,' William said wearily when he emerged from the bedroom. 'She doesn't want men around. That's all I can make of it.'

Christy recalled the preacher's vicious remarks and thought there was more to it. He wondered what sort of ugly tales he'd been spinning her in the name of salvation.

'Do you think you could get Sibell Hamilton to come over?' William asked. 'She might be able to talk some sense into her. Get her cleaned up at least.'

Sibell was surprised at the request but quickly grabbed her hat and coat. 'Of course I'll come with you, Christy.'

'What's going on?' Maudie asked, but for once could get no response.

'Oh my! We are travelling in style,' Sibell said as he handed her into the landau. 'I'm so glad Harriet is home at last. Did you say she was ill? Poor William, as if he hasn't had enough to deal with lately.'

Christy turned the horse about and began to explain the situation to Sibell, who was stunned. 'She's been there all this time?'

'It seems so.'

'Good God! But what's the matter with her now?'

'A nervous breakdown, I'd say. Overdose of religion. She's stuck in the bedroom, clutching a Bible to her bosom.'

'Dear oh dear. After you've dropped me, I think you'd better get Dr Byrne.'

Christy shook his head. 'I don't think she'd see him. Not yet anyway.'

While the men had lunch, Sibell managed to bathe Harriet, wash and dry her hair, and dress her. She had decided not to treat the girl as an invalid and have that thought lodge in her mind; she was already severely disoriented. During that time, though, Harriet had talked to her, rattling on about the evils of sin, men, life in general and her own sinfulness, and Sibell was appalled. She responded by smiling, soothing, quietening her when she became excited by the opportunity to pass on God's message to another woman.

But when Sibell brought her in some lunch – soup, fresh bread and butter, roast chicken, custard – Harriet ate the lot, leaving not a crumb.

'There's nothing wrong with her appetite,' she told William, 'so that's a good sign.'

Days later, after a great deal of fuss, Harriet finally allowed Dr Byrne in to see her. He was a matter-of-fact old gent, and once in the room would brook no resistance, pulling up a chair beside her to begin taking her pulse.

'Now, young lady, I'll check your heart and lungs and all that to see how you are, while you tell me how you feel.'

William was waiting nervously for him. Dr Byrne seemed to have been in there a long time, and when he eventually came into the parlour, he asked William to sit down.

'She's fit as a bull,' he announced. 'But bloody confused. I'd say yes, she is experiencing a mental breakdown, but she's not too far gone. Plenty of rest, good food, and give her things to do. She says she likes to read, and do quilting. Get her back on to that. And keep the bloody preacher away from her. She seems to think he's God.'

'You can bank on that,' said William grimly.

'Not much else you can do. Except no sex. She's not up to that. You understand?'

'Yes, of course.'

'Good. While I'm here I want to have a word with you about Myles. He knows you're only trying to help, so he doesn't want to upset you by disagreeing with you.'

'What does he want me to do?'

'He doesn't want you to bring up the feller to fit him with the leg. He wants to leave here and have it sorted out in Perth. In other words, he's shy about being here, learning to walk, with everyone watching him. He wants to work on that on his own, down there where he'll get a bit of privacy.'

'Why didn't he say so? He can do that. He can do whatever he wants.'

'No he can't,' Byrne said quietly. 'He says he doesn't have a bean of his own. And it means asking you to support him down there.'

'Is that all? Money's not a problem.'

'Maybe not, William, not to you. Now I don't want to go into whatever differences there have been between you two, not my business, but he's feeling pretty rotten about it. Making it worse by having to fall back on you for financial support.'

'That's tough luck, isn't it?' William said tersely.

'If you say so. But perhaps you should make it easier by suggesting this course yourself. Tell him it would be better for him to get to Perth to have the leg fitted. It won't kill you to volunteer. And you needn't say I mentioned this.'

'All right. Consider it done. It's late. Could you use a whisky?'

'I certainly could. It's been a long day. They say Mannering has put Jovial to stud. Have you heard anything about that? I wouldn't mind a little colt or a filly from that bloodline . . .'

Chapter Nineteen

Though he only inhabited the outskirts of the celebrations, Yorkey always enjoyed Christmas. As a little kid he'd been astounded when the rough old drovers had suddenly presented him with lollies, screwed up in paper bags, all for himself; and the boss, all smiles, had given him a penknife. He'd never forgotten that unusual day, nor its name, Christmas, which he'd figured meant feasting, because there was always plenty of tucker about too.

Because the big day came in the wet season, itinerant drovers, with no homes to go to, were gathered in camps with their families to wait out the laid-off months, and that in itself was an exciting time for the kids. A change from constant moving along the droving tracks. But Yorkey soon learned that the highlight of the season was that special day, and he looked forward to it, even when he was older, a fully fledged drover himself, remembering to buy lollies to distribute to the kids.

Over the years he'd often returned to the camp for a few weeks, to catch up on mates, and hear all the news, find a mate to go fishing, flirt with the girls.

This year, though, he was a bit lost. He'd left it too late to head down the track; the heavy rains had really set in now and Darwin was well and truly marooned, by the inland floods. The rivers would be rip-roaring by this, and the gorge would be a sight to see, with those cascades belting down. He wasn't finished with that gorge. One day he'd figure out how to get there in the wet. Probably have to call on a few mates to help him haul a boat to cross the flood plains, then hike up to the plateau to get an eagle's view of the falls and the fun in the gorge below. It could be done.

Meantime, though, he'd attached himself to Sweeney's stables. Might as well do something, pick up a few quid. Got a job as a rouseabout. And a bed in the hayloft. No problem.

That was where Zack Hamilton found him.

'I've been looking all over for you, Yorkey. Tomorrow's Christmas Day, we want you to come and have Christmas dinner with us.'

Yorkey was embarrassed. He'd never been to a Christmas dinner in a house, only in camps, where no one cared that you were a blackfeller, but this house business, with flash white folk. No fear. Not on your life.

'Ah . . . I'll be right here, boss. Got to work.'

'The horses won't miss you for a couple of hours.'

'I reckon I'll be right here,' Yorkey persisted, eyes downcast so as not to offend.

Zack understood, but this was Sibell's idea, and he was doing every damn thing he could to please her these days, these last few days, because she was still intent on leaving him. She had already bought her ticket and was due to sail for Perth on the *Australis* in the New Year. To make her decision even more irreversible, she had offered to take Myles Oatley to Perth with her.

William had been delighted that she would be accompanying his son, but also very concerned. When Sibell had first offered he'd insisted on discussing the situation with them.

'I don't want you to use Myles as an excuse to be leaving so soon, Sibell. What do you say about this, Zack?'

'It appears I don't have any say at all. But since she's dead set on leaving, she might as well make herself useful and look after Myles.'

William sighed. 'Then let me make myself clear. If you change your mind, Sibell, and decide not to take passage on the *Australis*, then I will send one of the nurses from the hospital with him. I have already spoken to Matron, and she has agreed to spare someone for a return trip if need be. And I have friends meeting him in Perth. So you are not obligated to this course, Sibell.'

'I realise that, William.'

'In other words,' Zack said coldly, 'she is leaving on the same ship.'

'Oh well, I'm sorry to hear this. Isn't there anything I can say that might help you change your mind, Sibell?'

'No thank you, William. How is Harriet?'

'She's settling down. I had thought about selling the house but I need to keep it now. For the time being. Then we'll move out to Warrawee station. Pop needs company, and I'm looking forward to station life again. A change of pace will do Harriet good too. She actually brightened up when I suggested living at Warrawee.'

No wonder, Zack thought. She got herself into such a pickle here, what with one thing and another, a gracious exit is a damn good idea. People were whispering, he knew, that it was good of William to take her back, but Zack disagreed. It was not 'good' of him, in that sense. The man was doing the right thing. She was his wife, and he was obviously still fond of her. William was, sensibly, intent on preserving his marriage. Zack wished he could say the same thing for his own wife. For the love of his life.

Yorkey was showing him around the stables, both of them sharing their love of horses. Most of the animals stabled here were owned by locals without stabling facilities on their town properties, and there were some fine mounts gazing out from their stalls. Zack wasn't above feeling a little smug, though. Any one of his own Thoroughbreds could run rings around this lot.

He was startled when Yorkey caught him out. 'Your horses better, eh?' he grinned.

366

Zack laughed. 'You think so?'

'Sure. These fellers a bit fat, need more work.'

'Talking of work, I've been meaning to ask you to come back to Black Wattle after the wet. I know you like droving, and you'd still get a bit from my station, but it's a tramp's life, Yorkey. You can do better than that.'

'Drovers get paid,' Yorkey said stiffly, knowing that most Aborigines working about the stations earned only their keep.

'I'll pay you a stockman's wage and your keep, you deserve that. Then it's up to you. If you stick to the job you could end up a boss stockman yourself.'

'Not likely,' Yorkey said shyly.

'Very likely. You know your job pretty good, and there aren't too many reliable blokes around. They come and go. You know that. I'd never turn my back on you. You could settle at Black Wattle, get a wife—'

'Jeez, you're rushin' things,' Yorkey snorted, feigning shock, and Zack recalled his own reaction to the mention of marriage, at the same age. You got spooked like a touchy horse.

'I'm talking to you the same way I'd talk to a whitefeller when I'm trying to recruit him to work for me,' he continued. 'I need good men, I always keep an eye out. I tell them they'll have a good life with me and my family at Black Wattle.'

But Yorkey was nervous. 'I dunno. Got to think about it now.'

'That's good. Plenty of time. We're not going any place until the wet eases up, but you do some hard thinking, mate. Do you want to end up an old bloke, hanging on the tails of young drovers? Or do you want to make something of yourself? Get some respect. It's up to you. And anyway, what about this Christmas dinner?'

Yorkey had lost interest in that invitation; his mind was winging back to Netta, and to a whitefeller word she'd so often hammered at him, a word she could never explain. It was something he had to find some-where, but she was unable to show him where to look.

'You gotta get reespek,' she had told him, but like so many of her stories it had faded into the years, that word.

But here it was now. In place. A real word. Respect. Yorkey tasted it, savoured it, because it sounded different coming from a white man, but he recognised it all right. Jimmy Moon, despite his terrible death at the hands of men unknown to him, had earned respect. By God he had. And so would his son, back there at Black Wattle, where Jimmy Moon had been invited into the homestead because he was so respected.

Yorkey decided he would take the job. Be bloody grateful for it, what was more, considering Zack's frightening alternative, and he'd make a real go of it too. But his own protocol required that a man shouldn't look too eager. Zack wanted him to think it over, so he would have to do that for a few days. And then accept. But as for that dinner, no. Jimmy Moon might have walked into the white world easy, but it was too soon for Yorkey. He wasn't ready.

'Hey, Zack. You tell the missus it's bloody nice of her wantin' me to come to her party, but I'm all right here, true. You explain, eh?'

Zack put an arm about his shoulder and walked with him to the gate. 'I'll tell her, Yorkey. She'll understand. It was just a way of letting you know she thinks you're a good bloke. But if you change your mind . . .'

Yorkey shook his head, but his parting smile was sheer joy and Zack knew that Yorkey would be coming home to Black Wattle where he belonged.

Christmas at the Hamilton beach house was always fun, culminating in a festive dinner set at long tables under the high-set house, but this year Lucy felt they'd have to be relying on their guests to keep the party going, thanks to her mother's decision to leave. She couldn't believe Sibell's selfishness. To leave her husband, her daughter and her home at her time of life was preposterous. And bloody selfish. It was a terrible thing to do to a fine man like Zack, who really loved her. He'd been angry at first, when he'd become aware that she really meant to leave, but now he was just plain hurt, you could see it in his eyes, and so he let her walk all over him.

He'd even offered to buy her a house in Perth, which Lucy thought was madness, only encouraging her, and she'd said so, but Zack wouldn't be drawn into criticising his wife, even to Lucy.

'This is your mother's decision. If she wishes to live in Perth, the least I can do is see she is comfortable there, Lucy. We can't have her moving into a rooming house.'

'Do her good. She might appreciate her home more!'

'And you might be better advised to look into your own affairs. What's going on between you and Myles?'

'Nothing,' she said, to avoid further questioning.

'I hope that's true.'

'What do you mean? I thought you liked Myles.'

'I did once,' he shrugged. 'Not so sure these days.'

'You never like anyone! You didn't like Christy either. If you have your way I'll end up an old maid.'

'Yes, you might,' he grinned. 'But I never said I didn't like Christy, I just wanted to give more thought to his proposal, especially when it comes to taking on station life. That's if the proposal's still on the table.'

'Why wouldn't it be?' she snapped.

'I haven't seen him around lately. Is he coming to dinner with us tomorrow?'

'Of course he is!'

'I see.' Her father nodded, but Lucy knew that doubting remark.

'What's that supposed to mean?'

He grinned. 'To quote my daughter, nothing.'

Lucy was shaken. It was true, she hadn't seen much of Christy lately. He'd been sulking because she spent so much time with Myles, but he'd get over it, especially with Christmas dinner coming up. His place was next to hers at the family table. They'd have a good time and everything would be back to normal. She'd have good news for him as well. Tell him that he should have another talk with Zack, who obviously would have no objections to their marriage as long as Christy was sure he'd be happy with the work and responsibility of the cattle station.

The more she thought about it, the better she felt. Christy was smart, he'd soon learn the ropes, and the property was so big Zack could do with the backup of another family man. And not to forget, she told herself crankily, with Sibell gone, their company would help her father get over the loss.

As for Myles, she admitted now, though only to herself, that she might have gone a little overboard in her efforts to help. But she had been shocked, and full of pity for her old friend, nothing wrong with that.

It had been strange, though. At first she'd thought she was falling in love with him all over again, but as he recovered she'd realised that it had only been a romantic notion. This man was not the Myles she'd once known, and never would be again. And that had nothing to do with the loss of his leg. But out of loyalty she stayed on, surprised that the doctors were right; once the fever left him, he did recover quickly and there were no complications with his wound. The poor stump was healing well.

She saw in him a determination that she admired. He was not about to let the loss of his leg get him down, to the relief of everyone. He even joked about it. But he began to take her for granted, expecting her to be there for him, and that worried her. She tried to do her best, staying with him as much as possible and further irritating Christy, and then came the talk of him moving to Perth, where he could have better assistance and rehabilitation. Lucy was relieved; this would extricate her from the situation.

But it didn't work that way. Myles began talking about 'us'. About Perth. And about how it had been decided that when he was able to walk freely again he could go down to Millford station, which had once belonged to his late mother's family, and prepare to take over eventually.

'You'll love Millford,' he said. 'It's great country. But of course you know it. You've been there plenty of times.'

Lucy had to laugh it off. 'I'd have to bring my fiancé, don't forget.'

'What fiancé? You haven't announced your engagement to that toy soldier. Get rid of him. The Oatley and Hamilton seniors will get their wish at last; we'll amalgamate all the properties, Lucy. It'll be some spread we'll have between us.'

Quietly she had to talk him down from his fantasy, recalling silently that he had dumped her before, and that horror about him and Harriet, but as she backed away, Myles became angry with her.

'It's the leg, I suppose! You don't want to be married to a cripple.'

'No it's not, Myles. I'm not in love with you, and you're not in love with me, so stop carrying on about the damned leg! It wouldn't have made any difference to me and you know it.'

'I don't appreciate your tone,' he said huffily.

369

'That's too bad. That's me. I'm a friend and we'll stay friends if you behave yourself. Now what's happening here tomorrow?'

She was still concerned for him. Her mother had said that William Oatley had not accepted her invitation to join them on Christmas Day because he planned a quiet dinner at home with Harriet, and that definitely counted out his father as a visitor at the hospital.

'They're having some sort of revolting bash, with paper hats and a pack of patronising do-gooders singing out of tune, you can be sure, but I've insulated myself against that.'

'How?'

'I still have plenty of mates here, you might recall. I'm entertaining two couples in my own domain tomorrow noon. They're bringing the liquid refreshments and Billy Chinn is sending round some decent food.'

'Oh God, Myles! Does Matron know?'

'I daresay she'll find out in time. But she won't be any bother. She's been doing handsprings all morning. The board has informed her that my philanthropic old man is underwriting a brand-new wing for this establishment. You're entirely welcome if you wish to join us. Even up the numbers, so to speak.'

She sighed. 'You know I'll be home tomorrow. As for evening up the numbers, don't kid me. Who are the two couples bringing for you?'

'Nancy Forrester,' he said, without the bat of an eye. 'Rather a good choice, I thought. She wants to be a nurse.'

'Goodbye, Myles.'

'You will come to see me off?' he called as she made for the door.

Christy was in his office. He leapt up from his desk with genuine pleasure when the butler showed her through.

'This is a surprise! How nice to see you, my dear.'

'I didn't know if you'd be in,' she began apologetically. 'But I thought I'd take a chance. The Christmas decorations in the lobby are just gorgeous.'

'Oh yes, even with the Resident and Mrs Mollard away, we have to keep the side up. Trot out the crib and statues and all, because people bring children to see our Nativity scene every year. Do sit down. Would you care for a glass of wine? No, what about a champagne in the garden? His nibs has excellent champagne.'

'I'd love it!'

The Residency, looking out over the harbour, had far and away the best uninterrupted view of the bay, but on this late afternoon the sea was shrouded in mist, the aftermath of heavy showers, or maybe just an interval.

'I think the gazebo would be best,' he said, leading her down the path. 'Not much to see, but at least it's dry. And may I say you brighten up a grey scene, my dear, you look lovely.'

Lucy took heart. The gown was one of four her mother had produced only yesterday. She'd had them sent up from Perth. It was a summery

Swiss voile, white, embroidered with tiny lemon and green flowers, and it had a swathe of soft white georgette around the neckline.

'Are these a payoff?' she'd asked Sibell angrily. 'Feeling guilty, are you?'

'They're nice dresses. I think you need them. If you don't like them, Lucy, give them away.'

She and Maudie had taken them from the large box, separating them from the masses of tissue packing, and hung them over the window curtains to look at them.

They were lovely, two evening dresses and two day dresses, but Maudie had turned her nose up.

'They're too frothy for you, Lucy. You need plainer clothes, a country girl like you.'

That got Lucy's back up. What Maudie really meant was that they were too feminine for her, and that wasn't fair. This time she was forced to admit her mother was right. The gowns were perfect for her. She tried them on, swanking before the mirror, choosing this one to wear this afternoon. And she'd made the right choice. This was the first time Christy had remarked so enthusiastically on any of her clothes. He even had her stand and swirl around to show off the satin-edged frill on the full skirt.

The butler brought down the champagne and some small biscuits, serving them quietly before departing.

'It's really dreamy here,' she said, 'as if we're in our own world with this mist all about us.'

'As it should be.' He smiled at her from the other side of the neat garden table setting. 'Happy Christmas, Lucy.'

He hadn't made any attempt to kiss her, not even the usual peck on the cheek, and the more they chatted about this and that, the more nervous Lucy became. This *was* a dreamy place; why wasn't he making the most of it?

She drank her champagne so quickly she felt she had to make an excuse. 'It's really delicious, isn't it?'

'Yes. The very best.'

She watched as he refilled the glasses, nibbling on a biscuit, casting about for something else to say, but Christy took the lead.

'And how is Myles?'

'Oh, he's all right. He's going to Perth in the New Year. With my mother.'

That brought disquiet into their seclusion. Lucy had no wish to discuss Myles and she knew Christy was too polite to venture into the awkward area of her mother's departure. She stared into the distance as if she were able to see ships in the harbour as the mists gave way to light silvery rain.

'I'm really looking forward to tomorrow,' she blurted suddenly. 'We should have a lovely day.' Then she remembered that she hadn't actually told him the procedure. 'Most people come about eleven and we sit down at twelve, but you can come earlier if you'd like, Christy.'

'Tomorrow?' He seemed startled. 'Is this to your Christmas dinner?'

'Yes.'

'But Lucy. My dear. I didn't know I was invited.'

'Of course you are. I invited you.'

'When was that?'

'Oh . . . ages ago.'

'No, I recall you did mention that your family likes to entertain friends on Christmas Day, but you did not invite me, Lucy. You've been very busy with other matters the last few weeks, and I seem to have been thrust into the background.'

She clasped her hands together. 'Please, Christy, don't be like that. I had to do what I could for Myles. But anyway, don't worry about it. You are invited. We're expecting you.'

'Thank you,' he said stiffly. 'But I have made other arrangements.'

'What? You can't! I wanted you to be with me.'

'That's not possible. Not tomorrow.'

'Why? Where are you going?'

'As I said, I have made other arrangements.'

'But I took it for granted you were coming to our place.'

'It isn't a good idea to take people for granted, Lucy. I am in love with you, and your behaviour of late has been rather hurtful. One could be forgiven for thinking you have had a change of heart.' He stood, reaching a hand out to her. 'I really ought to get back to the office.'

'But I haven't,' she cried.

'Then we'll talk about it another time, when you are more sure of yourself.'

Before she realised what was happening, Lucy was escorted up to the gate with a courteous kiss on the cheek. He handed over her umbrella and ushered her into the street.

'Have a happy Christmas, my dear,' he said.

'But when will I see you?'

'Would it be convenient if I called the day after Christmas?'

'Of course it would be,' she snapped, disappointed and offended.

When she arrived home she found a messenger had delivered a small parcel for her, an elegant gold fob watch and a card that read: 'May all your summers be happy. Merry Christmas, with love from Christy.'

Zack had done his duty. He'd swept and cleaned the area under the house, hung sheets of canvas on the beachside to prevent more sand blowing in, set up long trestle tables and benches borrowed from the local hall, and with utmost patience hung, tacked and hitched all the decorations exactly as Maudie wanted them. The foundation posts were now festooned with Chinese lanterns and streamers, and bunting swung giddily overhead in a riot of red, white, gold and silver. Then he collected masses of gum tips to place, at her direction, in kerosene tins camouflaged with coloured crêpe paper.

'Will that do?' he said at last.

'No. I need more gum tips to put along the other side. They'll give the impression of a small hedge. And perhaps you ought to go and get another table. It would be handy to have another serving table.'

'There aren't any more,' he lied. 'This'll do, Maudie. It looks very nice.'

'You really think so?'

'Oh yes, terrific. When the tables are all set up we'll think we're at the Ritz.'

Maudie beamed and Zack escaped.

Upstairs in the big kitchen, several ladies were hard at work with Sibell and Lucy, making preparations for the great day, so, with the invisible sun presumably over the yardarm, Zack slipped out of the house and made for the Victoria Hotel, where the first person he met was Christy Cornford.

'I wonder if I could buy you a drink?' Christy asked him, a little nervously.

'Best offer I've had all day.'

Christmas Eve was no time to find a quiet corner in any of the bars, so they took refuge on a side veranda, and after the usual small talk, Zack brought up the subject of the stolen rings.

'What happened there in the end?'

'We've alerted the Brisbane police. When the ship arrives, that woman Peggy Minto will be taken ashore and charged with theft and disposal of stolen property.'

'What about Walters? On the face of it, he kidnapped Harriet.'

'No. He's on safe ground unfortunately. She could have left. She was, after all, within a half-mile of her home. But I've prepared a report on the matter and it will go down to his bishop in Adelaide. I don't think we'll be seeing much more of Walters around here.'

'Poor William,' Zack said with a sly grin. 'What a thing to happen to a dead-set atheist. I think the next preacher to walk in his door will be met with guns blazing. By the way, he said you're joining him – sorry, I mean them – for Christmas dinner. He's thrilled to bits to have the company.'

'I was honoured to be invited. Besides which, Harriet isn't in any shape yet to be company for him, and he's very loyal. He wouldn't dream of going out without her.'

'That's true.'

'So he'd be stuck there on his own. He's a very interesting man. I'm looking forward to it.'

Zack nodded, approving. 'Lucy seemed to be under the impression you'd be dining with us.'

'I know. But you see, she forgot to invite me. Or rather she forgot until this afternoon, and I can't let William down.'

Zack put down his glass and laughed. 'She forgot? Not Lucy! She'd just expect you to turn up. You know we don't stand on ceremony. Was it Myles?'

'Yes,' Christy said candidly. 'And I'm still not sure what's happening there.'

373

'Don't worry about him. Lucy felt sorry for him, that's all. It was rather a good exercise for her to spend that time with him and find out once and for all that he's a spoiled brat.'

'Why? What did she say?'

'She told Maudie he had the bloody cheek to ask her to marry him. That put a fast halt to her benevolence.'

'I don't want to be offensive, Zack, but he must have had encouragement.'

'No fear. He's arrogant. He'd be taking advantage of her kindness. But anyway, forget Myles. I wanted to talk to you about the station. That's if you're still interested in marrying my daughter.'

Christy gaped. 'Yes, of course. Does that mean you approve?'

'As long as you promise to look after her,' Zack grinned. 'Or I'll come after you with the shotgun.'

'I'll take care of her. And thank you, sir.' Christy was so excited he was almost babbling. 'You can count on me, I promise you—'

'Then we have things to talk about,' Zack said, interrupting him. 'What about next week? Can we talk in your office? It will be quieter than my place, I can assure you. I want to give you a rundown on the station and how it operates. I have an excellent overseer, his name's Casey, you listen to him and you can't go wrong. Will tomorrow afternoon suit you?'

'By all means,' Christy said, wondering why the rush. Zack would be in town for at least another month yet. As for their wedding, he expected that would take place about six months after their engagement was announced. Lucy had given him the hint on that. She'd remarked that trying to arrange a wedding in a horrendous wet season was madness. That she hoped to be a June bride and enjoy the luxury of Darwin's clear blue skies.

'We'll shake on it then, Christy,' his future father-in-law was saying. 'And I'll buy you a drink, then I'd better get home to the great cook-in and see if I'm allowed to eat anything.'

Lucy thought she'd scream if anyone else asked her where Christy was. And Maudie wasn't helping.

'He's made other arrangements,' she chortled, amused by Lucy's discomfort.

'You knew he wasn't coming!' she accused Zack. 'You love to spoil things for me, don't you? So if he's not here, where is he?'

'Stop fussing and enjoy yourself. Go and look after the guests.'

Despite her disappointment, Lucy soon got into the swing of things and it turned out to be a wonderful day. Sibell and her helpers had excelled themselves, managing to serve Christmas dinner with all the trimmings to over thirty guests without a glitch, even though the temperature climbed to well above the hundred mark. The drinks flowed, great yarns were told and songs were sung, and Maudie, to groans, gave her recitation, as usual.

Zack walked quietly over to Lucy. 'I think you've earned a leave pass by this. Why don't you go and see Christy? I believe he's waiting for you.'

'Where is he?'

'Just down the road at the Oatley household.'

'You knew all the time!'

'Duty before pleasure,' he laughed.

'You forgot your hat!' he called as she rushed away.

'Where's she going?' Maudie asked.

'Forward,' Zack said, and Maudie, a little tipsy, blinked and wandered away.

At last they were on their own. Just the two of them. Everything cleared away, the house almost back to normal. Maudie fast asleep.

'There's some champagne left, would you like a glass?' Sibell asked him.

'No thanks. I've had more than sufficient. Why don't you come and sit with me on the veranda and we can contemplate your successful day.'

'Good idea,' Sibell said, taking off her shoes and following him outside. 'I'm exhausted.'

Zack sat next to her on the wide cane settee, and sighed. 'Don't look now, I think we've got a sea breeze.'

'Oh yes, it's wonderful.'

'So are you.'

'Thank you. You're not too bad yourself.'

'Then why are you leaving me?'

'Please, Zack, just for today, can't you stop?'

'It's not easy.'

They watched revellers stumbling down the street, returning their calls of 'Merry Christmas!' and settled back as the drowsy afternoon drew to a close. In the distance a curlew called mournfully and another answered. A glimpse of pink broke through the clouds, reminding Zack of Darwin's famous sunsets, a pleasure rarely allowed them in the wet season. Sibell, her feet up on a cushioned stool, was dozing. He put an arm about her, gently drawing her to him, and there he waited.

When she finally awoke it was dark, there being no time for twilight in this decisive land. She looked at the jasmine bush that she had planted the year before from cuttings Harriet had given her, its tendrils now reaching into the veranda.

'I'll swear that bush has grown a foot in a week. You ought to put up some wire so that it'll reach up instead of in.'

'And have it suffocate me with its perfume? No thanks. The one outside our window is bad enough.'

'I thought you liked it.'

'Well I don't. Sibell, can I ask you a question? Now listen to me, if you say no, it'll be all right, I'll understand.'

She looked at him carefully, pushing strands of hair away from her face, the way she did when she was nervous.

'What is it now?'

'It's about your move to Perth—'

'Please—'

'No. Hear me out. I was wondering. Can I come too?'

Sibell sat up, surprised. 'For heaven's sake, Zack. We already talked about that. I told you I'd love you to come down with me, to spend time with me until the end of the wet season, but no! You wouldn't have that. You were so pig-headed about it, flatly refusing. But if you've changed your mind, then we have to get a ticket for you right away.'

'I haven't changed my mind.'

She was puzzled. 'Then what?'

'I want to come with you. For good.'

'What? To live in Perth? You can't do that. You wouldn't leave the station.'

'Yes, I would – if you're not there. I don't want to live there without you.'

She was upset. 'Oh, Zack. You don't have to do that. Black Wattle's your life. You were born there. I couldn't ask you to leave.'

'You're not asking, I am. I've given this a lot of thought. Casey can take over as manager, I'll get him some extra staff. He knows the place as well as I do. And I won't have fallen off the face of the earth. I can come back and forth, keep an eye on the place.' He stopped suddenly. 'What do you say? I could come with you in the New Year. Help you find a house, get you settled, and then get back in time to take Lucy and Maudie home . . . sort them all out, pack my bags and go to Perth!'

Sibell stared. 'You mean it? You'd really come with me?'

'If you'll have me. It might be fun retiring. Safer, I suppose. No spears flying, no cattle to run me down. Only those new-fangled tramcars.'

She kissed him. 'I love you, Zack Hamilton.'

'Yes, but just don't try running off on me again. You see, it doesn't work. And look down the road. Here come Christy and Lucy.'

Sibell leapt up. 'I can't wait to tell them the good news.'

'We'll tell them tomorrow. I think they have good news of their own.'

They stood, arms about each other, as Lucy came rushing up the front steps ahead of Christy, her face shining with happiness. She didn't even notice that her previously warring parents looked very happy too.

'Ah well,' Zack said to his wife. 'It'll soon be time to move on anyway. Black Wattle doesn't need two bosses.'

Then he laughed. 'Three, including Lucy.'